# The Dog-walking Club

## LIZ HINDS

*For George,*
*the best dog in the world.*
*And for my lovely Husband,*
*with thanks for the original idea.*

# Chapter 1

Maggi's eyes were filling with tears. She'd known from the start that this was going to be a bad idea. If only she'd paid attention to the sensible part of her brain instead of the trying-to-please-everyone bit.

Her plan had been to make a preliminary enquiry on the telephone. If she'd stuck to her resolve and said, 'No, I don't need to visit the dogs' home. If you can just tell me if you have a suitable adult dog, not too old but well-behaved, good with people, and in need of a good home, that'll be enough for now.'

But, no, she'd agreed to go along to the dogs' home and meet some of its residents, and now she knew why the girl on the phone had been so insistent: at that precise moment Maggi was on the verge of saying, 'I'll take them all!'

First she'd been introduced to Tigger. 'His owner died and her son – who was more than happy to take the house – didn't want the dog that came with it,' the kennel girl said. 'Tigger used to be very playful I'm sure,' she added, as the black and white spaniel-cross stared listlessly at them through the mesh of the cage 'and probably would be again in the right home.

'Tyson here,' she said as she moved on to the next cage where a Jack Russell chewed frantically on the wires, 'has anxiety issues, probably as a result of mistreatment. A good caring home is all he needs though.

'Oh, and this is a sad story. Chloe's owner neglected her and we had to shave her. As you can see from the sore lesions on her back she needs some tender loving care.' The shorn brown and white whippet shivering in the corner of the cage had brought tears to Maggi's eyes.

The snarl from the next cage as they approached made both Maggi and the kennel girl jump back. 'Ah, yes,' the girl said. 'This is Casper. He's quite protective of his territory and can appear aggressive but …'

'All he needs is a good home?' Maggi finished her sentence for her.

'Yes,' the girl agreed, delighted that Maggi had understood. 'You did say you don't have children living with you, didn't you?'

'I don't but would that be a problem?'

The girl sighed. 'It depends on the dog. But mostly we like to find homes where the dog, for its own good, will take centre stage and get plenty of attention. A lot of our dogs have come from difficult backgrounds and need' she gestured with her hands, 'bringing out of themselves.'

'Oh dear.' It was Maggi's turn to sigh. When she'd contemplated getting a dog she hadn't realised she'd have to be a pet therapist into the bargain.

Maggi had never had a dog before. When her husband Jack had been alive they'd loved their holidays and their day trips and a dog had always seemed an unnecessary distraction. Their son Peter had begged for a puppy when he'd been a boy but then, he'd also wanted a giraffe and a baboon not to mention a boa constrictor, black widow spider and a panda, so they knew his enthusiasm wouldn't last and they'd be the ones left with the responsibility of looking after a dog. Or rather she would be.

Even after Jack died she'd not thought about getting a pet for company until she found herself talking to the microwave one day. 'Which wouldn't have been too bad,' she explained to Brenda, her best friend and co-worker, 'but it was answering back.'

She'd browsed the ads in the local newspaper and while there was any number of kittens going free to good homes there were no dogs. She'd had a cat as a child and remembered it as a sullen unfriendly animal who avoided all human contact as far as possible. 'They're not all like that,' Brenda assured her. 'Look at my Lucy, she always makes straight for my knees when I sit down.'

Remembering the kneading with sharp little claws that she'd suffered on more than one occasion at Brenda's Maggi wasn't convinced that was a good feature. 'No, I think it's going to have to be a dog.'

'But dogs are such a responsibility,' Brenda said. 'Who's going to look after it all day while you're in work.'

But Maggi had that planned. 'I'll arrange it so that I'm always on afternoons or evenings and then I can walk the dog before work.'

'But what about when you want to go out for the day? Or go away?'

'When do I ever go out for the day? Or go away for that matter? And if I do, I'll make arrangements. No, my mind is made up: I'm getting a dog.'

But now she was wavering. All the dogs she'd seen were too old or unfriendly, disturbed or in need of twenty-four supervision; that wasn't what she wanted or could cope with, dreadfully sad though their stories were. She'd just about decided to go away and have a rethink when the main kennel door fell open and a bouncing, yapping huddle of puppies flew in. They dashed up to Maggi and hopped up and down at her feet, nipping her toes with their pointy baby teeth, and wagging their tails so furiously they almost took off.

'Oh my word,' Maggi exclaimed, bending down to stroke each little head that thrust itself into her hand. 'How gorgeous are you?'

The kennel girl who'd come in from the exercise yard with the puppies said, 'Their mum's not so sure. She's knackered!'

And sure enough, trailing in behind them, looking every inch a befuddled new mum, was a pretty mongrel bitch. 'This is Sally,' the girl explained. 'Someone reported seeing what they thought was a dog in labour down a side street so we rescued her and brought her here.'

'Was she a stray?' Maggi asked.

'We don't think so. She looked well cared for. I guess the owner didn't want the bother of puppies.'

'Oh,' Maggi grimaced at the heartlessness of her race. 'So what will happen to her and her puppies?'

'We've already found a new owner for the mum and for four of the puppies. There's just the little one left.' She pointed to a puppy, slightly smaller than the rest being pushed around a little by his bigger siblings.

Maggi's heart went out to him. 'I'll have him.'

3

'But you said you wanted an adult dog,' the first kennel girl reminded her.

'I know but ... oh, look at the little mite. How can I resist?'

Two weeks later when she'd collected him, Bassett had settled in straightaway. 'It's as if he knows he's come home,' Maggi explained to Brenda who looked at the dog doubtfully.

'What is he exactly?'

'Hard to say. A bit of this, a bit of that. That's why I'm calling him Bassett.'

Brenda frowned. 'Why?'

'Because he's all sorts!' Maggi laughed and Bassett ran excitedly around her heels. As far as he was concerned life was there ready for the living. And the highlight of his life was his daily walk.

∞

'They say that owners resemble their dogs, you know.' Jemma looked in the mirror and sighed loudly. 'If that's true the outlook for me is pretty grim.' She sighed again and Pixie, sensitive as always to her mood, pushed his head gently against her leg. 'It's all right, Pixie, I do love you really.' Jemma bent forward to kiss the dog's smooth solid head. 'It's just that you're not a red setter.'

She'd always wanted a red setter. She wouldn't have minded resembling one of those, her long red hair blowing in the wind making passers-by gasp in admiration and liken her to a pre-Raphaelite painting. Except her hair was less red and more ginger, if you were being polite, or orange if you weren't. She'd gone through school suffering the embarrassment of being called 'Marma'. Her mother had overheard the nickname one day when she'd been collecting Jemma from school and she'd asked what it meant. 'Marmalade,' Jemma'd acknowledged miserably and to her horror her mother had laughed.

'Of course, that's perfect!'

'No, it's not!'

'At least it's original. They always called your dad Ginge.'

It had taken a great many tears - not to mention a few slammed doors - to convince her mother that she hated being called Marma.

Pixie licked her hand, his tongue rough against her skin. In return Jemma stroked him. 'And who calls a boxer Pixie anyway? You should be Rambo or Bruce or something manly and aggressive.' Pixie's eyes widened as if the very thought were abhorrent. He was a gentle dog through and through and Jemma hadn't minded taking him in when her uncle, Pixie's owner, had died suddenly. She'd been the obvious candidate, working from home and, as her mother said, 'having no responsibilities.' By which she meant no husband or children.

Not that Jemma wasn't without responsibilities, just not the sort of thing her mother considered real. For a start she had her work. As a freelance photographer she spent much of her time out and about, a situation that made Pixie very happy. Wherever Jemma went, Pixie went too and as a lot of the work she did involved being out in the countryside this made for one very contented dog. Jemma even took Pixie along on wedding shoots on occasion, often by special request of the bride who wanted her photo taken with the handsome dog. Only once did Pixie cause havoc when a rogue squirrel in the churchyard had taunted him and, fortunately, the happy couple saw the funny side of it although the vicar, who took his responsibilities very seriously, was less amused.

But as well as her work, which she loved, Jemma put herself at the beck and call of her next door neighbour, Gwennie, a not-as-sprightly -as-she thought widow of ninety-two. The day Jemma had moved into the tiny cottage Gwennie had knocked at the door with some fruit scones and the offer of help. 'Is there anything I can do, dear?' The quivering voice and obvious frailty made Jemma think of her own gran who died the year before but it turned out that Gwennie who'd been a seamstress could still see well enough to sew and was delighted to sit and take up the curtains that Jemma had brought from her old flat. 'You don't want to be spending your money on new curtains,' Gwennie had said. 'Not yet. If I take these up for you they'll do until you get yourself straight. I know what it's like when you first buy your own little home.' That had been five years ago and she still hadn't got round to replacing the curtains.

Gwennie had proved to be more help to Jemma than her mother had ever been and as the winters had been severe and Gwennie had come down with bronchitis badly for two years running, Jemma had been only too pleased to repay her neighbour by doing her shopping, making sure she had hot meals and fetching her prescriptions from the chemist. And since then most evenings Jemma had called in, ostensibly to tell Gwennie about her day while keeping a close eye on her well-being. The last time the doctor had visited he'd talked about a residential home and Jemma had been as adamant as Gwennie that she wouldn't be needing anything like that.

So with work, Gwennie and Pixie Jemma's life was full. If she occasionally found herself looking at the young couples she photographed with anything like envy she quickly pulled herself together. And every now and again when Gwennie would say, 'Any nice young men there? How was the best man?' Jemma would reply, 'I've got Pixie; what man could compete with him?'

Pixie's low sad whine brought Jemma back to the present and she glanced at her watch. 'Whoops, come on, Pix. Good job you reminded me of the time. The others will all be there before us again at this rate.'

Jemma pulled on her thick brightly-patterned jumper and took Pixie's lead from the hook by the front door. Then she sat on the edge of the sofa to put on her walking boots. She tied the laces tightly, grabbed a scarf, made sure she had poo bags and a few doggy treats in her pocket – although the chance of that was unlikely as every item of clothing she possessed had doggy treats in the pockets as the doctor had discovered when Jemma, undressing for a routine check-up, had inadvertently scattered mini biscuit bones all over the floor – and opened the front door of her cottage. She fastened Pixie's lead and they set off at a trot down the road towards the park.

∞

'Who's missing?' Angela's voice ran out across the car park. 'Who are we waiting for?'

The rest of the group looked around. 'Just Jemma,' Jon said.

Angela tutted. 'I don't know; she lives very close but is always the last to arrive.'

'Well, she does work from home,' said Jon. 'She may have had a phone call that she had to take.'

'Every time?' Angela looked sceptical just as Jemma and Pixie ran across the car park.

'Hi, everyone. Sorry, we're late.' Everyone smiled and greeted her and Jon made a special point of saying, 'No problem. We've only just met up.' Angela raised her eyebrows at him but good manners prevented her from contradicting him.

'Right, let's get on our way then,' she said. 'Come along, Mitzi, let's lead the way.'

As Angela and Mitzi, her beautiful French poodle, set off the others in the group fell in behind her obediently. They were all used to Angela and her ways and, irritating as she could be, they knew her heart was good. In one way or another they'd all benefitted from her kindness in the past. And it was thanks to her that the dog walking club had started.

Not that they were anonymous. It was just that the name had been suggested in the very beginning when they'd been trying to think of one, and it had stuck.

'Why do we need a name anyway?' Jon had asked.

'Because it's more official,' Angela had replied.

'But we're not an official group as such,' Jon had argued. 'We're just a gang of dog-walkers who've decided to meet regularly to walk together.'

'Precisely. How else would you define a group? No, we definitely need a name,' Angela was insistent and as she'd been the first to suggest that they should have a more formal arrangement than the accidental coming-together or crossing of paths that they seemed to have, it seemed only polite to go along with it.

'What about Dog-walkers Anonymous?' Maggi had suggested.

Angela had smiled tolerantly. 'But we're not anonymous.'

'So what? We'll be the DAs.'

'And we'll have a twelve step code like Alcoholics Anonymous.' Jon had entered into the spirit.

'Oh, it'll have to be more than twelve steps,' Maggi had laughed. 'The dogs will never put up with that!'

'True,' Jon said.

'What about something simple,' Sybil had said, 'that describes us like, I don't know, Doggers?'

Jemma, Jon and Maggi had all burst out laughing at that and it had taken them some time to calm down enough for Maggi to say, 'I'll tell you why we're laughing when we're on our own, Sybil.'

Sybil had looked puzzled while Angela had sighed and tutted. 'I suppose dog-walking club will do for the time being. Until we can think of something better.'

They'd been meeting to walk together now for nearly a year and the name had never been changed. Even Angela, if she had cause to phone one of the others, talked about it as the dog club.

And the others, though they sometimes laughed at Angela and her insistence on doing things by the rules, were grateful she'd brought them all together in the beginning.

Before that each of them had walked their solitary walks around the same piece of parkland at roughly the same time of day every day in all weathers. They'd see each other, nod and exchange pleasantries as dog walkers do, before carrying on, each following their own path. On the day that Angela, as she met each one in turn, had explained her idea, most had been disinclined to go along with her suggestion, and had made all sorts of excuses why they couldn't agree to anything as formal as a dog-walking group. Angela had returned home feeling more down than she had for some time, since before she'd had Mitzi in fact.

When her third and youngest child had started in university, though she wouldn't have admitted it for the world, she had lost some of her reason for living. Organising their lives, being chair of the parents and teachers' association, and running things generally, had filled a large part of her time and Angela was one of those people who needed to be needed. The doctor, when she'd consulted him about her listlessness – no, she wasn't depressed, just tired - had suggested taking up a hobby or going to the gym. 'Exercise releases endorphins, you know, and they help lift your mood.'

'I'm tired not depressed!' Angela had insisted and when he'd mentioned the appalling 'c' word (counselling) she'd stood and marched out of the surgery. Outside she'd bumped into an old friend, whom she'd dragged into the coffee shop in Marks & Spencer's. It turned out that the old friend had a French poodle that was due to give birth at any moment. 'That's why I can't stay long,' she'd said, looking at her mobile every other minute and jumping when it actually rang. She leapt to her feet in such a state that Angela took instant control. After driving her friend home she made endless cups of tea for the expectant 'granny' as she fretted over Lady Marigold de Silverre. The poodle did her stuff perfectly making far less fuss than her human owner and popped out puppy after puppy after puppy. Angela was so enchanted by the tiny bundles, so obviously in need of care and love, that she chose one and paid for it on the spot.

The next few weeks she made all the necessary preparations, including ordering a nest, dishes, toys and comfort blanket. At one point her husband felt it necessary to check with her: 'It is a puppy we're getting, isn't it? Not a baby?'

And when Mitzi was old enough to leave her mother and move in with Angela – or as Angela put it, 'to be born again,' although no-one was sure whether she was referring to herself or the puppy - suddenly Angela found all was well with the world.

Having a routine had been partly what Angela had been missing and now, with a puppy to feed and walk, she felt more herself and when she saw the opportunity to organise another different sort of group she couldn't resist it.

Sybil was the first of the dog-walkers to become acquainted with Angela when her Scottie dog had tried to hump Mitzi on one of the puppy's first forays into the country park.

'Oh dear, Jock, no!' Sybil called her dog in vain. The little white terrier, confused by the new smell of a strange puppy, wasn't having any of it, in more than one sense, as he hung on Mitzi's leg. 'Jock, come here, please! Oh, I am sorry. He has had the operation, you know. I'm afraid he just gets confused.'

'Don't worry,' Angela hurried to reassure the delicate figure before addressing the rogue Scottie, 'Off!'

Jock stumbled backwards blown by the force of the words and returned sheepishly to his owner's side.

'Jock, you're a very naughty boy.' Sybil put him on his lead and apologised again. 'He's normally very well-behaved. I don't know what came over him.'

'I expect Mitzi'll have to face much worse in the future. Please don't worry. There's no harm done. Maybe we could walk with you a little, help Mitzi get used to another dog?'

'Oh please do.'

Although Sybil looked frail she turned out to be a surprisingly fast walker and, chatting as they walked, in no time it seemed to Angela they were back at the entrance gate to the park.

'My car's over there,' she said, pointing to a large maroon estate. 'Did you drive here? Or would you like a lift anywhere?'

'No, thank you, I only live there,' Sybil pointed to the grand old house that occupied a corner of the park just next to the car park. 'In an apartment, you understand.'

'Right you are then. Maybe I'll see you again tomorrow.'

'Yes. Yes, that would be nice.'

And it was with that tentative beginning, and after Angela had noticed that it tended to be the same faces she saw each day in the park at the same time, that she had idea of the dog-walking group. The initial lack of interest from the others depressed her slightly until she realised that she needed to explain herself better, to help them see that it would be mutually beneficial. Once the others fully understood her idea they'd be on board, she had no doubt. It took a little longer but soon she'd won them all over and the Dog-walkers Club became a daily feature in all their lives.

∞

It was Sybil's habit when she returned from walking with the dog club to her small flat in the residential home to sit down with a cup of tea. Now she sat in her armchair next to the window that looked out towards the park. On the table next to her chair she'd carefully positioned the tray on which she'd placed a fine bone china cup and saucer in a dainty rose pattern, a matching milk jug and plate on which were two custard tarts, a small teapot kept warm in a knitted cosy, plus a spare saucer with the tea strainer on it. Although she'd lived alone since her husband had died, Sybil had never been able to adopt the modern habit of using a teabag in a mug. She'd tried; she was game to try most things – Reg, when they'd first been married, had been surprised but delighted when he'd discovered this characteristic of his new bride – but some habits were best left to others. 'Tea just doesn't taste the same, does it, Jock, when it's made in a mug? And anyway I'd have to make two mugs for us so I might as well make a pot.' Sybil and Jock enjoyed their tea times together, especially if Sybil had been to the village and bought one or two of their favourite custard tarts. Before Reg had died Sybil had baked her own cakes as he always said he much preferred them to shop-bought but since he'd gone there was no-one to bake for and, besides, a trip to the village made a welcome break in her otherwise empty week.

She'd thought in the past about inviting one or two of her neighbours in for afternoon tea but she'd never quite plucked up her courage to knock on their doors. They were always polite to her when she bumped into them in the hall but always seemed to be in a hurry. And she'd got used to her own company. And she had Jock, of course. 'We don't need anyone else, do we, old boy?' Though she dreaded the day, which she feared might not be too far away, when Jock would no longer be with her. Last time they'd visited the vet he'd pronounced Jock to be in fine fettle before adding the fateful words, 'for a dog of his age'. She stroked his head, gently caressing his silky ear. 'Better you go first though, Jock. I'd hate for you to be left behind after I'm gone. I'd never be able to rest in peace.' She chuckled at her own joke but the chuckle was laced with a sadness she couldn't shake off.

She and Reg had bought Jock as a puppy when their previous dog, a dark chocolate brown Labrador called Chunks, had died. They'd had him for fifteen years and before that they'd had a golden lab for about the same length of time. They'd been undecided about getting a new dog when they lost Chunks. 'We're getting on, love,' Reg had said. 'They need a lot of exercise, dogs do. Maybe it's time for us to hang up the lead. Or perhaps we could get a cat. They're independent, don't need anybody.'

Which was exactly why Sybil didn't want a cat. She loved the feeling of being needed. She knew Reg needed her but he'd never completely filled the gap she felt from not being able to have children. They'd both been distraught when the doctor had said it was unlikely they'd ever have a family. She'd wanted to adopt but Reg put his foot down. 'I couldn't love a child that wasn't mine.'

'Of course you could,' she'd argued. 'You'd grow to love him. Or her. We both would.' And Sybil knew that for her it would only take a second, to hold a baby in her arms, to look into a tiny face so helpless and trusting, to fall in love for a lifetime. But Reg didn't look it at it like that.

So they'd made do with doting on dogs. And she'd persuaded Reg that while getting another Labrador might be unwise a small dog that wouldn't need so much exercise would be ideal. So Jock joined their family and, like Chunks and Bessie before that, had more than repaid the love. And now, just when she'd thought that her life was gradually sliding into a world that was somehow separate from real life, she'd made new friends. And all because of Jock. She lifted the terrier onto her lap, crumbled the second custard tart and fed him bits of it, while she reminded herself how lovely it was to be part of a group, and such a friendly group at that. 'It was very kind of Maggi, wasn't it, Jock, to see us right to the door? I think she was worried about you as you had that little attack today.' Jock looked up at Sybil, his eyes, cloudy, and she felt that familiar pang again. 'No, no, it's all right. Nobody minded stopping and waiting until you felt better.' As if reassured Jock returned to eating out of her hand as she stroked him with the other. 'It was fine. You were just a little tired, that was all. We all get tired sometimes.'

∞

Maggi was feeling very tired at that moment. She'd been in work since noon and was there until ten. She yawned and then stretched and shook herself. 'Pull yourself together, woman.'

'You okay, Maggi?' Brenda was watching her.

'Yeah, thanks, Bren. Just knackered. Doing double shifts three times in four days is finishing me off, that's all.'

'I don't know why you want to volunteer for so many. I'm worn out after a normal day here what with everything else I've got to do.'

'Yeah, well, you know I'm saving. And anyway you have your grandkids every day after school. That's much more knackering than an extra shift.'

'True,' Brenda nodded, yawning. 'Oh look, you've got me doing it now too. That's the trouble with yawning; it's catching.'

Both women leaned on the trollies they propelled, heavy trollies laden with boxes of biscuits to be neatly arranged on the shelves. Brenda sighed, 'Can't believe we're putting out Christmas tins already.'

'I know. It's starts earlier every year.'

'You know what you're doing for Christmas yet? Any chance the family might come over?'

'No, no chance. Much too expensive to bring three kids over from Australia.'

'It's been a couple of years now since you've seen them, hasn't it? They must be getting grown up by now.'

'More than a couple, more like four,' this time it was Maggi's turn to sigh. 'Still,' she brightened up, 'if I can get enough shifts between now and Christmas I may be able to save enough to go over there for a holiday next summer.'

'As long as you don't wear yourself out in the process.'

It wasn't that shelf-stacking was particularly arduous work; it was more the long hours. Bassett didn't help, of course. By the time she'd taken him for his morning walk it was time for her first shift of the day. If she was doing doublers, as she seemed to be doing most days, she'd take Bassett in the car with her and pop outside in her breaks to let him have a quick run around and a wee. By the time she got home in the late evening she was fit for nothing except a toasted sandwich, half an hour's telly and bed, with Bassett sprawled alongside her. Indeed, if it hadn't been for Brenda and the dog club she wouldn't have a social life.

'Maggi.'

She glanced around. Suzy, the shift supervisor, had a suspiciously friendly look on her face.

'Maggi, how you getting on?'

'Fine, thanks.' It was obvious Suzy could see how she was getting on; no doubt she'd get round to what she really wanted in her own time.

'I really appreciate all the overtime you're doing, Maggi. The youngsters don't have the same work ethic as we oldies and it's impossible to get them to do any extra.' She laughed. 'You'd think they'd be glad of the money.'

As Suzy seemed to be waiting for some sort of response from her, Maggi said, 'That's kids for you. Rather be out enjoying themselves.' She sighed and added quietly, 'I know I would.'

'But you and me, we know the value of a wage coming in, especially in these times.'

There was no denying that so Maggi just smiled and carried on stacking the biscuit tins. They wouldn't stack themselves and if she stopped to wait for Suzy to get to the point it'd be home time.

'The thing is, Mags,' Maggi cringed: she hated people calling her that, 'one of the girls has phoned in to say she can't work tomorrow morning. Says she's going down with flu.' Suzy raised her eyebrows in disbelief. 'She looked fine when she clocked off – very promptly – at lunchtime, but there's nothing I can do if that's what she says. So I was wondering …'

'Oh, no,' Maggi groaned. 'I was looking forward to having my day off tomorrow. It's the first full day I've had off for two weeks, and I was going to start Christmas shopping.'

'Christmas shopping? It's a bit early for that, isn't it?'

'I've got to get my presents done early as I have to send them off to Australia.'

'Oh yes, of course. Well, I wouldn't ask you normally as you've done so much extra recently but I've tried the others and they've all already made arrangements that they can't get out of.'

'I bet they have,' Maggi thought to herself. 'Why didn't I think of that?' To Suzy she said, 'Oh all right then. What time do you want me to come in?'

'Half past seven okay with you?'

Half past seven was anything but okay with her but she nodded. If she kept telling herself it was all in a good cause it wouldn't seem so bad. But the thought of getting up and into work by that time made her feel even wearier. And she'd have to arrange with one of the dog clubbers to pick up Bassett and take him with them. Thank goodness for the dog club. Knowing that, whatever the circumstances or difficulties, there'd always be someone to walk Bassett for her if necessary made life so much easier.

When the idea of a dog-walking group had first been mooted by Angela Maggi hadn't been keen. She didn't want to be tied down to walking with the same bunch of people every day but as Angela had said, they all seemed to be creatures of habit, preferring to walk the same time and in the same places each day, and there was no denying that Bassett loved his doggy friends. And they helped wear him out.

When she'd chosen him from the rag tag bunch at the dogs' home she hadn't realised quite what a bundle of energy she was choosing. It had been a good choice and Maggi had never regretted it but she would never have thought it possible for one small scruffy mongrel to eat so much, poo so much and run around so much. She smiled to herself at the thought of him. He was such a good companion and he adored his daily walk.

Which was why, in her break, Maggi phoned Angela and arranged for the dog club to walk Bassett the next day. 'I'll leave the key in the usual place for you.'

'That's no problem,' Angela said. 'But, Maggi, I thought tomorrow was your day off, the day you were looking forward to.'

'Ah well, can't be helped. There'll be other days off.'

'I think they take advantage of you in that place. How many extra shifts have you done recently?'

'One or two, but that's my choice, Angela. You know I'm trying to save up to go to Australia.'

'Yes, I know that, Maggi, but I hate to see you looking so … tired. You've been looking really worn out of late.'

'Have I?' Maggi didn't think anyone had noticed. Actually she hadn't realised it was that obvious but if others were noticing she must be looking tired. Maybe she had been overdoing it. But a trip to see her son and his family would soon put her right. That was her aim, her dream, the thing that kept her going on the days when she was so tired she couldn't keep her eyes open.

'You don't want to make yourself ill. Fatigue will lower your resistance to illness. I heard a fascinating program on Radio 4 the other day …'

'I'm sure you're right but thanks, Angela, I'll have to go now. My break's over.' When Angela got started on one of her hobbyhorses there'd be no stopping her; Maggi knew that of old.

'Yes, of course. Now don't worry, we'll take good care of Bassett. Mitzi will look after him for you.'

Maggi laughed. It was a strange sight: the French poodle and the mongrel playing together. Yet of all the dogs in the group they were the two firmest friends. All the dogs got on all right; there were no problems. It just seemed like a special bond had formed, a bond that paid no attention to class.

Oh yes, Maggi was grateful to the dog club for the … she hesitated to call it friendship as she couldn't quite imagine Angela under any normal circumstances having a friend like her. But it seemed it wasn't only the dogs that ignored the class divide.

Maggi was proud to call herself working class. She'd seen her dad struggle to keep the money coming in and the hours both he and her mam had worked when the kids had been that much older. Just so they could have holidays in Butlins. Over the years they must have visited every Butlin's holiday camp in the country and they'd loved them. When she thought now of her planned – hoped-for – trip to Australia she had to smile. What would her dad have said? He strove to give his family everything and to see them move up in the world. She was sure he'd have been dead pleased and proud of her. Although he hadn't been so pleased to see her Peter move out in the world. Any more than she and Jack had. When Peter and Linda had called in to see them unexpectedly one weekend they'd been delighted as always until Peter broke the news that he'd got a fantastic new job and they were emigrating to Australia. 'It's a great opportunity for us. A fresh start in a vibrant young country. And the weather's so good there too.'

What could they say except well done? Jack had stood up and congratulated Peter on his new job and Maggi had hugged them both.

'You'll be able to come and visit us, Mum,' Linda had said. 'And if you like it you can always move out there too.'

But how could they even think of that with Maggi's dad who'd already had one bad heart attack and her mum who seemed to be ageing even faster since her husband had been unwell? But as it turned out it was Maggi's own husband who followed her dad to the grave. Peter had come home for the funeral and he'd come again with the family two years later. The grandchildren that Jack never saw. Grandchildren who were growing up fast. Maggi shook her head to clear the gloomy thoughts circulating in there. 'That's why you've agreed to come in early tomorrow,' she told herself. 'To increase the fund. If you keep this up, girl, you'll be out there before you can say Crocodile Dundee.' She yawned and stretched back her shoulders. 'Two more hours and I'll be able to go home.'

# Chapter 2

'Come on, kids, you're going to be late,' Jon yelled up the stairs, adding under his breath, 'as usual.'

'Daddy, what have you done with my gym kit?'

'It's in your drawer where it's supposed to be.'

'Daddy, I can't find my toothbrush.'

'Gracie, you've already cleaned your teeth. I watched you.'

'Oh yes.' His younger daughter appeared at the top of the stairs and smiled at him. 'I forgot. Oh, Daddy,' she said as she made her way downstairs, 'we have to take something for harvest festival today. Did I tell you that already?'

'No, you didn't but Rosie's mum told me.'

'Oh good.' She sat halfway down the stairs. 'What am I taking?'

'I have tinned pears for you.'

'Bleurgh,' Gracie made a face. 'I don't like tinned pears.'

'That's why I'm giving them away,' Jon explained patiently.

'But that doesn't seem fair.'

'What doesn't? And get your shoes on, please. Sophie, is there any chance you'll be ready soon?' Jon was gathering lunch-boxes and coats together. 'I don't know why they say only women can multi-task,' he grumbled.

'Why should old people have to eat something I don't like?'

'What old people? What are you talking about, Gracie?'

'Mrs Hunt said all the food we take to harvest will be given to old people but maybe they don't like tinned pears either.'

'I'm sure they will. Most people like tinned pears; it's only you who doesn't.'

'Who doesn't what?' Sophie asked as she skipped down the stairs.

'Gracie doesn't like tinned pears.'

'Oh yuck, nor me. I don't like them either.'

'See, Daddy, it's not just me.'

'Okay, okay, I'll get you a tin of baked beans as well then, shall I? Now, will you please put your coats on?'

'I don't need a coat.'

'Yes, you do, Sophie. It's going to rain later.'

'We've been studying rain. Miss Jones says the weather is changing so it might not rain.'

'I think Miss Jones was probably talking about climate change not what it's going to do today so take your coat, and come on, the pair of you!'

Jon eventually managed to get them both out of the house and was steering them towards the car when Sophie screamed, 'I haven't said goodbye to Benji!'

'Nor me,' Gracie shouted as they both turned and ran back to the house. Jon sighed. Was he ever going to get them to school today?

'Come on, but be quick!' He unlocked the door and the two girls ran into the kitchen where Benji, their black and white spaniel, had settled back into his bed to wait for his master's return.

'Bye bye, Benji, see you later, be a good boy.' They showered him with kisses until their dad grabbed them both by their coat collars and hurried them back out to the car.

Jon got them to school with seconds to spare. The bell had already gone and lines of children were rapidly disappearing in through the old wooden school door. They both kissed him goodbye before running in to find their school friends.

'Only just made it today,' Rosie's mum, Cathy, who'd been standing on the edge of the crowd of parents, grandparents and carers, strolled over to join Jon. She laughed at the look on his face. 'Bad morning?'

'I swear they get worse. Sophie lives in a world of her own and Gracie, well, she's on a different planet. A planet where there is no concept of time.'

'Well, I think you should be proud of yourself,' Cathy said. 'You get them here on time each day ...' she acknowledged the doubt on his face, 'just about! And they have their packed lunches and everything they need. It's an achievement.'

'You mean for a man? It doesn't seem to be a problem for any of the mums here. And they all have to do the same things.'

'Don't you believe it. Most of us only manage to arrive a few seconds before you do; we've just learned the knack of making it look easy.' She leaned forward conspiratorially, 'None of us wants to admit that we're not in total control but it's all play-acting. I bet if you went to any of our homes the kitchen would look like a bombsite.'

Jon laughed. 'Maybe, but I bet a bigger bomb hit my home.'

'You haven't seen mine!'

'No, believe me, I don't need to. I know mine would win.'

'Come back with me now then. Have a coffee – if you're happy to take a chance when you've seen the risk of catching something nasty.'

Jon hesitated. 'I'd love to,' he said, 'but I've got to get back. Things to do before I walk the dog.'

'Couldn't you do that a bit later?'

'No, we always meet at the same time.'

'We?'

'The dog club.' He smiled at Cathy's look of puzzlement. 'The dog-walkers group,' he explained. 'A gang of us all meet up same time every day.'

'Oh, well, they wouldn't miss you for once, would they?'

'Huh!' Jon couldn't help exclaiming. 'They would - and I'd have Angela to answer to and trust me, she makes Margaret Thatcher look like a pussy-cat.'

Cathy laughed. 'Maybe another time, then, Jon?'

'Yeah, sure.'

And why not, he thought as he walked back to the car. Coffee with a friend, a mum from school. If he were a woman it's what he'd be doing. The only difference being that he was a man. And a happily married man at that. But what harm could a coffee do? He'd ask Tilly if she'd mind. After all, in her job she was mixing with attractive men all day. Attractive? Why did he say attractive, he wondered? Sure Cathy was good-looking if you liked slim blonde types in jeans and boots and shaggy cardigans. But he wasn't looking for anything more than friendship. Being a stay-at-home dad was still a lonely occupation; the likes of him were few. In fact he didn't know any others. There certainly weren't any in Sophie or Gracie's classes. And he was the only man in the dog club. Tilly didn't object to his gang as she called them so he couldn't think of any reason why should she mind him having a coffee with Cathy.

Back home when he'd put the breakfast dishes in the dishwasher, the dirty clothes in the washing-machine and tidied the kitchen as best he could – which meant wiping jam off the kitchen table and gathering up the books and comics that the girls had been reading over breakfast and dumping them on the floor in their bedroom to be sorted out later – Jon took Benji's lead from the door by the back door. Calling the spaniel, he stuffed a few doggy treats in his pockets and they were ready to be off.

He only lived a short five minutes' drive from the park and he was nearly always the second one of the dog club to arrive. Sybil was always first.

'Morning, Sybil,' he said cheerfully. 'There's a real autumnal feel to the day today, isn't there?'

The wind was blowing around the few leaves that had already fallen and the air had a fresh crispness about it. The rain that had been threatening for the past few days had held off but the cloudy nights had prevented it feeling too cold.

'Yes, indeed,' Sybil replied. 'Ideal walking weather.' She bent over carefully to give Benji a scratch behind the ears. 'And how are you, Benji?'

The spaniel wagged its tail enthusiastically as he and Jock sniffed at each other as if looking for clues as to how the other had spent the intervening twenty-four hours.

Sybil straightened up. 'And how are your beautiful daughters, Jon?'

'Driving me mad as usual. Every morning it's the same performance; they spend ages eating their cereal and reading their comics and then it's a great big rush to get to school on time. Do you like tinned pears, Sybil?'

'Very much. It always used to be our Sunday afternoon treat, tinned pears and Farmer's Wife cream. I don't suppose they even sell that any more. Why do you ask, Jon?'

'Long story, Sybil. You see it's their harvest festival …' Jon began talking as Angela's car pulled into the car park. The blast on the horn she gave them drowned out his voice and they both looked up and waved. 'It looks as if she's got Bassett with her today.'

'Oh dear, I hope Maggi's all right. She's been looking very tired lately.'

Just then Pixie gallumped in through the park gate with Jemma hanging on his lead. 'Am I here before Angela?' she panted. 'Yes!' She made a triumphant gesture.

Jon laughed. 'Only just. She's in the car park now.'

'Only just is fine. I have time to get my breath back and look as if I've been here ages.'

'You don't want to worry about Angela, dear. We don't mind waiting for you; we know you sometimes have work to do.'

'No, I know, Sybil. And I don't really worry. But, to be honest, I'm not often delayed by work; it's more usually bad timing on my part. It's just nice to feel … nice to not have to apologise as I arrive!'

'Apologise? For what?' Angela didn't wait for an answer. 'Morning all. It's just us today I'm afraid. Maggi's had to work this morning, hasn't she, Bassett, old boy?' She bent over and tickled the dog's back.

'She's working a lot, isn't she?' Sybil said anxiously. 'I was just saying to Jon that she looks very tired.'

'Precisely what I told her, but, you know what she's like. She's determined to save enough to go to Australia.'

'It's a shame her family out there don't help her with the air fare.'

'Indeed, Jemma.' Angela's face said it all. 'Ah well, let's get on our way.'

And they set off up the path. After about a hundred yards they reached the point where the path split and the park opened out. Here, safely away from the car park, they let their dogs off their leads and the spaniel, the boxer, the French poodle, the Scottie and the mongrel could run free into the open space. The owners stood and watched for a few moments as each dog completed its regular routine.

Mitzi and Bassett always ran as fast as they could until they reached the trees at the edge of the park; there they stopped, turned on their heels and sprinted back again, screeching to a halt somewhere just beyond Angela.

Jock liked to plod around slowly, sniffing here and there and looking around every few steps to make sure Sybil was in view.

Every day, the instant Benji was let off his lead, he would look around frantically as if to make sure his favourite tree hadn't disappeared overnight before running to it, cocking his leg and releasing a stream that seemed never-ending. Jon used to tell his girls that he worried that one day they'd arrive there to find the tree had been cut down after being deemed a danger because its trunk had been weakened. And then how would Benji cope if his beloved tree went missing?

Meanwhile Pixie would stand regally, sniffing the air, until Benji bounced back and then the two of them would begin a game of rumble tumble, chasing each other around, knocking each other over, and growling fiercely at each other as if they were the greatest of enemies instead of the best of friends.

Then after the initial excitement the dogs would calm down and the walk could continue more sedately with them sniffing, exploring, running, investigating all the fascinating smells and tastes – 'Don't eat that horse poo, Benji!' – and occasionally rolling in some of them – 'No, Mitzi, no!'

The choice of paths in the park meant that those who felt less energetic could take a slightly shorter, easier path. That was usually Sybil and most days it seemed that at least one of the others would feel 'a little weary today' so she rarely walked alone. Not that she minded; she had Jock after all. But it was very nice to have human company as well. Especially such lovely company. She and Reg had never been great ones for socialising, being content with each other's company, and the few friends they'd made had all died now, so it was lovely to have young people to take an interest in.

Angela laughed when Sybil said this to her as they walked past the old Japanese bridge, a feature of the park. 'Hardly young!' she said. 'Well, Jemma and Jon are I suppose but Maggi and I are no spring chickens.'

'You seem like it to me,' Sybil replied. 'Now tell me how your youngest daughter is getting on at university.'

After Mitzi her children were Angela's favourite topic for discussion and Sybil was happy to listen to her concerns as well as the occasional boasts, this time that Emma had been awarded a distinction in the university summer exams.

'That's marvellous, Angela. You're right to be proud of her.'

'Thank you, Sybil. I don't like to bore people so it's lovely when someone asks.'

Sybil smiled and they carried on walking in companionable silence for a while before Angela, who'd been watching the Scottie dog, said, 'How old is Jock now?'

'Just over fifteen.'

'A good age.'

'Yes, Scotties tend not to live much longer.'

Angela glanced at Sybil. She'd stopped in her tracks. 'Are you all right, Sybil?'

'I'm sorry; I was just recalling the little turn he had yesterday.'

It had been a shock to all of them, a worrying moment particularly for Angela who'd been first to kneel down next to the little dog's still body. He'd seemed to collapse, before shuddering violently for a few seconds. She'd surreptitiously felt for a pulse and had been relieved to feel it getting stronger as he blinked his eyes and looked around for Sybil.

'Did you call the vet when you got home?'

'No, I didn't think there was any point. Jock was back to normal and what could the vet say anyway? Only that he's old and it's to be expected.'

Angela was surprised with the calmness with which Sybil was saying this. She thought, if it had been Mitzi who'd collapsed, she'd have been a wreck. What she didn't know was that Sybil had sobbed herself to sleep the previous night and, in the morning, had resolved to make the most of Jock's last days however many there were and not to spend them moping around waiting for him to die.

Sybil saw the look of surprise that flitted across Angela's face before she could stop it. 'What? Do you think I should be in mourning already?' She smiled gently.

'No, of course not. It's just that you seem so serene.'

'We've had a lovely life together, Jock and me, and I don't want to spoil it now by grieving before he's gone. It won't do either of us any good.'

'No, absolutely not. That's an excellent prescription for life.' Angela slipped her arm through Sybil's, even though she had to bend very slightly, and she changed the subject, asking Sybil if she agreed with her opinion that the fuss everyone seemed to make about Halloween these days was just shocking.

∞

'Do you have a boyfriend, Jem?'

The question came out of the blue and the surprise must have shown on Jemma's face because Jon hurriedly said, 'I'm sorry; I didn't mean to pry. It's just that I don't know much about you. Or about any of the dog clubbers really, which is strange as we've been walking together for a long time now.'

'Yeah, must be about a year at least. Yes, I'm sure it was autumn when we started.'

'So it's odd how little we know about each other.'

Jemma studied his face and wondered how to tell him that she and the other women knew plenty about each other; it was just him who didn't. She decided to be gentle. 'I think we know a fair amount. We're only a gang of dog-walkers after all. We're not trying to be bosom buddies.'

'I suppose not,' Jon nodded his agreement. 'But now I'm curious: what do you know about me?'

'Well, I know you're married to Tilly and you have two children, Sophie and Gracie. Tilly is a barrister – I think?' Jon nodded and she continued, 'And your children go to Beauville First School. You used to work in IT but you gave it up to be a stay-at-home dad when Sophie was born. You bought Benji when the girls were still tiny because you'd never had a dog and you felt it was good for them to grow up with one.'

Jemma stopped for breath and looked as though she was going to continue but Jon said, 'Okay, okay, I believe you: you know lots about me. But how? I don't remember ever setting out to tell everyone my life story.'

'It's just stuff you pick up from everyday conversation. Like osmosis; it just seeps in.'

Jon didn't look convinced. 'But I don't know anything about you.'

'I bet you do really. What do I do for a living? You must know that.' A big clue should have been the camera that Jemma was never without 'just in case' but Jon frowned and tried hard to think what he could remember from snatches of conversation.

I should be able to work this out, he thought. She's nearly always available in the morning to walk the dogs so it must be some sort of shift work. Perhaps she's a bar-tender. Or an exotic dancer. He shook his head to rid himself of the image. No, he couldn't see her draped around a pole.

'Well, she said. 'Any thoughts?'

He drew an idea out of the air, 'Nurse?'

'What with me fainting at the sight of blood? I don't think so.'

Jon remembered then how she'd told them she'd been to give blood but had fainted before they even got the needle in. 'I don't know then. I'm sorry I have no idea.'

Jemma waved her camera at him, 'I'm a photographer.'

There was something vaguely familiar about this information but it wasn't something he could have dragged out of his brain. He shook his head, 'I'm sorry. How bad am I not remembering that? What sort of photography do you do?'

'All sorts. I do a lot of landscapes, scenery, nature and stuff, and I do weddings. I'd like to do more portraits but I'd need a studio for that.'

26

'What do you do with the photos you take? The scenery I mean, not the weddings.'

She smiled. 'Sell them to magazines if they're exceptionally good or sometimes they're used in brochures, advertising blurb, that sort of thing.'

'You must be very good.'

'Do you know something?' Jemma said. 'I am. It's taken me a long time to appreciate that and have faith in myself but I'm getting there. Oh, look at the pair of them!'

Benji and Pixie were both splashing in the stream that ran through the park. The sunlight was shining through the trees and there was a fairy grotto air to the picture. It almost looked as though they were deliberately trying to splash each other. Jemma quickly took out her camera and snapped away. 'There should be some nice ones,' she said. 'I'll bring some copies for you if you'd like.'

'That would be great, yeah. I don't have any good photos of Benji. We've got loads of snaps of him with the girls but nothing special enough to frame.' Jon stopped in his tracks. 'I don't suppose you'd take some of Benji and the girls, would you? We'd commission you properly, of course.'

'Certainly, I'd love to. But as I said, I don't have a studio so I'd either have to come to your house or do it outside, which I'd prefer as I like to use natural light whenever possible.'

'Outside would be fine. I'll speak to Tilly and we'll arrange a date.'

'Excellent.'

'So I've found out you're a photographer …'

'Yes, and to answer your original question, no, I don't have a boyfriend. I do however have an interfering mother and an elderly neighbour, both of whom have made it their mission in life to see me settled down, which to them means married, preferably, in my mother's case to a millionaire.' She paused. 'What else? I'm twenty-five and when I was little I told my mother I wanted to be the handsome prince in Sleeping Beauty. When she asked me why I told her it was because he was the one who had all the adventures while

Sleeping Beauty slept. In fact I still dream about having adventures one day.'

'Some day your prince will come,' Jon said, very solemnly, 'and carry you off on his white steed.'

'Hm, maybe,' Jemma replied equally straight-faced. She giggled, 'But in the meantime I have Pixie to curl up with and he's in no hurry to give up his place on my bed for anyone.'

'Now will you tell me all about the others, please?'

'Certainly not! I think you should find out for yourself.'

'Aw, how do I do that?'

'Same way you've found out about me.'

'Just ask them you mean?'

'You could do or you could be a bit more subtle. Listen to conversations instead of drifting off because you think it's just going to be boring old female talk.'

'I don't drift off … always. Okay, I'll listen more. Anything else?'

Jemma shrugged. 'Maybe it's a woman thing. We pick up bits here and there and store them away like squirrels do with nuts. And sometimes we add our own hypotheses as well of course.'

'Oh really, and what do you hypothesise about me?'

Jemma blushed, 'Oh nothing really. Nothing specific. It's Maggi more than me anyway. She likes to make up stories for people.'

'So does she think I have a secret life as a drug dealer?'

Jemma looked at him and raised her eyebrows, 'Don't be daft. We don't think you're that …'

'That what?'

'Nothing.'

'Come on, you can't leave it there. What don't you think I am?'

'Daring, or stupid I suppose.'

'Oh, I'm too boring to be a drug dealer, am I?'

'Not at all! You're just … too nice.' She hurried to finish the sentence before Jon could interject. They both laughed and were still laughing when the path they were on re-joined the main one and they met up again with Angela and Sybil.

'A funny story? Do share,' Angela said.

Jemma and Jon looked at each other. 'Jemma was just giving me some lessons in being more like a woman,' Jon said.

It was Angela and Sybil's turn to look at each other and shake their heads. 'Reg could never make himself go to a unisex hairdresser,' Sybil said. 'He always insisted on a proper barber's.'

'A wise man,' Angela said. 'They should be banned.'

'What? Wise men should?' Jon gave her a puzzled look.

'No! Unisex hairdressers. A woman doesn't want to be seen by a man when she's in the hairdresser's. It's our time to let our hair down, so to speak.' She chuckled at her own words. Falling in behind them Jemma whispered to Jon, 'And Reg is?'

He took a deep breath, 'I'm guessing that would be Sybil's husband.'

'That's right, but alive or dead?'

'Oh dead. From the way she spoke.'

'You see, you're getting the hang of this already.'

∞

Tony was in his favourite chair watching *Top Gear* on television when Angela took him in an after-dinner coffee. He took it from her distractedly and put it on the table next to him.

'Tony! Use a coaster, please. You know how hot mugs mark the wood.'

'Hm? Oh, okay.' He moved his mug as Angela settled into her chair.

'I was wondering, Tony, if you'd had any more thoughts?'

'Hm?' Jeremy Clarkson and the other presenters on the television show were about to destroy yet another perfectly good car in their quest for fun. Tony couldn't decide whether to disapprove or apply for a job with them.

'Have you thought any more about my birthday?'

'Hm?' There it went. Boom. And they were giggling like schoolboys who'd let off a stink bomb. Tony grinned and pressed the Pause button on the remote. It was obvious Angela wasn't going to let him watch the rest in peace until she'd had her say.

'Have you thought any more about we can do for my birthday?'

'Your birthday? It's not for weeks yet, is it?'

'No, I know but it's my fiftieth so I want it to be special.'

'Wouldn't you rather forget about it? I know that's what I wanted.' But he hadn't been allowed to forget his: Angela had planned a surprise party. They'd been married twenty-seven years; he'd have thought she would have worked out that he didn't like surprises.

'No! I want to celebrate. I can't do anything about it so I may as well make the most of it.'

'Whatever.'

'Oh Tony, you sound like one of the girls when you say that!'

'Sorry, what do you want me to do?'

'I want you to take an interest in my birthday and to help me plan it. Is that too much to ask?'

'You're usually good at planning these things without my help.'

'But it's my birthday! I shouldn't have to plan it.'

'Okay whatever, sorry, I mean, what would you like to do?'

'Well I was thinking about getting the family all together. It's so hard to do these days with the girls all over the place.'

'Okay, invite them here then.'

'No, I was thinking it would be easier if we all met up in London. Stay in a hotel, see a show, have a meal together, that sort of thing.'

'How much is that going to cost? I assume we'll be paying for it all.'

'Yes, of course. It'll be a bit but we can afford it and it's not every day I'm fifty.'

'Okay, you plan it and I'll pay. How does that sound?'

Angela sighed. It sounded as it always did: he was hiding his lack of interest behind his credit card. It wouldn't hurt him, surely, to show a little enthusiasm for a family gathering. They so rarely saw their daughters all together. Still he'd be there, that at least was something. And she'd plan such a marvellous trip that everyone would have a simply amazing time and it would be a birthday she'd never forget.

30

# Chapter 3

The next morning, before she set off to meet the dog club Angela switched on the computer and searched for London theatres. Mama Mia was showing in the West End: she'd love to see that but the film had been so good it would be hard for the show to exceed that, and anyway she thought Tony might prefer something a little less girly. She browsed through the range of drama, murder, musical and avant garde. That last definitely wasn't to her taste. She'd recently seen an updated version of Hamlet where gangs of hooligans seem to have been let loose on the set and a butcher on the script. She liked to think she was open-minded but sometimes the gate to her mind wasn't quite wide enough – which was fine by her. She decided she'd seek the advice of her daughters. They were more in the know as to what was what on the fashionable arts scene. Not that fashionable necessarily meant good in her experience.

Angela was so engrossed in her search that she didn't notice the time and so, for once, she was the last to arrive at the park entrance.

'Sorry all, hope you haven't been waiting too long.'

'Not at all,' Jemma said. 'Don't know about the others but I only just got here.'

'Oh good, come on then, let's be off.'

The sky, which had been bright for the early part of the morning, was beginning to cloud over and the clouds were darkening as they thickened. Rain didn't bother the dog club; they were always prepared for the worst. It was one of the joys – or miseries - of being a dog-walker: the dog had to be walked whatever the weather so you soon learned to deal with any conditions. But as they set off it was still dry.

'If we're lucky we may make it around before the rain starts,' Maggi said.

'Or not,' said Jon whose slightly balding head was ultra-sensitive to rain drops.

Maggi and Angela fell in next to each other. 'Thanks for picking up Bassett yesterday,' Maggi said.

'It's no trouble, you know that. He's always so good.'

'I think you may be exaggerating there a little,' Maggi laughed, 'but we do both appreciate it.'

'So how was your extra day in work?'

Maggi shrugged. 'Same as usual. Same shelves to be stacked, same boxes to be emptied. Still it's a job and anyone with a job these days has to be grateful.'

'That's true,' Angela agreed. 'Tony said they'd have to lay more men off if business doesn't pick up soon.'

'His job's safe though, isn't it?'

'I hope so. But these days …' Angela didn't have to finish her sentence. They both knew men and women who'd thought they were in jobs for life who'd found themselves on the scrap heap before their time.

They were quiet for a moment and then Maggi said, 'It's the thought of going to Australia and seeing the grandchildren that's keeping me going.'

'I bet. But that won't be before Christmas, will it?'

'Oh gosh no. I'll be lucky if it's in the springtime. No, realistically I'm aiming for summer.'

'Which is their winter.'

'That won't matter to me. The winters, where they live, are still better than ours – often better than our summers! Oh, what's Bassett seen?' She'd spotted Bassett looking unusually attentive and alert. She followed his line of sight and saw an elderly greyhound they sometimes saw on their walk. Maggi knew the owner worried that undue exercise or excitement might be harmful to the old dog so she called Bassett to her. 'You stay here with me, Bass. Don't go charging off.' Bassett looked at her with a puzzled expression on his face. 'I know you just want to say hello and play but Ned doesn't want to play with you.'

She and Angela both waved a greeting to Ned's owner who responded likewise. 'Do you know what his name is?' Angela asked.

'The old man? No, I only know the dog's called Ned.'

'It's funny, isn't it, the way we all learn the dogs' names before the owners'? I knew Bassett's name long before I found out yours.'

'That's because you heard me screaming it all over the park!'

'True.' Angela laughed. 'He's calmed down a lot now, hasn't he?'

'Yes, he has, but he still has his moments. No, Bassett, stay here. Ned must be getting on now; he's looking very frail. How long do greyhounds live, do you know?'

'I don't know. I should think about twelve years on average. But you're right about Ned; he does look weary.'

Maggi glanced behind them. Sybil and the others were a way back but she still lowered her voice. 'I can't see Jock lasting much longer either. I wonder how Sybil will cope with that.'

'I think she'll be all right. She's prepared for it.'

'It's one thing being prepared for the worst; it's quite another when the worst happens.'

They walked on a little way and Angela told Maggi about her birthday plans.

'Sounds wonderful. Lucky you to have the family to spoil you.'

Angela suspected Maggi wouldn't be quite so impressed if she knew all the planning and the idea itself was not from her loving husband and family but from Angela herself. Still, she thought, I am lucky to have them. Maggi is right there.

They'd reached the split in the path. 'Shall we go up?'

Maggi nodded her agreement. 'One of the others will stay with Sybil, I'm sure.'

While Jemma and Sybil took the shorter route Jon caught up with the other two. 'Hey, wait for me,' he said. 'I've had an idea. I want to see what you think about it.'

They waited and he walked in between them. 'I was talking to Jemma the other day; did you know she's a photographer?'

Both women nodded.

'Oh. Well, anyway, I've asked her if she'll do some shots of Benji with my kids.'

'That's a good idea. I've seen some of her photos; she's very good.'

'I'm sure she is, but that's not my idea. What do you think about her taking some photos of Jock?'

'Shouldn't you be asking Sybil this?' Angela said.

'I thought if we could do it sneakily then if Jock dies …'

'When he dies,' Maggi interrupted, shaking her head sadly.

'When Jock dies we could give her a framed photo of him. I bet she doesn't have any good ones.'

'That's a lovely suggestion,' Maggi said, 'but would a surprise photo be a good idea. It might upset her more.'

'Do you think?'

'I don't know, I think it might if not heal then at least lessen the pain,' Angela was unsure but her instinct, from her conversations with Sybil led her to say this.

'I suppose so. What does Jemma think?'

'I haven't asked her. I only had the idea this morning when we were walking back there.'

'And how would she be able to take photos sneakily?' Maggi was still wary.

'Jemma's always got her camera and often just takes snaps when she's out with us,' Angela said.

'Does she?' Jon was surprised. 'I've never noticed.'

The two women looked at each other and raised their eyebrows. 'You're a man,' Maggi said.

'True. So what do we think? Shall I ask Jemma her opinion? And whether she thinks she could do it.'

'Or whether she'd want to do it. Maybe we should offer to pay her?' Angela was conscious that a freelance photographer – unless a member of the paparazzi - wouldn't be rolling in money.

'I'll ask her that as well.'

'Even if we just chipped in for the cost of printing and a frame. I think we should do that at least.'

'But you're saving all your pennies, Maggi; you don't need to. It won't be that much.'

'Excuse me, if the dog club is giving Sybil a present I'm paying my whack.'

Angela sighed. 'Okay, okay, well, let Jon speak to Jemma first before we start talking about money. Okay, Jon?'

'Yes, I'll do it tomorrow – oh no, wait, I forgot. I meant to tell you: I won't be dog-walking tomorrow morning.'

'Oh?' Both women looked at him expectantly.

'I'm, um, you're not going to believe this, I've been invited to a coffee morning.'

'Excellent, glad to see you're properly getting into being a stay-at-home parent,' Maggi laughed.

'Is it in aid of anything?' Angela asked.

'In aid of anything?' Jon frowned.

'Yes, PTAs quite often organise coffee mornings to raise money for a new library or the rugby team trip to France.'

'Oh, no, no, at least I don't think it is.'

'Ah well, enjoy anyway. And don't eat too much cake.'

The conversation then turned to favourite cakes and handed-down recipes. Jon admitted he'd never yet tried baking although he prepared all the main meals and the women offered him tips.

'Do you have to take a cake to the coffee morning? If you do you can't beat a Victoria sponge,' Maggi said.

'As long as it's well-made,' Angela added. 'You're better off with cookies if it's your first time at baking; they're less easy to make a mess of.'

'That's true,' Maggi agreed.

Jon listened attentively to the women's advice and promised he'd nip out to the corner shop and buy some chocolate chips for cookies as soon as he got home.

'And do you want us to collect Benji and walk him for you?'

'No, thanks. I'm not planning to be at the coffee morning for that long; I'll take him when I get home. I might even see you on your way back.'

∞

The next morning Jon was a little distracted as he prepared the girls' breakfasts.

'Daddy, you've put sugar on my Frosties!'

'Sorry, Gracie, love. You can eat them like that, can't you?'

'Yuck! They're much too sweet. What would Mummy say?'

Mummy had already said a lot about the children eating sugar-coated cereal for breakfast and how porridge or muesli was much healthier. Jon had pointed out that he didn't have time to make porridge and that the girls hated muesli.

'You'd have time if you got up when I do,' Tilly had said pointedly. 'Instead of grabbing an extra thirty minutes in bed. Think what you could do with that thirty minutes.'

Jon had thought and, worryingly, images of Cathy had popped into his head. Cathy naked in his bed. He shook his head to dispel the vision but not before a warm glow that had nothing to do with porridge had suffused his stomach.

He tipped the bowlful of extra-sweet cereal into Benji's bowl to Sophie's horror. 'Daddy, you can't do that! You'll give Benji a heart attack.'

'Daddy, it's parents' evening on Thursday and you haven't made an appointment with Miss Brown yet.'

'It won't hurt him this once, Soph, and I thought I'd sent the letter back with an appointment time, Gracie.'

'Yes but Miss Brown can't do that time so you have to talk to her. Where's my breakfast, Daddy?'

Jon stopped, rested his head in his hands for a moment then took a deep breath. Why was everything going wrong today of all days? Just when he wanted to leave the house in a calm frame of mind. He glanced at the clock: they were still early by their standards. He was doing okay. He just had to get them fed and to school and then he could … have coffee with Cathy.

He'd felt just a smidgen of embarrassment when he'd told the Maggi and Angela that he was going to a coffee morning. Not that it was a complete lie: he would be having coffee and it was morning. It was just that he knew he'd given them the impression it was something more organised and there'd be more than two people there. Well, there might be, he told himself. You're only assuming you're the only one Cathy has invited. There may be other mothers there. And even if there weren't it didn't mean there was anything wrong with it. Tilly would have gone in his place if circumstances had been reversed. It was a well-known fact that parents alone at home needed company. He was sure he'd read something along those lines. Somewhere.

He somehow managed to get the girls to school early and he waited as they lined up to go in. Other mothers milled around him, chattering, and he nearly didn't hear the almost-whispered 'hello' from Cathy.

'Hi.' He sounded abrupt. He must calm down. 'How are you?'

'I'm fine; are you okay?'

'Yes. I'm good.' Again his voice had that nervous edge.

'I just wondered as you got here early,' she laughed. 'For once.'

'Oh,' he tried laugh with her but no sound came out of his mouth. 'Is it …'

'Are you …' Their words jumbled into each other.

'I'm sorry,' Jon said. 'Go on.'

'I was just going to ask if you were still okay for coffee this morning.'

'I was going to ask the same thing. That is, I mean, if you were up for it. Coffee, I mean.'

She leaned slightly into him, 'I'm always up for it, coffee that it.'

He was embarrassed to realise he was blushing. Cathy laughed again. 'Relax, we're only having coffee; we're not having an affair.'

'No, of course not, I was just … um … shall we go to the Costa by the market?'

'Costa? No, I thought we'd have coffee at my place. If that's all right with you?

'I don't want to put you to any trouble.'

'You're not. In fact Rosie will be very sorry if you don't come to ours. She and I made some little cakes yesterday specially for coffee time with my friend.'

'Well, in that case, I certainly can't refuse.' Jon relaxed a little. If Cathy's daughter knew he was going there for coffee it was all out in the open. There was nothing sneaky about it.

'Can I come in your car with you? My house is only round a couple of corners so I always walk here.'

'Yes, of course. Come on.'

'I'll give you directions. It's not far.'

He opened the door on the passenger side for her and she slipped in. She was still struggling to fasten her safety belt when he'd settled into the driver's seat.

'Let me help you.' He took the end of the belt from her. 'Oh, your hand's freezing!'

'You know what they say: cold hands, warm heart.'

She had twisted slightly in her seat to try to fasten the belt and now her face was very close to Jon's. He looked down and tried to concentrate on the job. He stuttered, 'It's orange juice.'

'What is?'

'Gracie accidentally tipped a carton of orange juice over the catch and now it's really hard to do up. I've tried to clean it using all sorts but it's impossible to get rid of the sweet stickiness. No-one usually sits here so it's not a problem because if we all go out we go in Tilly's car so … there!'

He'd finally managed to fasten the safety belt and he sat up and took a deep breath. 'There, as long as you don't ever want to get out we'll be fine now,' he laughed tremulously and turned the key in the lock. 'Now which way?'

∞

Like Jon, Cathy lived on the Beauville New estate, which bore the name New but had been in existence for nearly thirty years. Her house was a modest semi-detached not far from the school that had been built to cater for the young families that would move into the estate. One of the original houses, the estate had grown around it over the years and catered now for a wide range of incomes and life styles.

She showed him into the lounge while she made the coffee. He glanced around at the photos on display. Most were of Rosie, sometimes with her mum, sometimes on her own. Jon had picked up one of the both of them to have a closer look when Cathy returned to the room with a tray laden with a cafetiere, mugs and a plate of small brightly-iced cakes. She apologised for the garishness of the cakes, 'Rosie was a bit generous with the food colouring.'

'Don't worry; I'm sure they'll taste fine.'

'Please sit down. Anywhere is fine. Oh I haven't brought sugar.' She went to go back into the kitchen but Jon stopped her, 'No, I don't take sugar, thanks.'

'Oh, plates. I've forgotten those too.'

She hurried back into the kitchen and returned a moment later. 'I'm sorry, I'm not usually such a bad hostess. I think I'm out of practice.' She seemed to have picked up on Jon's unease even though they were on her home territory. Jon, on the contrary, had now relaxed and he strove to put her at ease.

'She's very pretty, your daughter.'

'Thank you, I think so.' She smiled for the first time since coming into the house. 'But your daughters are too. I think all little girls are!'

'At least in their parents' eyes.'

The conversation turned to school, teachers, Christmas and dogs.

'My husband hated dogs. He was bitten by a corgi when he was about six and he held that against all dogs. "They're all potential killers," he'd say. So even though I'd have loved to have had one we never did. And since he's been gone, I don't know, I suppose life has just been a bit too hectic to consider it.'

'Gone?' Jon wasn't sure what her marital status was.

'Divorced. Oh not dead, if that's what you were thinking!' She giggled. 'I might have wished him dead but my wishes rarely come true.'

'That's a shame.'

She raised her eyebrows at him.

'I don't mean that your husband's not dead; I mean generally not having wishes coming true is a bit sad.'

'Who knows? Perhaps my luck will change.' She looked intently at Jon, a little smile playing on her lips.

The phone rang and they both jumped.

'Excuse me, I'd better answer it.'

'Of course.'

'Hello … oh hi mum … why? What happened?'

There was alarm in her voice and then she said, 'Hang on a mo, Mum.' She put her hand over the mouthpiece and said to Jon, 'I'm sorry, it seems my dad has fallen so this going to be a long call.'

'I'll go, don't worry. Unless you need a lift anywhere?'

'No, I think he's fine; it's just that Mum will have to tell me all the details and how much inconvenience he's put her to.'

Jon laughed, 'Okay, well, thanks for the coffee and I'll thank Rosie for the cakes when I see her at school'

'Oh, no, don't do that. She doesn't know it's you. She thinks it's just one of the other mums.' Cathy had the grace to look shamefaced. 'Not that … well.'

He smiled, 'Okay, this'll be our little secret. And … thanks again, Cathy. I've really enjoyed it.'

'Me too. Maybe we can do it again?'

'I'd like that.'

∞

Jemma loved the idea of taking a photo of Jock and refused to accept payment. 'Don't be daft,' she said, when Jon asked her. 'I'll be delighted to do it for Sybil.'

'But we want it to be a surprise.'

'That may be tricky but I'm sure between us we can find a way to do it. They don't call you Sneaky Jon for nothing!'

'What do you mean sneaky? I'm not sneaky. I'm …'

'Okay, okay, I was only joking.' Jemma was surprised at his reaction.

'Sorry, I didn't mean to snap. I'm just a bit edgy. School stuff, you know.'

Jemma smiled. 'No problem, but how are we going to get this photo?'

'Angela is putting her mind to it,' he replied.

'And if Angela is putting her mind to it, it'll get done.'

'Absolutely.'

'I'll bring my other camera tomorrow - it's got a better lens - and we'll see how it goes.'

∞

The next day Jemma arrived early at the park entrance. Sybil and Jock were already there but Angela was only just pulling into the car park. Jemma wandered over and whispered to Angela that she had her camera and was ready. Angela nodded, 'Right, this is the plan. You and I will walk with Sybil and when we get to the bog garden I'll get a stitch and want to sit down. I'll persuade Sybil to sit with me awhile and then you can walk on with the dogs and do your stuff. How does that sound?'

'Fine. That sounds perfect.'

Which it would have been if Jock hadn't refused to walk anywhere without Sybil. He sat down at her feet and would not budge. When Sybil said, 'Why don't you sit here with Angela, Jemma, dear, and I'll walk the dogs on a bit instead?' Angela suddenly found her stitch had gone and they could all continue on the walk.

The next day Maggi asked Sybil if she knew anything about the very smelly flowers that grew in the bog garden, persuading her to veer off the path a little in order to get a better look and sniff. This time Jock was happy to stay with the other dogs but was decidedly unco-operative and none of the photos Jemma did manage to take came up to her high standard.

They were beginning to think that they'd have to tell Sybil of their plan when misfortune or good luck, depending on your point of view, befell them. Sybil phoned Angela early in the morning.

'Angela, could you possibly walk Jock for me today, please?'

This was unheard of: in the months that the dog club had been in existence Sybil had not missed a single day. Angela was worried. 'Sybil, whatever's wrong? You sound dreadful.'

'I have a tummy upset.'

'Oh no.'

'It's not too bad and it seems to be easing but if you could collect Jock and walk him for me I would be most grateful.'

'Of course, Sybil. What number's your flat?'

'No, I don't want you to come to my room and risk catching anything. I'll leave Jock in the foyer just before the usual time. The receptionist here is a nice girl; she'll keep an eye on him till you get there.'

'If you're sure, Sybil. Is there anything else you need? Anything I can get for you? You must make sure you drink plenty even if you don't feel like eating.'

'I will do and I have everything I need, thank you. If you just walk Jock and then drop him back to reception when you finish I'll be happy.'

'Well, if you're sure?'

'Yes, honestly. He's my main concern.'

∞

When the others arrived at the park and found Angela with both Mitzi and Jock they looked around anxiously. 'Where's Sybil?'

Angela explained and after they'd all murmured sympathetic words one by one they realised that this was the opportunity they'd been waiting for.

They took Jock up to what they knew was Sybil's favourite spot on the walk, where the stream ran down over some rocks creating a mini waterfall that in spring time was surrounded by daffodils. They couldn't arrange for the flowers to be there but they could get Jock to pose magnificently.

'It's as if he knows this is his big moment,' Maggi said, as they stood and watched.

'Yes,' Angela agreed. 'Even his eyes are shining.'

He turned his head this way and that as Jon called his name and Jemma snapped away. At last, she was happy that she had a good collection of photos from which to choose and Angela returned him to the residential home. As she was going in she noticed her own doctor was just leaving. She frowned and spoke to him. 'Morning Dr Peters.'

'Good morning, Mrs Richards.'

'Dr Peters, I know you can't discuss your patients but could you just tell me if you've been to see … oh dear, I don't know her surname. Sybil's her first name but we've never been more formal than that.'

'I can reassure you that I haven't been to see a Sybil, whatever her surname might be. Now I must hurry, more calls to make.'

'Of course, good day, doctor.'

The young receptionist on the desk had heard the exchange and she said to Angela, 'It's food poisoning.' She dropped her voice and looked around anxiously. 'Several of our residents have gone down with it, some quite badly.'

'Oh no, that's dreadful. But how do you know it's food poisoning and not a bug?'

'We've had a couple of doctors here and they agreed that the timing and symptoms all suggested it so we asked everyone who was feeling ill what they'd had to eat and it turned out they'd all had the salmon last night.'

'Dear me, what a dreadful thing to happen.'

'Yes, the chef is pulling his hair out. He's so careful and nothing like this has ever happened before. He thinks it must have been a dodgy bit of salmon.'

'But that means Sybil doesn't have a bug and isn't infectious so I can pop up and see her. What number is her flat, please?'

'Number 8. On the second floor. The lift's over there.'

'I think we can manage to walk up the stairs, thank you.'

∞

When Sybil opened the door to find Angela there she tutted, 'I told you you weren't to come up here and put yourself at risk.'

At her feet Jock's little tail wagged so furiously that his whole body shook. When Sybil bent to lift him up he licked her nose and made such a great fuss of her that she exclaimed, 'Good heavens, Jock, you'd think you hadn't seen me for months!'

Angela smiled at the pair of them and then said, 'Well, the receptionist said it's food poisoning, Sybil, not a bug and I can't catch that.'

'Oh, no, of course you can't. How foolish of me.'

'Although I thought you did your own cooking,' Angela said, suddenly remembering.

'I do usually but if there's something I like the sound of on the menu – like a nice bit of salmon - I eat in the dining room. But I don't think I'll be doing that again in a hurry. But I'm keeping you standing on the doorstep, do come in – if you'd like to?'

'Thank you, yes, I will.'

The wave of heat that greeted Angela caused her to undo the zip on her anorak before she could look around. The room she was in was a high-ceilinged sitting-room from which three doors led. There were china and glass ornaments on almost every flat surface and each chair wore an antimacassar. There were richly patterned rugs on the plain-carpeted floor and deep blue velvet curtains hung at the windows. On the mantel-piece above the mock fire amongst the china dogs and vases there was an ornate clock that ticked loudly. Angela was surprised; most pieces looked old but of good quality. Everything spoke of a previous very comfortable lifestyle.

Unaware of Angela's surprise Sybil said, 'Would you like a cup of tea?'

'No, thank you, I've left Mitzi in the car and though she's very good it isn't fair on her I feel. I just wanted to make sure that you haven't thought of anything you need.'

'Thank you but no. I don't feel very hungry at the moment …' then seeing Angela was about to lecture her on the importance of eating, Sybil hurriedly continued, 'but I'm making myself regular drinks of tea and hot blackcurrant juice. And it seems to be passing. I only had a very mild bout. Some of the old people in here have it much worse.'

When she'd extracted a promise from Sybil that she would call her if she felt worse or realised she needed anything Angela prepared to be on her way. 'I'll collect Jock same time tomorrow.'

'Oh no, dear, I'm sure I'll be fine by then. If I'm not I'll phone you.'

When Angela finally left, Sybil made herself a glass of hot juice and sat down in her favourite chair. She wrapped her shawl over her legs, Jock curled up at her feet and together they fell asleep in front of the afternoon television.

∞

'That's odd.'

'What is?'

'Isn't that the gentleman who usually walks Ned, you know, the greyhound?'

Jemma followed Maggi's line of vision. 'Yes, I think it is. But I could be wrong. All old people look alike to me.'

'Huh, charming,' Maggi grinned.

'What?'

'All old people look alike, do they? I'm surprised you can tell the difference between Sybil and me.'

'Oh no! I don't mean that. I mean … '

'Yes?'

'Well, you're not old! And actually,' Jemma put her head on one side as she thought about it, 'I don't think of Sybil as old either.'

'Good save,' Maggi grinned again then frowned. 'I'm sure it is him though. I wonder if something's happened to Ned.'

'He was quite old, wasn't he?'

'Yes, that's what worries me. I think I'll run over and ask him.'

'Is that a good idea? If Ned's died he might not want to be reminded.'

'On the other hand, he may appreciate sympathy. I would if anything happened to Bassett. I'll just go over.'

Maggi hurried across the grass to catch the man as he made his way towards a gate. 'Excuse me,' she waved, 'excuse me.'

The man stopped and smiled as he recognised her as a fellow dog-walker. 'Good morning.'

'Hi,' Maggi panted. 'Phew, I didn't realise that bit of grass was so steep.' She took a few gulps of air. 'There, that's better. Good morning. I hope you don't mind me asking but I couldn't help noticing that Ned's not with you today. Is everything all right?'

The man sighed. 'No, I'm afraid not. Ned passed away last night.'

'Oh no, I am sorry.'

'The end was very peaceful when it came and I was sitting by him so that makes me feel better. But I shall miss him.'

'Of course you will. We get so attached to our pets.'

'He was nearly sixteen you know, an exceptional age for a greyhound, so I must be grateful for that.'

'And he always looked so … happy – if a dog can look happy. He seemed content from what I saw of him.'

'Oh he was I think. I wasn't going to walk this morning but then I thought, no, Bernard, you need the exercise. Ned would want you to.' He laughed. 'How silly that sounds.'

'Not at all.' Maggi took his hand in both hers and squeezed it. He nodded in acknowledgement of the empathy that only another dog-owner could express. 'If you ever want to walk with us, please do. We walk the same way and the same time each day so we're easy to find!'

He smiled. 'I might just do that. Thank you.'

# Chapter 4

Angela's birthday weekend wasn't quite going to plan. Their train had been severely delayed and, as a result, it was gone nine o'clock when they reached their hotel. Their daughters had given up waiting and had gone out to eat, the hotel restaurant had stopped serving and Tony had started grumbling.

'Never mind,' Angela said, trying to make the best of it. 'Claire texted to say they were going to find a pizza place; we'll go and join them.'

'You know I can't eat pizza at this time of night; it gives me indigestion.'

'You don't have to have pizza; you can have pasta.'

'I'm knackered. I knew it wasn't a good idea coming to London on a Friday.'

'If you'd had the whole day off instead of insisting on working a half-day we could have been here earlier.' She hadn't wanted to begin the same old argument but Angela was finding it hard to remain cheerful in the face of such blatant misery.

Her husband sighed. 'Don't start that again. I told you that work is really difficult at the moment. I can't be taking days off willy nilly. Not without a good reason.'

'I'd have thought your wife's fiftieth birthday celebration may have counted as a good reason.'

'Not to the bosses it doesn't.'

Angela took a deep breath. 'Let's not argue. Let's just go and eat.'

'I'm not hungry now. Let's just go down to the bar and have a drink.'

'But I'm hungry!'

'You can have a bag of crisps.'

By the time the girls returned to the hotel, Angela and Tony had gone to bed, Angela having enjoyed a steak baguette and chips at the bar while her husband sipped miserably at his beer.

They finally met up at breakfast the following morning. Claire, the oldest and bossiest, was there with her husband, Sam, while Miranda and Emma both had current boyfriends in tow.

'Dad, can we get something clear, please?' Claire had requested everyone's attention before speaking. 'Are you paying for everything this weekend? Only Sam keeps fussing; he thinks we all ought to chip in.'

'Well, that's very nice of Sam,' Tony began but before he could continue Angela spoke, 'But of course Dad's paying. We invited you after all.'

'Sam's got a point,' Miranda said. 'It's going to be expensive for everything. And we could all afford to help pay.'

'Speak for yourself,' Emma said. 'Ben and me are students remember.'

'No apparent lack of money the way you were drinking last night,' Claire said.

'Girls, it's fine, honestly,' Angela interjected before sibling war broke out. 'It's my fiftieth treat and we're paying.'

'How is it a treat for you if you're paying?' Sam asked.

'It's a treat for me to have us all together. We so rarely manage it these days, so no more discussion. We're all going to enjoy ourselves.'

∞

'I swear gremlins were at work this weekend.' The look on Angela's face spoke more than her words could ever have done. Any reticence she might have felt about opening up to the rest of the dog club had been worn out of her by the weekend. 'For the final stage of our journey home last night we were transferred to a coach. There was vital work being done on the line, they said. At eight o'clock on a Sunday evening? I ask you. But really it was the perfect way to end the weekend, completely in keeping with the rest of it.'

'Oh dear,' Maggi spoke for the group. 'So it wasn't the best birthday celebration then?'

'Celebration? With Tony cringing each time he had to pay for anything, the girls bickering – the like of which I haven't seen since they were teenagers arguing over who had used whose make-up – the entire weekend and the boys sneaking off whenever they could to watch football on the big screen in the hotel bar.'

'Oh dear,' Maggi said again.

'How was the show?' Sybil asked tentatively.

'The man sitting in front of me must have been 6'6" if he was an inch. I had a crick in my neck by the end of the evening and the play, well, what I saw of it was clever but not entertaining. Certainly not funny, which is what I felt in the mood for - and needed - after a day wandering around London with the girls. "Come on, mum, let's go and buy you a birthday present," they said, but it was very odd as all the shops we visited were trendy clothes shops selling nothing I'd even consider wearing. The girls all found something but I came away with nothing except a very large credit card bill.'

Maggi was about to oh dear again when she thought better of it. Angela took a deep breath. 'Let's just say that I'm putting this weekend down to experience and hoping that I'll never have to repeat it. Now, let's walk!'

They set off at a sprint, Sybil – and Maggi - struggling to keep up with Angela. After a while the group settled into its more usual pace and when it came to the parting of the paths Sybil and Maggi took the lower while Jemma and Jon marched on with Angela. 'Wish us luck,' Jemma whispered back to the remaining two.

Maggi laughed, 'They're going to need it. Poor Angela. It sounds like she had a rotten birthday weekend.'

'Yes, such a shame. She was so looking forward to it.'

'I've bought a card for her, by the way. I'll need everyone to sign it without her seeing. I've got it in the car so perhaps you could sign it after she's driven off, and I'll get the others another time.'

'Yes, certainly. It's not her birthday until Thursday is it?'

'That's right.'

'I was wondering …' Sybil paused.

'What?'

'Oh no, it's just a silly idea of mine.'

'What is, Sybil?'

'Well, it occurred to me that it might be nice if we had a cup of tea and a piece of cake together after we've walked on Thursday. To celebrate Angela's birthday. But I expect she'll have something else planned.'

'That's a lovely idea. Where would we go? To that little park café?'

'Well, the park café isn't up to much these days I'm afraid. No, I was thinking you might come back to my flat. It's just across from the car park as you know and that would mean we wouldn't have to walk any further or drive anywhere.'

'That would be great! If it wouldn't be too much trouble for you?'

'Not at all, I'd be delighted. It would make a nice change. I haven't had visitors for a long time.'

'But you're right: that café is looking a little run-down these days; I wouldn't fancy eating in there. But you shouldn't have to do all the work; would you like me to bring anything? Shall I get a cake from the supermarket when I'm in work on Wednesday?'

'No, no, you're my guests; I'll provide the cake.'

∞

'This is delicious, Sybil!' Angela exclaimed after her first mouthful of Victoria sponge. 'So light and airy. Mine always turn out like bricks.'

Sybil blushed. 'It's all right, is it? I haven't made cake for a very long time.'

'It's more than all right, it's gorgeous,' Jemma said, her words accompanied by much nodding of heads from the others.

Maggi said, 'I'm embarrassed to think I suggested buying a cake now. You've been hiding your light under a cake tin, Sybil.'

'I'm so pleased it's turned out okay. I wanted it to be perfect.'

'And it is,' Angela said. 'Thank you so very much, Sybil, and thank all of you for your cards.'

They'd decided as they were having a birthday 'party' they should each bring their own card – but definitely no presents, Angela had been insistent when they'd invited her. 'I know this is a bit presumptuous but I'd rather say it now so we don't have any awkwardness later: I don't want any presents. You probably weren't planning on buying me one but just in case.'

'No, you're right, we weren't,' Maggi said with such a straight face that, for a moment, Angela felt she might have spoken out of turn, but then Maggi grinned. 'We'll save those for your sixtieth.'

Angela was touched by the thoughtfulness shown by her friends and as she thought it she realised that she did think of them as friends. They were no longer just a gang of dog-walkers who kept each other company; they had a stronger link than that. Indeed she found she liked their company as much if not more than many of her older friends. She raised her cup of tea, 'Here's to the dog club, long may we walk!'

'And here's to you, Angela,' Jon said, 'without whom the dog club would never have started.'

'To Angela,' they echoed his words as they toasted the birthday girl.

The dogs meanwhile sat patiently, each by its owner, hoping against hope that a crumb would drop in their direction. It was a squeeze getting them all into Sybil's sitting-room but with Sybil in her chair, Angela and Maggi on the sofa and Jon and Jemma on the floor they managed it. The tea tray had to be passed from one to the other from the kitchen in the beginning but once they were settled – and as long as nobody wanted to move – it was a comfortable sort of squeeze. Certainly as far as Pixie was concerned. With his nose on a level with Jemma's he could watch intently each bite of cake Jemma took.

'He really is very well-trained,' Angela said. 'If Mitzi were that close to food I'm sure she'd make a grab for it.'

'My uncle had him from a puppy and he devoted a lot of time to training him. I think he would have liked to have shown Pixie, who unbelievable as it sometimes seems, is from Crufts prize-winning stock, but he died before he had the chance.'

Jemma had stopped eating to reply to Angela and the slice of cake in her hand halfway to her mouth proved to be too much temptation for Pixie. He stuck out his tongue and it was gone before she finished speaking. 'Oh Pixie! Just when I was singing your praises!'

Everyone laughed and Jemma said, 'I'm afraid I'm not as strict as my uncle was. I spoil Pixie and let him get away with too much.'

'I don't think dogs should be too perfect,' Maggi said.

'Not much chance with ours,' Jon said, and everyone agreed.

∞

When she left Angela kissed Sybil's papery cheek and squeezed her hand. 'Thank you again, Sybil.'

Downstairs in the foyer the manager of the home came out of her office just as Angela came down the stairs. 'Ah, good morning. I believe you're one of Sybil's guests.'

'That's right. We've had a lovely time with her.'

'Good, and I have to tell you how pleasing it is to see Sybil inviting guests into her apartment. She's never done so up till now.'

'Really?'

'Yes, I get the impression she and her husband kept to themselves – or were enough for each other maybe – so she doesn't have that many friends. None that she's invited here anyway. She seems to have come alive over the last year or so particularly.'

'She is a reserved lady but a delightful one. I'm so glad that our little dog-walking group has been good for her.'

'Most definitely. She told me she was baking a cake and she was very nervous as she hadn't made one since she's been here.'

'She needn't have been; it was delicious. Her husband was a lucky man.'

Sybil watched the members of dog club leave. Because her flat was a corner one she had a good view across the car park from her bedroom as well as a view over the park itself from the living-room. She waved to Jemma as she and Pixie walked past and watched

52

Maggi and Jon let their dogs sniff around briefly before getting them back in the cars and setting off. When Angela reached her car she turned and looked up at the block of flats to see if Sybil was watching. When she spotted her she waved and blew an exaggerated kiss. Sybil smiled to herself and said to Jock, 'We did all right, didn't we, boy?'

∞

From one old lady to another, Jemma thought as she knocked on Gwennie's door. Although she had a key Jemma preferred not to use it unless Gwennie was unwell. It seemed more respectful that way.

'Come in, dear,' Gwennie opened the door with a flourish and took Jemma's arm, 'quickly.'

'What's the matter? Is something wrong?'

'No, no, nothing wrong but I saw something in the newspaper I want to show you.'

'Oh,' Jemma sighed. Gwennie was always seeing 'something in the newspaper' and it was either to do with people she'd known years ago – and whom Jemma'd never met – who'd died or it concerned 'eligible young men' that she thought would be ideal for Jemma.

'Now sit down and look at this. I'll make you a cup of tea in a minute. Here, I cut it out of last night's paper.' Gwennie thrust the cutting into Jemma's hand. It was only a small piece of paper and not an article but an advert. Jemma flicked the paper over thinking she must be looking at the wrong side but the other side showed an unidentifiable part of a photo. She turned the paper back over and read the advert. 'Want to meet the love of your life?' She groaned, 'Oh, no, Gwennie, what's this?'

'Read it all, go on.'

Jemma read the rest aloud, 'Looking for the one who will make your heart beat faster? The one you want to wake up next to for the rest of your life? Then join us on Monday evening at Blackmill parish hall for an evening of speed dating!' The rest of the advert gave details of the date, times and whom to contact.

Jemma put her head in her hands, 'Oh no, no, Gwennie. '

'Why not? It's only down the road. And …'

'Do you even know what speed dating is?'

'Yes, I called the organiser to ask.'

'Oh Gwennie, you didn't?'

'Don't worry, I explained I wasn't enquiring for me but for my young friend, and she was very helpful. I don't see what harm it can do; you'll get to meet a lot of nice young men, and you never know.'

'Speed dating is only for losers and people who don't have any friends.'

'I'll come with you if you want.'

'No, Gwennie, that won't be necessary as I'm not going.'

'Are you doing something else on Monday night?'

'No, but that's not the point.'

Gwennie sniffed. 'You're never going to meet anyone if you don't go out.'

They both sat in silence until Jemma said, 'Shall I put the kettle on?'

'I'll do it,' Gwennie said huffily as she pushed herself up from her chair straightening her back as she walked into the kitchen. Jemma, watching her, smiled to herself. She knew the intentions were good and she also knew Gwennie was never going to stop interfering – 'I only want the best for you' – until she was in a relationship. No, make that until she was married with three children. Then Gwennie might be satisfied. But at least her intentions were genuinely for what she believed would make Jemma happy; her mother, on the other hand, wanted to see Jemma married to the right sort of person, like her brother who'd somehow contrived to marry the daughter of a millionaire who also happened to be a Sir. 'Not an hereditary title,' her mum had pointed out, 'a bit nouveau riche, but nevertheless, not to be sniffed at.'

Jemma stroked Pixie's head as she read the advert again. 'What do you think, boy?' Pixie lifted his eyes to her. 'I suppose it would make Gwennie happy. I could just show my face there and then leave.' Pixie nudged her hand; he had other things on his mind. Jemma shook her head. 'It's no good asking me,' she said. 'You know you have to go and ask Gwennie for your treat.'

The boxer jumped up and in three strides was across the room and into the tiny corridor that led to the kitchen. Jemma heard Gwennie say, 'Don't worry, Pixie; I've not forgotten. I've got your biscuit here.'

Gwennie kept a packet of rich tea biscuits in the pantry especially for Pixie along with the milk chocolate digestives for her and Jemma. She maintained the silence when she carried the tray back into the living-room and handed Jemma her mug of tea.

'Okay, Gwennie, you win.'

The old lady looked up hopefully.

'I'll go to the speed dating ...'

Gwennie clapped her hands excitedly, 'Excellent!'

'But if I get there and hate it I'm not staying, okay?'

'Yes, yes ... as long as you give it a good try. Have a biscuit.' She proffered the plate.

'I shouldn't really; I've just had cake,' she said, taking a biscuit.

Jemma explained about Angela's birthday and Sybil's cake-making skills. She'd told Gwennie previously about trying to take a photo of Jock.

'She still has Jock, does she?' Gwennie knew almost as much about the dog club as Jemma did, loving to hear all about their walks in the park.

'Yes, in fact, he seems a little brighter of late. He might have just had a bug. I suppose dogs are prone to bugs just like humans. Maybe he'll live longer than we think.'

'I hope so for Sybil's sake.'

As her young visitor took another biscuit Gwennie smiled to herself. Jemma was such a lovely girl and shouldn't be wasting her time with old women. She sincerely hoped the speed dating would have a successful outcome.

∞

'You're doing what?!' Jon spluttered and then seeing the pathetic look on Jemma's face struggled to pull himself together. 'I mean, it was a surprise, that's all. I didn't see you as a speed dating sort but I'm sure it'll be great.'

Jemma gave him a 'really?' look and he tried not to laugh. 'Well, maybe not great but it'll be … an experience.'

'I'm only going to please Gwennie, you know, the old lady next door.'

'Why do you have to go to please her?'

'Because she reminds me of my nan.'

There didn't seem to be an answer to that so Jon patted her on the back sympathetically. 'Couldn't you just pretend to go?'

'No, she'll be at the window watching me leave.'

'You could sneak back in.'

'No, I've got to go through with it; I've promised her I will.'

'Promised?'

'Oh, yes, she made me swear. She's taking this very seriously. She is convinced I will meet the love of my life.'

'Do you want to?'

'Doesn't everyone?'

'I don't know. You did give me the impression that, at the moment anyway, you were settled with your job and Pixie.'

'I am. I love my work and I love Pixie but … oh I don't know. Once upon a time I'd have said that was nonsense and a woman with a career she loved could be satisfied with that but now I'm getting older …'

'Older? You're what? Twenty-four?'

'Twenty-five, but soon I'm going to be older than all the brides I photograph. I do want to have a partner and children, I can't deny that; it's just that the effort of finding the right one is a bit much.'

'Well,' Jon said, 'I can't wait for Tuesday morning to hear the outcome of your night. Will she find love – or just louts? Pleasure or pain? A soul finely-attuned to hers? Or will he be tone-deaf?'

'Did I ever mention that Pixie is highly-trained? At a word from me he can kill with a single bite.'

Jon laughed and putting his arm around her shoulders gave her a cuddle. 'Well, don't worry if speed dating doesn't work; you've always got the dog club.'

∞

For once Jon arrived at the school to pick up the girls with time to spare. He was never actually late for them but it was usually a last-minute rush. He parked the car and strolled over to where a group of mums and grandparents were waiting. Several acknowledged him recognising him as Sophie's dad or Gracie's but he didn't feel comfortable about joining their conversations. That was partly why, when Sophie had started in school, that he had originally timed his collection arrival very carefully to avoid having to stand around and chat about washing powder or *Eastenders* or other tedious subjects he imagined the women discussing. He'd have been surprised - and flattered – to discover how often he was talked about and his status and availability discussed.

He spotted a grandfather he'd seen a few times standing on his own so Jon was about to walk over and join him for a 'manly' talk when a voice behind him said, 'Hi, stranger.'

Jon turned around quickly, 'Hi Cathy.'

'How are you?'

'Fine. You?'

'Yes, we're well again now.'

'You've been ill?'

'Tummy bug. Both of us went down with it.'

'That's why I haven't seen you at school then. I was wondering.'

'Did you think I was avoiding you?' Cathy looked up at Jon through her lashes and once again he was convinced she was flirting with him. When they'd had coffee in her home she'd been uneasy, certainly not flirtatious and he'd been wondering if he'd misread the signals. Now he wondered again.

'Did you miss me?' There it was again: that suggestion of intimacy.

'You know me,' he shrugged, 'always rushing. I thought I just might have missed you as I was late.'

'Would you like to do it again?' Her words tumbled out hurriedly. The first children were coming out of school and Rosie, Gracie and Sophie would appear soon. The opportunity would be gone for another day.

'Coffee you mean?'

'Yes, of course, what else did you have in mind?' She smiled teasingly at him. Now he was sure: she was flirting.

He laughed uncomfortably, 'Yes, coffee would be nice, but maybe an afternoon would be better. Can you do afternoons?'

She said she could and they arranged that Jon would go to her house the following Wednesday at two. 'That'll give us time for coffee and a chat before we have to pick up the girls,' she said.

'Daddy!' A little whirlwind threw itself at Jon's legs. 'Daddy, I'm going to be an angel!'

'How very inappropriate, Gracie.'

'What's inappopinate mean, Daddy?'

'Daddy, I'm going to be the ghost of Christmas presents.'

'Daddy, I'll need a pink dress with wings.'

'And I need chains. I have to carry lots of chains, heavy chains that make a clanking noise.'

'I don't think angels wear pink, Gracie, and are you sure that's the right ghost, Sophie?'

'Oh yes, Miss Jones said.'

'Miss Brown said I have to wear a floaty dress with wings. She didn't say it couldn't be pink.'

Jon looked over their heads to where Rosie was telling her mother that she was to be a shepherd in the Christmas panto. He caught Cathy's eye and they shook their heads and smiled at each other. 'See you Wednesday if not before,' Jon mouthed and Cathy nodded.

∞

'Drat you, you stupid car! Don't do this to me now!' Maggi leaned back in her seat and slammed her hands onto the steering wheel. Brenda's face appeared at the window next to her.

'What's up, Maggi? Car not starting?'

'No, I've tried everything and there's no sign of life. I could do without it this evening too. I thought I was actually going to get home at a reasonable time tonight.'

'It's probably the battery, that's all.'

'I'm sure it is. It's been dodgy for a while. I've been trying to remember to recharge it every now and again but I haven't done it for a while. I think I really need a new battery but that's going to cost a few pounds.'

'We've got jump leads in the garage. Come home with me and Steve can bring you back and get it started.'

'Thanks, Bren. I'm inclined to leave it until tomorrow but I know that's silly. Won't Steve mind you volunteering him?'

'Nah, course not. He can make himself useful for once. Come on.'

By the time they'd got to Brenda's, had a cup of tea and a chocolate bar, returned to the car with the jump leads and got it started it was gone eight. By the time Maggi had driven home, put the battery on charge and finally closed her front door behind her, she was worn out. She made herself some toast and took it to bed. She flicked on the television and watched it as she shared her toast with Bassett who approved greatly of this eating in bed habit. She woke up with a start some time later to find crumbs in the bed and the television still talking to itself. She yawned. 'I suppose I should clean my teeth, eh, Bassett?' The dog who didn't like being disturbed when he was comfortable closed his eyes and leaned further into her. Maggi yawned again. 'You're right; why bother? It won't hurt this once.' She switched off the television and the bedside light. 'Night, night, Bassett, sleep tight.'

Before setting off for the park the next morning Maggi checked the battery meter. The level of power in the battery had hardly improved at all. There was no escaping it: she was going to have to buy a new one. She groaned. That meant seventy or eighty pounds out of her hard-earned savings. And she'd already withdrawn a fair bit to pay for Christmas presents to send to the family in Australia. And the postage had cost nearly more than the gifts. She'd never accumulate enough to book a flight to Australia at this rate. She'd have to see if there were any more shifts going at work.

Only Sybil was at the park when Maggi arrived and she quickly realised that Maggi wasn't her usual cheerful self. 'What's wrong, Maggi?'

'Oh, nothing really. Just the stupid car.'

'Ah.' Sybil had never driven but she remembered the times Reg had grumbled about the car. 'My husband used to say they are very useful when they work properly but the devil's own tool when they don't.'

'He was right there. Still it's not a major problem; I just need a new battery. It could be a lot worse but I've only just had to replace the fridge – you remember the problems I had with that flooding, don't you? - and, well, nobody has much spare cash at this time of year, do they?'

'It's a very expensive season I fear especially for anyone with young children.'

Jon, who'd joined them, agreed. 'Tilly's got a well-paid job and we still struggle to pay the bills in January. I don't know how some people manage.'

Conversation about the growing commercialisation of Christmas took them and the rest of the dog club up to the parting of the paths. Maggi decided she needed a good long walk to walk out the frustrations so she and Angela set off leaving the other three to take the more leisurely lower path.

Jemma and Jon were fascinated by Sybil's reminiscences of Christmas from her childhood. They found it hard to believe that children had ever been grateful for an orange and a sixpence or, if they were very lucky, a single toy.

'My childhood Christmases weren't quite as spartan as that because my parents were comparatively wealthy but I certainly never received piles of presents,' Sybil explained. 'A book, a jigsaw and a doll and I was thrilled.' She sighed, 'I feel sorry for parents these days. And for Maggi.'

∞

The new battery cost slightly less than Maggi had been anticipating but it was still a big chunk from her savings. In work she asked the supervisor if there were any shifts going spare.

'More shifts, Maggi? You're already doing more than everyone else. You'll wear yourself out.'

'I keep telling myself it'll be worth it when I get to hold my grandchildren again. But, I admit, it's getting harder and harder to convince myself of that.'

'You won't be able to go if you make yourself ill.'

'No, I know, but I'm fit and healthy. It's just tiring and I can cope with that. So, are there any more shifts I could do?'

'I'll have a look at the rota and see if I can find one or two for you.'

∞

Jemma meanwhile had her own problem: the speed dating evening. She had given up trying to think of an excuse; she knew Gwennie wouldn't accept one. She'd resigned herself to going along. It might not be that bad, she thought. Just before she thought, who are you trying to fool? But if she went, she didn't have to stay long. Just long enough to persuade Gwennie that she'd tried. She'd only promised to go; she didn't promise to stay.

So on the evening she made an effort with her clothes – Gwennie had insisted she call in before setting off so she could inspect her – 'I know what you're like, young lady!' – had passed the inspection in a neat denim skirt, thick woolly tights and a dark green polo neck jumper, and was standing, or rather hopping nervously from foot to foot, outside the hall plucking up her courage to go in.

'There's no reason to be scared!' A voice behind her made her jump. She looked around to find facing her a man about two inches taller than her, with neatly parted generously-gelled flattened short hair, and a faceful of spots. 'I've been to lots of these,' he carried on enthusiastically. 'They're great fun.'

'Oh,' Jemma said. His excitement was beginning to show in the odour emanating from him.

He offered her his hand, 'I'm Simon by the way.'

Jemma took his damp hand and he held hers surprisingly tightly. 'I'm Jemma,' she said, keen to be released from his grip.

'Of course, we're breaking the rules now,' he said giggling.

'We are?'

'Yes, we're not supposed to meet until it we're all sitting down at tables.'

She tried to pull her hand away from his but still he hung on.

'Maybe it's fate.'

'What is?' she asked unable to help herself but dreading the answer.

'Bringing us together. Here. Same time. Same event. Our stars drawing us together.'

'I arrived before you and this is the only event on here tonight,' Jemma pointed out the flaws in his argument but he was beyond reason.

'I feel good about this evening. Don't you? I feel tonight the gods are on my side. Come on, let's go in.'

Still holding her hand he dragged her through the door into the brightly lit village hall. Inside, a number of small tables had been laid out each, at a discreet distance apart, each with two chairs on opposite sides. Jemma counted ten tables but only three men and five women including her and Simon. Another couple who both carried clipboards bore down on them.

'Good evening … both,' the woman seeing their hands linked frowned and Simon immediately released Jemma's hand and held both his hands in the air in an attitude of surrender. 'You got us bang to rights, gov!' he laughed as the clipboard couple looked at each other uncertainly.

'Just joking,' Simon went on.' I was just helping this lady pluck up her courage to come through the door. We've never met before this evening, I assure you.'

The man sniffed and said, 'Okay, Simon, we believe you,' before turning to bestow a beaming smile on Jemma. He took her hand in a strong cool grip. 'Good evening, Miss. May I say how delightful it is to see you here and I promise you that you won't regret your decision.'

'Okay, Malcolm, down, boy,' the woman, whom Jemma assumed to be Malcolm's wife, took over. 'May I have you name, please, Miss …'

'Jemma Cuthbert.'

'Welcome, Jemma. Have you ever been to a speed dating event before?'

Jemma shook her head, and the woman who introduced herself as Barbara explained the procedure for the evening. As she explained she wrote JEMMA on a sticky label, which she tore off and stuck to Jemma's jumper. 'We'll be starting soon,' she said. 'Obviously, as it's our first time in this hall, we've not got as many people as we'd have liked  but I'm sure once word gets around numbers will increase. Now if you'd like to wait over there we'll get you all sitting down in a minute. Oh, just one other thing: we do ask that you don't talk to each other until you're sitting at a table and we've commenced. Okay, Jemma?' Her voice rose at the end of the sentence.

Jemma nodded. She wasn't keen to talk to anyone whether they were sitting down or not. And now she could see that she wasn't going to be able to escape. She sighed and resigned herself to the rest of the evening, which, as there were so few contenders, – she wasn't sure if that were the right word but it seemed appropriate - shouldn't last very long.

She looked around. The other women were all older than her. She was sure of that. Although she could tell they'd made a special effort. One of them was wearing so much mascara she could barely open her eyes. The men, apart from Simon, also looked older. Both were thinning on top and one had a paunch that she'd have thought he would try to conceal but the striped sleeveless pullover he was wearing only drew attention to it. Thankfully she didn't recognise any of them.

She looked at the door. If she sneaked out now she could tell Gwennie the truth: that she'd gone in and enrolled but that there hadn't been enough men so she'd volunteered to leave.

But just as she was edging her way across the hall Barbara called for attention. She announced that owing to low numbers they'd decided to change the format this once. Instead of the usual three minutes per table they'd decided to increase it to ten. 'And as we're two men short Malcolm and I will join in.'

'How's that going to work?' Simon said. 'I'm not gay, you know.' He laughed loudly to make his point.

'No, of course not, Simon,' Barbara said. 'If you were you could come to our special gay evenings. Every Wednesday Cullenwell Town Hall. We alternate between male and female evenings. What are we on this week, Malcolm?'

'Er, men I think.'

'But,' she laughed gaily, 'to get back to this evening, Malcolm and I will sit in, as I said, so that the ladies don't feel left out. And it will be good practice for you. We can lead you through a typical chat.' She made the word sound very short and sharp with an exaggerated t at the end. 'So …' she looked around, beaming furiously, 'are we all ready?'

The assembled group muttered their assent. Except for Simon who gave a loud, 'Definitely!' And rubbed his hands together in anticipation.

Barbara handed each of them a sheet of paper and a pencil before telling the women to go and sit at adjacent tables. 'Now before I forget, please switch off your mobile phones. As there are so few of us we won't bother with numbers; just use people's names and indicate on the paper whether it's yay or nay, yay, of course, meaning that you'd be happy to see that person again and nay, well, I hope there won't be many of those.' Her head on a tilt she smiled widely and briefly before allocating the men to women.

Simon was first to arrive at Jemma's table. The upside of that was that she didn't have to contribute to the conversation as he was happy to talk about himself for ten minutes. When the buzzer went to move on, he exclaimed, 'But you haven't told me anything about yourself! Never mind, that can wait till our first date.' He winked in what she assumed he thought was an enticing way. Jemma smiled weakly, which Trevor, her next visitor took as a good sign.

'Hello,' he said, 'I'm Trevor. You must be …' he leaned close to her chest ostensibly to read her name tag but Jemma had her doubts, 'Jemma. I'm delighted to meet you.'

Then he sat back and waited for her to speak. She smiled and said, 'You too.'

After a few moments had passed Jemma said, 'Have you done anything like this before?'

'No.'

'Nor me,' she giggled. 'It's a bit silly, isn't it?'

'No,' he looked affronted.

'I don't mean you're being silly,' she said hurriedly in case he'd misunderstood. 'I just mean the idea of speed dating.'

'I think it's a good idea.'

Jemma tried to think how she could retrieve the conversation. Of course, Pixie. Men liked dogs; her boxer would be a good topic of discussion.'

'I have a boxer called Pixie. Do you have a dog?'

'I don't like dogs. I'm allergic to them.'

There was nothing left to say. They sat in silence for the rest of the ten minutes in spite of Barbara's stern glances.

When the buzzer went Trevor moved off without so much as a goodbye and, just as the third man was about to sit at Jemma's table Barbara pushed him aside. 'Would you like to do – so to speak' she giggled, 'Denise next, Brian? Then you can come back to Jemma.'

Brian obediently did as he was told and Barbara sat down opposite Jemma. She said, 'Jemma, do you have a problem?'

'No, I don't think so.'

'Only I've noticed you're not really entering into the spirit of this evening. You hardly said a word to Trevor or Simon. That's not a helpful attitude, Jemma. We don't organise these events for our own benefit, you know. You will only get out of them as much as you put in.'

Jemma was about to defend herself but Barbara continued, 'Now I hope I'm going to find positive answers from you on your response sheet. But for now, would you like to practise your technique on me? We'll start from the beginning; let's pretend my name's Tom and I've just come to sit down at your table. I've introduced myself; what are you going to say to me?'

Jemma tried to think of a suitably witty retort. She bit her lip and wished Maggi were there. She bet Maggi would be able to sort out this Barbara.

'Well, Jemma? I'm waiting.'

Jemma sighed. 'How do you do, Tom. Do you like dogs?'

It turned out 'Tom' was a huge dog-lover and, in fact, was enthusiastic about every topic Jemma raised. By the end of the ten minutes she was almost wishing Barbara were Tom so they could go on a date.

She was brought back to reality by Barbara saying, 'That was much better, Jemma. You see, you can do it if you try. Now I want to see you enticing, err,' she peered at the approaching man, 'Brian. Here, we are, Brian. She's all yours, you lucky man.'

Brian beamed at Jemma before squeezing himself and his paunch onto the chair. 'Hi Jem.'

As she told Gwennie later, the dandruff on his shoulders wouldn't have put her off necessarily if he hadn't kept scratching and shaking his head, causing clouds of white dust to fall at frequent intervals during their ten minutes.

'How many times?'

Jemma thought back. 'At least four. Honestly, Gwennie, I'm surprised he has any skin left on his head.'

'I'm sorry, Jemma. It obviously wasn't such a good idea of mine after all.'

The old lady looked so disappointed that Jemma gave her a hug. 'No, it was good for me to get out there, Gwennie.'

'Really? You mean that?'

Jemma sighed. 'No not really. But don't worry. It was an experience and I survived. And when I tell you all about it we can have a good laugh. So get that kettle on and bring out the biscuits. I need solace.'

∞

The dog clubbers were equally entertained by her tales of speed dating. That is once she'd explained what it was for Sybil's benefit.

'It sounds rather like a cattle market, dear,' she exclaimed.

'It's not quite that bad,' Jemma said. 'At least both parties get to opt in or out.'

'And did you?' Angela asked. 'Opt for one of them?'

'Good grief, no. The closest I got was with Barbara.'

They all stared at her, puzzled.

'I mean when she was pretending to be Tom,' she said. 'I'd better start from the beginning.'

So that day nobody took the shorter path. All were too amused by Jemma's stories, which were only very slightly exaggerated for her audience's benefit.

'Oh, Jem, it sounds like a nightmare,' Maggi said.

'I was wishing you were there with me,' Jemma said, 'whispering witty or sarcastic comments in my ear. It wasn't until I got home and was in bed that I kept thinking what I should have said.'

'Ah, well, you won't have to see any of them again,' Jon said.

'I certainly hope not,' Jemma agreed.

# Chapter 5

Maggi was delighted when her supervisor gave her extra shifts in the final run-up to Christmas but it did make dog-walking difficult. Angela insisted it was no problem for her to pick Bassett up and the others all agreed that they'd be happy to help out but Maggi didn't like to feel she was taking advantage so she took one extra morning shift and three late evening ones over the weekend. The shelves needed refilling almost constantly and the shop was so busy during the day that she preferred the late shifts simply because there was room to do her work without customers taking goods from her hands.

Brenda hated the late shift. 'I don't know how you can do it, Maggi,' she said one day as they stacked shelves together. 'Working at that time of night and then going home in the dark to an empty house.'

'I enjoy the solitude,' Maggi shrugged, 'and the house isn't empty anyway: Bassett is there waiting for me. He always makes me feel welcome, as if I've been away for a year, not a few hours.'

Brenda shook her head. 'I couldn't do it.'

They continued to stack and then Brenda said, 'What are you doing for Christmas this year?'

'Same as ever,' Maggi said. 'Get my phone call from Australia in the morning and then share a turkey joint with Bassett before going for a lovely walk in the afternoon. Fall asleep in front of whatever's on telly in the evening and then go to bed.'

'I do wish you'd come to us. We'd love to have you and we always have plenty of food.'

'I know you do, Bren, and it's kind of you to offer every year but I enjoy my Christmas days, really I do. Just a change from routine makes them special for me. Plus my phone call, of course.'

'Do your dog-walking gang still walk on Christmas day?'

'No, we all do our own thing. They've all got family around.' As she said that Maggi wondered about Sybil. She'd never asked her

68

what she did at Christmas; she probably enjoyed the festivities with others in the sheltered accommodation.

∞

At almost the same time as Maggi and Brenda were discussing Christmas plans Sybil was also thinking about Christmas and the next day when she found it was just Maggi and herself taking the lower path around the park she decided to be brave.

'Maggi, what are you doing for Christmas?'

Maggi told Sybil what she'd said to Brenda, that it was the same every year. 'Why? What are you doing, Sybil?'

'Usually most of the residents have Christmas lunch in the dining-room and then we sing some carols, listen to the Queen's speech and have a nap until they bring Christmas cake around at tea-time.'

'That sounds quite jolly,' Maggi said, hoping she'd never end up in a home.

'They try hard but it's basically institution food and I haven't enjoyed a Queen's speech since, oh, probably 1968.'

Maggi laughed, 'Oh dear, not so jolly then.'

'No, so I was wondering – and you must say no if you would rather not – don't feel obliged – I would hate that – but it seems a bit silly – when we're both on our own with our dogs – but I don't want to put you under any pressure ...'

'Sybil, just ask me whatever it is!'

'I wondered if you would like to come to me on Christmas Day. I haven't cooked Christmas lunch for years and I'd love to. Afterwards we could take the dogs round the park, and then maybe we could play a game of cards or something ...' Sybil faltered off.

'Sybil, I think that would be absolutely brilliant! I'd love to do that!'

'Really? You would? You're not just saying that?'

'Not at all. I think it's a great idea. As long as you're happy to cook but I can help if you want?'

'If you want to but I love cooking so you don't have to.'

'Okay, well, maybe I'll bring a box of choccies to eat when we're playing cards. How about that?'

'That sounds lovely. I shall look forward to it.'

'Me too,' said Maggi as she put her arm through Sybil's. 'And the dogs will love it!'

∞

The first Christmas, after they'd been walking together about four months, Angela had said that rather than give each other presents or even cards – 'if you were wondering what would be good etiquette' - 'may I suggest that we do Secret Santa for the dogs?'

'Secret Santa?' Sybil hadn't heard the phrase.

'We decide on a maximum amount – not a lot, a couple of pounds maybe – and then the dogs' names go into a hat and we each pick one out. We don't say which dog we have but then it's our responsibility to get a small gift for that dog.'

They'd all agreed that would be a good idea and on the day before Christmas Eve they held a little gift exchange ceremony at the end of the walk. The presents were as varied as the dogs. That year Mitzi found herself the recipient of a neon pink diamante-studded collar and Sybil helped Jock to open his present to find a tartan feeding bowl.

This year Maggi had Mitzi and, with money being in such short supply – and as she felt she had to take a small gift for Sybil as Sybil was refusing to take any money towards their Christmas lunch – she set to trying to think of a cheap but acceptable present for the poodle who had everything.

Browsing on the internet she found the answer: home-made dog biscuits. She had all the ingredients in her cupboard and they didn't take long to make. Being Maggi of course she had to add a little pink food colouring. And then a little more as the dough hadn't gone pink enough for her liking. But when she took the tray of bone-shaped biscuits out of the oven she was distressed to see they'd turned a dirty mushroomy sort of colour.

'Oh dear, Bassett, they don't look very good, do they?'

Bassett sat at her feet and looked up at her expectantly. He was happy to go along with anything she said if there was a chance he might be fed from it. And he usually was when Maggi was stood by the stove. But she shook her head this time, 'They're a bit hot at the moment; you'll have to wait until they cool down before you can sample them for me.'

Bassett understood the word 'wait' and wandered over to his bed where he flopped down.

'Oh, Bassett, don't look so hard done by!' The dog lifted mournful eyes to her and she laughed. 'You have the hang-dog look down to a T, you know.'

When the biscuits had cooled enough Maggi called Bassett to her and gave him one to try. There was a satisfying crunching sound as he bit it in half and, by the speed with which he devoured it, Maggi assumed it must taste better than it looked. Although Bassett's taste-buds were possibly under-developed as there was very little that he wouldn't eat. Or try once at least. In fact lettuce was the only foodstuff she could think of that he would leave on the floor untouched if he came across it.

She picked up another biscuit and sniffed it. She was pleasantly surprised: the smell resembled that of shop-bought biscuits she'd occasionally treated Bassett with. She drummed her fingers on the work-top as she thought. She didn't have enough flour to make another batch and the planned exchange of gifts was happening the next day. She shrugged, 'Oh well, Bassett, I'm sure they'll be fine if I wrap them up daintily.'

Bassett edged his bottom along the floor to be closer to her feet in case there were any more treats going. Maggi looked down at him, 'Oh go on then, just one more.' She picked out one of the more misshapen biscuits and gave it to him. 'Now, what am I going to wrap them in?'

∞

The next day the dog clubbers made a big show of concealing their gifts as they slipped them into the big black sack Angela had brought along for the purpose. 'All done?' she asked. 'Now, who's going to be Santa this year?'

'What about Sybil?' Jon said.

'I don't mind if someone else would like to do it,' Sybil demurred.

'Nonsense, come along, Sybil, let's begin.' Angela clapped her hands together, excited as a child on Christmas morning. She had always loved Christmas and everything about it from the cheesy songs to the Queen's speech, from midnight mass on Christmas eve to the cold turkey for Boxing Day lunch, but most of all she loved to choose presents for people and to watch as they opened them, hoping desperately that they'd love the gift she'd chosen with so much care.

'The first one is for …' Sybil peered at the label, 'Benji.'

'Hooray,' Angela said as she clapped enthusiastically. 'What have you got, Benji?'

'A new ball,' Jon said after he'd unwrapped the present that had been cunningly concealed in a square cardboard box. 'Excellent, just what he needs as he's chewed his last pieces. Thank you, Santa,' he said, looking at Jemma, who looked away feigning innocence.

The other dogs were all declared to be equally thrilled with their gifts: Jock with his low-fat senior treats, Pixie with his extra-large bag of doggie chocs, Bassett with his soft woollen blanket and Mitzi with her bag of strangely-coloured bones.

As they parted at the end of their walk they wished each other merry Christmas. Family commitments over the holiday season meant they wouldn't walk together until the day after Boxing Day and in Jon's case not until after the children had gone back to school.

'Although you could bring them along,' Angela suggested.

'Hm, I might do that. Give them a chance to let off steam. The holidays always result in at least one huge argument. And they're older now, old enough to manage a long walk. Yes, well, if we're coming I'll make sure we're here on time, so don't wait for us if we're not here.'

'Okay, everyone, have a wonderful Christmas and don't eat too much!' Maggi said, adding, 'And I'll see you on Christmas Day at about half past twelve, Sybil.'

'I'm looking forward to it, 'Sybil said.

And she was. For the first time for years Sybil was excited about the prospect of Christmas. For years when Reg had been alive they'd alternated spending Christmas first with one set of parents and then the other. Later they'd gone to Reg's sister. And always there'd been the unspoken assumption that, as Sybil was childless, she'd prefer to spend her time in the kitchen, preparing food or, more often, washing-up. She didn't mind helping and she did love cooking but she'd have much preferred to have got down on the floor with her nieces and nephews and played with their new toys with them, exclaiming over the shininess of the red car or the loudness of the Jack-in-the-box.

Eventually she and Reg decided they'd rather be on their own at Christmas. Between them they made it very special, spoiling each other and resolutely refusing to have the traditional sprouts as neither of them liked them. In fact, after the first couple of years enjoying Christmas on their own, they'd given up on the whole turkey idea and instead treated themselves to the best fillet steak they could find washed down with a delicious red shiraz. For weeks before Reg studied the Sunday paper supplements for recommendations and would search out what sounded to him like 'just the ticket'.

I think you'd approve of my Christmas this year, Reg, Sybil thought as she and Jock walked back to her flat. I'm doing what I want with someone I like. And, don't worry, I chose a good wine; it was recommended by that man you used to like in the Sunday paper. Yes, I think this year will be 'just the ticket'.

∞

Jemma was staying at her parents' house over Christmas and Jon was going to his in-laws; only Angela was planning a big family Christmas at home. She had dragged Tony out to the garden centre the weekend before so she could choose a tree and the house was now warm and welcoming, tastefully decorated and lit. The tree decorations included some that she'd had since the children had been tiny and even some that they'd made in school had survived the years and came out faithfully each December. To Angela that was part of the joy of Christmas, the traditions that they'd been brought up with and that she hoped had been passed on in turn to her own children.

It was Claire's turn to go to Sam's parents for Christmas this year so it was just Miranda and Emma who were both arriving home Christmas eve evening. Miranda was bringing Paul, her boyfriend. When Angela had asked why he wasn't going home Miranda had said that he didn't get on with his step-dad, and that, anyway, he wanted to be with her and was it a problem? Angela sighed; the girls seemed so touchy these days it was difficult to have a conversation with them sometimes without feeling she was treading on eggshells. She thought they were supposed to leave that behind with their teens. By now she'd hoped she would have three young women to whom she could relate not three stroppy females.

One of the traditions she'd fixed on over the years took place on Christmas Eve afternoon. Tony finished work at lunchtime and together they'd listen to the service of Nine Lessons and Carols on the radio while they prepared the vegetables for the next day. Normally Angela would never prepare vegetables in advance it having been drilled into her that they'd lose all their goodness if left to stand in water but she felt Christmas could be an exception.

She hummed carols to herself as she prepared prawn and mayonnaise sandwiches for the two of them. She opened a packet of crisps – something else she would never have in the house as a rule – and picked at a few while wondering what time Tony would get home. She glanced at her watch and tutted; he was normally home by now. She ate a couple more crisps and took the pencil she'd stuck behind her ear in her fingers and jotted on her to-do list: remind Emma it's her turn to collect Grandma from the home tomorrow morning. She won't be happy about that, Angela thought, having to get up early on Christmas morning but tough.

Miranda'd done it last year and it was only fair that the girls took some responsibility. Besides Tony's mum liked chatting to her grand-daughters.

Angela suddenly realised she'd eaten the entire packet of crisps and she'd planned to share them with Tony. She sighed. That wasn't a good start to the season. She must try not to over-indulge this year. She said that every year and every year something seemed to come over her and her resolutions to be sensible. Ah, well, it was only once a year and she was normally very controlled about what she ate.

She checked her watch against the kitchen clock. Where on earth was Tony? She gave up waiting and ate her sandwich. She'd have to start on the vegetables by herself.

By the time she'd finished preparing the root veg she was beginning to worry. In spite of the frankly scary television campaigns and the high police presence on the roads, some idiots still insisted on drinking and driving. Suppose Tony had had an accident? Would they know to contact her? Yes, she reassured herself: he carried next of kin details in his wallet. They both did; Angela had insisted upon it many years ago after a friend's husband had been knocked down and no-one had told his wife for two days.

When the phone rang she jumped and rushed to it. 'Hello?'

'Hi Mum, how are the sprouts doing? Have you put them on to cook yet?' The sprouts were a long-standing family joke as Angela liked to serve them still crisp while the girls insisted they could only eat them – if they really had to – if they were soggy and could be mashed up.

'Oh hello, Emma.'

'Well, I wasn't expecting a fanfare but you might sound pleased to hear from me!'

'I'm sorry Emma but it's your father. He hasn't come home yet.'

'So? He's probably having a Christmas drink with his mates.'

'He never does that. He always comes straight home to help me with the veg.'

'Perhaps this year he feels like a change. Why don't you ring him if you're worried?'

'I did but his phone's switched off.'

'Well, I wouldn't worry. He'll be home soon. Anyway the reason I'm calling is to say I'm going out with the girls this evening so I won't want supper. I thought I should let you know.'

'What are you going to have to eat then?'

'We'll get something in the pub. Gotta go now, Mum, see you later, bye.'

Angela could hear festive sounds in the background, Band-Aid's Do they know it's Christmas mingling with the buzz of excitement. She replaced the phone and then picked it up again and retried Tony's number. It was still switched off. She scolded herself. Pull yourself together, it's probably as Emma said, Tony's just having a drink. He'll be home soon. Now get on with what you've got to do; the sprouts aren't going to peel themselves.

∞

Angela had finally sat down with a cup of tea and a shortbread biscuit when the front door opened. 'Is that you, Tony?' She jumped to her feet. 'Where on earth have you been? I've been worried about you.' She hurried into the hall where her husband was hanging up his coat. Or rather he was trying to hang up his coat but each time he approached the hook he swayed and missed it. 'Stupid hook,' he slurred as he threw his coat on the ground. He turned around and saw his wife who was staring at him open-mouthed. 'Angela! My sweetness, light of my light of …. Come here, I've got something for you.'

When she didn't move he screwed up his eyes and leaned towards her. 'Okay, I'll come to you. Just stay there. Don't keep moving about.'

She caught him as he tumbled towards her. 'Tony, you're drunk!' She stumbled as the force of his weight fell against her and she had to struggle to keep her balance. With one arm wrapped around him she managed to half drag half carry him into the living-room and push him into a chair.

'You're drunk!' she repeated unable to believe the state he was in.

'I know' he smiled happily. 'It's Chrissmass, you know.'

'But you never get drunk.'

''Bout time I started then. Barman,' he waved his hand in the air, 'get me a large whishky and soda, oh, and have one yourself.'

Ignoring his request Angela made some strong coffee and put a mug in his hand. 'Drink that.'

He sniffed it. 'Thass not whishky,' he said.

'No, it's coffee. You need it to sober up.'

'Sober up? What makes you think I want to sober up? I don't think I'll ever sober up again.' He put the coffee on the edge of the table. Angela put it on a coaster and moved it further in.

'Whatever's come over you, Tony? Has something happened?'

'Hash something happened? Thassa a good question. Did you hear that?' he asked an imaginary friend. 'My wife – that's my wife you know – she's a good woman, everyone tells me so – but she won't get me whishky … you're right, I should get it myself.' He tried to stand up but Angela was able to push him back down easily.

'Tell me, Tony, what's the matter? Why are you in this state?'

'Becos …' he wagged his finger at her, 'becos I've been drinking.' He closed his eyes and laid his head back against the chair. Then he suddenly sat forward again. 'An do you know why I've been drinking?'

'No, Tony, that's what I want you to tell me.' Angela was trying hard to be patient.

He looked in her direction earnestly. 'It's not becos it's Chrissmass. No,' he shook his head then frowned. 'My head hurts.' He put his hand to his head then continued, 'No, it's not becos it's Chrissmass; I'll tell you why.' He beckoned her to come closer to him. Angela hesitated but it looked like he wasn't going to go on until she'd done as she was told.

'It's a secret,' he whispered. 'Only I know. But now you're going to know too.'

Angela gasped and put her hand to her mouth. 'Tony, are you having an affair?'

77

He looked at her and for a moment his eyes cleared and then he burst out laughing. 'An affair? Me? When do I have time to have an affair? I'm too bushy working to have an affair.' He put his head on one side, his eyes closed and his mouth open and then he laughed, 'But I could now. Now I'm not working any more.'

Angela felt a shiver running down her back. In the midst of the rambling there was sudden clarity. She knew why he was drinking. 'Tony, have you lost your job?'

'No! No, not lost it. I didn't lose it, honestly, Angela, I didn't. It wasshn't my fault. I didn't put it down somewhere and forget about it. I promish.'

'No, of course it's not, Tony, but it's gone?'

He nodded pitifully. 'All gone. The whole place gone. All of us.'

Worn out by the exertion of explaining he slumped back into his chair and fell asleep instantly. Angela put a stool under his feet and moved his head; she didn't want him to wake up with a crick in his neck. Then she took his coffee mug into the kitchen, emptied the dregs down the sink and rinsed it under warm water. Going back into the lounge she poured herself a large gin and tonic, sat down opposite him in the lounge and sat silently, sipping her drink and staring at the brightly-lit tree.

# Chapter 6

The dog-walkers' club didn't meet to walk together again until three days after Christmas and then they walked without Jon. Sybil and Maggi were still buzzing with the enjoyment they'd had in each other's company. Maggi'd had to work on Boxing day afternoon but they walked in the park in the morning and in the evening she went round to Sybil's flat again. Jemma was pleased to be back to the normal routine. She'd had a good Christmas with her parents, brother and sister, but was always glad to be return home afterwards.

'It's not that we don't get on,' she explained to the others. 'It's just the house seems small now and I have to share my sister's bedroom. And my mum, well, she's just a bit much. I can cope in small doses but after three days my nerves are frayed.'

'Oh dear, I hope it won't be like that when I get out to Australia,' Maggi said, 'It'll be a bit far to come home for a breather!'

'I'm sure you'll be fine,' Jemma said hurriedly. 'My mum talks a lot and spoils my little sister rotten, doing everything for her as if she's a child, and she's nineteen now.' Maggi wasn't looking reassured so Jemma went on, 'And, anyway, you'll have your grandchildren to lighten the situation. You'll be fine, don't worry.'

'Of course she will,' Sybil agreed, 'don't you think so, Angela?''

'Sorry, did you say something?'

'Are you all right, Angela? You don't seem yourself today. Are you coming down with something?'

Angela faced the three women who were all looking at her, concern written on their faces. She could feel tears pricking at her eyes and she blinked rapidly to dispel them. She would tell them but not yet. She was still struggling with the reality of Tony's redundancy and she couldn't talk about it. Not yet.

'I'm all right. Just tired probably after the busyness of Christmas. I'll be back to normal in a few days.' She said it with more confidence than she felt; she wondered if she'd ever be back to normal again.

'You haven't said anything about your Christmas,' Maggi picked up the quizzing. 'Did you have a good time? The girls get away safely?'

'Oh, yes, very pleasant. Same as usual you know. Very nice.' Which wasn't strictly true but, again, if she told them about the disaster that had been Christmas she'd have to explain how it came about. And it hadn't been entirely disastrous. Not if she discounted the facts that Tony slept through Christmas Day, his mother was even more of a pain than usual and the girls argued over what to watch on television until she ended up screaming at them all. From what she'd read in various magazines that was probably a good Christmas by some people's standards.

'Well, it's obvious Jon's not going to make it today so let's get going. I feel like stretching my legs,' Angela said as she marched off without waiting for anyone. The other three looked at each other. Jemma shrugged and Maggi said, 'We can't help if she won't let us.'

'No,' Sybil agreed. 'Angela is a very private person. She will tell us in good time I'm sure, when she's ready.'

∞

A couple of days later Jon brought his daughters along for some morning exercise and they thoroughly enjoyed walking with all the dogs, playing chase and throwing sticks.

'I'm not sure who's enjoying this more,' Jon said.

'They'll be worn out afterwards,' Maggi said.

'Excellent, perhaps they'll go to bed early tonight.'

At the parting of the paths, Maggi took the top path with Angela while Jon, Sybil and Jemma followed the lower route by the river.

'Can I throw a stick in the water, daddy? Are they all allowed to go in?'

'Yes, Soph, they love it. Go on.'

'Come on, Gracie, let's collect sticks.'

With the two girls and the dogs happily occupied Jon said, 'Is Angela okay? She seems a bit distant.'

Jemma clapped. 'Well done, Jon! You've come on a lot. Not so long ago you wouldn't have noticed that. You're becoming an honorary female!'

'Oh no!' he groaned.

Sybil and Jemma laughed and then Sybil said, 'But really it's no laughing matter. She's been like it since Christmas.'

∞

As they walked Maggi kept up a monologue mostly about what she and Sybil had got up over Christmas – including over-indulging on the sherry by the sound of it – but after a while she gave up and the two women walked in silence over the hill. At last Angela said quietly, 'Tony's been made redundant.'

Maggi stopped in her tracks. 'Oh no, Angela! That's terrible. When did that happen?'

'Christmas Eve.' Seeing the look of horror on her companion's face, she added, 'They timed it nicely, don't you think?'

Maggi put her hand on Angela's shoulder. 'No wonder you're distracted. Christmas must have been a nightmare for you.'

'Oh we made the best of it. We – or rather I – decided that we wouldn't tell the girls until after Christmas so they could enjoy the day at least. Tony got very drunk on Christmas eve and slept through the next day so he wasn't there to let the cat out of the bag. I told the girls and his mother that he'd eaten something dodgy and had food poisoning. His mother insisted on going up to see him but fortunately he was asleep.'

Angela stopped and stared into space for a moment. 'When we did tell the girls all they could think of was how it would affect them. You think you're doing the best for your children and you never imagine you're creating selfish monsters.' She spoke with such vehemence that Maggi squeezed her arm tightly.

'You didn't create monsters, Angela; society does that. And I'm sure it was shock speaking. Don't we all think of ourselves first, about how something will affect us, if we're honest? But when they think about it and realise what it will mean to you and their dad they'll be phoning and asking what they can do to help, you wait and see.'

'I'd love to believe that, Maggi, but I can't honestly see it. I think it was their attitude more than the shock of the redundancy that upset me most.'

The tears were beginning to slip down Angela's cheeks and Maggi hugged her as she sobbed loudly. When the sobbing had subsided a bit Maggi rummaged in her pocket. 'Here,' she said, handing Angela a handkerchief. 'It is clean. I always keep a clean hankie in my pocket just in case.'

'Just in case of what?' Angela sniffed as she took the proffered hankie.

Maggi frowned. 'I don't know really. It was something my mother always drummed into me. I use tissues myself but I like to keep a clean hankie in all my coat pockets.'

Angela smiled weakly. 'And finally your mother was proved right; you did have need of a hankie.'

She wiped her face once more then put the hankie in her pocket. 'I'll wash it and return it to you freshly ironed.'

'There's no need to do that.'

'I insist. But will you do something for me?'

'Of course.'

'Will you tell the others for me, please?'

'Of course, if you want me to.'

'They have to know. I want them to know. But I can't tell them.'

'Then I will.' Maggi slipped her arm through Angela's. 'Now let's get walking again. Mitzi and Bassett are looking bored and you know they'll find mischief to get into if we don't get a move on.'

∞

Maggi waited until Angela had driven off before she told the others the news.

'No wonder she was looking so rough,' Jon said.

'Poor things and what a horrible time to happen,' Sybil was shocked. 'Why would they do that on Christmas eve of all days?'

Maggi shrugged. 'Who knows? Maybe it would have been worse if he'd been told a few weeks earlier.'

'Or they could have waited until after Christmas,' Jemma said.

'When a business gets in trouble they don't have time for sentimentality.' Jon was ever the realist.

Maggi sighed. 'Well, whatever the rights or wrongs, it's happened and they're going to have to work out what they're going to do now.

∞

Angela felt as if a huge weight had been lifted. Having told Maggi it was as if she'd been released, as if she'd been living in a box and she'd finally managed to poke a hole through the side. She could see daylight again.

When she got home she found Tony sprawled on the sofa in front of daytime television. She marched across the room and switched it off.

'I was watching that!' Tony said indignantly.

'A programme about no-hopers sharing their innermost secrets with the world? Tell me, were you enjoying it?'

Tony fumbled in amongst the cushions looking for the remote control. 'I was waiting for the antiques programme to come on.'

'Ah yes, that's much more worthwhile. Come on, Tony, we're going out for lunch.'

'Lunch?'

'Yes, come on. Go and shower and put some clean clothes on: you've been wearing that t-shirt for three days at least. Then we'll go to the pub and have something nice for lunch.'

'I've been made redundant; have you forgotten? We can't afford to go out for lunch.'

'Nonsense, we've got all your lovely redundancy money. We might as well spend it. I'm not planning on leaving any for the girls.

Now go on, get a move on, we've got things to discuss, plans to make.'

She hustled her husband off the sofa and upstairs to the bedroom. 'You shower in the en-suite and while you're doing that I'll freshen up in the bathroom.'

Angela began to take off her clothes, chattering all the time. 'I was talking to Maggi today and she's given me some brilliant ideas. She suggested that now the girls have more or less moved out we could adapt their rooms and open a little bed and breakfast place. Or, and this is the idea I really like, maybe buying a little café; the one on edge of the park is up for sale. I pointed it out to Maggi weeks ago and said how I'd always wanted to run a café and she remembered me saying that. And now we have the money to do it. And why are you still standing there? Come on, I'm hungry.'

Within two weeks Angela had contacted the estate agent selling the café and arranged to go and see around it. She'd spoken to the bank manager about temporary loans and business plans, and she'd met the previous owner – the café always closed for three months in the winter – who was retiring to go and live in the Costa del Sol. He'd shown her his accounts and talked of his plans for the place – before he'd decided to retire on the money he'd made rather than invest it and put off his retirement for many years. It seemed to be, as he described it, 'a nice little pocket money earner.' Tony, who was coming round to the idea of running a café, said they'd have to get an accountant to check the figures but he agreed it looked promising and that more could be made of the café's potential.

'The thing is,' Angela explained to Sybil one morning, 'that he's 56. The chance of him getting another job is remote. IT is a young man's game; the technology changes almost daily and keeping up with it is stressful. And even if anyone would consider him at his age the chances are we'd have to move and we love it here; we're too old to uproot now.'

'It would be hard work running a café too though, for both of you.'

'Yes but I've always loved catering for people and Tony is – or used to be before work wore him out – a great host and conversationalist. I really believe we could make a go of the café, make something special of it.'

'But will you be able to work together? Some couples can't do that.'

Angela nodded. 'I know. I have thought about that and we've talked about it. I think we can. We're going to give it a try anyhow.'

'Good for you,' Sybil said. 'I for one will be delighted to call in regularly – oh, but will dogs be allowed?'

'Of course!' Angela answered promptly. 'I'm going to put a sign on the door saying we welcome children, dogs and muddy boots.'

∞

It had been raining and although it stayed dry for their walk by the time Sybil and Jock reached her flat Jock's short legs were layered in mud. 'Stand still, Jock, let me wipe your paws,' Sybil said, reaching for the towel that she kept just inside the front door. 'Oh bother,' she exclaimed. 'I put it to be washed. Stay there for a minute, there's good boy. I'll go and get a clean one.'

Sybil retrieved a fresh towel from the airing cupboard and when she got back she found Jock lying on the hall rug. 'Oh Jock, you poor thing! Did we have a long walk today? Are you worn out?' She lifted one of his paws to wipe it and then stopped. 'Jock? Are you all right, Jock?'

∞

Maggi's phone was ringing but the house was empty. The supervisor had offered her an extra shift at the last minute and Maggi had jumped at the chance. Even though she'd had a comparatively frugal Christmas it, combined with extra car and house expenses she hadn't budgeted for, had taken a big chunk out of her savings. She'd popped home long enough to feed Bassett and let him out for a pee before rushing back to work so missing the phone call.

Sybil decided against calling anyone else. Angela she knew would come round but she had enough to contend with in the light of Tony's redundancy; Jon had his young family and Jemma her work. She'd tell them all the next day; that would be soon enough. Tonight she'd just have her thoughts and memories, and she had plenty of good ones to look back on.

The vet had called and taken Jock's little body away. He'd lost weight gradually over the last months and it was only when she held his lifeless body to her one last time that she appreciated how little flesh was on his bones.

He would be cremated and his ashes returned to Sybil if she wanted. She did. She'd scatter them in the park, in his favourite spot by the river. He loved to play in the water. For a Scottie that was unusual but then, Sybil thought, he was an unusual dog. People said Scotties could be bad-tempered and snappy but only once in his life had Jock ever shown his dark side. Sybil had been walking on her own along what was then an overgrown path in the park. It was a path she didn't usually venture along but she'd decided to explore it that particular day. She and Jock had been quite a way along it when a man stepped out of the bushes. She'd realised later that he was the local tramp, a character who was well-known in the village, who kept to himself and never bothered anyone. But at the time his sudden appearance had frightened Sybil and she'd given a little cry of alarm. Jock had instantly been at her side, his hackles up, snarling fiercely. The man had given them one look and hurried back into the bushes but it had taken Sybil some time to calm down.

She'd been so thankful at the time that Jock had been there, and even later when she knew that she'd not been in danger she'd been grateful for his protection, for knowing that he would leap to her defence should she ever need it.

And she was grateful to Jock for being the means by which she met the others in the dog club. Shall I continue to walk with them, she wondered. There was no reason why not. She enjoyed the exercise and the company but, she thought, we have been holding them up. She knew it was no coincidence that one of the others always felt 'like taking the shorter path' and she blessed them for their kindness but if she weren't there then they'd all be able to have a longer – and faster – walk. She could stroll later on her own; that way she'd get the exercise she needed to stop her joints ceasing up, and she'd get a daily dose of fresh air. From childhood that necessity had been drummed into her. She decided she'd meet the dog club in the morning, tell them the news and then come back to her flat on her own. 'Yes, Jock,' she said out loud, 'that's what I'll do.' And then she remembered that her faithful companion was no longer at her side and she wept.

∞

The next morning Sybil was first to arrive in the park as usual. It felt strange to be there without Jock so she read the noticeboard she'd never paid much attention to before. She was just discovering more about the history of the wonderful collection of rhododendrons for which the park was famous when Angela drove up. She jumped out of the car, a spring in her step that had been missing for some time, and walked Mitzi over to Sybil.

'Morning, Sybil, morning …' Angela stopped. 'Oh, where's Jock today?'

Sybil had been bracing herself for this and had rehearsed the words she was going to say. 'I'm afraid Jock passed away yesterday afternoon,' but when she opened her mouth she was only able to get as far as 'I'm afraid …' before she found herself struggling to hold back the tears. She began again only to falter again. Angela wrapped Mitzi's lead around the arm of the wooden bench and hugged Sybil. 'It's all right, Sybil. You don't have to say any more.'

When Sybil had stopped crying Angela made her sit down on the bench where Mitzi licked her hand softly and sympathetically, causing Sybil to cry again. Jon and Jemma were next to arrive; they quickly guessed what had happened. Jon put his hand on Sybil's shoulder and squeezed it while Jemma sat down and held the hand that wasn't being held by Angela.

Maggi came rushing in, apologising for being late but she stopped mid-sentence as she took in the tableau. 'Oh Sybil,' she cried, 'when did it happen?' She knelt before the frail elderly woman.

'Yesterday afternoon,' Sybil replied between sniffs.

'Why didn't you call me? I'd have come round.'

'I did try but when there was no reply I thought, well, it'll wait until tomorrow.'

'You could have called any one of us,' Angela said.

'I know but you all have your own busy lives. And it's not as if it were unexpected.' She gulped, trying hard to stay in control. 'The vet was very good and I have so many lovely memories of Jock.'

'Come on,' Maggi said, 'you're getting cold sitting here. Let's walk.'

'I'm not coming. I'll go home; I just wanted to let you all know about Jock and to say, well, to say how much your friendship has meant to me.'

They all looked at her and Jemma spoke for them, 'We've loved getting to know you and Jock. It's been a privilege.'

'Bless you for saying that, dear.' Now it was Sybil's turn to pat Jemma's hand.

'Why aren't you walking with us?' Jon asked.

Maggi gave him a look and raised her eyebrows, 'She's too upset today..'

'But you will keep on walking with us, won't you?' Jon persisted.

'Of course she will,' Angela said. 'Won't you, Sybil?'

'I don't think so, dear.'

'Why ever not?' Maggi asked.

'Well, I know I slow you down. I appreciate the fact that you've made allowances for an old lady and her dog but you don't need to any more.'

'But you told me that exercise was good for your hips,' Jemma said. 'I remember you saying that.'

'I can take a stroll later on; I don't have to be holding you up.'

'Don't you like our company?' Angela asked.

'You know I do.'

'That's settled then,' Jon said. 'You're walking with us.' He paused. 'You can have today off if you want but I think Jock would want you to keep fit.'

Maggi could see tears filling Sybil's eyes again and she said, 'Come on, take my arm. You and I'll reminisce about Jock while the younger ones go speeding around the park. You're not getting rid of us that easily.'

∞

Two weeks later when they were walking Sybil said, 'The nurse at the vet's called me yesterday afternoon; I can pick up Jock's ashes now.'

'I'll take you,' Angela said. 'We can go straight after our walk today if that's okay with you.'

'That would be wonderful, thank you.'

'Have you decided what you're going to do with the ashes?' Jon asked.

'I'd like to scatter them by the river; he loved that spot just below the bridge.'

'We could do that tomorrow,' Maggi suggested. 'If you'd like that.'

'Oh yes, please. I'd love to say goodbye to Jock in the presence of his special friends.'

'Then we'll do that and, perhaps, if anyone has any special memories we could share them,' Angela said.

∞

Sybil lifted the box off the mantelpiece where she'd left it overnight. It had been another bitter-sweet evening for her, happy memories vying with the sorrow she felt at losing her canine friend. Maggi and Angela had both offered to sit with her but she'd declined their offers saying she would be fine. And she was. Contentment was her over-riding emotion: contentment that she'd had such a long and happy time with Jock, that he hadn't suffered and that the end had been peaceful. 'I have such a lot to be grateful for you know, Reg,' she said as she put her coat on ready for Jock's final walk. She smiled. She still talked to her dead husband and, no doubt, she'd talk to Jock too. 'There might be some folk who'd find that strange, Jock, but then they never knew you.'

It wasn't that she believed their spirits were with her, nothing as foolish as that she'd have said if anyone had asked, but it brought her comfort 'and it's better than talking to myself,' she laughed as she pulled on her furry boots. She put on her hat and then took it off again. She rummaged in the drawer until she found the hat she'd had when Jock had been a puppy. He chewed it in the way that puppies do and she hadn't worn it for years, but because it had been her favourite hat she'd never thrown it out. She put it on her head and adjusted it so the chewed part could barely be seen. 'Right,' she said. 'I'm ready. Let's go, Jock.'

The dog clubbers talked quietly until they reached the spot Sybil had chosen to scatter the ashes, then, as one, they stopped, and gathered in a small circle.

'Thank you all for coming with us today,' Sybil said, 'for joining me and Jock on his final walkies. I know how much he loved walking with his friends. Every morning, at the same time, he would fetch his lead from the stand by the front door and bring it to me. If ever I was engrossed in a newspaper article, he would nudge me very gently, as if to say, you can read that later; it's time for walkies now. So it was thanks to Jock that I was never late for our walks.'

There was a moment's silence and then Jemma said, 'I think Jock was the first one to befriend Pixie. When Pixie first came to live with me I didn't know much about dogs but thanks to Jock bringing us into contact with all of you I now feel part of something special.'

'I know what you mean,' Jon said. 'Jock sniffed out Benji when he was digging in some leaves under a tree. When Benji followed Jock – and didn't come back when I called him – it led me to Sybil and in turn to all of you too.'

'Jock was so funny at Christmas,' Maggi said. 'When we sat down to eat Sybil told him he'd have to wait for his Christmas dinner until we'd finished and he obediently went and lay down on his bed. I had a bigger dinner than Sybil so I was last to finish and the moment I put down my knife and fork, Jock came trotting back up to us. Do you remember, Sybil? I said his hearing certainly hadn't gone!'

They all laughed and Jemma said, 'I wish Pixie was that well-behaved. He embarrassed us both at Christmas with his greed!'

'It's true,' Angela said. 'Jock was very well-behaved. I take pride in Mitzi's behaviour but Jock could teach her a thing or two. I have to admit I was a little unsure about having a Scottie in our group because I'd heard they didn't get on well with other dogs but whether that's an exaggeration or whether he was an exception that rule certainly didn't apply to him. I think in his own quiet way Jock brought us and held us all together. '

'He certainly brought us together, Angela,' Sybil said, 'when he began humping poor Mitzi.'

'Yes,' Angela agreed. 'He never really got over that habit, did he?'

Everyone laughed and then gradually silence fell over the small group. They stood silently for few minutes and then Sybil opened the box. She walked to the edge of the river and sprinkled the contents into the flowing water. 'Bye bye, Jock,' she whispered. 'Sleep tight.' She blew a kiss after him before wiping away a solitary tear.

Maggi walked to her and took her arm. 'You okay?'

Sybil nodded, 'Yes, yes, I think I am. Thank you.' She turned and faced the others. 'Thank you all so much.'

Jemma looked at Angela who nodded and then she took a packet out of her back-pack. 'Sybil, this is for you. We hope you like it.' Jemma handed the parcel across to Sybil who looked puzzled.

'What is this?'

'Open it and see,' Jon said.

She unwrapped the framed photo and they all stood anxiously waiting, hoping she wouldn't be too upset by the picture of Jock sitting almost exactly in the spot where Sybil was now standing. The sun shining on his coat he looked every inch a mature but healthy dog.

Sybil continued to stare at the photo. At last Maggi said, 'Sybil, if you don't like it or find it too upsetting we'll take it away, don't worry.'

'Upsetting? Not like it? Oh no, I love it.' The tears started slipping down her cheeks and Maggi hurried to hand her a hankie. 'It's absolutely the best present anyone has ever given me. It's magnificent. Thank you so much. But how did you get the photo? Who took it? When?'

Angela explained the subterfuge they'd gone through in order for Jemma to take the photo. 'But it was all worth it if you like it, Sybil.'

'Oh I do. So much. How talented you are, Jemma, dear. I never realised.'

Jemma blushed. Only Jon had seen the photo before that day and now they all wanted Jemma to take photos of their dogs. Jemma produced some snapshots she'd taken, on the same day, of the dogs all in a group. 'They're not brilliant photos; it was difficult to get them all looking the same way at the same time.'

'Not to mention smiling!' Jon added. 'How on earth did you capture that grin on Benji's face?'

'I think that's your imagination, Jon, but I brought these copies in case you'd each like one.'

They were all delighted and Angela and Jon said they'd both definitely like to commission her to do some photos. Jon wanted Benji with his children and Angela thought Mitzi outside the café would be good for advertising when they opened.

'You haven't bought it yet, Angela,' Jemma pointed out.

'No but there's no harm in being prepared.' She turned to address Sybil. 'And you definitely like the photo?'

'It shall have pride of place on my mantelpiece.'

∞

It had become a regular arrangement for Jon to go around to Cathy's on a Wednesday afternoon for coffee. They had begun to relax with each other and enjoyed each other's company. Jon still hadn't found the right moment to mention this arrangement to Tilly but, whenever he thought about it, he managed to find an excuse. She was too busy or had other things on her mind, or, well, it just wasn't important; there were always plenty of reasons for him not to tell her.

If I were meeting a male friend she wouldn't be interested, Jon told himself. In fact she's very rarely interested in anything I do. It's all about her and her clients and the important cases she has to work on. 'She seems to have forgotten I have a life too,' he grumbled to Cathy one afternoon. 'Although,' he sighed, 'sometimes it doesn't feel as if I do. Do you know how many loads of washing I had to do after last weekend? Because some of her friends came to stay I had all the extra towels and bed linen to wash, and you know how damp it's been. It's impossible to get clothes dry out of doors so I have to use the tumble dryer and then she has the nerve to tell me off. I should be thinking of the planet apparently.' Jon finally stopped ranting and looked at Cathy. 'What's so funny?'

'You are! You should hear yourself. You sound like a hard-done-by little wifey.'

Jon pretended an indignant air. 'I thought you as a woman would sympathise.' He tossed his head. 'I'd flounce out – if I knew how.'

Cathy laughed. Jon shook his head running his fingers through his hair. 'I'm sorry. Have I been going on?'

'Just a bit.'

He sighed again. 'All I want is a bit of sympathy,' he said looking so much like a little puppy dog that she leaned over and stroked his head. When, instead of moving her hand, she left it on the side of his face he turned his head very slowly so that her palm was on his lips and he kissed it. She quickly pulled her hand away.

Jon stood up suddenly. 'I'm sorry; I should go.'

He was out of the door before Cathy could speak.

# Chapter 7

He was still breathing faster than usual when he got to the end of the street. He stopped and tried to calm himself down. You're a fool, he told himself. It was perfectly innocent. If you'd not made a fuss … what would have happened, he wondered.

He looked at his watch. He was too early for school; the girls wouldn't be out for another half hour or so. He wandered over to the park and sat on one of the benches near the entrance. He put his head in his hands. What had he been thinking of? The trouble was he hadn't been thinking of anything: it had been a perfectly natural and un-thought-about reaction, the sort of thing he'd do to Tilly – if she ever stroked his face that was. Did that mean it was innocent? Or was he somehow replacing Tilly, if only in his mind, with Cathy? He ran his fingers through his hair and leaned back against the bench.

He enjoyed the afternoons with Cathy and, up till now, they'd done nothing more risky than mild flirting. The blatant flirting she'd done in the beginning had settled into a more innocent and jokey thing – as far as he was concerned. Yes, it was a two-way flirtation but it was innocent. There it was again, that word, innocent. But did he really believe that?

But what matters is my relationship with Tilly and that's solid. Isn't it? Is it? He thought about how he'd been grumbling to Cathy but told himself that didn't mean anything. Everyone in a long-term relationship complains at some point or another.

Jon looked at his watch again. It was still a little early but maybe Cathy would get there early too and he could apologise again and they'd laugh it off and make a date for the following week, the same as normal. He hurried along to school and scanned the faces in the school yard but there was no sign of her amongst the mums already there. He hung around near the gate hoping she'd arrive with time to spare but when the bell went and the children began coming out she was still not there. He gave up and walked around to where his daughters would be coming out. Gracie still got upset if she couldn't quickly pick out his face amongst the crowd. She smiled when she saw him and ran over. 'Daddy, I have to practise my reading tonight. Will you help me? We had a new girl in class today. She's from somewhere else and her name is Soraya and she's very pretty and nice and I want to ask her for tea, please, soon, Daddy. And it's Timmy's birthday next week and I'm going to his party and it's going to be a pirate party in the leisure centre and we'll have to get him a present. What shall we get him do you think?'

Half-listening to his daughter Jon nodded occasionally and said 'right,' whenever she paused and seemed to be waiting for an answer.

'What, Daddy?'

'What?'

'What shall we get Timmy for a present?'

'Oh, I don't know. We'll find something.' Out of the corner of his eye Jon spotted Cathy hurrying in and looking around anxiously and then wave. He half-raised his arm to return her wave but as her daughter ran over to her, he realised it was Rosie she had been waving to. His arm dropped back to his side as mother and daughter turned and left the school grounds.

'Where on earth is Sophie?' He wanted to run out after Cathy and put things right; he couldn't bear the thought of any awkwardness between them.

Gracie was hopping over the gaps in the paving stones. 'Oh, I nearly did ten! She's got gym club tonight. Don't you remember, Daddy?'

'Oh yes, of course,' Jon sighed as he saw Cathy disappear across the road. 'Come on, then, miss, let's get you home and see if we've got time to get you changed at least before we have to come back to pick Sophie up.'

∞

For once Tilly was home before six that evening. She was in a good mood. She'd won an important case and, not only was the money good, but it also helped her reputation, which was growing and spreading beyond the city. 'You should have seen him in the witness box, Jon; he went to pieces under my questioning.'

'Who did?' Jon was busy crushing garlic as his wife poured herself a large glass of wine. 'Don't use too much of that! I need some for the sauce.'

'The accused, Richard Bellington, of course.'

'And he's who?'

'Do you listen to anything I tell you? He's been fiddling the books for years. His company went down the pan and all the shareholders lost their money but somehow he came out of it untouched. It's so rewarding to be able to put a man like that behind bars.'

'Ah, yes, I do remember you telling me.'

The phone rang and Tilly answered it. 'Hello ... oh hi Giles. ... Yes, thank you, I was pleased ... I'd love to ... okay, I'll get our clerk to call yours and arrange a meeting. I'll look forward to it.'

'Dinner's ready,' Jon called up the stairs just as Tilly was dialling a number. 'Can't you do that later?' he asked. 'Dinner's ready.'

'I'll call from the bedroom; dish up, I'll be down in two ticks,' she said. 'I just want to ring Jeremy and tell him Giles is after us for the Winstone case. Careful, girls, what's your hurry?' The two girls burst into the room as she was leaving.

'It's Daddy's lamb with red sauce!' Sophie declared. 'It's my favourite.'

'And mine,' said Gracie, not to be outdone.

'No, it's not, Gracie. It's my favourite, not yours.'

'It can be my favourite too, can't it, Daddy?'

'Of course it can. Now have you washed your hands, girls?' Four upturned palms were presented to him for inspection. 'Okay, sit down and I'll dish up.'

The girls had both almost cleaned their plates by the time Tilly re-entered the room. 'I think you both deserve a treat,' she said.

'Yay!'

'What for?' Jon asked.

'For being my favourite girls in the whole wide world.'

Sophie and Gracie hugged their mum. Jon continued eating his dinner. 'Your dinner is getting cold,' he said. 'Sit down, girls, if you want any pudding.'

The three females sat at the table, the girls giggling and chattering excitedly. Their mum was in a good mood and who knows what they could get out of her. But before they could start the pestering Jon took away their empty plates and gave them a carton of yogurt each.

'Oh, Daddy, couldn't we have ice cream tonight?' Sophie tried.

'You can have banana with your yogurt if you want.'

'Oh go on, let them have ice cream,' Tilly said. 'It won't hurt them once in a while.'

'They had ice cream last night which you'd have known if you'd been home in time for dinner.'

'Oh oh,' Tilly looked at the girls and giggled. 'I think Mummy's in trouble.'

Gracie was indignant. 'You mustn't be cross with Mummy, Daddy.'

'No, Daddy,' Sophie joined in, 'Mummy has to go out to work to earn money.'

'Do you want banana or not?' Jon knew he sounded short with them but to have them siding with their mother against him - and just for the sake of ice cream. It was enough to make a man … he took a deep breath. And tried again, 'Well, do you want me to chop up bananas for you?'

'Yes, please, daddy,' Gracie said, her indignation turning out to be short-lived when it came to a choice between yogurt and banana and just yogurt.

'Me too, please,' said Sophie.

The rest of the dinner-time conversation revolved around what had happened in school and how pretty Miss Brown's dress was, Tilly joining in enthusiastically. When the girls had finished, Jon sent them to get ready for their bath, while he cleared the table. Tilly remained seated, slowly finishing the last mouthfuls of dinner between large swigs of wine.

'What's the matter with you tonight, Jon?' she asked when the girls had left the room.

'Me? Nothing.'

'Yeah, right. You're grouchy as Mr. Grouch.'

'I just think it's interesting the way you feel able to comment on Miss Brown's dress when you've never even met the woman.'

'The girls were telling me all about it. Of course I had to comment. I'm their mother; I'm supposed to be interested.'

'But only when it suits you; when you can fit them into your busy schedule.'

'What is all this about, Jon? Aren't you pleased I'm doing well at work? Making a good living so we can afford all we need?'

He gripped the edge of the work surface and hesitated before replying. At last he said, 'Of course I'm pleased. I'm, I don't know, maybe I'm going down with something. I'm sorry. I didn't mean to sound so grumpy.'

Tilly moved to stand behind him and slipped her arms around his waist. 'Well, I'm home early tonight so let's get the girls off to bed and settled and we can have the evening to ourselves.' She rubbed her face against his back. 'Maybe we'll have an early night too.'

He turned round to face her and smiled. 'Yeah, yeah, that would be nice.'

She kissed him on the lips and backed away. 'I'll even go and bathe them while you load the dishwasher.' She blew him another kiss before she left the room.

When she'd gone Jon leaned on the back of the chair and took a deep breath. What was the matter with him? One innocent kiss – on the hand at that – and he was incapable of behaving normally. What would he be like if he ever had an affair? He laughed to himself at the thought.

But it wouldn't go away.

∞

Sybil was preparing for bed. As she pulled the curtains at her bedroom window, the one that overlooked the park entrance, she remembered seeing Jon on the bench in the afternoon. He'd looked troubled. She'd considered going out and speaking to him but had thought better of the idea. He knew where she lived if he needed immediate help and she doubted if an old lady would be much good when it came to advising a young man. She didn't know exactly how old he was but guessed it was early thirties. He was a lovely boy – she thought of anyone less than fifty as a boy – and a wonderful father. His daughters had been a delight when they'd joined the dog club walking in the park during the school holidays and they obviously adored their father. She hoped it wasn't a serious problem that he was wrestling with. So many marriages broke down these days; people didn't seem to be willing to work at it. Didn't want to put in the effort. It was easier to give up and try again with someone new. She thought back to her own marriage. Her darkest days came when Reg had been unwilling to consider adoption. She hadn't thought about divorce - the scandal would have killed her mother – but there had been times when she'd considered running away. If she'd thought that would have healed the ache in her heart she would have done. What made it worse was that she never knew whether it was a problem with her or with Reg or whether they could have done anything about it. He'd refused to do the tests the doctor had offered them and had told her she shouldn't do them either. 'It's the will of God,' he'd said. 'If it was meant to happen it would.' Sybil had never been sure of God's existence up till then; from that moment on she decided she didn't want to believe in the existence of a god who would be so cruel as to deprive her of the greatest blessing a woman could have. She never told Reg that and she carried on with the ritual of Sunday morning church until he died when she gave up altogether in spite of frequent visits from the vicar. When, at last, she told him why and when she'd stopped believing he'd come out with some nonsense that she'd had no difficulty in pooh-poohing.

But she'd never left Reg or given him cause to think she was unhappy. Putting on a brave face, that's what her mother called it.

And she'd loved Reg, loved him with all her heart, so that made it easier to bear the pain. Almost. But there was something else too, a memory, a possibility that she'd buried with her dreams, something she'd had to put behind her, but someone she could never forget.

Reg was an old-fashioned man and she'd loved him for that. Their early married life began before women's lib started, when the man was the bread-winner and the woman stayed at home to keep house and look after the children. Even in the fifties there were rumblings of discontent as women who'd done men's jobs during the war, objected to being returned to the house but Sybil was an old-fashioned girl too and she loved the way Reg wanted to provide for her and look after her. His delightful manners had been one of the things that had attracted her to him initially. But when the babies didn't come along and Sybil suggested that perhaps she could do a typing course or find a job in a shop Reg had been affronted. She'd tried to explain that housework didn't consume all her time and energy and she just wanted an outlet for it but he'd been adamant: no wife of his was going out to work. So Sybil began to look for other things to do to amuse herself. Some afternoons she'd go to the pictures or wander around a museum. And some days she's just shop; Reg was a good provider and there was plenty of money for her to spend. It was during an afternoon's shopping that she met Bill. It was raining and she'd called into her favourite tea-shop. She was sitting at a table in the corner, watching raindrops running down the window, when a man, about her age, spoke to her. 'Excuse me, I wonder if this seat is free?'

She glanced around the café: all the other tables were occupied by like-minded shoppers wanting an escape from the rain. 'It's free, yes.'

'Would you mind if I sat here?'

'Um, no, I suppose not.' Sybil shifted her tea things onto her half of the table to make room, then she returned to staring out of the window.

When the waitress had brought his order and he'd poured his tea he said, 'I think this must be my favourite tea-shop in the whole of the town. Their madeira cake tastes just like my mother used to make.'

Sybil smiled briefly at him and sipped her tea.

'That's why,' he went on, 'I'm so grateful that you let me join you at your table. I would have hated to have to go elsewhere.'

She smiled again and poured herself another cup of tea.

'I'm sorry, you must think I'm a dreadful nuisance but I just have to say something else.'

Sybil looked up, curious to hear what was so urgent.

'I'm also glad the only available seat was at your table. I saw you from outside and thought you were both the prettiest and saddest girl I've ever seen.'

Sybil laughed and shook her head. 'What nonsense,' she said.

'No really, I mean it.' He frowned, 'Is life so very bad?'

Her first impulse was to laugh again, finish her tea and leave politely but there was such an earnestness in his face that she found herself saying, 'I suppose I am sad but it's nothing you'd understand.'

'Try me.'

She laughed. 'Don't be silly.'

'No, I mean it. Isn't it so often easier to talk to a complete stranger than to your closest friend?'

Reg was her closest friend and every time she tried to talk about babies, he would stop her and say that it was done with, and weren't they happy just as they were? And she was – or would have been if there hadn't been a gaping hole somewhere in the region of her heart.

Suddenly she heard herself saying, 'I can't have babies,' and the relief of saying this out loud to someone she'd never see again so it didn't matter what she said, was so enormous that the tears, which she'd kept under control for so long, began to trickle down her face. And the trickle turned into a flood.

The man, instead of rushing away hurriedly as Reg tended to do whenever she cried, calmly took a handkerchief out of his pocket and offered it to her. 'It is clean,' he assured her, before calling the waitress and ordering another pot of tea for two.

He sat silently while she wept yet she sensed his sympathy. When the tears at last began to subside, she sniffed, 'I'm sorry. This is a terrible bore. You must be regretting sitting at my table now.' She tried laugh but only a strangled sound came out.

'Not at all,' he said. 'Here.' He poured a cup of tea and pushed it across the table to her. 'Do you take sugar?' he asked as if they were in a parlour and it were a perfectly normal social situation.

She shook her head. 'No, thank you.'

'Would you like more cake? I think I am rather Pooh-like and I find a little something often helps.'

She laughed aloud this time. 'You are familiar with Winnie the Pooh?'

'Of course! What well-brought-up young man isn't?'

'I think you're right,' Sybil smiled. 'A little something may be called for.'

The young man summoned the waitress again and ordered more madeira for himself and 'What would you like?'

'I think I'll have a slice of madeira too.'

'Excellent choice. Make that two large pieces, please, miss!' He beamed at the waitress who simpered.

'Now,' he said, 'as we're almost family …'

Sybil frowned, 'How do you work that out?'

'We share a love of Winnie the Pooh; what better bond could there be? Okay, let's be book brothers then, oh, and sisters, I think introductions are in order. I'm Bill.' He stood up and bowed very slightly in a gentlemanly way, holding out his hand. Sybil took it and said, 'I'm … Mrs Wright.'

'Of course you are! I know that, but what's your name?'

Sybil laughed out loud again. 'You are an idiot! It's Wright with a W.'

'Just for today, as we're book brothers and sisters, may I know your Christian name?'

She hesitated. But what harm could it do? She'd never see him again. 'Sybil.'

'Sybil, the very essence of femininity and beauty. I should have guessed.'

The waitress brought their cake and for a moment Bill was quiet as he concentrated on cutting the slice into bite-size pieces with his cake fork. 'I like to do this in advance,' he explained seeing Sybil watching him, fascinated. 'It saves time later.'

There was no comment she felt she could make so Sybil ate a mouthful of the madeira. It was really very good. When Bill had eaten his first portion he said, suddenly serious, 'That is very sad, you know. Thank you for telling me.'

For a moment Sybil couldn't think what he meant then she blushed as she remembered. 'I shouldn't have said anything; you were just being polite. I don't know why I did. I think it must be because ...' she paused.

'Because what?'

'You have a sympathetic face.' She laughed. 'You have the sort of face that attracts confidences. You must have women all over town telling you their secrets.'

'Believe it or not, I don't usually approach women I don't know.'

She looked at him disbelievingly.

'No, really. In fact I've never done it before. It was only because you looked so sad that I felt I wanted to. Because a girl as pretty as you shouldn't have anything to be sad about. But now I see you have every right to be sad.'

He tactfully changed the subject then and told her a little of his story, how he was one of five sons and his family had always lived in the country but now he was trying to break into journalism. 'That's what I've always wanted to do, to write,' he explained. 'I thought it would be simple: I'd just arrange to see an editor who'd love my writing and would hire me on the spot. I don't suppose you know any editors, do you?'

'Ah I see,' Sybil said. 'This was all a ruse to try and meet someone who could help you.'

'No, no!' he was appalled at the suggestion even though Sybil had made it in jest. 'I swear that thought never entered my head.' He paused. 'I don't suppose your husband is editor in chief of the Times, is he, by any chance?'

Sybil laughed and shook her head. 'Afraid not. He's a bank manager.'

'Ah well, I suppose he could still be useful when my savings run out and I'm destitute and down and out on the streets.'

Their conversation continued in this light-hearted way until Sybil glanced at her watch. 'Oh my goodness,' she said. 'Look at the time! I have to get home to get Reg's dinner on the table.' She stood up to leave. Bill leapt to his feet and helped her on with her coat that the waitress brought over. 'How much do I owe you?' Sybil asked the girl, who glanced at Bill before saying, 'It's all right, madam, it's all been settled.'

'Oh no, I can't let you …'

'I insist.' Bill shook his head vehemently. 'Anyway you can pay next time.'

She laughed, 'There won't be a next time.'

'We'll see.'

She resisted the temptation to return to the tea-shop the next day and the day after but on the following day she had to go into town to collect some shirts she'd ordered for Reg and stopped at the tea-shop afterwards. She was disappointed to realise Bill wasn't there and then was angry with herself for feeling disappointed. You're a happily married woman, she told herself, who should never have indulged in such flirtation, but she couldn't get rid of the empty feeling in her tummy. She was toying with a piece of madeira when a voice behind her shoulder said, 'Wasn't I right about that cake? Doesn't it taste just like your mother used to make too?'

She looked around to find Bill smiling down at her and her heart gave a small leap. From that day they met regularly in the tea-shop where Bill would tell her of his latest rejection. Nothing seemed to bring him down though. He could find a bright side to every situation. 'They'll be sorry when I'm a Pulitzer-winning journalist. All these editors who turned me down. They'll be begging me to work for them. But by then I'll be freelance and highly-paid and doing just the work I want to do and winning more awards, the Nobel prize maybe.'

He always had such self-belief.

Sybil suddenly realised that she was still standing at the window, the curtains half drawn. She shook herself as if waking from a dream. She'd not given Bill more than a brief thought for many years though there had been times when she'd scanned every newspaper desperately hoping to see his name. But that was a long time ago, a whole lifetime past. She wondered why the sight of Jon in the park that morning had brought these memories back and then she realised it was the look of confusion and uncertainty in his face. She'd seen those emotions in her own face before she'd made her decision; after she'd made it a mask seemed to slip into place. Had she ever been truly honest since?

But the love that she and Reg shared was worth fighting for. She'd believed that at the time and still thought so. Was Jon's? She hoped so. Although she was making assumptions: there could be any number of reasons for his sudden appearance in the park and his disturbed state of mind. Perhaps she'd mention in the morning when they were walking that she'd noticed him. She'd see what he said. It was probably just her imagination working overtime again.

She looked at the photo of Jock in pride of place on the mantelpiece and stroked it. 'Night, night, lovely boy,' she said. 'Sleep tight. See you in the morning.'

∞

The next morning Jon phoned Jemma to say that Sophie was unwell and off school so he wouldn't be walking with them and could he drop Benji off to her on his way back from dropping Gracie off at school. When she opened the door to him Jon greeted her gratefully, 'Thanks, Jemma. It's such a relief not to have worry about how I'm going to manage to walk him.'

'No problem. Are you okay for picking up Gracie from school? Do you want me to? Or I can stay in your house and look after Sophie while you go if you like.'

'Thanks but I'm hoping Sophie will be up to coming in the car with me. I don't think she's too poorly.'

'Well, call me if you need me to. Come on now, Benji, Pixie's in the kitchen waiting for you.'

∞

At the park Jemma told the others that Sophie was ill. 'But Jon looked really ropey too. I think he might be going down with the same thing.'

'Perhaps he was up with her in the night,' Angela said.

'Maybe, he looked as though he hadn't slept much.'

Sybil listened to their conversation. 'I do hope he's going to be all right,' she said.

'Oh I think it's only a cold Sophie's got so even if he does get it he'll soon recover,' Jemma said.

'I hope you're right,' Sybil said thoughtfully.

∞

The following Saturday afternoon Angela and Tony stood in the middle of the park café and hugged each other. 'Well, old girl, we've done it.' Tony kissed his wife on her forehead. 'We've bought ourselves a café.'

'I can't quite believe it.'

'You better had because the hard work starts now.'

'I know.' Angela broke free and twirled around. 'Where are we going to begin?'

'Well, we know the kitchen needs a bit of updating …'

'And tables and chairs in here are past their best, not to mention the walls need painting and the floor needs …' she looked at the stained carpet and grimaced, 'replacing. And we'll have to think of a new name and plan the menu and decide when to open and …'

'Okay, okay, you're putting me off this idea!'

They both laughed. 'We knew it was going to be a lot of work to get it ready for reopening,' Angela said. 'But you don't regret it, do you?' She looked worriedly at her husband.

'I haven't notice you do that for years.'

'Do what?'

'Bite your bottom lip. You always used to do it when you were anxious.'

'Did I? Do I? I wasn't aware I did.'

'There have been lots of things I haven't noticed.' Tony suddenly looked serious.

'But are you regretting it?' Angela persisted.

'The only thing I'm regretting is stopping noticing what an extremely attractive and sexy wife I have.'

'Oh Tony, be serious!'

'I am perfectly serious. But to put your mind at rest I have no regrets: I think this café is going to be a great success. How can it fail with a dynamic duo behind it? You know something, Angela? I'm beginning to think that being made redundant is the best possible thing that could have happened to me. To us. We've another chance in life, a new start.'

'I'm so glad you think so. Oh drat, I meant to bring that bottle of champagne that's been sitting in the larder for months with us to drink a toast.'

Tony slid his arm around his wife's waist. 'I can think of another way, let's say, christen the place.'

'Really? What's that?'

He nuzzled her neck and his hands began exploring her body.

'Tony! We can't do that here!'

'Why not? We own the place.'

'Someone might see us through the door.'

'We'll go in the kitchen then.'

'That's not very hygienic!'

Tony stopped, put his hands on his hips and said, 'Excuse me? We're having the kitchen refitted so we can do what we like in there.'

'Oh yes, so we are,' Angela giggled. She wasn't used to her husband in this mood and she rather liked it. 'Come on then, last one to get undressed makes the coffee after,' she said as she ran into the kitchen.

# Chapter 8

Afterwards as they lay on the makeshift bed Tony had constructed on the floor out of towels and table linen Angela shivered. He pulled some more towels off the shelf and threw them over her. She smiled contentedly.

'We haven't done anything this foolish for a long time.'

'Not at all foolish,' Tony contradicted her.

'Come on, we're in our fifties. Only teenagers make love on the floor.'

'You're only just fifty, and why should youngsters have all the fun?'

'Very true. Oh, I agree wholeheartedly,' she said as he pulled her to him and kissed her soundly on the lips.

They lay back, relaxed and almost comfortable. 'What do you think about Jock's?' Angela asked suddenly.

'Jocks? I don't really have any particular feelings about them. Why? Have you heard something? Are there lots of them moving into the area; do we need to cater with porridge and deep-fried mars bars?'

'What on earth are you talking about?' Angela raised herself on one elbow and stared at her husband.

'You asked me what I thought about jocks.'

'Oh, no, not the Scottish variety,' she laughed as she realised the misunderstanding. 'I meant, what do you think of Jock's as a name for the café?'

Tony considered it. 'It's okay. Short, easy to remember. Any particular reason why though?'

'After Sybil's little Scottie dog. He died, I told you. I thought it would be a nice little tribute. The first one of our dogs to go.'

'Oh right. Yes, I've no objection. Would she mind though, seeing his name on the café every time she passed?'

'I don't think so. She's quite pragmatic. I'll ask her first anyway.'
She stretched. 'Now, nice as this is, do you think we could get up
before my joints seize up?'

∞

When they'd dressed Angela brought out the notepad she'd put in
her handbag specially. 'I'm going to make a list. What do we need to
do first?'

'Kitchen I think, don't you?'

'Yes but while that's being done we can carry on decorating the
rest of the place. I was thinking something restful for the walls with
bright splashes of colour from the crockery and the blinds.'

'Do we need to replace the tables and chairs straightaway?'

'Yes, I think so.'

'Or maybe we could paint them at first and then, depending how
business is going, when we close over the winter ...'

'Oh we can't close in the winter.'

'But Mr. Thomas said he closed for four months every year. And
he still made a living.'

'But there are loads of dog walkers out every day. They'd be
grateful for somewhere to have a warm drink. And a piece of cake. I
know I would be and all the dog clubbers agree with me. Honestly,
it's a large market, the dog-walkers.'

'Hm,' Tony said, 'I was looking forward to spending a month in
Spain each winter.'

'A month in Spain? We're not ready to give up and die yet! I'll
ask the dog club and maybe I'll bring them all in so we can have a
look and talk about colour schemes. Jemma's a photographer, you
know; she has an eye for artistry. Oh, maybe we could sell some of
her photos of the park! In all the different seasons! I bet they'd go
down well with tourists and locals. I must add that to my list. Ask
Jemma about photographs.'

'As long as they're all going to be giving us their custom.'

'Of course they will.' Angela paused. 'Not that I'd charge them
of course.'

109

'What? How are we going to make any money if you give everything away.'

'Oh don't exaggerate! They're my friends. You'll love them when you meet them.'

∞

Jemma was thrilled with Angela's idea that she should frame some of her photos of the park and sell them in the café – that was to be called Jock's to Sybil's obvious delight.

'Maybe you could stock some of her doggy photos too,' Maggi suggested. They'd all had a portrait although Jemma had only charged them for the cost of printing professionally. 'If people see them they could commission her to take photos of their pets too.'

'What an excellent idea, Maggi. Would that be all right with you, Jemma? I know you prefer doing landscapes.' Angela didn't want Jemma to feel coerced into anything.

'That would be fab. I really liked doing the dog portraits. And they're outside so it's not like a posed studio shot.'

'Oh, no, you capture the dogs so naturally. I love my photo of Jock,' Sybil sighed.

'And I'd like a copy of that too, please,' Angela said. 'It's only fitting to display a photo of the café's namesake after all.'

'When do you hope to open, Angela?'

'I think realistically we need to allow at least a couple of months for kitchen refurbishment and decorating, and Tony and I both have to do a food hygiene course, but I'm already investigating suppliers. We want to use as much local produce as we can.'

'Will you be organic?' Jon asked. Tilly had been nagging him to take more care when he was shopping for food. 'Do try and buy as much organic as you can,' she'd said. He had tried the organic baked beans but the girls had turned up their noses at them.

'No, but I'm planning a mix of wholesome and healthy food with sweet treats. We're going to start off by just doing tea, coffee and cakes and then when we've got our feet a bit, we'll begin light lunches, toasted paninis and baguettes and soup, that sort of thing.

The sort of food dog-walkers would like to round off their walk with.'

'I think it's a brilliant idea to aim at the doggy market,' Jemma said. 'I could never understand why the old owner closed all over winter. That's just the time people need something warming when they're in the park.'

'Precisely,' Angela agreed. 'Oh, I'm so excited! And Tony and I, well,' she hesitated, 'we're getting on much better now he has a new interest and enthusiasm for life again.'

Maggi grinned, 'Plenty of rumpy pumpy, eh?'

Angela blushed. Maggi couldn't possibly know about the kitchen floor incident … could she?

Jemma and Jon laughed and Sybil, seeing Angela's embarrassment, sought to rescue her. 'I'm surprised you didn't call it Mitzi's – although I'm thrilled that it's to be Jock's.'

'I did consider it,' Angela admitted, 'but when I mentioned it to Tony he said it sounded like a massage parlour.'

They all laughed again and, this time, Angela joined in.

∞

'Good morning. I wonder if I may be allowed to join your little group?' The dog clubbers had gathered as usual and were about to set off around the park when a middle-aged man with a greyhound on a lead approached them. They all turned and peered at him and suddenly Maggi said, 'Oh it's Ned's dad, isn't it?'

'I hadn't really thought of myself as being his dad – though maybe his adopted father, yes,' he smiled.

'You know Ned, the greyhound,' Maggi said to the others. 'We used to see him and – 'she indicated the man 'his dad sometimes but he died - just before Christmas, wasn't it?'

'That's right, yes.'

Angela and Sybil both remembered Ned and they expressed their sympathy to his owner.

'But who's this lovely boy?' Angela asked.

'This is Whisky, another rescue dog.'

'Oh, how sad,' Jemma said.

'Not too sad in this instance,' the man explained. 'Whisky broke his leg racing so his owner didn't want to keep him and he went to the greyhound rescue centre. I've been popping in and out there since Christmas and when I saw him I just knew he was the one for me.'

'Ah,' said Maggi. 'How lovely. How old is he?'

'Just four.'

'Plenty of life ahead of him then.'

'Absolutely. But I used to see you all walking when I'd come here and you seemed such a jolly bunch that I thought I'd enquire whether you were taking new members.'

Angela laughed. 'Oh golly, we're not as formal as that! We're just people who all had the same routine so it works out well for us. If one of us is ill or can't walk for some reason, because the dogs are used to each other and to all of us, there's no problem and the dog can still be exercised. I think it works rather well.'

Everyone agreed.

'I, for one, shall be glad to have another man in the group,' Jon said. 'I've been accused of becoming more feminine, I'll have you know. Me!' he said, putting on a butch market-trader accent. 'I ask ya?'

The dogs were beginning to get restless so Angela said, 'Let's get walking then. We can introduce ourselves and the dogs as we stroll.'

The man told them his name was Bernard and with some less than subtle questioning they discovered that he had lived alone since his divorce thirty years earlier, he had two grown-up children and four grandchildren, whom he saw regularly. 'I quite often pick them up from school and they come home for tea with me,' he explained.

'Oh lucky you,' Maggi said wistfully. 'My grandchildren live in Australia and I haven't seen them for years, one of them not at all. But that's going to change this year because I'm going to visit them!'

'How wonderful. When are you going?'

'I haven't actually booked yet,' Maggi admitted. 'Every time I think I've nearly saved enough something breaks down in the house

and I have to pay for repair. Last week my oven gave up on me.'
She sighed. 'But I'll get there. One day.'

'Of course you will,' Jemma said. 'You certainly work hard enough. You deserve it.'

They'd reached the separation of the paths. Angela, Maggi, Bernard and Jon decided to take the longer path while Jemma walked with Sybil. At one time Sybil had worried that they put up with her and her slowness and that it was a duty that each took in some sort of turn, but now she knew she had her place in the group just as much as Angela the organiser, Maggi the joker, or anyone of them, and she felt none of the anxiety she had in the early days.

As they walked Jemma told her about the latest commission she'd been given, taking photographs of a collection of old churches in the county. 'It's all the old Methodist churches,' she explained, 'for an exhibition that the local history society is putting on in conjunction with the museum.'

'That sounds  fascinating,' Sybil said. 'But are there many Methodist churches in the county?'

'Oh yes, you'd be surprised. They're celebrating the anniversary of a visit that,' she stopped to think, 'Was it John Wesley? That he made, I think. He was the big Methodist man, wasn't he?'

'I think you're right, but I'm not a good person to ask; I'm not a church-goer.'

'Neither am I but that doesn't bother them so they're happy and I'm happy. At least I hope they'll be happy with my images.'

'I'm sure they will.'

They walked on a little way in silence, watching Pixie frolic in the water.

'People often assume that as I'm an old lady and therefore close to death that I'd be a church-goer or at least a believer.' Sybil waved away Jemma's protestations. 'I am old, my dear. I'm eighty-two. Even if I stay in good health I'm not likely to live that much longer.'

Jemma hadn't thought about Sybil being old. She was just one of the dog club, older than the others, it was true, but not that old. Now it seemed she was that old.

'You don't look it,' Jemma said, still amazed.

'Thank you, dear, but you should see me struggling to get out of bed some mornings.' Sybil smiled. 'But I'm glad Jock went before me.'

'To doggy heaven.'

'Oh I don't believe in such a thing, not for dogs or for people. I believe we all just …' she spread out her hands, 'rot away in the ground.'

'Oh, no, I can't believe that.' Now Jemma was shocked. 'There must be something more.'

'I stopped believing in God when I couldn't have a baby.' Sybil stopped walking and turned to face Jemma. 'You're only the second person I've ever told.'

Jemma put her hand on Sybil's arm and gave it a squeeze. Then she linked arms with her friend and they walked on each occupied with their own thoughts.

They were almost back at the point where the paths re-joined when they heard a pounding and panting behind them. Jemma glanced over her shoulder to see a jogger running up the path with a slightly overweight golden retriever panting along behind. Jemma edged Sybil to the side of the path to let them pass. The jogger grinned at them and said, 'Thanks.'

The retriever stopped to exchange sniffs with Pixie – and to get his breath back – but his owner turned and yelled, 'Come on, George, you lazy lump! No slacking!'

'Poor dog!' Sybil said, as the retriever sniffed at their pockets hopefully before he plodded on his way.

'He was struggling to keep up with such a fit owner.'

'Yes, very attractive too.'

'Mm.' Jemma nodded in a non-committal way.

'Didn't you think so?' Sybil asked.

'Do you mean the dog or the owner?'

Sybil smiled, 'Well, both were but I actually meant the owner.'

Jemma laughed. 'I didn't really notice.'

They walked on in silence for a few moments then Jemma said, 'I'd like to be the sort of person people notice.'

'But you are, my dear.'

'Huh, only because my hair is bright orange.'

'You have beautiful hair.'

'Nobody, not even you Sybil, can think ginger hair is beautiful.'

'I do. And anyway your hair's auburn. I envy your gorgeous tresses. I always wanted auburn hair when I was growing up. I wanted to look like a pre-Raphaelite painting. Just like you.'

'And I've always wanted someone to say that to me!' They both laughed but then Jemma shook her head. 'But even if you don't think my hair is ginger most people do and it puts them off.'

'More fool them then.'

They walked on a little further and then Jemma asked, 'Why did you ask me if I thought that jogger who passed us was attractive?'

'I don't know, dear. I thought, well, I thought it might have been mutual attraction.'

'What do you mean mutual attraction?'

'Even an old lady like me could see she gave you a very appreciative stare.'

'Really?' Jemma bit her lip. 'But what makes you think I would be interested in her?'

Sybil stopped walking and grasped Jemma's hand. 'Oh, I'm sorry, my dear. Have I offended you? I wouldn't have wanted to do that for the world.'

'No, Sybil, don't worry, I'm not offended. A little surprised maybe.'

'As I said, Jemma, I'm an old lady and I've seen a lot of life but sometimes I see things or I imagine things that aren't there.'

They had reached the join in the paths and they could see the others approaching down the hill. Sybil leaned into Jemma and whispered, 'Now what do you think about Maggi and Bernard? Or am I seeing things that aren't there again?'

'What about them?'

'As a couple. Don't you think they'd be perfect together?'

'Sybil, you little matchmaker you!'

Sybil smiled smugly. 'I could be wrong but let's wait and see.'

∞

Since Jon had kissed her hand Cathy seemed to be avoiding him. At first he imagined she was angry with him – although the more he thought about it the more innocent the kiss appeared – but then he wondered if she were simply embarrassed. Maybe she'd felt he was making fun of her - or taking their friendship too seriously. He had no idea: women were definitely from another planet as far he was concerned he decided. Living in a house with three women, even if two were still in the making, you'd have thought he'd have picked up hints on understanding the female mind. He shook his head. If anyone believed that they'd only have to study him for a short while to find out the truth.

He stopped ironing for a moment and stared out through the window. Should he seek Cathy out and apologise – for whatever it was – or should he just let it go? The trouble was that he had enjoyed their afternoons together; he missed them – and her company. He considered asking Jemma's advice but soon thought better of that. She was sure to misunderstand his motives, innocent though they were. What about the other women? He paused, no, Sybil was too old – she'd definitely disapprove- Angela was too preoccupied with the opening of the café and her newly-revived love life – apparently, according to Jemma – and Maggi, well, she was alright but she did talk a lot and she might let it slip to the others. And he'd only just met Bernard so could hardly land this on him straightaway.

What about his other friends, mates he'd known since school? He thought hard but realised he'd virtually lost touch with anyone he might once have considered a mate. Since he'd become a house-husband his life had revolved around the home and the children not football, computer games and eyeing up the talent at the pub they used to visit most evenings for an after-work drink. Good grief, Jon thought to himself, what has happened to me?

The smell of singeing brought him back to the ironing with a start. He lifted the iron to find a big black mark on one of Sophie's school polo shirts. One day Tilly had asked him why he bothered ironing polo shirts as they were quite presentable if folded flat in the airing cupboard. Jon recalled he'd replied saying, 'I want my

children to look as if they've got someone who cares for them.'
Sophie certainly would look uncared-for if she turned up at school
with a black iron print on the front of her shirt. He sighed. That
was something else Tilly always accused him of: being unable to
multi-task. He'd always denied it but it seemed he couldn't think
and iron at the same time.

He tried to concentrate on the rest of the ironing without
thinking about Cathy but her laugh kept whispering into his ear. He
looked at the clock. It was only half past one. He made a decision:
he'd phone her. If she answered then he'd play it by ear; if she was
out then he'd forget about her. He'd let fate decide.

He dialled the number he'd written on a slip of paper in his
wallet. She'd insisted they exchange numbers in case something
cropped up and one of them wasn't able to make their Thursday
afternoon date - 'I mean meeting,' she'd corrected herself hurriedly.
He dialled without planning what he was going to say; fate could
decide that to.

'Hello.'

He gulped. 'Hi, er Cathy, it's me. I mean, um, it's Jon.'

'I know who me is.'

'Oh, okay, um, how are you?'

'I'm well, and you?'

'Er fine.'

There was a moment's silence.

'Did you want something, Jon?'

'Um, Cathy …'

'Yes?' She wasn't making this easy for him.

'Er, I miss you.'

He could hear the smile in her voice when she replied, 'I miss
you too.'

'I don't know what I've done – well, no, I do know but I didn't
think it was that bad and it wasn't meant to be and it wasn't really
meant to be anything but if it upset you then I'm sorry. For
whatever it is. No, I shouldn't say that. Tilly says I shouldn't make
blanket apologies; I should know what I'm apologising for but I
mean it, whatever it is.'

'Tilly knows you're apologising to me?'

'Hell, no. I just mean generally when I say sorry to her. You know what women are like; they get upset and men are supposed to know what they've done but I never do but apparently that's not good enough. I'm rambling, aren't I?' He stuttered to a halt.

'Just a bit.' Now he could definitely hear the laughter in her voice.

'But am I forgiven?'

'There's nothing to be forgiven for; if anything I'm the one who should be apologising.'

'You? Whatever for?'

'Behaving the way I did.'

'What way? You didn't do anything wrong.'

'I over-reacted.'

'Did you?'

'When you kissed my hand.'

'Oh.' Jon wasn't used to being on the receiving end of an apology. And he still wasn't sure why she felt she needed to but it seemed she did. 'Well, let's just forget it, shall we, and go back to how we were?'

'Is that what you want?'

'Yes, definitely. Don't you?' He suddenly thought that maybe she'd been happy of an excuse to be rid of him and his visiting.

'I'd like you to come round for the afternoon again.'

'Great,' Jon breathed a sigh of relief. 'I'm so glad. When shall we make it?'

'Next Wednesday?'

'Great. One thirty as usual?'

'Yes, that'll be lovely. See you then.

'I'll look forward to it. Bye, Cathy. Oh and see you at school this afternoon.'

'Yes. Bye, Jon.'

He smiled as he put down the phone. Good old fate.

# Chapter 9

'Yes, Bernard said he'd seen the new James Bond and it was a good film.'

Maggi and Brenda were chatting as they filled the cereal shelves. Brenda was wondering if she could persuade her husband to take her to the pictures. Now she stopped and looked at Maggi.

'Bernard enjoyed it, did he?'

'Yes, he said Judi Dench was wonderful as always and that it was the best Bond film he could remember.'

'Oh, yeah?' Brenda was smirking now.

'Yes. What's the matter?' Maggi asked. 'What have I said that's funny?'

'It's not what you've said but the fact that you've mentioned Bernard's name in just about every sentence you've uttered today.'

'Go on with you, I haven't.'

'And now you're blushing!'

'Don't be ridiculous, Bren! I'm not blushing. I'm having a bit of a flush, that's all. You know what it's like. Women of our age.'

'It's all right, Maggi, there's nothing with fancying a man.'

'I do not fancy him. I haven't even thought about him like that. He's just one of our dog-walking club now.'

'You don't bring the others into every conversation we have. I'd be hard-pressed to remember all their names.'

'You're just being silly now. Bernard's just …'

'See? There you go again!'

'Well of course I'm going to say his name now: you've just accused me of saying it so I have to defend myself.'

'So what's he like then?' Brenda wanted to know.

Maggi sighed. She obviously wasn't going to be able to convince Brenda there was nothing in it if she refused to answer her questions. Best to get it over with. 'He's in his early sixties, divorced with two children and four grandchildren. And he has a rescue greyhound called Whisky.'

'What's he look like?'

'A good head taller than me, he walks a bit like a military man – although he's not - very straight-backed. He's got wavy grey - almost white – hair and he's quite trim.'

'All sounds good so far. Is he sexy?'

'For goodness sake, Bren!'

'Oh come on, don't tell me you haven't thought about it?'

'Well,' Maggi paused before placing the last box of corn flakes on the shelf, 'I think some women would probably find him attractive.

'Some women? Either he's attractive or he's not. Do YOU think he's attractive?'

Maggi sighed and raised her eyebrows, exasperated with her friend. 'I suppose I do.'

'Yes!' Brenda punched the air. 'So what are you going to do about it?'

'About what?'

'Oh, Maggi, are you deliberately being thick to annoy me or have you really forgotten what the mating game is about?'

'I thought it was the dating game?'

'Dating, mating, one leads to another if you play your cards right.' Brenda gave a dirty laugh.

Maggi shook her head. 'I'm not going to do anything.'

'Why not?'

'Because … I'm not interested and neither is he.'

'How do you know?'

'Have you looked at me recently, Bren? What man in his right mind would give me a second glance?'

'Are you serious? You're a good-looking woman, Maggi. I've seen men in here look you over when their wives aren't looking.'

As if on cue a man interrupted their chat. 'Excuse, where can I find … um, tea-bags?' He directed his question to Maggi who said, 'Aisle seven. This is aisle 22 so it's way back there. Would you like me to show you?'

He looked anxiously over his shoulder where a woman had appeared with a shopping trolley. 'Er, no, it's all right, thank you. I'll find them.' He hurried back to join the woman and Brenda said, 'See?'

'See what?'

'He only wanted an excuse to talk to you.'

'Nonsense! He wanted to know where the tea-bags were.'

'He didn't really want to know.'

Maggi frowned, genuinely puzzled. 'Why would he ask then?'

'To start chatting you up.'

'Oh for heaven's sake! He was with his wife!'

'And did you notice how he changed his mind about wanting tea-bags when she appeared and saw him?'

Maggi frowned again. 'Do you really think so?'

'Yes! That wasn't the best example I admit but think how often you're approached by men. They never ask me anything!'

'That's probably because you scowl if anyone comes near you while you're busy.'

They both laughed at the truth of that and then Brenda said, 'But seriously, Maggi, if you like this Bernard you should ask him out.'

At that Maggi burst out laughing. 'I never burned my bra, Bren; I'm not going to become a new woman now.'

'You've been alone for a long time. Wouldn't you like someone to share special occasions with?'

'Like you and your Steve, you mean?'

As each new day brought a new complaint from Brenda about what her husband had done now she had to smile. 'Okay, I admit he drives me around the bend but I wouldn't be without him though, you know that.'

'Okay, then I'll admit that I am attracted to Bernard but as all my energy is focused on my trip to Australia I don't have any left for dallying with handsome strangers. And anyway,' Maggi went on, 'Bernard has shown no sign of being interested in me.'

''Hm,' Brenda sounded doubtful. 'You wouldn't notice if he had.'

'Course I would.' Maggi paused. 'I think. Anyway I've got to fetch some more boxes to unpack; are you coming?'

Brenda looked at her trolley. 'No, I've got a few more to do. But don't think I'm giving up on this Bernard idea!'

∞

'Oh no! At this rate we're not going to be ready in time for the opening!' Angela felt like screaming. Since the workmen had started on stripping out and refitting the kitchen in the café they seemed to have been on stop for longer than they were actually working. One problem after another had cropped up: the wrong parts had been sent; bits got broken in the fitting; the oven had been too big to get through the door; and now the electrician who was being brought in to check all the electrics had fallen and broken his leg.

'Can't he come in in plaster?

'Poor chap's only just done it. He's going to be in a bit of pain for a while.'

'Why? He'll be on lots of pain-killers.' Angela was usually more sympathetic but the stress of the delays was wearing her patience.

'Sid said he can get someone else but it'll take a day or two to organise. But it's all right because they can carry on with the tiling. Or most of it at least.' Tony tried to comfort her but his words were falling on ears that could only hear the potential problems.

'What do you mean most of it?'

'The bits around the sockets they need to leave in case there are any problems.'

'Are there likely to be problems?'

'No, of course not, but no point tiling just in case anything's not quite up to standard.'

'But why wouldn't it be up to standard? Is our electrician no good?'

'Angela, calm down! I can't say anything to reassure you if you're going to find a problem in everything. It's very unlikely that there'll be anything wrong with the electrics and everything else is going smoothly.'

'Going smoothly? How can you say that? With all the problems we've had.'

'Every project has its difficulties; it's expected. Now why don't I put the kettle on so we can all have a cup of tea?'

Angela's mobile rang just as Tony was filling the kettle with water. She answered it.

'Hello?'

'Good morning, this is Jenny Burrows, features editor at the Daily Post. I received your press release about the new dog-friendly café and we'd like to come and interview you.'

'Oh! Really? That would be marvellous. When would you like to come? We're not quite ready for opening yet but …'

'That's okay. I'm thinking of including the article on the Features page the week after next, which I think would tie in with your opening?'

'Yes, it would. Perfectly.' Angela crossed her fingers as she spoke: the way it was going the café wouldn't be opening any time soon.

'I'd like to send a photographer to the interview and then again for the official opening. You did say a local celebrity would be performing the ceremony, didn't you?'

'Er, yes.'

'And who is that?'

'Oh, um, I'd like to keep it a secret until the big day if that's all right?'

They agreed that a reporter – probably the editor herself who as the owner of a couple of Jack Russells was very interested in the idea of a café that welcomed dogs – would meet Angela at Jock's the following day at 11.15. Angela suggested the time as she hoped she could persuade some if not all of the dog clubbers to be there in attendance to support her. She definitely wanted Sybil to be there, and Maggi, and Jemma too. And Jon as the only male in the group for a long time.

Tony brought her cup of tea just as she came off the phone. 'That was the features editor from the Daily Post. Someone's coming to interview us tomorrow and bringing a photographer – oh dear, maybe I should have told her to wait for photos  but perhaps I can get Jemma to bring some of hers in – and writing a feature about us and she has Jack Russells and she sounded very interested and this could be great publicity. I wonder if I should get my hair done.'

Tony smiled. This was better; Angela was usually very determined and not easily deterred by minor setbacks. He'd been concerned that she might have been burying her disappointment about his redundancy and her anxiety about the long term prospects, by putting all her hopes into the café's future. He nodded. 'I think you should go to the hairdressers. A bit of pampering will do you good, help you get things into perspective. And you haven't been for ages.'

'While I'm there I can make notes, remind myself what I need to make sure I say. You know what reporters are like, especially local ones. They often make mistakes. I'll phone the hairdressers' now.'

While Angela was in the hairdressers' waiting for her colour to take she called all the dog clubbers and explained what she wanted them to do. 'Just hang on after our walk tomorrow. Come back to the café with me – Tony can make us all a hot drink while we wait – and then we can all have our photograph taken.'

'Why do you want us to be in the photo?' Maggi asked.

'Because it's because of you – especially you, Maggi - that I had the idea of the café. And it's because of the dog club that we're putting the emphasis on being dog-friendly. And, well, you're all important to me.'

They all agreed although Sybil was reluctant at first to be in the limelight. 'It's Jock really,' Maggi said, when they were walking the following day. 'You just happened to be his owner.'

'I suppose so.'

'And you'll be helping Angela,' Jemma pointed out.

'That's true,' Jon agreed. 'We're all doing it to help Angela.'

'I feel rather awkward about it though,' Bernard said.

'Why?' Maggi asked.

'I appreciate being asked by Angela but I'm a newcomer to the group. I didn't even know Jock and all this was planned before I came along.'

'That doesn't matter,' Jon said. 'If Angela invited you she must want you there.'

''No, she just felt she had to.'

'Rubbish!' Maggi said. 'When you get to know Angela better you'll realise that she doesn't do things because she feels obliged to.'

'That's right,' Sybil said. 'You're part of our group; you have to be there.'

Bernard was touched by their generous spirits. 'Well, I'll come along but I'll have a quiet word with Angela and say I'm happy to stay out of the photos.'

'If you want to but I bet she says the same as us.' Maggi was certain.

∞

Angela wasn't intending to do much tidying-up of the café as she'd explained to the reporter that the builders were still in but being Angela she couldn't help herself and by seven the following morning both she and Tony were in the café. 'Tell me again why we're here so early,' Tony asked, yawning as he scrubbed the floor.

'We want the public bit of the café to at least look tidy. No-one's going to want to come otherwise.'

'But we still have the decorating to do in there.'

'Yes, I know, which is a shame as it won't give the right impression but we have to make some effort. You've missed a bit, look!'

'It's too early; my eyes haven't woken up yet. Let's have a cup of tea.'

'In a bit.'

'We've got hours before she comes. A cup of tea won't slow us down. In fact it'll speed me up.'

'Oh, okay, I'll put the kettle on,' Angela said as Tony put his mop down. 'No, don't you stop! You carry on scrubbing while I make the tea. I should have bought some flowers.'

'Flowers? In a builders' yard?'

'Tony, you're not helping! Flowers will improve the look of the place.' Angela glanced at her watch. 'I'll pop out and get some when the shops open.'

∞

By the time the dog clubbers arrived back at the café after their walk they were amazed at the transformation. Angela had put out some tables and chairs and arranged small posies of flowers on each table. She'd hung some of Jemma's photos on the wall arranged so that the one of Jock took centre stage and she'd brought some of her prettiest china from home. With the cups and saucers laid out on the tables as well as the cake Sybil had made and brought along at least one corner of the café looked presentable.

'Wow!' Maggi said. 'It looks fab, Angela.'

The others all agreed.

'Well, it's not ideal,' Angela said, 'but I hope it will give newspaper readers some idea of what to expect when we do open. It's a shame we won't always have Sybil's cake to offer our customers though.'

'Why not?' Maggi asked. 'If Sybil wanted to make you a cake or two a week would you be able to sell it?'

'Of course,' Angela said, 'but you wouldn't want to do that, would you, Sybil?'

Sybil frowned. 'Oh I don't think my cake would be good enough for paying customers.'

'You're joking,' Jemma said. 'Some of the cakes I've bought have been horrible and if the one you made us for Angela's birthday is anything to go by, your cakes would be much better.'

Jon was nodding and Maggi said, 'Absolutely, Sybil.' Turning to the others Maggi continued, 'And the Christmas cake she made for us was delicious – and the shortbread. I've never tasted any so crisp and rich and buttery.'

Just then the door opened and a young woman stuck her head around the door. 'Hello, is Angela here?'

'Yes, I'm Angela. You must be Jenny. Do come in.'

The reporter entered followed by a man with a very large camera bag. 'I wonder, Angela, if Mark – this is Mark our photographer by the way – could take some photos before we do the interview? He has to dash off afterwards for the opening of a new store.'

Mark arranged them in various groups - all including the dogs - and took what seemed like an inordinate number of shots. Then Angela showed him the framed photo of Jock on the wall and explained this was where the name had come from. Mark duly took more photos that included Jock's image but saying he couldn't guarantee which ones would be used in the feature.

When at last he was satisfied that he had enough shots Mark left and Jenny was able to conduct her interview with Angela. The rest of the dog clubbers sat quietly in the background listening intently and answering the reporter's questions when they were put to them. Jenny was very taken with Jemma's pet portraits and booked a 'sitting' with her before she left. 'Although I suppose you can't call it a sitting if they're going to be running around in the park,' she said.

She explained that she intended to include the feature in two weeks' time in the Friday edition. 'That will be the day before you open, won't it?'

'Yes, that's right,' Angela said brightly and with more confidence than she felt.

'And are you willing to tell me who your local celebrity is yet? The one who's going to perform the opening ceremony?'

Angela laughed, 'Oh I don't know.'

Jenny, the reporter, thought she meant she didn't know if she should tell her. 'Oh go on, I can plug the opening then in the feature. Make more of it.'

'No,' Angela said, 'I um … er …'

'She's reluctant to tell you because it hasn't been confirmed yet,' Bernard interrupted. 'As soon as it has been you'll be the first to know,' he said nodding sagely.

'Okay, I shall hold you to that … Bernard is it?'

He nodded and said, 'I'll make sure of it.'

When the reporter had left Angela said to Bernard, 'I wish you hadn't said that.'

'What?'

'That you'd make sure she knew about the local celebrity opening the café. I should never have put that in the press release; I just wanted to attract attention. But it's my fault really; I should have come clean and admitted I hadn't organised anyone.'

'Well, I'll have to check with him but I know my nephew is home for a few weeks between shows and I'm sure he'd be happy to help out and I think he'd probably count as a minor celebrity.'

'Your nephew?'

'Simon Brewer. He won a …'

'Simon Brewer?' Maggi interrupted. 'Simon Brewer? He's your nephew?'

'Yes, have you heard of him?'

'Have I heard of him? Who hasn't?'

'Even I know Simon Brewer,' Sybil said. 'He has a wonderful voice. I was delighted when he won that talent show on television. Especially as he's from this town. And it's so unusual for a proper singer to do well.'

Yes,' Jemma added. 'I bought his cd for my mum for Christmas. She loves it – and even I think he's gorgeous!'

'Tilly worships him too,' Jon said. 'Wait till I tell her.'

'Well, let me ask him first,' Bernard said, 'although I have chatted to him about the dog club and he loves dogs. He'd have one himself but he's in his flat in London or touring most of the time. As I said he just happens to have a few weeks off.'

'Bernard, you would be an absolute life-saver if you could arrange this,' Angela said. 'You can have free tea for life if you can pull this off!'

∞

Jon was looking forward to his Thursday afternoon date with Cathy. He laughed to himself as he called it a date. It wasn't a date as such; it was just the day they'd arranged to get together again. Now that he had the afternoon to look forward to he was able to admit to himself how much he'd missed their weekly chats. He got on well with all the dog clubbers and they never ran out of conversation topics but none of them currently had children in school so weren't in the kind of routine he was. Tilly always seemed too busy as well as not really interested enough to chat about how long it had taken him to do the shopping or how hard it had been to dry the washing outside with the weather they'd had. Sophie who'd been learning about energy in school had started to nag him about using the tumble dryer.

'Now every time I switch it on I hear her voice in my head, "Is that absolutely necessary, Daddy?" I bet her teacher doesn't think twice about using her dryer when she's trying to fit all the housework in one weekend. They should think about the poor parents before they brainwash the kids.'

He smiled at Cathy. 'I'm so glad we're back to normal,' he said. 'You understand what it's like.'

She smiled but not as broadly as he had. 'Would you like more coffee?'

'Thanks, Cathy, that would be great. Any more of those biccies too? Tilly won't let us have chocolate biscuits in the house. I have to eat them while I can!'

This time Cathy didn't smile back at him. Instead she got up from her chair opposite him and went to the kitchen. Jon was puzzled: Cathy didn't seem very comfortable and hadn't been since he'd got there. In fact, she seemed to be a bit on edge. He wondered if it were hormone trouble; he always knew when Tilly was best avoided but it hadn't been noticeable with Cathy before. Perhaps she'd done her best to conceal it when they were getting to know each other. Yes, he nodded to himself, maybe that was it. It might even be a good thing if it meant she felt she could be herself with him.

But, he sighed, it didn't make for a pleasant afternoon for him. He wondered if he should make a note of the date and find an excuse each month to avoid seeing her. That might be a bit obvious though. He sighed again: why were women so complex?

'What's the matter?' Cathy had come back in with his coffee and another plate of biscuits and had heard his sigh.

'Oh, I didn't hear you.' He was flustered. He could hardly tell her what he'd been pondering. If it were her hormones any mention of them would only go against him; he'd learned that much from Tilly.

'Are you okay?' she asked.

'Yes, I was just thinking, um, I mean I was wondering er, if everything was okay with you actually?'

'In what way?'

'You've seemed a little on edge this afternoon.'

'Have I?'

'Um, yes, I think so.'

She didn't say anything but sat down next to him on the sofa. He turned slightly so that he could look at her. She was staring into the distance.

''I was so pleased after we'd spoken on the phone,' he said. 'I thought everything was going to get back to normal.'

'To normal?' she asked sharply.

'Yes, well, to the way it was before.'

'Is that what you want?'

'Yes, of course.' Suddenly it became clear to him. 'Isn't it what you want?'

'No.' Cathy shook her head.

Jon stood up. 'I'm sorry. I misunderstood. I'll go.'

'No wait,' she caught his hand. 'Don't go. Please sit down.' She tugged gently on his arm. He let himself be pulled back.

'It's my fault,' she said. 'I wasn't clear.'

'No, no,' Jon argued. 'It was my fault. I should have realised that this wasn't what you wanted.'

'What do you think I want?' She looked at him, her eyes wide.

'To be honest, I don't really know.'

'When I say I don't want things to go back to as they were what I mean is …' she stopped, then leaned forward, took his face in her hands and kissed him urgently on the lips.

Jon's first instinct was to draw back, to pull away but as he tasted the toothpaste-fresh tang of her breath and felt the softness of her lips he began to respond. He put his arms around her and pulled her to him. He felt her body relax and shape into his. His hands that are been gripping her shoulders began to move down towards the small of her back. He could feel her arms around his neck and her fingers as she ran them through his hair. Everything felt so right, fitted together so perfectly, he didn't want to let go.

In the end Cathy was the one who drew back. She sank back against the sofa and brushed her hair away with her hand. Her breath was coming quickly through her open mouth as she smiled at him. She reached out and stroked his leg. 'That's what I want,' she breathed. 'What do you want?'

# Chapter 10

Most days now, somewhere on the walk, Jemma saw George, the retriever, and his jogger. Whether she took the top path or the shorter one she'd see them en route. She mentioned the coincidence to Maggi one morning just after their paths had crossed.

'It's strange how often we see them.'

'Not really,' Maggi said. 'We see lots of walkers when we're out.'

'Yes, but not on a regular basis. They're always out at the same time as us.'

Maggi, who'd been wondering how Bernard was getting on, made herself concentrate on what Jemma was saying. 'Well, they're not going to want to join the dog club, not if they're running.' She paused. 'Wasn't it amazing that Bernard turned out to be Simon Brewer's uncle?'

'What? Oh yes, I suppose so, although most people have got uncles.'

'Yes, but what's the chance of having a dog-walker in our group who has just the right contacts when you need them?'

'He hasn't spoken to his nephew yet.'

'No, that's what he's doing this morning. That's why he's not here and why we're walking Whisky.'

'Oh I wondered where he was.'

'Angela explained when we met up.'

'Oh, I must have missed that.'

'Are you okay?' Maggi looked at her young friend, concerned. 'You do seem a bit distracted.'

'Yes, I'm fine. I just didn't hear that bit.'

Jemma felt the blush rising and was grateful that Pixie chose that moment to run up to her and present her with a big stick. She leaned over, took the stick and threw it into the distance. She watched for a moment while both Pixie and Bassett bounded after it before turning around, hoping the colour had gone from her cheeks.

Whisky, who was walking with them, didn't care to chase sticks. He preferred to walk gracefully along, looking around almost as if he were appreciating the scenery. Bernard had explained that since breaking his leg Whisky had been nervous about running anywhere.

'It's strange, isn't it,' Jemma said, 'having a greyhound who doesn't run?'

'Maybe he'll have a go one day. It's not that long since he broke his leg – and it was a severe break. The vet suggested putting him down.'

'Really? Just because of a broken leg?'

'He was a racing dog. Not much use with an imperfect leg. Lost his value. Bernard said he was lucky that the owner put him into the rescue home rather than destroy him. Lots of racing greyhound owners are less caring.'

'That's sad.' Jemma bent over and stroked the dog's sleek back. Whisky lifted his head to allow her to tickle under his chin and she said, 'How could anyone destroy a young healthy dog?'

'I know,' Maggi agreed. 'It's beyond me too. There are some strange people in this world.'

She too stroked the dog. 'You were lucky to be given a home by Bernard, weren't you, Whisky?'

They carried on walking towards the top of the hill, chatting as they strolled.

'How's the saving going?' Jemma asked.

Maggi groaned. 'Oh don't ask! This week it was my iron that gave up the ghost and my fridge is making funny noises as if it really finds it too hard to keep cool. A bit like me. I'm having to keep the bare minimum in it otherwise it overheats. I'm living out of tins at the moment. It's fantastic how many things you can have on toast. Now I have my new toaster that is.'

'If you dry and fold things carefully you don't need an iron anyway,' Jemma said.

Maggi raised one eyebrow. 'My mother would turn in her grave if I went out in un-ironed clothes, and, anyway, I'm old enough to be of the have-to-iron brigade. Have you noticed how nicely Bernard is always turned out? Makes me feel quite a scruff.'

'There's no point dressing up if you're going to get muddy, which I always seem to. I can't say I've noticed how Bernard dresses particularly but what I have noticed is how often you mention his name.'

'Oh not you too!'

∞

'You know, Sybil, Tony's redundancy is the best thing to happen to us in years.'

While the floor in the café was being done, Angela had grabbed the chance to walk with the dog club. For over a week the others had taken Mitzi out for her to let her get on with café preparations and Angela felt in need of some fresh air. She was getting plenty of exercise from all the scrubbing, painting and cleaning she'd been doing but she definitely missed the fresh morning air and getting together with friends. They didn't stop when they collected and dropped off Mitzi as they didn't want to get in the way of the workmen who were filling the place so Angela's contact with them had been intermittent.

Sybil had called in to discuss cakes and she and Angela had enjoyed a pleasant few minutes sitting outside in the sunshine before Angela's instruction was needed inside; Jemma had been around a few times to photographically record the progress and advise Angela on the best spots on the walls on which to hang photos; Jon had taken some of the tables home with him and sanded them down ready for re-painting; Maggi had put in a few hours' helping to clean whenever she wasn't working; and Bernard had brought the wonderful news that his nephew would be delighted to perform the opening ceremony.

Angela had hugged him delightedly when he'd told her. 'Oh, Bernard, that's wonderful! And he really doesn't mind?'

'No, he's happy to help out. As I said he loves dogs and the idea of a dog-friendly café in this location appeals to him no end. So, would you like me to get on to the features editor at the Daily Post? Let her know the celebrity and all the opening details?'

'If you don't mind that would be a huge help.'

'It'll be my pleasure. Make me really feel like one of the club.'

The others had all shared her delight when she told them, making a big fuss of Bernard as she did so. He insisted it was no bother and he was pleased to be of help. Maggi and Jemma were full of questions about Simon Brewer so at the parting of the paths they opted for the top path with Bernard. Jon decided to go that way too as he needed to walk out some of the tension that had built up inside him since his last meeting with Cathy.

So it was just to Sybil that Angela confided her thoughts about Tony's redundancy. 'We had, I think, got stale. Our marriage I mean. Oh, we got on all right or maybe it was just that we tolerated each other enough to make life bearable but there was no excitement. Tony'd come home from work, we'd have dinner that I'd prepared and then we'd sit and watch television. Occasionally we'd go out with friends or to the theatre but we didn't really enjoy each other's company.'

Angela went quiet and seemed to have drifted off into her own head but then she said, 'I don't think we'd ever have divorced - we didn't have the energy for anything so dynamic – but if we'd had to think about our marriage we'd – rather I'd – have said that it just was. I suspect Tony would have been equally apathetic. So, as I said, his redundancy was the best thing to happen to us.'

'It was hard at first though, wasn't it? Coming out of the blue on Christmas eve.'

'Oh my word, yes. I'm not sure how we got through Christmas. I suppose I was on autopilot and Tony was on whisky.' She laughed. 'Fortunately I'd forgotten to stock up so we soon ran out and even he wasn't depressed enough to start on the Greek holiday ouzo.'

Sybil smiled but then looked serious. 'We were all worried about you. We could tell something was wrong.'

'I know,' Angela gave her a heartfelt smile. 'Walking with the dog club kept me sane. Tony would have lain around in bed all morning – possibly all day – and that sort of inertia is infectious. Because of having to walk Mitzi and do so at a set time each day I knew I had to get up, get dressed and get out. Without that incentive … who knows where we'd be now. And without Maggi's suggestion I'd never have thought of doing something different. Something completely out of the blue.'

'I thought you said you'd always liked the idea of running a café?'

'Oh yes, I have. But having a vague idea that you might think about think about doing one day and actually doing it are worlds apart.'

'What did Tony say when you first suggested it?' Sybil was curious. She'd met Tony at the café and he'd seemed full of energy and enthusiasm. It was difficult to imagine he'd been the lethargic man Angela spoke about.

'He wasn't keen,' Angela admitted. 'In fact he said that I'd lost my marbles. He said, and I quote, "There's absolutely no way you'll get me spending all my hard-earned redundancy money on running a café." I must remind him he said that.' She chuckled to herself.

'So your marriage isn't so …' Sybil hesitated. It was one thing for Angela to suggest her marriage was boring but she may not take kindly to Sybil reminding her. 'Sleepy?' she finally settled for.

'Sleep is the last thing I'm doing these days.' Angela shook her head. 'I tell you Sybil when I'm not in the café working I'm at home thinking about the café or ordering supplies or adding to my numerous lists. And when I finally get to bed - let's say we do a lot more cuddling than we used to.'

'I see,' said Sybil. 'Good for you. There's nothing like … cuddling to revive a tired marriage.'

'In fact,' Angela glanced over her shoulder to check there were no walkers nearby. 'In fact, it's not only in bed that we're cuddling.'

Sybil's eyebrows shot up. 'Well, jolly good for you then! There's nothing like doing it in the fresh air to bring a flush to your cheeks.' She leaned in towards Angela. 'Reg and I had our own favourite spot.'

Angela who'd been remembering sex on the café floor was amazed to find she was rather shocked by Sybil's confession. 'You mean you did it out of doors?' she whispered.

'Only in the springtime, when the bluebells were out. A bed of bluebells is the sweetest thing.'

'Aah,' Angela said. She and Tony had never done it out of doors. She would have to mention this to him and see if they could rectify it. She giggled at the thought. 'Oh Sybil, you are a star!' she said. 'A blessing to the dog club in general and to me in particular.'

Sybil looked amazed but smiled happily. Her life since meeting the others in the dog club had improved no end and she was glad if she'd helped it improve for others too.

They could see the others making their way down the path towards them and Sybil frowned. 'Is everything all right with Jon do you think?'

Angela looked over at him as he approached. 'I can't say I've noticed but I haven't seen much of him recently and I've been preoccupied.' As they were speaking he tossed a ball for Benji and was obviously laughing at something that had been said. 'He looks okay.'

'Yes,' Sybil agreed. 'It's probably my imagination.'

'We were just discussing the opening, Angela,' Jemma said, when they were close enough to talk. 'We'll all be there obviously but is there anything special you'd like us to do or wear?'

'Oh I don't think so. Just having you there will be enough. That reminds me the feature should be in the paper this weekend.'

'I'll have to order a copy,' Sybil said. 'I usually read the one in the communal lounge but I shall want to cut this out and keep it.'

Maggi said, 'I'm in work Saturday; I could get copies for anyone who wants one and drop them off if that helps.'

'That would be good,' Jon said. 'When the girls are home at the weekend my brain goes to mush trying to make sure I deliver them to the right ballet class, netball practice, violin lesson at the right time.'

Bernard said, 'I won't need one, thanks, Maggi, as I have mine delivered.'

'But you could get several for me, please,' Angela said. 'Let's see, one for me, one for each of the girls, one for my mother and one for Tony's dad; how many's that? Six. Perhaps you'd better get ten for me to be certain.'

'You'll need to frame one,' Maggi said. 'I've been in lots of places where they display reviews.'

'This won't be a review of course, but that's a good idea, Maggi. Shall I pay you now? My purse is back at the café.'

'No, pay me afterwards. That'll be fine.'

∞

On Wednesday morning Jon sprang out of bed. He'd made his decision.

'Come on, girls! Rise and shine!' he shouted brightly. 'The sun has got its hat on, hip hip hip hooray.'

'Oh Dad, don't be so cheerful,' Sophie groaned as she appeared from her bedroom door. 'It's too early.'

'It's a beautiful day and we should be out there enjoying it.'

Sophie looked up at her father hopefully. 'Does that mean we don't have to go to school today?'

'No, it doesn't! It just means we should be grateful for days like these and make the most of them.'

Sophie poked her tongue out at her dad. 'Why are you so cheerful?' She turned to go back into her bedroom but Jon took her by the shoulders and steered her towards the stairs. 'Downstairs, miss, I've poured your orange juice and got your cereal and bowl, ready. I'll come and make toast when I've tipped Gracie out of bed.'

Sophie wandered downstairs only stopping once to go back for her book.

'Sophie, I said, get downstairs!'

'I'm on my way, Dad, but I have to have my book to read while I'm eating.'

At weekends Tilly made a fuss about the girls reading at the breakfast table but Jon, who thought reading of any sort was to be encouraged, tended to ignore it during the week. Besides when they were engrossed in books he could get them to eat porridge, which they normally turned their noses up at, so it was win win as far as he was concerned.

'Come on, Gracie,' he poked his younger daughter who was still curled up embryo-like under her quilt. 'Time to get up, sleepyhead.' He opened the curtains as she groaned.

'Oh, Daddy, I don't feel well.'

Jon sighed. Gracie occasionally didn't 'feel well' if someone or something had upset her at school the day before. She hadn't mentioned anything the previous evening but she was like her dad in that respect: she would put bad things out of her mind for as long as she could.

'Come on, Gracie. You know you've got to go to school.'

She didn't move so he sat on the edge of her bed and pulled the quilt down just far enough so he could see her eyes. 'What's up, sweetie? Has someone been upsetting you in school?'

'No, Daddy, really I don't feel well.'

He put his hand on her forehead and frowned. She did feel hot. 'What hurts, Gracie?'

'Everything. And I'm itchy.'

He drew back the cover further and pulled up her pyjama jacket: her back was covered in spots.

'Oh no.' It was his turn to groan.

'What is it, Daddy? What's the matter with me?'

'I think you might have chickenpox.'

He'd heard one of the mums say that it was going around the school and Sophie had said she wished she could catch it because she wanted to stay in bed and watch television and eat ice cream. It looked like that dream was going to come true for Gracie.

'Daddy!' Sophie called up the stairs to him. 'Are you going to make my toast?'

'Yes, I'll be down now.' He covered Gracie back up and told her he'd be back in a few minutes. Downstairs he quickly put some bread in the toaster before ringing the doctor. The receptionist was sympathetic and said, yes, chickenpox was going around and that if he popped her to the clinic just before surgery hours the doctor would have a quick look to confirm.

When he explained to Sophie she was indignant. 'How come Gracie's got it and I haven't? That's not fair.'

'You'll probably get it next,' Jon said, sighing as he anticipated two weeks of keeping grumpy itchy children entertained.

When Sophie had finished her breakfast he sent her up to dress with strict instructions to make sure she cleaned her teeth properly, while he phoned Jemma to ask if he could drop off Benji again. Then wrapping Gracie in her dressing-gown and a spare duvet, he carried her to the car. As he struggled to open the door with her in his arms he said, 'Why am I carrying you?'

'Because I'm poorly, daddy,' she said, very pathetically.

'But you can walk.' He'd managed to open the door and dropped his daughter into the seat.

'Will you put my strap on, Daddy?'

'You can do it.'

'No, I can't. Not with my duvet on.'

Jon took a deep breath; this was going to be a long week.

When he'd dropped Sophie off at school –after withstanding the barrage of her well-thought-out arguments: I might as well get it sooner rather than later and you'd don't want to keep coming back and for to school when Gracie's so ill, do you, daddy? – and the doctor had confirmed his diagnosis of chickenpox, and Benji had been dropped off, the two of them returned home with helpful advice but no medicine, which made Gracie feel instantly better. She hated medicine in any shape or form and ever since she'd been a baby had managed to make herself vomit whenever they'd tried to dose her. Even now when she was at an age to understand that medicine would make her feel better at the very least, she chose not to believe it.

He settled her on the sofa, thanking his stars for children's television, and left her with a long glass of squash and the promise that he was only in the kitchen doing things if she needed him.

Then he made his phone call.

He drummed his fingers on the work surface as he waited for the phone to be picked up. At last it was.

'Hello.'

'Cathy, hi, it's me.'

'Hi Jon.' He could feel the warmth in her voice.

'I'm not going to be able to make it this afternoon.' He lowered his voice though he was sure Gracie wouldn't be able to hear him over the television.

'Oh.'

'The thing is …'

'It's okay, Jon. I understand. You don't need to make excuses.'

'No, really, it's not an excuse: Gracie's got chickenpox.'

'Oh.' It was amazing how differently a single syllable could sound. 'That's okay then. I mean it's not okay that Gracie's unwell,' she said, hurriedly, not wanting to sound like an uncaring woman, 'but obviously you can't come round if she's ill. That's fine; we can make it another time. Maybe next week?'

Jon sighed. 'As long as Sophie doesn't go down with it too.'

'Oh yes,' she couldn't hide her disappointment. 'Yes, of course. Well, if it's – we're - meant to be …'

'I'm sure we are,' Jon said firmly.

'Are you? Are you really?'

'Yes, I've been doing a lot of thinking this last week and I keep coming back to the same place.'

'Which is?'

'With you in my arms.'

'I thought – I feared – I was the only one hoping that.'

'Oh no, I want … you very much.'

A small cross voice behind him made him jump. 'Daddy, I'm itchy.'

'Okay, I've got to go now, nurse the patient,' he forced a jolly laugh. 'So, um, sorry, about that and I'll see you around some time.'

When he'd put down the phone he looked at his tiny daughter and wondered how much she'd heard.

'Were you telling Mummy that I'm poorly?'

'What? Oh, yes, that's what I was doing. Mummy said to give you a nice cool bath and put on lots of calamine. That'll make you feel better she said.'

He carried her upstairs and left her on the bed while he ran the bath. He was still feeling guilty, caught out, flustered. Which is ridiculous, he told himself, I haven't done anything. Not yet, the other voice in his head told him, except kiss her. 'Shut up!' he muttered to himself just as Gracie wandered in to the bathroom. She burst into tears.

'Oh, sweetheart, I wasn't talking to you,' Jon said as he hugged her.

'Who were you talking to then?' she sobbed.

'Myself. You know sometimes grown-ups do silly things.'

'Like shouting at yourself?' She sniffed.

'Yes, like that. And I've seen you talking to yourself in your bedroom sometimes.'

Gracie frowned . 'I'm not talking to myself; I'm talking to Miffy.' Miffy was her favourite bear, the one who slept in her bed and the one they had to make sure they took on holidays with them if they didn't want long sleepless nights.

'Well, let's get you undressed and into this bath.' When she was sitting in the water he could see just how many spots she had. 'Wow!' he said. 'I think you've got more spots than Leopard.' Leopard was another bedtime favourite of Gracie's and she looked down at her tummy and smiled for the first time that day.

'Have I?'

Jon nodded. 'Easily. Do you want to count them?'

They tried but kept losing count. In the end Gracie decided to settle for 'more spots than leopard'. 'When everyone asks me how many I had I'll be able to tell them that, won't I?'

'You certainly will.'

He encouraged her to lie down and he splashed water over her tummy. 'Is that making it feel better?'

She nodded. 'Can I stay here all day?'

'I think the water might get a bit cold if you did that, but we'll put some of this special cream on the spots when you get out. That should make you feel better too.'

Spots had appeared on her face as well so the only parts of her body not spotty were the soles of her feet. As Jon patted her dry gently she wriggled. 'Careful, Daddy! That hurts.'

'Come on, let's get this cream on and then we'll get you downstairs and I'll make you a drink; what would you like?'

'Can I have hot chocolate?'

Her favourite drink she was usually only allowed to have it once a week on Saturday mornings. Jon smiled, 'Yes, okay.'

'And can I watch Sleeping Beauty?'

'Yes, of course.'

'And will you watch it with me?'

He sighed.

'Oh please, Daddy.'

'Well, just for a little bit then.'

Sleeping Beauty had just met the prince in the woods and Jon's eyes were beginning to close when the doorbell rang. It was Jemma returning Benji.

'Thanks, Jem. Has he been a good boy?'

'Wonderful. How's the patient?'

'She'll live; I may not.'

Jemma laughed. 'The joys of being a parent.'

'You wait,' he said. 'Your turn will come.'

'Everyone sends their love to you both. And I thought that, tomorrow morning, I could call in and pick up Benji and take Sophie to school for you.'

'No, it's okay. That would be a nuisance for you.'

'I don't mind, honestly. You don't want to be dragging a sick child back and for to school. I would offer to pick Sophie up tonight but I've got an assignment to do.'

'That's fine. I'll manage but … yes, if you could take her in the morning that would be a help. I hadn't really thought about the logistics.'

They arranged the time for Jemma to be there and Jon went back into the lounge where Gracie had fallen asleep. He switched off the film, made sure she was neither too hot nor too cold, and left her to sleep.

Minutes later the phone rang. 'Hello, Jon, it's Bernard.'

'Oh hello, Bernard.'

'I hope you don't mind me ringing you; Maggi gave me your number. I was going to volunteer to collect your other daughter from school. Maggi would have done it but she's in work this afternoon and Angela is up to her eyes in the café.'

'That's very kind of you, Bernard.'

'I suppose you'd have to tell the school that a strange man would be picking her up, and, of course, she doesn't know me. But Sybil's offered to come with me; she's met Sybil I believe?'

Jon was incredibly touched by the kindness of his dog-walking friends. 'I really can't ask you to do that.'

'You're not asking: we're offering. Those of us who've had children know how jolly difficult it can be when one of them's ill. It's no fun dragging a little one in and out. Especially when there's no need.'

When he'd accepted Bernard's offer Jon called the school and explained to the secretary who said she'd make sure that Sophie was told who would be collecting her. By the time he'd come off the phone Gracie had woken and was moaning again about the itchiness. It was going to be a very long day.

# Chapter 11

'Jock's looks set to become a favourite not just with the dog-walking brigade. With the promise of home-made cakes, fair-trade tea and coffee and locally sourced ingredients, this soon-to-be-opened and refurbished café is sure to be a hit with the many crowds of visitors who frequent Beauville Park all year round.'

Angela put down the newspaper. 'There! What about that? Isn't that excellent? She's done us proud.'

Tony put his arm around his wife. 'Only speaking the truth. You've transformed this café already from the slightly run-down place only frequented by a small group of regulars that it was. Look at it!'

They looked around together. They were finally beginning to believe that they might be ready for their grand opening the following week. The comfy leather sofas and low coffee tables had been delivered – Angela had insisted on splashing out on those – and the other tables and chairs that Jon had sanded so thoroughly had been re-painted cream. Jemma had decorated some of the chairs with delicately-painted ivy vines and all had new cushions, covered in hard-wearing but pretty material in a variety of woodland colours. For the walls they'd – or rather Angela – had chosen what the paint manufacturer called Natural Wicker interspersed with Muddy Puddles, which looked a lot better than it sounded, Tony had to admit. They'd decided the counter would be fine as it was – once freshly painted - but had invested in a new computerised till to replace the antique the previous owner had used. All that was left to do in the public area was to hang Jemma's photos and she was bringing those the following Monday.

'Oh, I must remember to place an order for daily newspapers. Which ones did we decide on in the end?'

'Independent and Mirror.'

'Is that enough?'

'It'll do to begin with. If they prove to be popular we can order more.'

Angela took out the small notebook she'd taken to carrying with her at all times. She wrote newspapers in large letters in it then asked, 'Is there anything else I need to remember? I'm sure there was something in my head earlier. I thought I must write that down.'

'I'm sure it'll come back to you if it's important,' Tony reassured her. 'There can't be much left that we've forgotten.'

'Oh, I know what it is: posters to put up around the park and in the local shops. I'm not sure whether we'll be allowed to stick posters on trees so maybe we'd better just use gate-posts and railings. They can't object to that, can they? Not if we're going to be encouraging more people to come to the park for longer? But perhaps I should phone the parks department; I don't want to get on the wrong side of anybody. But what if they say no?'

'Don't ask them.'

'Do you think? Oh, I don't know.'

'If you don't ask them you can plead innocence if they object. Not that they're likely to object if you only put them on railings.'

'Yes, I suppose you're right. Print out posters.' Angele added it to her list. 'Oh and I must confirm with the baker how many and which sort of loaves I want.' She added that to her list too. 'I think a mix of white and granary, don't you? Oh it's so difficult when we have no idea how many will come or whether they'll eat anything.'

Tony pulled his wife to him and hugged her. 'Angie, calm down. It'll be trial and error at first; it's bound to be. It'll take us weeks, probably months, to get into a routine.'

'But what if …?' she stopped and bit her bottom lip. His use of his pet name for her – a term he hadn't used for a long time – brought her to the edge, and she could feel tears welling up.

'What?'

'What if it's all a disaster? What if we spend all your redundancy money and it flops? What will we do then?'

'Then we'll cope. But it's not going to be a disaster. You read what the reporter said: this is just what the park needs. Now come on, this isn't like you to be so negative. It's just approaching first night nerves. Everything will go wonderfully, you'll see. And the girls are going to be here to support us – and they'll want feeding even if no-one else does. You know what gannets our children are.'

Angela smiled tearfully. 'Yes, that's true. I'd better order plenty!'

Then Tony said, 'Listen.'

'What? I can't hear anything.'

'Precisely. That's the first time for weeks that there haven't been workmen in here making a noise.'

'They're coming back on Monday to finish in the toilets though.'

'Yes, I know, but they're not here now.'

'No,' Angela nodded.

'So …' Tony pulled her tighter still, 'maybe we should take advantage of having the café to ourselves: it may never happen again.'

'Tony! What are you suggesting?' Angela grinned and looked up at her husband through her fluttering eyelashes.'

'Have you got something in your eye?' he said.

She slapped him across the shoulder. 'I was trying to be alluring!'

'I know,' he laughed. 'But you don't need to try: I find you alluring first thing in the morning so I can hardly need any encouragement, can I?'

'That's true,' Angela agreed, smiling as she remembered the early morning bed romps that were becoming a new habit for them.

'Shall we adjourn to the store-room? I would suggest christening the leather sofas but you'd probably object to people watching us through the windows.'

She tapped him gently again. 'You are a bad man! Leading me astray like this.'

So saying she took his hand and led the way to the store-room.

∞

Jemma and Pixie were walking in the park. It was Saturday and as the dog clubbers didn't walk together at weekends they were alone. Seeing Angela's car at the back of the cafe, she'd knocked on the door. She wanted to check again which prints Angela wanted to hang on the walls. She could see Mitzi inside – and Mitzi saw her and began to yap excitedly – but there was no sign of Angela. Jemma thought that was strange but maybe she was on the phone and didn't want to be interrupted so she shushed through the glass at Mitzi, blew her a kiss and carried on her way.

She'd been busy of late with photo commissions and hadn't walked in the park alone for some time. She missed the company of the other dog clubbers but was quite happy to stroll around, snapping flowers in bloom or occasionally dogs playing. Pixie also missed their regular companions and he bounded around, seemingly searching for them. Although she took him with her when she went on assignments and he was used to her company alone, he wasn't used to being in this park without the others.

Every time he saw another dog he was off like a bullet to check out the potential for play fun. Jemma was beginning to think she'd lose her voice the number of times she had to call him back. He was very friendly and loved to play but because he was a large dog some park visitors, and particularly parents of young children, were wary of him. She understood that but she hated to see a parent instilling a fear of dogs into a child. It was fair enough that they might have had a bad experience themselves and she appreciated that children did need to be taught not to approach strange dogs without caution, but to scream, 'Come away, Tracey! Don't go near that dog; he may bite. Hey, you, get your dog away from my daughter.' Which was what had just happened to her.

She'd called Pixie who'd instantly run to her side (for once demonstrating his obedience and making Jemma feel proud of him) and walked on next to her. She no longer tried to remonstrate with parents like that as she once did. She'd given up the battle to persuade them that a boxer, even one as large as Pixie, could be a gentle softie. Instead she muttered to herself as she walked along, keeping Pixie next to her until they entered the woods at the top of the park.

'Go on then,' she said. 'You can run now,' and Pixie dashed off into the undergrowth. Jemma could hear the rustling of the dry twigs and leaves underfoot. No matter what time of year it was there was always a leafy covering on the floor. As she walked she remembered an old piece of mining equipment left from an earlier era when the woods had been an industrial site rather than the pleasant environment it now was. She'd always thought it would be a great subject for a photo but had never got round to going there. She frowned as she tried to recall its location and then headed off into the trees following a narrow path that grew narrower and more over-grown the further in she went. Even Pixie, who usually insisted on being in front, let her go first. 'Where's your spirit of adventure, Pix? Come on, I'm sure it can't be far now. Ouch!' Jemma yelped as a particularly vicious thorny branch scratched her arm and got caught on her t-shirt. She was just beginning to think she should give up and go back when she spotted the old iron contraption through the trees in front of her. 'Yay, Pixie! We've found it.'

The path by now had completely disappeared so she had to fight her way through brambles and shrubs. 'It feels like we're in a magical land, Pixie. Maybe we have to save the princess from the wicked witch. Shame we don't have a sword though.' She giggled as she stroked the dog's head. Pixie was now convinced he'd be safer if he stuck close to her side while in such unknown – and potentially dangerous – territory.

The old winding gear was on the edge of a bank that teetered away into a large hollow but by creeping carefully Jemma was able to get close to it. She was delighted she'd made the effort as the sun was shining through the leafy branches and creating a wonderful dappled effect on the rusty metal. 'This will look brilliant in black and white too, Pixie,' she explained to the dog who looked suitably unimpressed. It was impossible for him to run around or venture far from her side and, even though he was usually very patient when Jemma stopped to take photographs, something seemed to be making him uneasy. He whined pathetically.

'Honestly, Pixie! Be patient. I spend long enough waiting for you; you can wait for me for once.'

He whined again. Jemma shook her head. 'I won't be long. I just want to try to get a little lower down the slope so I can get that angle.' She scrambled closer to the edge of the hollow clinging onto branches from the various shrubs that overhung the edge. She was so intent on getting her shot that she didn't notice the holly bush until she grabbed its prickling branch. 'Ow!' she yelled, but as she tried to find another less spiny hand-hold she felt the earth beneath her foot give way. 'Oh no!' She tumbled and fell through the bushes down and down to the bottom of the hollow. 'Ohhh,' she groaned.

Pixie, still at the top of the ridge, peered over the edge at her and started to howl.

'It's okay, Pixie, I'm all right' Jemma shouted with more conviction than she felt. 'You stay there,' she said as she saw the dog desperately trying to find a way down. 'No, Pixie, stay! I'll climb back up.' She looked around. There were no obviously easy routes back to the top but, she figured, I got down so I must be able to get back up. She didn't want to think too hard about that statement as she was afraid she'd find flaws in it, so, instead, she stood up. She instantly fell back down as the pain in her ankle screamed its way up her leg. 'Aaaaahhhh.'

Pixie seeing his mistress in distress became even more agitated and desperate to reach her. His howling developed into a continuous and high-pitched whine.

'It's okay, Pixie, it's okay, boy, I'll …' Jemma's sentence floundered to a stop: what was she going to do? Suddenly she remembered her mobile. She always carried it with her for moments such as this, she realised. She'd had it drummed into her by Gwennie whose imagination could leap from an innocent walk to a cliff fall in seconds. As she rummaged in her pocket to find her phone she wondered whom to call?

The other dog clubbers were her first thought but she didn't want to be an inconvenience: they all had so much going on in their lives – except maybe Sybil. She smiled weakly to herself as she tried to imagine Sybil carving her way through the undergrowth with a machete, and then carrying her out. And knowing Sybil she probably would try to be a one-woman rescue party.

Perhaps she should call the police or ambulance. She'd never called an emergency service and wasn't sure if this constituted an emergency. As Pixie continued to whine, and Jemma became aware

of the brambles she was lying on, she decided it was especially as …
she patted herself all over, 'Oh no, I don't have my phone!'

'What have I done with it?' Jemma felt frantically again in all her
pockets and in the camera bag but there was no sign of the phone.
She felt herself beginning to panic and tried to take some deep
breaths. 'Calm down now, don't be silly, just think.' She forced
herself to go through her movements before leaving the house: she
definitely remembered putting her mobile in her pocket, the side
one she always put it in. 'Right, so, it must have fallen out as I fell.'
She scanned the ground around her. Long grass grew in the few
gaps between the brambles and the chance of spotting a tiny phone
seemed remote. Or maybe I dropped it somewhere else on the walk,
she thought. 'Shut up, Pixie!' she screamed at the dog who was
silenced momentarily by the sudden sharpness in her tone.

Jemma tried to calm down and assure herself she must have
dropped it in the fall; any other possibility was too bad to
contemplate. It wasn't that large a hollow. Even if she had to crawl
all over it on her hands and knees it shouldn't take that long. Even
if she was cut to bits by the thorns. She shivered. Although the sun
was shining and it was a warm day outside the trees in the depths of
the hollow she was beginning to feel the cold. Probably shock, she
told herself, remembering one of her mother's sayings. 'You need a
nice hot cup of sweet tea when you've had a shock.' If only she
could have one now. If only her mother were there with her. Tears
came to her eyes and slipped down her face. She didn't even have
the comfort of Pixie to cling onto. She looked up the side of the
bank. Maybe Pixie could get down if she called him - and then
maybe he could pull her up. No, she shook her head; that was too
risky. She'd have to start looking for her phone even though her
ankle was throbbing painfully now. 'If only you were Lassie,' she
said to Pixie. 'I could send you to get help then.' She sighed and
shifted her weight onto her side so she could pull herself along
more easily.

She was amazed how much pain her ankle was giving her. If she
thought about it she could imagine herself fainting with it. Better
not to think. At least it stopped her noticing the tiny scratches and

cuts she was collecting from the brambles. Just keep looking, she told herself. She tried to think logically and work out where it was most likely to have landed. Assuming it's here at all, the mean little voice in her head kept whispering. 'It is here, it must be here,' Jemma kept repeating the words to herself like a mantra as she felt in amongst the sharp thorns and dangerously-sharp broken branches and twigs with her bare fingers.

What with her chanting and Pixie's howling Jemma didn't hear at first the voice calling to her.

'Are you all right?'

And when she finally did hear it she couldn't believe anyone would ask such a stupid question.

'Yes, I'm fine. I love scuffling through brambles with a probably broken ankle. There's nothing I like better.'

The owner of the voice peered over the edge of the hollow. 'I'll go then, shall I?'

To Jemma's horror it was her jogger. Pixie had, of course, been delighted to see George, the retriever, and the two of them were already playing precariously close to the edge. 'Oh be careful, Pixie!' she shouted when she saw him.

'He's fine. Dogs are more sure-footed than humans,' Jemma's jogger assured her. 'Now, how are we going to get you out of there – assuming you were being sarcastic before?'

'Er, yes, sorry.'

'I think we'll need the air ambulance. You haven't already called them, have you?'

'No, I lost my phone when I fell. That was what I was looking for when you arrived. But are you sure I need the air ambulance? Couldn't …' she glanced around, 'we somehow manage between us?'

The jogger shook her head. 'I've had a good look round: there's no easy way to get down there and certainly not get you out again. We definitely need help.'

Jemma sank back on her bed of thorns. 'Can you call the air ambulance? Is that one of the emergency services?'

'I'm calling 999. They'll decide what's needed.'

Jemma lay back against the bank and tried to brush her hair with her fingers. I must look as if I've been dragged through a hedge forwards – which I have, she thought.  Not that it matters anyway. Then the pain that had temporarily subsided started again in earnest, she forgot about her appearance and yelled, 'Please tell them to hurry. My foot really really hurts.'

'No, she's not dying,' she heard her rescuer say. 'Her life's not in any danger but you'll need some lifting equipment to get her out of the hole.'

Huh, she thought. Rude.

Her jogger gave the emergency services instructions how to find them and confirmed that she'd stay there until they arrived.

'Okay, they're on their way.'

'How long will they be?' Jemma shivered. She was very cold now.

'They'll be as quick as they can be. Are you cold? I could give you my hoodie but it's a bit sweaty and smelly I'm afraid.'

'That's okay, I'll manage.'

'I'm Claire by the way.'

'Hi, Claire. I'm Jemma with a J.'

'Hi Jemma with a J. And this is George.'

'I know. I mean I've heard you calling him. That's Pixie.'

'I've heard you calling him too. It's an unusual name for a Boxer.'

'He was my uncle's dog originally and he called him that. I don't know why.'

'Didn't you ask?'

'I didn't see much of my uncle until he died. I mean, I … oh, I don't know, I mean Pixie came to live with me when he died. My uncle that is. Who died. Not Pixie. Obviously.'

Claire took off her hoodie and threw it down to Jemma. 'Here, if you can put up with the smell I think you need extra warmth.'

She caught it and felt the body heat lingering on it. She held it to her chest and pressed her arms firmly against it. She could smell Claire on it but it wasn't the acrid smell of stale sweat, more a sweet tang, a mixture of body odour and deodorant spray. Gratefully she pulled it over her head.

'Is that any better?' Claire asked.

'Yes, that's much better,' Jemma smiled up at her. 'But won't you get cold?'

'I'm okay. My body takes ages to cool down. I have very good circulation.'

She also had a very good body Jemma couldn't help but notice. Lean but not skinny, toned and tanned. 'Mm,' she murmured then shook herself.

'What? Did you say something?' Claire asked.

'No, nothing. I was just thinking you look tanned. Have you been away?'

Claire had just begun to say, 'Not long back from Tenerife,' when her mobile rang, jarringly. It made Jemma jump and remember the pain in her ankle.

'Hi,' she said, quietly, into the phone. 'No, I won't be there for a bit.' There was a pause then before she said, 'I'm still in the woods.' The person on the other end was obviously expecting her to be somewhere else as she replied, 'I can't help it. I'll be late. You'll just have to explain. I've got to go now; I need to keep this line free. I'll explain later.'

'Are you supposed to be somewhere?'

She shrugged. 'It's not important.'

'Are you sure? You can go if you want to,' Jemma said, praying Claire wouldn't take her at her word. 'I'll be all right.'

'No, I told the emergency services that I'd stay with you and they might need me to direct them once they get closer. I'll stay until you're sorted; that'll be fine. They shouldn't be long now anyway.'

'I hope not.' Jemma spoke slowly and sounded sleepy.

'Try not to fall asleep,' Claire said. 'I don't think it's good for you if you're in shock. Or that might be if you've banged your head. Did you bang your head?'

'I don't remember. I don't think so.'

'I suppose if you did bang it you might not remember anyway so we won't take any chances. Why don't you tell me all about yourself?'

'What do you want to know?'

'Anything, everything. What your favourite subject in school was, who's your favourite film star, which side of your bed Pixie sleeps on.'

'What makes you think he sleeps on my bed?' Jemma tried to sound indignant through her chattering teeth.

She shrugged. 'You look the sort.'

'Huh, what sort is that?'

'Soft.'

Jemma didn't know whether to be annoyed or pleased. She was struggling to think clearly. 'So where does George does sleep then?'

'On the left side.'

'Left side of what?'

'My bed of course.' Claire grinned down at her. 'I'm soft too.'

Their conversation continued covering dogs – and of course the dog club, work, family, and books it turned out they'd both enjoyed.

The sound of approaching engines made them both look up. 'Here comes the cavalry,' Claire said as a helicopter appeared and hovered overhead. They watched as a man was slowly lowered down right into the base of the hollow next to Jemma.

'Okay, my love,' he said with a warm reassuring smile, 'let's have a look at what you've done.'

When he'd assessed the damage he said, 'Looks like a broken ankle to me. I'll strap you up and then we'll take you to hospital.'

Jemma was so relieved that help had arrived that she completely forgot about Pixie until he began whining as she was being strapped to her rescuer.

'Oh no, Pixie! What's going to happen to my dog? Can he come in the helicopter with me?'

'I'm afraid not, love.'

'Don't worry, I'll look after him,' Claire called to her. 'I'll take him home with me.'

'I can't ask you to do that. Oh, wait, could you take him to Sybil's? She lives in the sheltered accommodation at the entrance to the park. He knows her and she'll look after him for me until I get home.'

'Okay, I'll do that. The big house just by the gate you mean?'

'That's it. She's in flat … oh, I can't remember the number. Just ask for Sybil at reception.'

'Okay.'

'I hate to be a nuisance. Are you sure you don't mind?'

'Well, I do really so I'll just leave Pixie here in the woods, shall I?'

'What? Oh no!'

'Don't worry! I'm joking. Not a very good joke obviously. I'll take Pixie to Sybil's. You go and get plastered.'

Jemma smiled weakly. 'Thank you.'

∞

'It was just fortunate that the hollow was exposed and they could see us clearly from the air,' Jemma told Sybil the next day when the old lady called in to return Pixie and to see the invalid.

'And they lifted you up to the helicopter, did they?'

Jemma nodded. 'I thought I'd be petrified but I felt perfectly safe as I was strapped onto Terry - that was the name of the man lowered down to assess me,' she explained. 'Then I was whisked off to hospital, plastered and back here in no time.'

'Would you like another cup of tea, Sybil?' Jemma's mother, who'd travelled down to stay with her daughter as soon as she heard the news, was acting hostess.

'No, I'm fine, thank you, Marjorie. It must have been a nasty shock for you hearing that Jemma was in hospital?'

'It would have been worse if it had been someone else calling me but as she phoned me herself just hearing her voice reassured me. She's always been a bit accident-prone though.'

'Really?' Sybil was surprised. 'She hasn't shown any signs of it before.'

'That's because I'm not,' Jemma said. 'Mum is basing that statement on one accident I had as a child when I fell and cut my hand badly. She feels bad because it was her fault for letting me carry a bottle of milk when I was only toddling. Isn't that right, Mum?' she grinned across at her mother who was playing with the teaspoon in her saucer.

'That wasn't the only incident. What about the time …'

'Mum, I don't think Sybil wants to hear a litany of my mishaps. Now have you decided? Are you going to walk Pixie on your own or go with the dog club?'

'Or we can just take Pixie if you'd prefer?' Sybil added.

'I think I'd rather like to walk with the dog club,' Marjorie said. 'I've heard so much about you all I'd like to meet you in the flesh, so to speak.'

'That will be lovely,' Sybil said, 'and don't worry, Jemma, we'll get you to the café opening one way or another – even if we have to get the air ambulance in again! Or maybe George and his jogger,' she added mischievously.

Jemma flashed her a 'don't say anything in front of my mum please' look but it was too late; her mother had already picked up the hint. 'What's this? Is there more to this little adventure than is meeting the eye?'

'I'll be off now,' said Sybil, standing and smiling conspiratorially at Jemma. 'Lovely to meet you, Marjorie, and I'll look forward to seeing you again tomorrow morning in the park with Pixie.'

When she'd seen Sybil to the door Marjorie sat on the armchair opposite her daughter. 'So? What did Sybil mean?'

'About what?' Jemma tried to look innocent.

'About the jogger, what was his name? George?'

Jemma laughed. 'No, George is …' she gave a big yawn. 'Actually, Mum, I'm really tired now. Talking to Sybil must have worn me out. And the doctor did say I should get plenty of rest, so I think I'll just close my eyes for a bit. If you could just pump up my cushion for me.'

Her mother hurried to do as she was asked and, after checking if Jemma wanted anything else, like another cup of tea or a book or the television remote, said she'd make herself useful then. 'I notice your kitchen cupboards are looking a bit grubby. I'll just give them a quick clean out.'

Jemma would have argued but her desire to have a few minutes to herself, so she could think about Claire, and the emotions she felt, was too great.

# Chapter 12

The morning of the grand opening dawned clear and bright. And Angela was up to see it.

'Come back to bed, Angie,' Tony groaned. 'It's not light yet.'

'It is, and I have too much on my mind to sleep so I may as well get up. Would you like a coffee?'

He groaned again. 'I suppose so. Unless there's any chance you're going to let me go back to sleep.'

'No chance. I want this to be perfect.'

Their daughters had travelled down the night before so Angela crept down to the kitchen. She didn't want to wake them and have them grumbling about the place all morning: she'd had enough of that the evening before. They might have come down to support her but she'd got the distinct feeling they were expecting the whole event – and the café itself – to be a disaster.

'Honestly, Mum, did you really think this through?' Miranda asked. 'It's going to be hard work and you're going to be dreadfully tied down.'

'Yes,' Claire joined in, 'You could have gone travelling or simply invested your money. You could have sat back and watched it grow.'

'And what would be the point of that?' Angela asked. 'So we could leave it all to you?'

'No, of course not, but there are easier ways of making money than running a café.'

'But it's not all about making money,' Tony chipped in.

'What is it about then?'

'It's about living life to the full.' He smiled across to his wife. 'We've never been happier, have we, darling?'

Angela shook her head.

Miranda wasn't convinced. 'That's all very well now but the café's not open yet: you've been able to do things in your own time. You'll have strict timetables to work to when it's open.'

'And we'll manage. When we're established we can take on staff – even get a manager in for the day to day stuff if necessary and to run it when we take holidays. We have thought this through, you know.'

Tony's reassurances, which seemed to be directed at her as much as the girls, had fallen on stony ground which was part of the reason Angela found it hard to sleep that night. She'd tossed and turned wondering if they were crazy, if they'd taken on too much, if the girls were right and they should be taking it easy at their age. The only conclusion she'd come to by the morning was that the opening – if nothing else – had to be a great success, not just for her and Tony but for Sybil and the rest of the dog club.

Cutting the ribbon was scheduled for just after 11. Tony would make a short speech about their plans for the café before handing over the scissors to Simon Brewer to do the official opening. Then they'd have to rush to get behind the counter ready to serve their first customers. Angela had suggested that all the customers on the first day should have a complimentary cup of tea or coffee but Tony had managed to persuade her to limit it to the first hour. 'We don't want to start our new venture with a loss,' he'd laughed. And the dog clubbers had all agreed with him.

'Listen to your husband,' Maggi said. 'You'll have to watch her, Tony; she'll be giving free cake to every passing walker, not to mention their dogs.'

'I'm not that stupid,' Angela said indignantly. 'But you're all definitely special guests and don't pay. Ever.'

They all tutted and Sybil said, 'We'll see about that.'

Sybil had been very busy and made a Victoria sponge, a lemon drizzle cake and a malt loaf. She'd also made a rich fruit cake that she'd had iced and decorated by a local woman that the manager of the retirement home knew. She'd had 'Good luck to Jock's café' written on the top. Angela had been touched and thrilled. Sybil refused payment for the fruit cake saying the other dog clubbers had all chipped in for the surprise.

The dog clubbers walked early that day and then gathered at Angela's invitation in the café. Only Bernard was missing as he was bringing the guest of honour later.

'I just wanted to say thank you,' Angela said. 'For all your support and help and … love. I've always been a bit of a doer and never really stopped long enough to appreciate those around me or to make friends.' She swallowed, 'But the dog club – all of you – have become …' She couldn't continue and Tony stepped forward and put his hand on her shoulder. 'Let's toast Jock's,' he smiled as he produced a bottle of champagne. He was about to shake it when all the women, as one, shouted, 'No!'

'It'll make a mess all over your lovely café!'

'Ah, yes, okay. I'll shoot it out the back door then shall I?'

Once they'd toasted the success of Jock's – using small glass tumblers – 'I knew I'd forgotten something,' Angela moaned – the dog clubbers decided they should go and stand outside.

'In case people don't know about the opening they'll see us and wonder what we're doing hanging around and we can tell them.'

'In fact, we could give out some flyers if you have any left,' Jon suggested. 'Tilly and the girls will be here soon and the girls would love to go round handing them out, I'm sure.'

'I'm not sure if flyers will be of any use,' Maggi said, after she'd lifted a corner of the blind and peeped out.

'Oh no,' Angela groaned. 'There's nobody around, is there?'

'I think you should take a look for yourself.'

Angela sighed and walked across to Maggi. 'It's too late to do any more advertising if there no people about.' She lifted the blind and gasped. 'Oh my gosh!'

The others all hurried to peer out too. 'Wow!'

There were people everywhere. People of all ages, many with dogs, and some with banners saying, 'We love Simon'. They spotted the reporter and photographer from the Daily Post as well as Tilly and the girls, a number of elderly men and women from Sybil's sheltered accommodation, and just pushing through the crowd,

Claire, Miranda and Emma who were staring around at the crowd with looks of total amazement.

There were still fifteen minutes to go. Bernard had planned to arrive about ten minutes before eleven. He'd seen for himself the effect his nephew had on people: they'd lunched together the previous day and a crowd had quickly gathered outside the restaurant when they heard he was in there.

He pulled into the car park to find it almost full. 'This looks promising,' he said to his nephew. 'Let's hope they all come into the café too. Come on, Whisky; you're coming too.'

They made their way up the path the short distance to the café. Even on that short trip there were people stopping Simon and asking for his autograph. After he'd signed five Bernard said, 'If you don't mind, everybody, we have to be at Jock's café before 11. I'm sure if you join us there, Simon will be happy to sign more autographs for you.' He looked at his nephew questioningly. Simon nodded. 'Yes, of course.'

They hurried on and tried to make a way through the crowd that by now was six deep. Tony saw them coming and called to Jon to help them get through. At last they made it, just in time. Bernard introduced Simon to Angela and was about to introduce the rest of the dog club when Tony cleared his throat and shouted out, 'Good morning, ladies and gentlemen. We're delighted to see so many people here today for the opening of Jock's café and we're especially delighted to have Simon Brewer' – here a few girls screamed – 'to perform our opening ceremony. But before I hand over the scissors I'd just like to say that a lot of people have been involved in this project from its very early days and I want to thank them for their support and help. We are determined that Jock's will become the very best in its park ...' he paused for his audience to get his joke and when they'd groaned he carried on, 'and will become renowned for its good quality food, friendly service and open door to all visitors and walkers whether on two legs or four.'

There was a round of applause when he finished and then he handed the scissors to Simon Brewer.

'When my uncle told me about Jock's and asked me if I'd be willing to come along here today I was delighted to be able to say yes. This is just what every park needs: a dog and walker friendly café. I wish Angela and Tony much success and I'm delighted to declare Jock's Café open.'

He cut the ribbon with a flourish amidst much noisier applause, cheering and shouts of 'Give us a song, Si!' He smiled good-naturedly and stepped aside as Angela and Tony moved to open the front door. As he went in, Tony turned around and shouted, 'Complimentary tea and coffee for the first hour!'

Although some people, mainly young girls, had only come to see Simon, the majority of the audience wanted to sample Jock's for themselves and there was some unseemly pushing and shouldering as they tried to get into the café. The dog clubbers stood back and let the others go in first but still all the chairs were taken quickly leaving half the crowd – including Angela's daughters - queuing at the door.

'This is ridiculous,' Miranda shouted to her sisters. 'Let's go home and have a coffee there.'

'Yes,' they agreed. 'We've done our bit.'

The dog clubbers watched as the girls and their partners and children headed away. Maggi shook her head. 'Little madams,' she said in disgust. Then she turned and said, 'Right, I think Angela's going to need a bit of help in there. I'm going to offer. I can wash dishes if nothing else.'

Sybil said, 'I'll come with you, Maggi. You can make sandwiches or take orders and I can do the dishes.'

Jemma sighed. 'I don't think I'd be a lot of use not with my ankle in plaster.'

'No, you'd only get in the way, 'Maggi agreed. 'It's only a small kitchen.'

'I'd offer,' Jon said, 'but … 'he glanced across to where Tilly was waiting and tapping her watch, 'I think Tilly wants to go now.'

'Don't worry, either of you. The two of us will be enough, we'll cope, won't we, Sybil? We're resourceful women. You both get off.'

Jemma's mother, who'd been as keen as Jemma to attend the opening when she'd found out that Simon Brewer would be there, was reluctant. 'Couldn't we just stay until we can get inside? I'd love to get Simon's autograph.'

Seeing Jemma's hesitation Maggi said, 'I think Jemma's been standing for long enough already and she's not properly used to those crutches yet. Come on, I'll help you back to your car. You wouldn't want her to damage anything else, would you?' She addressed Jemma's mother.

'No, of course not but I do think special seats should have been reserved for members of the dog club. And their families.'

Maggi ignored her. 'Come on, Pixie; you've got to go too.'

The boxer who'd been enjoying the warm spring sunshine sprang up at the sound of his name, beginning a chain reaction with Bassett and Mitzi, who was spending the day with Sybil.

'Oh that's a point,' Maggi said. 'What are we going to do with the dogs if we go and help Angela in the kitchen? We can't very well leave them outside; it wouldn't be a good advert.'

'We'll take them with us,' Jemma offered, ignoring the horrified look on her mother's face. 'Don't worry, Mum. They're very good and they're used to each other's company.'

'Will we get them all in the car?'

'Yes, we can manage.'

Maggi walked to the car with them, so Jemma's mum wouldn't have to manage all of them, and as they were piling into the car, a familiar voice said, 'Have you taken up dog-napping now?'

Jemma who was half-buried in the car trying to rearrange her junk so all the dogs had a bit of space, straightened herself up quickly – too suddenly - and wobbled on her crutches. Claire stretched out her hand and caught her by the elbow to steady her.

'Careful! I don't want to have to go calling the ambulance again.'

Jemma's mother, who'd hurried around from the other side of the car, was looking at Claire curiously. Jemma was just wondering if she could get away without introducing them when her mother stuck out her hand and said, 'Hello, I'm Marjorie, Jemma's mother. You wouldn't happen to be George by any chance?'

Claire and Jemma both burst out laughing and the retriever who'd been sniffing an interesting piece of grass, hearing his name, trotted over and stuck his nose in Marjorie's crotch.

'George! Don't do that! I'm very sorry, um, Marjorie.'

'Mum, this is Claire. And I think you've just met George.' She giggled again.

Marjorie hadn't been president of the WI for nothing; she knew how to handle herself, and she calmly pushed the dog's nose away before wiping her hand on the back of Jemma's jacket and holding it out again to Claire. 'Claire, of course. I'm so pleased to meet you and to have the opportunity to thank you for coming to Jemma's rescue. She's so accident-prone it's just what she needs: a knight in shining armour.' She beamed while her daughter turned an attractive shade of red.

'Mu-um.'

'It was my pleasure, Marjorie, although perhaps pleasure isn't the right word for an accident.'

'Mine too.' Marjorie managed to endow the two words with a whole ton of meaning. She raised her eyebrows at Jemma who hurriedly said, 'I haven't thanked you properly both for coming to my rescue and looking after Pixie.'

'I must admit I was a little worried about Pixie when they started lifting you up to the helicopter. I thought he was about to climb the nearest tree to follow you. He didn't really calm down again until I got him to Sybil's. Then I would have called to see how you were doing except I didn't know where you lived.'

'Well, you must come round one day soon,' Marjorie said. 'We'd like to thank you properly, wouldn't we, Jemma? Maybe you could join us for dinner one evening? What about this evening in fact?'

'No, Mum!'

Claire grinned. 'That's very kind of you, Marjorie, but I'm afraid I'm working tonight. But maybe another evening?' She looked directly at Jemma as she spoke.

Jemma blushed and said, 'Yes, I'd like that. We'll have to fix a time – when Mum's gone home.' She added the last bit pointedly.

'How did the opening go?' Cathy had crept up behind Jon as he waited for the final turn and wave from Gracie before she entered school. He jumped.

'Oh, sorry, Cathy, you startled me! Yes, it went very well. There was a huge crowd there, mostly come to see Simon Brewer but lots of them called in to the café too. I think Angela was very satisfied with her first day. I did wonder if you might have come along.'

'I thought about it and we almost did but,' she shrugged, 'I guessed Tilly would be there.'

'Yes,' Jon nodded. 'She and the girls came. Tilly was as bad as the teenagers wanting to see her idol.' He waved again to Gracie and watched her little blonde head bobbing along the corridor. He waited until she'd disappeared and then turned to Cathy, 'How are you anyway? It's been ages since we … last got together.'

'I'm okay.' Her voice didn't sound convincing.

'Is anything wrong?'

'I don't know; is there?'

Jon thought about sighing. He didn't know much about the female psyche but he knew a loaded question when he heard one. And he had no idea what was wrong, whether he'd done something - or maybe he hadn't, which could be the trouble. At least Tilly was blunt; when she was mad at him she told him why. He tried to think what could be at the root of this coldness: and he definitely sensed a coldness. He and Cathy had spoken on the telephone – enjoyed flirtatious conversations - and at the school gates a few times but he'd not managed to get to visit her since the girls had been ill. Looking after them in turns and then helping Angela with her café preparations had taken up all his time. He thought he'd explained this to Cathy.

When they met at the school gates their conversation was necessarily innocent but their phone calls had been much less chaste. Cathy seemed to be promising him so much. So now why this?

He shook his head. 'I'm sorry, Cathy. I'm a man; I have no idea if there's anything wrong. As far as I'm concerned there's not but if I've done something to upset you please tell me. Don't make me have to guess.'

It was Cathy's turn to sigh. 'Look, can you come round to my place this week? We can't talk properly here.'

'Yes, I'd like that. Wednesday as usual okay?'

She nodded. 'I'll see you then.'

As Jon walked back to his car he noticed a few of the other mums watching him. Recognising them as parents of children in Gracie's class he raised his hand to wave goodbye but dropped it again as, as a group, they walked across to him. There was some jostling and one of the women was pushed forward; she seemed to have been appointed as spokesperson for the group.

'Jon, hi,' she said a little too brightly.

'Hi, how you doing?'

'Good. Ah, we couldn't help noticing you chatting with Cathy.'

'Yes.'

'Again.'

'Yes. Is there a problem with that?'

She paused; one of the others nudged her. 'It's just that ... well ...'

'What?'

'She's a bit of a man-chaser.'

'Oh come on, she's lonely that's all. If some of you tried talking to her she wouldn't have to chat to me!' Jon's embarrassment, a sense of being found out, fuelled his anger.

'We have tried talking to her and making friends!'

'Yes,' one of the others joined in, 'and she repaid us by flirting with our husbands.'

'Big time,' the third woman added. 'She practically cornered my husband in the garage when I suggested he could go round and look at her car for her because she was having trouble with it.'

'That's what he's telling you,' Jon continued to defend Cathy.

'And when my husband went round to look at her washing machine because it was broken and she'd told me she couldn't afford to get it fixed she was all over him!'

'She was grateful. Your husband probably misread her gratitude, made it into something more.'

'He came home telling me if I wanted a divorce there were easier ways to go about it than setting him up with a tart. And that was his word.'

'Look, Jon,' the first woman took over again, 'we're only saying this to warn you. If you value your marriage be careful. Things aren't always what they seem.'

Jon shook his head. 'My marriage is fine, thank you, and it's nobody's business what friends I choose to make. Good day, ladies.' He turned and marched away.

He was angry. Angry with himself, with Cathy, with those women. Interfering bitches. Sticking their noses in. Making something out of nothing.

He drove home, did his usual quick round of the kitchen, putting cereal dishes to soak, and mopping up the milk spills before gathering up Benji's lead and setting off again.

Sybil was waiting in the park when he arrived. She had Pixie and Mitzi with her.

'No Angela today?' Jon asked.

'No, they were so busy all over the weekend that she wanted to try and get the café straight before they opened this morning. She's hoping that soon she'll get herself into a proper routine and will be able to join us again.'

Maggi and Bernard pulled into the car park one after the other, quickly let their dogs out and walked over to join Sybil and Jon.

All the talk was of the cafe opening and how successful it had been and what a wonderful thing it was that Bernard had been able to get his nephew to come along.

'It really drew the crowds in,' Maggi said.

Bernard nodded, 'A little fame is a frightening thing I've discovered. Simon was hardly able to leave his home without being photographed or pestered. But he was delighted to open the café and he's promised to visit next time he's home.'

'And as soon as people have been there once they'll see how good it is and will come again,' Sybil said.

'Oh yes,' Maggi agreed. 'The café will easily stand on its own merits, especially with your cakes, Sybil.'

'Go on with you,' the old lady blushed but looked pleased. 'A pleasant environment in which to have a short rest and refreshing cuppa after your walk is just what this park needs.'

They'd reached the separation of the paths. Maggi and Bernard both wanted a good walk. 'Shall we take Mitzi and Pixie with us over the top?' Maggi asked.

'If you're happy to,' Sybil said. 'They'd probably enjoy a good long run.'

Pixie as it turned out had his own ideas and refused to budge from Sybil's side.

'I think he sees me as his special friend since Jemma's accident,' she explained.

So Sybil, Jon, Pixie and Benji took the more leisurely stroll around the lower lake while Maggi and Bernard strode off up the hill.

'It really was good of you to ask your nephew to do the opening,' Maggi said.

'Why does everyone keep saying that? All I did was ask a favour; everyone else put in much more hard practical work. How often were you there, helping to scrub and paint?'

'Oh, that was nothing. It's what friends do for each other.'

'Nothing my foot. It was above the call of friendship.'

'You must have had some strange friends then.' Maggi laughed.

Bernard stopped and considered this. 'I've never really been much for friends. My family has always been enough for me.'

'You're lucky to have them near.'

'Yes, I am.' He paused again. 'Would you like to meet them one day?'

'Me?'

She sounded so surprised that Bernard quickly said, 'Well, I mean you and all the other dog clubbers, of course.'

'Oh. Yes, I'm sure that would be lovely. We all could all meet in Jock's.'

'Indeed, that would be ideal. I'll find out when they can all make it. It would probably have to be a weekend, that's the only thing, as they work during the week.'

'That wouldn't be a problem I'm sure.'

'Excellent.'

They carried on some way in companiable silence, both grateful for the chance to catch their breath on the uphill walk. The dogs, Bassett, Whisky and Mitzi, were happy to do their own thing: Bassett tended to fall behind as he had to check out each tree, sniffing it carefully to determine who'd passed by recently; Whisky, who'd overcome his previous anxiety about running, loped gracefully ahead until he was almost out of sight before turning and haring back to his owner – and each time under-estimating the distance it would take him to stop and skidding straight past Bernard; while Mitzi strolled, like the lady she was, next to Maggi, as if listening to the conversation and ready to join in at any moment.

When they'd reached the flatter ground at the top Bernard said, 'Now tell me: how's your saving going?'

Maggi groaned. 'Don't ask.' She shook her head. 'No, that's not fair. I suppose it hasn't been too bad for the last month or so really. I've had very few expenses I wasn't expecting so I'm hoping it will mount up miraculously when I'm not looking.'

'If you have family to stay with in Australia, it's only the plane fares you need I assume.'

'And a bit of spending money. I want to be able to treat the grand-kids.'

'Of course. Goes without saying. I'm sure you'll get to your target soon.'

Maggi sighed. 'Yes, of course, but,' she hesitated then continued, 'then there's the question of the flight itself.'

'The flight itself? It is a long one, it's true, but watching the on-board films, sleeping, reading and, of course, eating all take up time. You'll be surprised I'm sure how quickly the journey passes.'

'It's not really the length of the flight that's bothering me: I haven't got as far as worrying about that yet. It's more the actual flying. I've only flown once, you see – well, twice if you count both ways. Me and Jack went to Majorca for a package holiday after Peter had grown up and left home. Before that we'd always gone to Cornwall or the Isle of Wight.'

'And you didn't enjoy it?'

'Enjoy it? I was terrified! At one point the whole plane dropped out of the sky, miles it felt like. Things fell out of the overhead lockers, the stewards fell into passenger's laps and the drink I was holding flew out of my glass – like in a cartoon – in slow motion, shot up into the air and then splashed down all over me. I was soaked. But the discomfort was nothing to the terror I felt. And that was on the way out there. I had to go to the chemist and get doped up before I could fly home again. I swore that was it; I was never going on a plane again.'

'I don't blame you. It sounds dreadful.'

'I'd been anxious before getting on the plane, and then I was listening to every little squeak and rumble, imagining a wing was about to fall off.' Maggi shook her head. 'I haven't told anyone else about my fear. I feel so silly. But if I'm honest my attempts at saving may not have been quite as rigorous as they could have been because of it. But I'm determined not to let it stop me going to Australia. If I have to be knocked out first I'll get there somehow.'

'Of course you will. Grandchildren are a tremendous incentive.'

'You're lucky to see yours regularly.'

'Yes, I'm very fortunate, but, hopefully, they'll come along when I arrange the get-together for us. I've told them about you.'

'About the dog club you mean?'

'Well, yes, but especially about you – and Bassett,' Bernard added quickly. 'I explained where his name came from and they thought it was lovely. The only trouble now is I think they expect to see a dog that looks like a liquorice allsort.'

'Ha ha,' Maggi laughed. 'Do they like liquorice?'

'I don't know if they've ever had it but they love chocolate.'

'I'll bring some with me then when I meet them to make up for the disappointment.'

'You don't have to do that! Think about your savings.'

'If I'm saving so hard I can't buy a bit of chocolate for children my life's not worth living. Now, are we going up the next bit or back down?'

'I'm rather enjoying myself. Shall we go up? If you're not too tired?'

'No, I'm fine. Just don't talk to me again until we've reached the top. I can't climb hills, breathe and talk.'

# Chapter 13

Pixie and Benji were both dripping. They'd been racing to get the sticks Jon had thrown into the lake for them. Although Pixie had the advantage of size and strength Benji was an excellent and fast swimmer. He was also wise enough to watch where the stick went before he launched himself into the lake unlike Pixie who began running before Jon had even thrown the stick.

'Oh dear,' Sybil said. 'I hope Marjorie won't mind having a wet dog in her car when she collects Pixie. I'll give him a good rub-down with a towel before she arrives but short-haired dogs seem to absorb more water.'

'I'm sure she'll be fine with it,' Jon said. 'How is Jemma doing now? Does her mum say?'

'She's hobbling around well I think and, reading between the lines, I get the impression that Marjorie is keen to get home again.'

'I bet Jemma'll be keen to see her go too,' Jon chuckled. 'Her mum's quite a … um,' he tried to think of a polite description, 'character.'

Sybil nodded smiling broadly. 'It's difficult for them both I imagine. Jemma is used to her independence.'

As they spoke Claire jogged past with George in pursuit. She nodded a greeting to them but didn't stop.

'That's Jemma's rescuer you know,' Sybil said.

'Is it? I wondered who it was who'd found her. I knew she was a jogger and guessed I must have seen her in the park.'

'Yes,' Sybil gave a sly smile. 'I've come to the conclusion that things have a habit of working themselves out sometimes. If you let them.'

'Mm.' Jon went quiet.

They were approaching a bench on the far side of the lake. Sybil recalled seeing Jon in the park on his own, looking … she wasn't sure what it had been. 'I'm feeling a little tired. Would you mind if we sat here for a moment or two?' she asked him.

'No, of course not.' He looked anxiously at her. 'Are you all right? Do you want me to get help or … anything?'

'No, no, no, I'm fine. A moment here to get my breath back and I'll be ready.' She patted the bench next to her. 'Will you join me? Or would you prefer to walk on?'

Jon sat next to her and stretched out his legs. 'No, it's a pleasant morning and the dogs are happy. I'll sit too. We can enjoy the view.' He smiled at the old woman. It shocked him to realise that she was very elderly; it wasn't something he thought about as a rule. Sybil was just one of the dog clubbers and she always seemed healthy and active. He hoped she wasn't going to become frail; he enjoyed her company as much as any of the others.

It was strange, he thought, how such a mixed bunch had become good companions in a comparatively short period of time. He said as much to Sybil.

'I suppose we had the dogs in common although, as you say, we're an unlikely gang when you think about it: a young father, a busy photographer, a shelf-stacker, an old woman and,' Sybil hesitated, 'Lady Muck.' She put her hand over her mouth as she said it.

'Lady Muck? Is that what you call Angela?' Jon laughed out loud.

'Not any more but that's what I used to call her to myself, before we'd ever started walking together. She always looked like the lady of the manor, in her big car and with her poodle, strutting around. Now I know her better of course I see how wrong I was. My Reg used to tell me off for judging people too quickly and he was right.'

Jon laughed again. 'What did you think of me then?' he said. 'Did you think I was an unemployed layabout?'

'Oh good heavens, no. You never had that look about you. You were always walking purposefully, with a schedule. There was no unemployed got-all-the-time-in-the-world look about you. No, I had you down as someone who worked from home. I know a lot of people do it nowadays.'

'But not a stay-at-home dad?'

'No. They didn't really have those in my day so it didn't cross my mind.' She looked at him steadily. 'Jon, I'm an old woman; I've lived a long life.'

'With plenty more to live I hope,' he interrupted her.

'Yes, indeed, I hope so too, but, well, I'd like to tell you about someone, a man I once knew. Would you mind putting up with an old woman's whimsy?'

The dogs had relaxed and were both lying by the bench, drying off in the warmth of the morning sun. Jon shrugged. He had no idea where this was going but it was peaceful sitting in the park next to the lake; it took his mind off Cathy and Tilly.

Sybil began, 'Reg and I were unable to have children.' She held up her hand to stop his commiserations. 'I came to terms with it a long time ago. Reg was happy enough as we were, just the two of us. It was different in those days. We were of the generation that didn't make a fuss; you just got on with whatever life threw at you. At least that was the impression you gave people. I think I even fooled Reg into thinking I'd accepted our lot. But I hadn't.

'And then I met Bill. He was a young journalist trying to make his mark in the world and I fell in love with him. At least I think I did. I was so confused by my own misery that a kind word could bring me to tears.

'Bill was different. He listened to me; he understood. Or he seemed to understand. I suppose journalists have to demonstrate empathy to draw stories out of people. Anyway we met regularly, oh, only for tea and cake in a little tea-shop in town, but those afternoons came to be all that I was living for. They made the rest of the week bearable.

'But then Bill had his big chance. He was offered a job with a prestigious publication. When he came to the café and told me he could hardly contain his excitement.' Sybil smiled as she remembered Bill that day. 'He ordered two extra large slices of cake and two teas "in your best china, please, miss!" Even the waitress wanted to know his news.'

Sybil's face had taken on a dreamy look and now it dropped. 'The only trouble was that the job was in New York.'

175

She paused and stared across the lake, then shook herself and continued. 'He asked me to go with me. I told him he was crazy, that I was married – as he knew – and that we'd never even as much as held hands. He said none of that mattered. He was in love with me and now he could offer me a real future, in a new country, away from my sadness.

'But I told him my sadness would be with me wherever I went. Then he said that I didn't know that: it could be that the problem was with Reg. I may be able to have babies with him. Can you imagine it, Jon? A man I thought I loved offering to try and make my dreams come true.'

Sybil's voice trembled with emotion and she stopped speaking, staring into the distance, seeing not the ducks on the lake but the past that could have been. After a few moments she said, 'I think we should walk on now,' and she got to her feet. Jon standing next to her took her hand that was frail and cold and put it on his arm. They walked on slowly and silently. The dogs didn't need to be called; they stood up and followed behind.

When she was able, Sybil began to speak again. 'I'm sorry, Jon, you must think I am a silly old woman letting the events of the past – and such a far distant past – affect me like this.'

'Not at all, Sybil. They were momentous days for you.'

She looked him in the face and smiled. She squeezed the arm her hand was wrapped around and said, 'I don't expect you to understand.'

'Maybe I can't but I can see the pain you still feel.'

Sybil chuckled. 'Jemma would be proud of you.'

'Jemma would? Why?'

'She dismisses most men as insensitive creatures.'

'Oh, yes, well, she's been giving me lessons,' Jon chuckled in return.

'Do you know, Jon,' Sybil began, suddenly serious again, 'you're the very first person I've ever told about Bill?'

'I'm honoured.' He pressed her hand close to his side. 'And I won't tell anybody else, I promise.'

'Oh it's all in the past now. Maybe it would do me good to talk about it more. That's what they do these days, isn't it? Everyone needs counselling for something it seems.'

'I'm not sure it's always helpful. But then I'm a man; men don't talk about their feelings, everyone knows that.'

They were approaching the bench where they'd sit and wait for the return of Maggi and Bernard. They'd already been a long time and Sybil knew she wouldn't have much longer with Jon on his own.

'The thing is, Jon, I didn't run away with Bill.'

Jon laughed. 'I'd sort of guessed that. Otherwise you wouldn't be here today – or if you were you'd be talking with an American accent.'

'Yes, of course, but I was tempted. Very tempted. I told Bill I'd have to think about it. It wasn't as clear-cut a decision for me as it should have been. I was a married woman, for goodness sake. I'd made vows on my wedding day and I took those seriously. I'd believed in God on my wedding day but even though I no longer believed in God they were still vows, made to Reg, the man I'd promised to spend my life with. The man I loved. I never stopped loving him but I had lost sight of our love. Does that make sense?'

Jon nodded.

'So I stayed. I'd like to say I never regretted it but, of course, there were days when Reg and I would have a row or I'd see another friend with a bonny baby and I'd think and I'd wonder, what if? But I made the right decision. As the years went by the love Reg and I had grew, if that were possible. I suppose only having each other to give it to made it easier.'

They'd reached the bench just as Maggi and Bernard came into sight. Sybil turned to face Jon. 'I saw you one evening in the park on your own. You looked anxious as if you had the world's problems on your shoulders.'

Jon went to speak but Sybil held up her hand. 'I have no idea what your dilemma is or was, or even if you have one; it could be an old lady's imaginings. But some things are worth fighting for, hanging on to. That's all I wanted to say in this long roundabout

177

way. And that things have a habit of working themselves out for the best in the end.' She tutted. 'Listen to me, I sound like my own grandmother. Oh, hello, Mitzi,' Sybil smiled as the poodle bounced up to her. 'Have you had a good walk? Oh my, you look ...' She grimaced.

'I know,' Maggi said as she arrived at the bench. 'If hedge and backwards are words that spring to mind it's because we had to pull her out of one. Backwards! I don't know what Angela's going to say when she sees her.'

Mitzi had twigs and leaves sticking out of her curls at all angles. Of her normally immaculate appearance there was no sign.

Jon and Sybil both burst out laughing.

'What happened?' Jon asked.

'She chased a squirrel through a hole in the hedge, across a field and then through another hedge. But there wasn't a Mitzi-sized hole in the second hedge. She got wedged in and couldn't move either way. We called and whistled and shouted but all that seemed to happen was that she got herself even more firmly stuck.'

Bernard took up the story. 'We walked around the field until we found a gate, which was padlocked, so we had to climb over it and leave Bassett and Whisky on the other side.'

'I bet they didn't like that,' Sybil said.

'No, indeed, they set up a mournful wail from their side while Mitzi was howling on hers. In our hurry to reach her we weren't looking where we were going and ...'

'I stepped in a pile of cow poo.' Maggi held up her boot, which still bore the tell-tale smears. 'Anyway when we got to her she was so excited that she wriggled even more frantically and got even more wedged. We tugged on her rear end and tried to move branches and twigs aside but we weren't doing any good. Fortunately Bernard had his Swiss army knife on him ...'

Bernard looked slightly embarrassed. 'I never leave home without it, I'm afraid.'

'And a good thing too or we'd never have got her out. Bernard had to hack away at twigs ...'

'And her hair I'm afraid.'

'Until we finally set her free. And by now, of course, our dogs were practically hysterical so we hurried back to the gate where …' Maggi collapsed in giggles, 'Bernard had to …' she giggled some more.

'I had to lift Mitzi over.'

'And as he gave her the final push to get her to jump down on the other side …' It was no good, Maggi couldn't continue speaking; she was helpless with laughter. Bernard sighed and carried on, 'I fell onto my backside in the mud.'

He turned and displayed a filthy mud-layered jacket and trousers.

They were all laughing now until Bernard said, 'But really it's no laughing matter. Angela is going to have to cut chunks of hair off to get rid of all these tangles and twigs.'

Sybil frowned. 'I think, at one time, Angela would have been very annoyed but she's mellowed a lot. She'll just be grateful you rescued Mitzi. You wait and see.'

And Sybil was right. After her initial shock on seeing the walking scarecrow and then hearing the tale behind it, Angela insisted on everyone having not only their usual free cuppa but free slices of cake as well. She pressed them to have sandwiches too but they all declined.

'Seriously, Angela, you'll never make any money if you give all your food away,' Maggi said.

'I don't give it away to everyone,' Angela said indignantly. 'Only to my special friends. And you deserve it after what you've been through. You must both let me pay for your clothes and boots to be cleaned properly.'

'Don't be silly!' It was Maggi's turn to be indignant. 'It's only a bit of mud …'

'And cow poo,' Angela pointed out.

'Well, that was my fault for not looking where I was going, and it'll all brush off when it's dry.'

'And these are old clothes I only keep for dog-walking,' Bernard said. 'There's no harm done.'

The others looked at Bernard's outfit. Either he was lying to ease Angela's concerns or his wardrobe must be full of extremely smart suits.

'Hmm,' Angela said, unconvinced but touched by the sentiments. 'Okay but you must have some cake. We have Sybil's lemon drizzle today.'

Nobody was going to turn down a piece of Sybil's lemon drizzle especially if it were free so they took a table inside the café near the window.

Two of the tables were already occupied, one by a group of four well-dressed women who were having an animated discussion and the other by a couple and their dog, a Jack Russell, who looked up excitedly at the entrance of the other dogs.

When Angela returned with the tray of cakes and cups Maggi said, 'They don't look like your average park walkers,' nodding towards the four women.

'No,' Angela whispered excitedly. 'They're a reading group and they've decided to come here each week for their meeting. They came to the opening and were so impressed with the place decided straight away. They came to see Simon,' Angela added, 'so his appearance is already having a knock-on effect on our business. I can't thank you enough, Bernard, for bringing him along.'

Bernard raised his hand in a 'don't thank me' manner but Angela continued, 'Honestly, he made such a difference. So many people came to the opening and several have been back again since.'

'And when they've been once they're sure to come again,' Maggi said. 'You've brought about such a change in this place.'

'Oh and I must phone Jemma,' Angela said. 'Two of her prints have sold and another woman asked me for her telephone number as she wanted to commission her. Jemma needs to get some business cards printed to leave here.'

'She will be pleased,' Sybil said. 'But it's only what she deserves: she has a real knack of capturing the dog's spirit in her portraits.'

∞

When Jemma's mother called to pick up Pixie she stayed as usual for the cup of tea Sybil offered her.

'I'm going home tomorrow, Sybil,' she said. 'Jemma's getting about okay now and, well, to be frank, we're beginning to get on each other's nerves. I think it's time I packed my bag if we want to maintain a good relationship.'

'That's very sensitive of you, Marjorie. Not many women would be able to acknowledge that.'

'Hm,' Marjorie pressed her lips together. 'To be honest, Jemma said it.'

'So it's gracious of you to accept it,' Sybil said gently.

Marjorie sighed. 'I'll be glad to get home anyway. I can't imagine what sort of mess Trevor will have the place in.'

Sybil smiled to herself. She could imagine how trapped Jemma was feeling and how tense things must have got to have reached the point where she would say something to her mother. She was very grateful that she hadn't reached the being dependent on others stage. Not yet anyway. And there was no point letting her mind run along those lines. If it happened she'd have to cope with it; but she hoped she'd die before that.

Marjorie was still grumbling about the mess that was likely to greet her when she got home. 'I don't know why men who are very successful executives in their working lives and turn into such slobs the minute they step through the door to home. And it's not just men. Jemma is as bad. I don't think she's given that house of hers a spring clean since she moved in.'

'But she's happy there.'

'That's as maybe but what if she ever wanted to invite,' she paused, 'anyone home with her?'

Sybil could see she was in for a prolonged visit. 'More tea, Marjorie?'

Jon made himself a sandwich for lunch and, as it was a pleasant day, sat in the garden to eat it. As he bit into a tomato he thought about what Sybil had said. It had been an almost surreal conversation; he wasn't used to being a confidante so, though his first reaction had been to phone Jemma and tell her about the strange conversation, he stopped himself. Sybil had admitted that he was the first person she'd told – in fifty, sixty years – so it probably wasn't his place to discuss it with others.

No, there was a reason she'd told him. She'd said that herself: she'd seen him in the park looking anxious. He tried to recall the occasion, not that he had to try very hard: he remembered it well. It had been when he'd kissed Cathy and rushed away afterwards. How odd that Sybil had spotted him. Even odder that she'd correctly identified his mood. Or maybe not that odd as he recalled being fairly distracted.

Tilly hadn't noticed anything amiss though. She'd been too engrossed in her own work to notice him. As she always was these days. When she was home that was, when she wasn't working late. But although she talked a lot about the men at work he didn't suspect her of having an affair; she was too intent on getting on in the firm to risk anything that might get in the way.

When they'd first married and talked about children Tilly had been a great believer in parents being at home to look after children rather than farming them out to childcare. 'It's important for the child but also for the parent,' she'd said. 'And really, why would you have children if you're not going to be there to bring them up? 'Jon had agreed with her but it hadn't been until she'd been on maternity leave and the public relations firm Jon had worked for had closed down that there'd been any talk of her going back to work.

Jon's redundancy pay had been good but not good enough to support a young family for very long so it had seemed sensible that Tilly would go back to work as a temporary measure until a job that Jon would enjoy came up. At first each week he'd buy the Guardian and the Independent on the days they featured media and PR jobs but after a while he got used to being at home and gradually, without noticing, they stopped saying, 'When you get a job,' 'when I give up work,' and life drifted on.

And as he sat in the warm sunshine enjoying his cold orange juice Jon thought that that was no bad thing. He closed his eyes and Sybil's earnest face and her words drifted into his head. 'Some things are worth fighting for.' She'd been talking about her marriage to Reg but had she meant him to think about his own relationship? He was enjoying life as it was. He loved looking after the girls and being there when they got home and being first to hear about the ups and downs of their days, but, he had to admit, the time in between them leaving in the morning and arriving home in the afternoon could drag. He was very grateful for Benji, for the excuse the dog gave him to get out of the house and especially thankful for the dog club. He smiled to himself and shook his head. Who'd have thought he'd find friendship with such an unlikely bunch? Certainly not any of his ex-colleagues he was sure of that. Their world – and his when he'd been part of it – had involved late nights working on clients' briefs, eating takeaway curry and drinking lager while they tossed publicity ideas around. And most of the older men had indulged in affairs while he'd been too newly-married and in love to contemplate such a thing.

Was he really contemplating it now? For that's what it would be if he took his relationship with Cathy any further. Affair was such a harsh word, an unforgiving word. What he'd done up till now had been … playing, fun, with nobody likely to get hurt. But even if he took it further what harm would there be? Tilly would never know and Cathy was unattached so …

But did the fact that he was even considering it say something about his marriage? Did his contract with Tilly cover more than housekeeping, fathering and occasional late-night sex? But if nobody knew, who would it hurt? No-one. He argued this but struggled to convince himself.

He adjusted his position in his chair and glanced at his watch. He could squeeze in another five minutes in the sunshine and still have time to change the beds as he'd planned and put the sheets in to wash before picking up the girls. He shook his glass rattling the ice cubes that had almost melted and tried to push Sybil's words out of his mind. He was seeing Cathy on Wednesday. For coffee. He'd see how that went, let the afternoon develop as it would. He tried to ignore the playground gossip jostling for head-room. He sighed. Gossip, that was all it was. Insecure women jealous of an attractive

– and available - rival. He stood up. His peace was spoiled; he might as well get on with the housework.

# Chapter 14

Jemma struggled to get out of her chair. 'Don't hang up,' she shouted at the phone. 'I'm on my way.'

She'd meant to put the hand-piece next to her chair – as her mother had told her she should – 'Yes, mum, you were right as always' she muttered under her breath - but had forgotten and usually by the time she'd got up, crossed the room and picked up the phone, the caller had rung off. This time she made it.

'Hello?' she gasped down the phone.

'Oh hi, is that Jemma?'

'It is, yes.' She was still breathing heavily from the effort of rushing.

'Hi, Jemma, this is Claire. The jogger. With George.'

'Yes, I know who you are, my rescuer! How are you?'

'I'm fine, thanks. How are you? You sound a little breathless.'

'That's the effect you have on me,' Jemma laughed, then realised she might have come over as desperate. 'I mean, thanks for not ringing off. Mum's gone home and it takes me ages to get to the phone.'

'Maybe you should keep it by you.'

'Yes, I should.'

'Sorry, you've probably already thought of that.'

Jemma laughed. 'Well, my mother had but I didn't do anything about it, as you noticed, to my cost.'

'I guessed you'd be struggling. I hope you don't mind me calling you.'

'Oh no, I'm delighted. I mean, it's not a problem.'

'I called into Jock's today and saw the dog portraits you've taken. I was hoping I might be able to commission you to take one of George.'

'That'd be fab! He's such a handsome dog.'

'Hm, you wouldn't say that if you could see him now, covered in mud.'

185

'Actually it would be a way for me to repay you a little for helping me. Just a small thank you.'

'Oh no there's no need for that. I must pay you.'

'We can argue about that when my foot's better.'

'Are you planning on kicking me into submission then?'

Jemma laughed. 'No, of course not. I meant when I take George's photo. I can't realistically do it until I'm fully mobile again as it usually involves getting into strange positions and scrambling around in bushes.'

'What a fun job you have.'

Jemma could imagine Claire smiling on the other end of the phone. 'I like it.'

∞

When Gwennie appeared at tea-time with a plate of cottage pie, peas and carrots Jemma who'd been trying to decide which of the frozen pizza her mother had filled her freezer with to have - four cheese or meat feast –welcomed her delightedly. 'Oh that smells good.'

'I told your mother I wouldn't let you go hungry,' Gwennie said.

'I don't think there's much chance of that, not with all the food she's stuffed in the freezer. But I'd much prefer your cooking,' Jemma added, as Gwennie looked a little downhearted. 'Not that you must make a habit of it! I'm quite capable even though my mother thinks I'm an invalid.'

'She's just worried about you. It was a nasty shock for her.'

'It was quite a shock for me too.'

Gwennie had called in each day since Jemma's accident but the presence of her mother who loved to talk had made it impossible for Gwennie and Jemma to have a good catch-up. Jemma told her visitor to sit down.

'Unless you have to get back. Have you eaten your dinner yet?'

'No, I plated them both up at the same time.'

'Why don't you fetch yours in then and we can eat together?'

When Gwennie had fetched her dinner in on a tray and had made sure Jemma was settled in comfortably and had everything she needed, she sat down in the chair opposite and they began to eat companionably, watched by Pixie, who drooled lavishly as he lay on the rug next to Jemma's chair.

Talking was mostly deferred while they concentrated on the pie, which was too good to let go cold. 'Sorry, Pixie, no chance you're getting any of this,' Jemma said, through a mouth full of tasty mince. The unexpected words gave Pixie a spark of hope and she quickly sat up and gazed at her owner keenly instantly making Jemma regret speaking.

When they'd both cleaned their plates – Jemma was tempted to lick hers but settled for running her finger around and gathering up all the gravy – Gwennie said, 'There's apple crumble and custard for afters.'

'Oh my,' Jemma sighed. 'I'll be stuck in this chair for ever if I eat like this all the time!'

'Shall I get it now?'

'No, let's wait a bit, shall we? Let our dinners go down. I want to tell you who phoned me this afternoon.'

Gwennie was instantly alert. 'A man?'

'Sorry but no.'

'Ah well. Who was it then?'

'My gallant rescuer. The jogger who called the air ambulance and stayed with me in the woods.'

'Ah yes, the nice-looking girl.'

'What makes you think she's nice-looking?'

Gwennie looked a little embarrassed. 'I happened to be glancing out of the window when she called in to see you.'

Jemma was well aware that little escaped Gwennie's eagle eyes even though she always claimed that she couldn't see further than her nose.

She chuckled. 'And you think she's nice-looking, do you?'

'With those eyes? I should say so. Not to mention that figure.'

'Gwennie!'

'What? I might be old but I can still see.'

187

'Anyway, my rescuer, Claire, wants me to take a photo of her dog, George. Of course I can't do it until I'm properly fit but she saw the portraits in the café. Angela gave my number to some other potential clients too so it could be a new side-line for me. If the other people phone me that is. But Angela said she'd told them I was injured but that they seemed very keen so maybe they're waiting for me to recover first. So that's what I wanted to tell you. About my burgeoning career.'

'Very nice too but what else did Claire say?'

'What do you mean what else?'

'I'm sure she didn't phone just to ask you to take her dog's photo.'

'Why else would she phone?'

'To see how you are. She did rescue you after all and she'll want to be sure you're getting better.' Jemma, who'd been hoping this and much more, was pleased to hear the old lady say it but needed more convincing.

'Yes, I suppose so. Almost like a professional interest?' She said this tentatively, desperately wanting Gwennie to deny it. Her visitor was pleased to oblige. 'I'm not sure professional interest extends to big bunches of flowers.'

'You saw those too, did you? When you happened to be glancing out of the window?'

Gwennie studied her hands. 'I might have noticed them.'

'It was very nice of her and quite unnecessary.' Jemma glanced across to the yellow tulips in the jug her mother had gone out and bought specially. The flowers were beginning to droop now and lose their petals but standing on the window-sill in the pale green jug they looked perfect. She sighed. Rather too deeply. Gwennie stood up. 'I'll get the pudding now, shall I?'

'Yes, please, Gwennie.'

While the old lady popped next door to dish up, Jemma considered the flowers. 'Oh Pixie, it's a bit sad though, isn't it, that I have to break my ankle before anyone buys me flowers?'

The boxer put his head on her lap leaving a trail of drool down her trouser leg. She stroked his silky coat. 'Am I going to turn into a dog lady, Pixie? Not that there's anything wrong with dogs,' she hastened to reassure her pet, 'it's just that it would be nice to have someone else around to stroke my head now and again.'

∞

As Jemma and Gwennie settled down to watch Casualty together Jon was putting the girls to bed.

'Come on, settle down now.' He tucked Gracie in tightly. She loved to feel secure, wrapped up, unable to move; her sister was just the opposite hating to feel trapped, as she described it. 'What if there was a fire and I couldn't get out of bed?'

'Then Daddy would come and rescue you.' Gracie was still young enough to believe her dad could do absolutely anything.

'But what if he couldn't get up the stairs and it was just you and me and we couldn't move?' Sophie had a vivid imagination. Her teachers commended her for it, praising her story-writing skills but Jon sometimes wished she were a little less imaginative.

'Sophie, that's not going to happen.' He tried to reassure her but she was warming to her theme. 'We'd have to watch big flames coming through the door and we'd be screaming …'

'Sophie, that's enough! No more. You're scaring Gracie and there's no need for it.'

He needn't have worried because Gracie was unconcerned. She cuddled her teddy to her and said, 'I'm not scared. I know Daddy would find a way through. And Benji would warn us. He always barks when Daddy burns the toast.'

Sophie yawned. 'Will you tell Mummy to come and say goodnight when she gets in, Daddy?'

'I will do but you'll probably be asleep.'

'No, I won't go to sleep until Mummy gets home.' Sophie was adamant but Jon knew that within minutes of putting out the light she'd be fast asleep.

'Okay, I'll tell her.' He kissed both girls again and left the room, putting the light out as he went.

'Night night, Daddy,' Gracie called.

'Night night, sleep tight.'

'Don't let the bed bugs bite,' Sophie finished the rhyme as she always did.

He could hear them chattering away for a few minutes after he'd left but soon all was quiet.

Tilly had phoned just before tea-time to say she had an urgent meeting that was likely to go on into the evening. They'd have sandwiches in the office so he wasn't to worry about cooking any food for her. As there was already a large pan of Bolognese sauce bubbling on the hob Jon was tempted to thank her for the short notice but he restrained himself and instead told her to drive home carefully.

He'd noticed the last few mornings that she'd been very pale. She was over-working, he knew that, but she seemed to enjoy it, to find it preferable to being home with him and the girls. But she needed a holiday. They all did. They'd not had a proper break since – he tried to remember – it must have been June the previous year when he'd booked a cheap package holiday to Menorca without telling Tilly until the last minute. She'd been mad at first, insisting she had important cases that needed to be dealt with but he'd dragged her away and, after the first few days when she'd been unable to relax the sun, good food – and plentiful wine – worked the trick and they'd had a great time. Maybe he should do that again. He'd look on the internet for somewhere warm and sunny. In fact he'd do it that evening before she came home.

When he'd loaded the dishwasher and cleared away all the debris that seemed to accumulate with two children in the house he sat down at the computer and searched for holidays. First question was where did he want to go? Menorca again? He'd liked it but there were plenty of places he'd never visited. But as he browsed through the options he realised that not only were there places he hadn't visited, there were places he'd never even heard of. Brand new resorts in unfamiliar countries that were trying to build a tourism industry for themselves.

He stopped after an hour and poured himself a gin and tonic. He stretched his back and settled down in front of the computer again. The website he clicked on was offering holidays in Florida, in Disneyworld. The girls would love that! But would he and Tilly enjoy prolonged exposure to Sleeping Beauty, Snow White and their friends? He doubted it. Maybe he and Tilly should go on their own, get her parents to have the girls for a long weekend and they could go to New York. Tilly'd always wanted to see New York.

New York, New York, so good they named it twice. He thought about Sybil and her Bill. What a different life she'd have had if she'd run away with him. What an amazing story and much more astounding that it was genteel respectable Sybil who'd lived this out. Jon paused and sat back in his chair thinking about her. You could see that she'd once been a very attractive woman; she still was, in a duchess-sort of way – as he thought of her - with her clear eyes and upturned mouth. Jon thought about his own daughters and how very much he loved them. He couldn't imagine life without them. One of the men he'd worked with had been childless; he'd always claimed it was a blessing, meant he and his wife could enjoy themselves with their expensive holidays and posh cars. Jon hadn't given it another thought: he knew there were some women who chose not to have children – though how empty their lives must have been he couldn't imagine. He smiled to himself as he could almost hear Tilly reprimanding him: it's their decision; not everyone's made the same way. Whatever he wouldn't have been without his children for the world.

Almost without realising it he found himself typing 'Bill Walters journalist' into Google. He didn't expect to find anything or if he did, it was a common enough name, it would probably be the wrong man but in less than two seconds the screen was filled with references to Bill Walters journalist. Award-winning journalist at that. Jon clicked on the first link that took him to a Wikipedia entry:

Bill Walters won the Pulitzer Prize in 1957 for his 'Russia Today' series in the New York Times.

Jon went on to read that 'the journalist of English descent lived in Russia for five years during which time his reports made a significant contribution to America's understanding of the Soviet Union.'

Clicking on another link Jon found a website for the journalist that suggested that he was still alive and active. By the time Tilly finally arrived home he'd discovered that Bill Walters was on Facebook and, without pausing to reflect on the wisdom of his action, had sent him a message.

∞

Sybil was watching Casualty but her mind wasn't really on the dramatic scenes on her television; she was reliving her own dramatic moments of all those years ago. If she closed her eyes she could still hear Bill's voice, with its west country lilt. She was glad she'd told Jon about him. It was as if she'd finally acknowledged his importance in her life. She'd always been ashamed, ashamed of her actions, the secrets she'd kept from Reg, the thoughts she'd allowed in her head. But she'd never been ashamed of her feelings for Bill.

They had been real and had kept her going through the dark months that followed his departure. And, at first, there'd even been that lingering hope.

When she'd met Bill in the café on the day they'd arranged, when she would give him her answer, she'd already made her plans. When he walked in through the door he was still expectant; he hardly dared to allow himself to be but he was sure his feelings were reciprocated. He'd seen it in her eyes. He was a journalist, trained to investigate, to observe, taught not to accept what was obvious on the surface but to look deeper, to ask questions, even, one tutor had said, to be guided by instinct.

His instincts as he pushed open the door, saw her look up and smile at him told him her answer was going to be yes. He rushed across the room and kissed her in front of everyone.

'Bill, what are you doing?' Sybil spluttered as he finally released his grip. 'You can't! Not here. Not in front of people.'

He made a show of looking around. 'I don't know anyone here; do you?'

'No, but …'

'Then what's the harm? And soon everyone will know.' He paused and took her hands. 'Won't they?'

'Sit down, Bill.'

Her tone of voice sent a cold spear through his heart. It was gentle but firm. Releasing her hands he sat down opposite her. Almost at once the waitress appeared. 'Same as usual, sir? And you, madam, will you have a slice of madeira now?'

Sybil had arrived early, sick with nerves, and had already ordered a pot of tea for herself. She shook her head. 'No, thank you, not today.'

Bill hadn't taken his eyes from her face. The waitress repeated her question. 'Tea and cake for you, sir?'

'Oh, yes, please. No, I mean, just tea, thank you.'

They sat in silence until Bill's tea had arrived and then, finally, he said, 'So? What's your answer? Yes or no?'

'Oh Bill, it's not as easy as that.'

'Why not? Yes, you'll come or no, you won't. Seems straightforward to me.'

'I'm a married woman, Bill. You're asking me to …' she couldn't go on.

'I know full well what I'm asking of you. I wish it didn't have to be like this. I wish you were a single girl and there was no-one to get hurt. But that's not the way it is. You and I both know that. Knew that when you left me last week and said you'd have to think about it. Nothing's changed. So the answer is simple.' His voice got louder as he spoke.

'Ssh, people are looking.'

'So what?' he said but lowered his voice. 'Sybil, I love you. I want to be with you always. Maybe I didn't tell you this clearly enough last week. I'm not a cad; I didn't deliberately set out to destroy your marriage or hurt your Reg. When I first saw you in this tea-shop it was just that you looked upset and I wanted to cheer you up but love is inconvenient. It came along and crept into my heart when I was busy making you laugh.'

'You did, Bill.' Sybil smiled weakly.

He grabbed her hand again. 'Tell me, I can't bear it any longer. I think I know but I want you to say it. Is it yes or no?'

She hesitated.

'Are you worrying about the scandal? We'll be in America; it's different there, a young and forward-thinking country. But no-one need ever know that you're divorced if that's what you prefer.'

'Reg wouldn't divorce me.' She said it quietly.

'But if you left him for another man?'

'He's old-fashioned like that.' Her words weren't said in anger but in acceptance and, even if Bill didn't want to admit it, love.

'Well, that's okay. Like I say we'd be far away. We could live as man and wife and no-one would be any the wiser.'

'No, Bill.'

'Okay, then I was just thinking what options we had if Reg does refuse to divorce you.'

'I mean my answer's no, Bill.'

He dropped her hands, sank back into his chair and lowered his head. At last he said, 'I know. I think I knew before I came in through the door. I guess I always knew I was fooling myself.'

It was Sybil's turn to lean forward and take his hand. 'The thing is, Bill, it's not that simple.'

'I know, I know. You have a husband, responsibilities. I understand.' He shrugged.

'That's not what I mean. I mean ...'

As he looked up at her his face suddenly hopeful she hurried to explain. 'I mean I can't come to America with you.'

'Yes, that's what you said.' His face dropped again.

'But I ... oh, this is so hard. Could we go for a walk in the park, do you think?'

'Of course.' Bill paid the waitress and gave her a generous tip. He forced a smile onto his face as he said, 'Next time you see me I'll be a famous reporter. I'm off to make my fortune in America.' He winked at her and took Sybil's arm. 'See you round, doll,' he said in an American drawl.

'Good luck to you both,' the waitress called after them, her words carrying on the air.

They walked along the pavement before crossing the road and entering the park. The sun was shining and the paths were filled with mothers and their prams and pushchairs, elderly couples and a few young men and women taking advantage of the weather. It was a small well-maintained city park with a bandstand, a duck pond and some flower-beds, in which brightly coloured dahlias vied with each other for space.

Bill kept quiet, uncertain, wondering what Sybil had to say, desperate to know but allowing her to say it in her own time, although waiting was driving him crazy.

'Let's sit over there.' She pointed to some trees. 'In the shade, on the grass.'

It was late morning and children were still in school so the grassy areas were relatively empty apart from one or two courting couples wrapped up in each other in their own world. Bill glanced across at one such couple enviously. The world he and Sybil had created wasn't as simple as theirs. But they could build a new one. He allowed his hopes to rise briefly before quashing them. She's already said no, he reminded himself. She's not going to America with you. Whatever it is she wants to say now is only … what? A pretty farewell? A gesture? He let go of her arm. She glanced at him then carried on walking towards the trees.

She chose a spot and sat down before he had time to take off his jacket and put it down for her. He held it out belatedly but she shook her head. 'I'm all right.'

Sybil patted the ground next to her. 'Please sit down - and don't look at me.'

'What?'

'What I have to say I won't be able to if you're looking at me.'

'Okay.' He made himself comfortable and stared straight ahead. 'This all right?'

'Yes, yes, that's fine.' Sybil too then stared ahead and for a few moments didn't say anything. When she finally spoke her words came out in a rush. 'The thing is, Bill, I think I love you. I know I'm married and I shouldn't but I don't know how else to explain the way I feel about you. I love both of you. That can't be unique, can it?' Without thinking she turned to look at him as she said that but as he turned his head towards her she quickly looked away again. 'No, don't look at me.

'So what I'm going to suggest isn't as bad as it might sound. I don't think it is anyway. I've told myself it's not that bad because I love you. Maybe that's just an excuse but what if … what if we had something to show for our love, Bill?'

'What are you talking about, Sybil? I don't understand.'

She took a deep breath. 'Will you sleep with me?' She released her breath in a flurry. 'There, I've said it. You probably think I'm a hussy or a tramp or worse, I don't know, but I love you and suppose if we slept together, just suppose it's not me but Reg, and maybe, just maybe … oh, wouldn't it be wonderful, a miracle?'

'I don't understand. What would be wonderful?'

'If I had a baby!'

Bill jumped up. 'That's what this is about? You want a baby? And you think I could father it?'

'Shh, Bill, people are looking.'

'I don't care who's looking. I can't believe you've suggested this. You want me to father your child and then clear off out of the way and leave you to it? And I suppose you'd tell Reg a miracle had happened and that it was his child. And …' he flopped down on the grass again, shaking his head, anger replaced by pain. 'I thought you loved me.'

'I do, Bill, I do love you. That's why I'm suggesting this. I couldn't suggest something like this if I didn't love you … and think you loved me.'

He stood again, still shaking his head. 'Goodbye, Sybil. I hope you have a good life. With Reg.' He turned and strode away.

Sybil's tears didn't begin to fall until she'd watched him walk out of the park. She kept thinking, he'll turn back, he'll come back, he won't leave me – us - like this. But he did. He was gone.

She sat weeping quietly until a child ran up to her and asked if she'd like a daisy. 'I'm picking them for my mum but you're crying,' the infant said, holding it out to her.

Sybil smiled through her tears. 'Thank you. I'd like that very much.' She took it expecting the child to leave but he continued to stare at her.

'Are you going to stop crying now?' he asked.

Sybil laughed and nodded. 'I'll try.' She took her handkerchief out of her handbag and wiped her face before blowing her nose. 'There, is that better?' she asked her concerned young friend. He nodded and ran off to join his mum who'd been watching him carefully. Sybil waved a hand to her and stood up. She glanced at her watch: it was getting late. She needed to buy something for Reg's tea before she caught the bus home. She brushed her skirt and straightened herself up. She'd call in to the butcher's on the way to the bus stop. Planning something extra special for her husband's tea would stop her thinking, for a little while anyway.

'No, I'll do the washing up,' Reg insisted. 'It's the least I can do after that treat of a meal. You put your feet up and listen to the wireless. I'll come and join you with a cup of tea when I've done in here.'

Sybil switched on the wireless and picked up her knitting. She'd just got comfortable when the phone rang. Reg had had the phone installed at their house and at her mother's when her mother had been so poorly. 'You won't have to worry then,' he'd said. 'She can get in touch with you at any time she needs you.'

Since her mother was still the only person they knew who had a phone she answered it saying, 'Hello, Mum. How are you tonight?'

'Sybil, it's me.'

'Bill?' She gasped and turned her face away from the kitchen door. 'What are you doing phoning me?' she whispered. 'Reg is here.'

'I'm sorry, Sybil, I was an idiot this afternoon. I have to talk to you.'

'We can't talk now.'

'Meet me in the café tomorrow? Please?'

While she hesitated Reg called out, 'Say hello to your mum for me.'

'Okay,' she whispered, 'but I've got to go now. Good bye.'

Sybil hung up and quickly dialled her mother's number and was listening to the goings on of various family members when Reg came into the hallway carrying a cup of tea. 'Do you want this here?' he mouthed at her.

She shook her head and gestured for him to take it into the living-room. 'Mum, I've got to go now. Reg has just made me a cup of tea and it'll go cold.'

She finished the phone call grateful that her mother's long-winded witterings had given her time to calm down before facing Reg. She went back into the living-room to find he'd put her favourite cup and saucer on the little table next to her chair and the pouffe in front of it.

'Put your feet up, love,' he smiled across the room at her with such tenderness that she only just managed to stop herself crying again.

∞

Sitting in her cosy little flat now Sybil was barely aware of the hospital drama happening on the small screen in front of her. She was remembering Bill's tiny bedsit. The bed, narrow though it was filled half the room. A wardrobe, its doors hanging off, leaned precariously in one corner, while a chest of drawers doubled as a kitchen worktop, holding a hotplate, kettle, teapot and the essential crockery for one. She had only just managed to refrain from gasping in horror when Bill had pushed open the door for her.

'It's not much,' he'd explained beforehand as they walked there from the cafe. 'It was only ever meant to be a temporary base until I got my big chance. I wish you'd let me take you to a hotel.'

'No!' Sybil exclaimed. She felt bad enough as it were; if they'd gone to a hotel she'd had felt even more like a tramp. Already as she perched on the very edge of the bed as he boiled the kettle for a pot of tea she felt like a scarlet woman. She thought back to what he'd said in the café.

'If this is all I can have, so be it. After I'd left you yesterday afternoon in the park I walked and walked until I didn't know where I was and I finally realised I love you so much I'll take anything.'

He handed her a mug of tea. 'I'm sorry I don't have a cup and saucer to give you.'

'That's all right,' she smiled. 'Aren't you having one?'

'Um, I only have one mug.' He looked embarrassed. 'I've never brought anyone here before so never thought about it.'

She smiled again. He looked so uncertain of himself, so unlike the confident young man who'd first approached her in the tea-shop all that time ago. Her smile changed into a frown as she realised it wasn't really that long ago that they'd first met. She bit her lip. Was this so very wrong? What she was doing. She tried to reassure herself that her motive was good: if a baby came from their union what joy that would bring. To her and to Reg. But not to the baby's father. She wouldn't allow herself to think those thoughts: he'd be far away, enjoying his new life, meeting a woman who'd be free to love him as he deserved to be loved. Then she realised Bill was speaking, his voice anxious.

'Are you okay? You didn't want sugar in your tea, did you?'

'No, I don't take sugar.'

'I didn't think you did - only you were frowning.'

She shook her head to get rid of the unwelcome thoughts. 'No, everything's … fine.' She looked for somewhere to put down her mug. Bill reached out and took it from her. He turned from her and put the mug in the bowl on the makeshift worktop. It took so long for him to turn around again that Sybil began to think he was changing his mind.

At last he faced her and spoke. 'You see, Sybil,' he stopped. He seemed to be finding it hard to find the words. 'I've … I'm not like you … that is, I mean I'm not married, not … experienced.' He looked down at his hands.

Sybil was relieved. She smiled again. 'Come and sit on the bed next to me.' She patted the coverlet. Bill sat but as far away as it was possible to be on a bed. 'Come here, you idiot,' she laughed now and grabbed his hand, pulling him towards her. She took his face in her hands, brought it close to hers and then kissed him softly on the lips.

At first his response was tentative but soon he was kissing her eagerly. His arms wrapped around her and held her close. 'Oh, Sybil,' he breathed. 'I've wanted to do this for so long.'

At last he released her and said, 'I'll go to the bathroom while you …' his eyes flicked to the bed.

She nodded, grateful for his sensitivity. When he was gone she removed her cardigan, dress and petticoat. She folded them neatly and put them on the floor at the end of the bed. She was undoing her suspenders when there was a quiet tap on the door. 'Can I come in yet?' Bill whispered outside.

'Oh, give me two more minutes!' Sybil hurriedly took off her stockings and added them to the pile of discarded clothes then leapt into bed, pulling the coverlet up over her. 'You can come in now.'

Bill had already taken off his shoes and socks and now without saying a word he took off his braces, shirt and trousers and threw them on the floor. Sybil squeezed herself against the wall and pulled back the bedding to allow him to scramble in besides her. 'This is snug,' she giggled.

Bill raised an eyebrow. 'Are you saying I'm fat?' he said sternly.

Sybil giggled again relieved that the tension that had built up had gone. 'Well, let me see,' she said as she stroked his lean abdomen. 'Oh no, you're not fat at all. You're just about perfect.'

He kissed her with more urgency and, encouraged by her obvious delight, began to explore her body. He slid his arms around her and gingerly tried to undo her bra, struggling with the hooks, until she burst out laughing and said, 'Here, let me do it!' She tossed the offending item out of the bed and slipped out of her knickers. She pressed against him and slipped her fingers into his shorts. He groaned with pleasure.

∞

Sybil smiled to herself. She could see Bill in her mind's eye. Could remember the surprise he showed when she took the lead in their love-making. Those had been heady days when all she could think of was Bill and she counted down hours until they could next meet in his bedsit. It had been a struggle each time Reg had turned to her in bed and kissed her on the lips, the polite signal that he wanted sex. She didn't begrudge him - quite often and more usually in different times she was the one who would instigate it - but she was fearful that she may, in the heat of the moment, say the wrong name. She and Bill were being so careful not to be found out and the very last thing in the world she wanted to do was to hurt her dear kind husband.

'It was because I wanted a baby so much,' Sybil spoke aloud into her empty flat. 'That was why I did it.' Then she shook her head. 'No, Sybil, be honest at least with yourself. That might have been how you excused your behaviour but truth be told you wanted Bill.' She stood up and crossed the room to the sideboard which housed a collection of silver photo frames. She picked up her favourite of Reg. It had been taken on holiday at the seaside somewhere, she couldn't recall where, and he was standing on the promenade leaning against the sea wall and beaming at her. She smiled at the memory and the man. 'I loved you, Reg,' she said. 'I never stopped loving you. I hope you know that.' She kissed his face and a tear fell on the smudged glass.

# Chapter 15

Maggi whistled and called again, 'Come here, Bassett!' But of her dog there was no sign. He'd disappeared as soon as she'd let him out of the car. His nose had twitched and following what was obviously an irresistible smell he'd vanished into the bushes. 'Oh, Bassett, where are you? What are you doing, you ratbag?'

'You've lost Bassett?' Bernard's voice was incredulous. Bassett was usually such an obedient dog.

Maggi turned to greet him. 'Oh hi, Bernard. Seems like it.'

'Has he been gone long?'

'Not really but you know what he's like, he usually stays close by me. So I worry when he does a runner in case he gets himself lost.'

'That's understandable. Have you searched anywhere yet?'

'No, not yet. He went off as soon as we got here. Before I had time to turn round. Stupid dog.' Maggi was annoyed but couldn't hide her concern.

'Well, let's go into the park, tell the others what we're doing and then go and look for him.'

'There's no need for you to come and look for him. You'll want to walk with the others. I'll look if you just tell them where I am.'

'Nonsense. Two pairs of eyes are better than one and we'll get a walk one way or another. Besides, Whisky might be able to help sniff him out.'

They both looked at the greyhound who was staring absently into space.

'He's smarter than he looks, you know,' Bernard said.

Maggi laughed. 'I'll believe you. Well, if you're sure you don't mind it would be helpful.'

They joined Sybil, Jon and Jemma inside the park gates.

'Jemma, how lovely to see you out with the dog club again,' Bernard exclaimed and kissed her on the cheek. 'But are you going to be able to walk far?' He indicated her stick.

Jemma laughed. 'No, not really but I was determined to get out of the house for a bit. I'm going to sit on the bench just up the path and, maybe take some photos of passing dogs if their owners don't mind. I'm hoping you lot will take Pixie for me and then I'll join you in Jock's at the end. Where's Bassett by the way?'

'Just what I was going to ask,' Sybil said.

Maggi explained he'd done a runner and that she, Bernard and Whisky – here she cast a doubtful glance in the dog's direction – were going to look for him. 'You carry on and we'll meet you later in Jock's. And we'd better get hunting now actually. I don't know where he'll have got to by now.'

'I'll sit on the bench by the gate then,' Jemma said. 'I can see into the car park from there and if Bassett makes his way back I'll call him to me and then let you know. You've got your mobile with you, have you?'

'Would you? That would be brilliant. Thanks, Jem. Yes, I've got my phone.' Maggi felt in her pockets to make sure. 'Right, when I catch this dog he's going to be in big trouble.'

Maggi and Bernard followed the hedge around the park until they spotted a tiny gap in it.

'Do you think that's where he came through?' Maggi said.

The hedge was high and they couldn't see over it but Bernard nodded. 'It must just about be the right place in relation to the car park.'

'Basseeeeeetttttttt!' Maggi yelled so loudly that Bernard jumped back surprised.

'Oh sorry, didn't mean to frighten you.'

'You didn't frighten me; I wasn't expecting such a loud shout, that's all.'

'I can be a right loudmouth when I have to be. And I have to be now.'

The park as far as they could see was empty of Bassett.

'Do you want us to separate? To go different ways?' Bernard asked.

Maggi shook her head. 'I know that makes more sense but I'd rather have company if you don't mind.'

'Not at all.' Bernard smiled at her. 'I understand. Now, Whisky,' he led the dog to the gap in the hedge, 'have a good sniff. We're looking for Bassett right? That's his scent, so you take us to him.'

He took Whisky's lead off and stood back and watched the dog expectantly. Maggi also looked at the dog but with less expectation. In a promising move Whisky sniffed the grass and then trotted off. Maggi was amazed. 'Do you think he's picked up the trail?'

Bernard who was also amazed was uncertain but, he reasoned, the direction Whisky was taking was as good as any. 'He might have done. Shall we follow him?'

The three of them made their way further around the park, Whisky stopping every now and then to sniff and cock his leg, and Maggi stopping to take a huge breath before calling Bassett's name as loudly as she could.

They were approaching a wooded area. Bassett preferred wide open spaces and, when they walked through trees, always kept close to Maggi's legs – unless he were with his doggy pals – but Whisky was heading towards the wood.

'I'm not sure, Bernard,' Maggi said. 'I don't think Bassett would go in there on his own.'

'Not even if he were following a strong scent, which he must have been to run off in the beginning?'

'Hmm, I suppose that might lure him.'

'Maybe the scent was of a bitch and he's followed her in there.'

'Maybe. Okay, perhaps we'd better go in a short way.'

At that moment Whisky's ears flicked upright, alert. He stopped and turned then began racing in the opposite direction. Straight towards Bassett who was pelting down the slope towards them for all he was worth. He almost leapt into Maggi's arms, knocking her backwards onto the grass. With his mistress incapacitated Bassett made the most of his opportunity and covered her face with sloppy licks.

It wasn't until Whisky tried to join in too that Bernard took any action. 'No, Whisky. Come on, Bassett, let your mum get up. We know you're pleased to see her but I think she has something to say to you.'

He helped Maggi to her feet. 'Bassett, you …' she began. 'You stupid great dog.' And she knelt down and hugged him tightly to her.

∞

'So Whisky wasn't actually following Bassett's trail then?' Angela asked when they were all safely back in Jock's and she's heard the story.

'He could have been,' Bernard said defensively.

'What?' Jemma said. 'Even though Bassett finally appeared from the opposite direction?'

'Well,' Bernard stroked his chin. 'He might have started off going in that direction and then gradually looped back on himself. I fully believe that Whisky would have led us to him eventually.' He sat up straighter in his chair. 'I have perfect faith in my dog.'

For a moment they took him seriously but when they realised his eyes were flickering from one to the other waiting to see who would challenge him, they all burst out laughing.

'Okay, Bernard,' Jon said. 'We believe Whisky could have done it.'

'Eventually,' Jemma gurgled.

Sybil was stroking Whisky's head. 'He tried, that's what counts, isn't it, boy?'

They all looked at Whisky who had his nose raised and his eyes closed, an expression of vacant bliss on his face, and they burst out laughing again.

As they left the café afterwards Maggi thanked Bernard again. 'I was really worried about Bassett and having you, having someone, with me made me less anxious. So thank you very much.'

'It was my pleasure. I'm just glad the rascal turned up safe and sound.'

'Yes, me too. I wonder where he went.'

'Or what adventure he had.'

Looking at Bassett sitting obediently at Maggi's feet it was hard to believe he'd run away earlier.

'I wonder …'

'I was thinking ..'

They spoke simultaneously. 'After you,' Bernard said.

'No, you go first,' Maggi insisted.

'Well, I was wondering if you'd like to go to the cinema one evening. I noticed the latest James Bond film is on and I remember you saying you wanted to see it when it came out. That is, if you have a free evening. I know you work shifts and do a lot of evenings so if you'd rather not or it's impossible that's fine.'

'No, I'd love to. I don't work every evening.'

'Wonderful,' Bernard beamed. 'Maybe we could call in somewhere and have a bit of something to eat before the film? If you'd like to that is.'

'Strangely enough I was about to ask you if you'd like to come to my place for a meal. As a thank you for your help today,' she added hurriedly. 'Maybe we could combine the two.'

∞

Angela could see Maggi and Bernard talking outside the café and she noted the flush rising to Maggi's cheeks. She hurried back into the kitchen where Tony was preparing paninis for customers.

'I do believe Bernard's asked Maggi out!' she declared.

'Eh? Tony looked at her blankly. 'Does he fancy her then?'

'For goodness sake, Tony, it's been obvious for ages to anyone with eyes that they like each other. I was beginning to think I might have to help them along.'

'Angela!'

'No, it's all right because, as I said, it looks as if Bernard's taken matters into his own hands. They're perfect for each other, don't you think?' She sighed, staring out of the small window at the back of the kitchen. 'I do love it when things fall into place.' She began to load dishes into the dishwasher. 'I may phone Maggi later.'

'Angela! No interfering!'

'I'm not interfering. I'll just be phoning to enquire how Bassett is after his escapade.'

Tony sighed. 'Here, take these out to the customers on table three. Then you can prepare their tea tray. They said they wanted to eat their paninis first.'

What they had started to call the lunch crowd was beginning to arrive. They'd found that the first customers they had were very early morning walkers (tea, coffee, toasted teacakes), followed by the elevenses (tea, coffee, scones and Danish pastries) brigade. This group would be leaving just as the lunch crowd (paninis, baguettes, tea, coffee) appeared. Although they grouped them together the lunch crowd came in in dribs and drabs and took over the café for the best part of two hours in the middle of the day. The last lunchers would be going as the first of the afternoon teas (tea, coffee and cake) turned up. Then the café would gradually empty and they'd be able to clean up ready for the next day when it would begin again.

In between taking orders and serving customers, Angela said to Tony, 'You know I think we might have to get someone in to help us. It's still quite early in the summer and we're already busy with extra visitors.'

They hadn't had any time off since they'd opened after the first few weeks when they'd closed on Mondays. Though they were loving it they were both beginning to feel the strain.

'What sort of help?'

'A waitress, someone to be on the counter, so I can help more back here.'

'But you're so good with the customers. It would be a shame to give that up. And you like that bit, don't you?'

'I do,' Angela admitted. 'I love it. But we need help of some sort so maybe in the kitchen then. We need someone reliable for when we go on holiday anyway though when we're ever going to get a holiday I don't know.'

'I thought we said we'd holiday in January, when it will be quiet.'

'Mm, yes, but you know what it's like, even on rainy days we still do good trade. And, as we said when we took over, dog walkers do it all year round.'

Tony gave a dirty laugh. Angela gave him a mock frown. He put down his carving knife and grabbed her round the waist. 'So do café owners I believe.' He kissed her on the nose as she pushed him away.

'Behave yourself! There are customers out there!' But she wiggled her bottom at him as she pushed her way through the swing doors.

∞

Later that evening, true to her word, Angela phoned Maggi.

'Hi Maggi, I was just wondering if you and Bassett are both recovered after your adventure today.'

'Oh yes, we're fine, thanks, Angela. Bassett's here curled up on the sofa next to me – though I've told him he'll have to move soon as I've got work to go to.'

'It was kind of Bernard to help you on your hunt.'

Maggi smiled to herself. She'd already had Sybil and Jemma on the phone saying much the same thing. She told Angela what she'd told them. 'He's coming here for dinner tomorrow evening and then we're going to see the new James Bond film.'

Angela squealed. 'Oh that's wonderful, Maggi. I'm so pleased. I've thought for ages you were made of each other.'

Which was exactly what Sybil and Jemma had said.

'Don't go getting carried away now, Angela. The meal is just a thank you from me to him.'

'And the cinema?'

'Well, he did suggest that first,' Maggi admitted. 'And you can take that "I knew it" smirk off your face.'

'Really! What makes you think I'm smirking?'

'I can hear it in your voice. But we're just friends, that's all.'

'Of course you are, Maggi. For the moment.'

They chatted a little more about what Maggi was going to cook for dinner the following evening when an idea began to form in Angela's mind. She interrupted Maggi's conversation saying, 'Would you mind telling me how much you earn as a shelf-stacker, Maggi?'

'That's a strange question. Why do you want to know?'

'I'm just doing some research. For the café you know.'

'Oh.' Maggi told her and Angela was appalled at how little she earned for so many hours.

'Well, it's all I can get. There's not much in the way of employment around here. Not for a woman with five o-levels and a degree in gossiping, as my Jack used to say.'

'All the same ... well, thanks for telling me, Maggi. It's useful information to have. Now, what did you say you were planning for dessert?'

When she came off the phone finally Maggi sighed. 'You know, Bassett, you don't know how lucky you are not having to explain everything to all and sundry.' Then she smiled and stroked him fondly. 'It is rather nice though, having friends who care. Not to mention a gentleman friend who is polite, kind and, well, gentlemanly.'

Bassett stretched out, his four legs up in the air and his head leant back onto Maggi's lap. 'Yes, and who likes dogs,' Maggi added. 'Too good to be true almost. But let's not get carried away. It's only a bit of food and the cinema. It's not as if we're getting married.'

She glanced at the photo on the sideboard of her and Jack on their wedding day then slapped herself on the wrist. 'Pull yourself together, woman. Let's not get ahead of ourselves.'

But the excitement – and anticipation – expressed by Sybil, Jemma and Angela was catching and by bedtime Maggi was in a tizzy. It had been years since she'd been out with a man; in fact there had been no-one since Jack. Come to that, there hadn't been that many before him either.

But it's not as if you're going on a date, she told herself. You've invited him here as a thank you. Yes but, she argued with herself through a mouthful of toothpaste, he asked you to the cinema first. She continued the argument in between spitting out, but only because you'd said you wanted to see it. Yes, but he'd remembered and, whichever way you looked at it, it was a man and a woman going out together. Like on a date. But not exactly on a date as they were both in their sixties. She wiped her face with the towel. And what on earth was she going to wear?

The thought had only just entered her mind. She scurried into her bedroom and threw open her wardrobe door. The contents served only to depress her. She had nothing that looked remotely smart. She'd bought very little in the way of clothes since she'd started saving for Australia and everything she took out of the wardrobe looked drab and matronly. 'Not that I want to look glamorous,' she muttered to Bassett who was already curled up on her bed. 'Just presentable.'

The slacks and top she'd worn to Sybil's at Christmas were comfortable and, one big plus in their favour, not used for dog-walking so lacking the usual mix of dog hair and mud. They were nowhere near glamorous but tidy and clean – another thing in their favour as she'd not managed to do a good load of washing for over a week. They'd have to do, Maggi decided. Bernard's used to seeing me in my walking gear so he'll not expect much.

She climbed into bed and plumped up the pillow arranging it to support her as she sat up. She picked up the novel she'd been reading while Bassett, quickly identifying all the signs, snuggled in a bit closer, stretched and settled down. But he'd barely had time to get comfortable when Maggi slapped down her book and sat bolt upright in bed. 'It's no good, Bassett! I can't wear those trousers. I'd forgotten: they split when I was at Sybil's. All that good food took its toll on my seams. Oh, no, now what am I going to do?'

She scrambled out of bed and went through her wardrobe again. When its entire content was on the floor she shook her head sadly. 'There's nothing for it; I'm going to have to wear walking or working clothes. For my first date in … forever. Ah, well, it'll probably be my last date too.'

Bassett jumped down off the bed and curled himself around her legs. She bent down and picked him up, tickling his tummy as she did so. He flopped back in her arms exposing his belly for more tickling. Maggi laughed. 'Is that what I should do, boy? Throw myself on Bernard's mercy? Take pity on me, kind sir, I am just a poor hard-working maid.' She laughed again. 'Ah well, he'll have to take me as he finds me.'

She climbed back into bed, gently placing Bassett next to her. 'Lights out I think. If I try and read I'll keep worrying so best to catch up on some beauty sleep – and let's face it, Bassett, I need as much as I can get.' She kissed the dog on the nose, turned out the light and within minutes was fast asleep.

∞

The walk the following morning was incident-free. At the end of it Jemma and Jon both had to rush off and Bernard also made his excuses so Maggi decided she'd call into Jock's with Sybil who was going to return Mitzi.

'Hello, my beautiful girl,' Angela hugged the big poodle who returned the greeting enthusiastically. 'Have you missed mummy? Mummy's missed you.' Angela kissed Mitzi on the nose then said to Sybil and Maggi, 'Thank you so much – as usual. I do hope I'll be able to join you walking regularly again one day soon. I'm sure I'm going to put on pounds if I don't get some exercise soon.'

'Put on pounds?' Maggi exclaimed. 'Looks to me more like you're losing weight.'

'Really? Do you think so?' Angela peered down at her figure.

'Yes, my dear,' Sybil agreed. 'You're positively fading away. It's all the running around you're doing in the café.'

'I'm certainly on the go all day. And I do take Mitzi for a short walk first and last thing too.'

'No wonder you're losing weight then. I could do with losing some too,' Maggi said, as they sat down and Tony brought them all tea and generous slices of Victoria sponge.

'Nonsense,' Sybil said. 'You've a very shapely figure.'

'Huh, remember Christmas? All that food we ate? And I split my trousers?'

'Oh yes, but that was special.'

'And those were my special trousers, or at least the only decent ones I've got and I planned to wear them for my date, I mean

211

evening out with Bernard tonight, until I realised I never got round to mending them.'

'So what are you wearing?' Angela asked.

'Haven't worked it out yet. I'll have to go through my clothes – again -and find something clean. I've not had time to do a wash recently I've been working so much.' Maggi looked embarrassed.

'I thought you might say something like that,' Angela said. 'So I took the liberty of bringing a couple of items along with me today. I hope you don't mind?' It was Angela's turn to look hesitant.

'Um,' Maggi was doubtful. It was a kind gesture but her world and Angela's were miles apart; Angela's clothes were sure to be far too smart and immaculate for her. Not to mention too small.

'Bring them out, why don't you?' Sybil said, seeing both of them felt uncomfortable, needlessly she was sure.

'Shall I?'

Maggi nodded. 'Yes, please, Angela, if you're not too busy.'

The café was enjoying a momentary lull. Several tables were taken but everyone had been served and as they were still on the elevenses the orders weren't too arduous, even if Tony had to cope on his own for a short while. Angela hurried out to the small store room where she'd left the holdall. She took it back to the table and opened it. 'I think we're roughly the same size,' she said, 'so I picked out a few things I thought might suit you.' She drew a loose fitting very pale blue silk shirt out of the bag. Followed by dark blue linen trousers and a mottled purple and blue scarf.

'I thought these might go well together and bring out the colour of your eyes. I've also got …' she dug into the bag again, 'this cardigan. It's light but surprisingly warm and the evenings can still be chilly. Do you have some sandals you could wear? If not I've got some you can borrow. Alternatively …' she reached into the holdall again, 'you might prefer this skirt and top.'

The navy blue cotton skirt was fitted around the hips but swirled out attractively; the top was a simple white t-shirt covered in tiny blue forget-me-nots. 'You could wear the same cardigan with either outfit. Or not if you don't like it. And you don't have to wear these at all. I just brought them in case you were desperate. I don't want to interfere.'

Maggi stood up. 'Come here you,' she said to Angela. She hugged her closely to her and Angela realised Maggi had tears in her eyes. 'I'm overwhelmed; I've never had friends like you lot before. These clothes are fabulous. I thought … well, I thought you might have brought clothes that I'd feel uncomfortable in but these look just like the sort of thing I'd wear. If I can get into them that is. It's nice of you to say we're the same size but …'

'Try them on, Maggi, before you turn them down,' Sybil urged.

'Yes, go in the store room. It's not very big but you should just about be able to turn around in there.'

When Maggi had disappeared into the tiny room Sybil said, 'The same size, Angela?'

Angela blushed. 'I have to admit they were from my slightly larger days but Maggi doesn't have to know that.'

Sybil smiled and patted her hand. 'No, of course not.'

'I love this!' Maggi twirled her way across the room to them, looking very glamorous – for her – in the linen trousers and silk shirt, with the scarf draped loosely around her neck. 'I think this is perfect, don't you?'

The other two women agreed it suited her. 'But try on the skirt as well, 'Angela said.

'Yes, do,' Sybil agreed. 'You may as well.'

When Maggi had done as she was bid, again she was thrilled with her appearance. 'Oh goodness, I don't know which outfit I prefer.'

'Borrow both,' said Angela. 'Whichever one you don't wear tonight you can wear on your next date.'

'Oh Angela! You're awful! I keep telling you we're just friends.'

Angela and Sybil looked at each other and nodded knowingly. 'Yes, Maggi, whatever you say.'

# Chapter 16

On Wednesday morning Jon had taken the girls to school, walked Benji and was sorting out the laundry when the phone rang.

'Hello.'

'Jon, it's me.'

'Oh hello. What's up?' His wife rarely phoned him during the day unless something had cropped up and she needed to work late or was being taken out for a meal by clients.

'I was wondering if you'd planned dinner tonight yet.'

So that was it: she wasn't going to be eating with them. He sighed. 'Not really. I was going to get some chops on the way back from school this afternoon but if you won't be here …'

She interrupted him, 'Actually I was wondering if we could go out and eat.'

'What? Us? All of us?'

'No, just you and me. I've spoken to Mrs Taylor and she said she'd be happy to sit in with the girls.'

'Oh, um, I suppose so then.'

'Don't sound so enthusiastic!'

'You've just taken me by surprise. I can't remember the last time you and I went out on our own.'

'No, that's what I thought and …' she paused, 'I thought we could talk better on our own.'

'Okay, I'll give the girls pizza then. They'd prefer that anyway.'

'And I'll make sure I'm home by six.'

∞

When he'd put the phone down Jon frowned. This was very un-Tilly-like behaviour. A sudden thought occurred to him. 'Oh no,' he groaned out loud. Benji looked up at him, his head on the side, ears alert. 'I'm okay, Benji, but I bet one of those gossiping bitches has been on the phone to her. "You should watch out for that Cathy;

she's got her eyes on your Jon.'" He mimicked a female voice. 'I bet that's what happened.' He shook his head. 'Honestly you can't move around here without someone watching you.' He recalled Sybil's words. 'Even Sybil watches me like a hawk.' He kicked the table leg making Benji jump up and growl.

'Sorry, boy, it's not your fault.' He bent over to stroke and reassure the dog and when Benji had settled down again Jon stood and stared out of the kitchen window. He thought for a while then made his decision. He returned to the phone and dialled Cathy's number. The answering machine came on.

'Oh, hi, Cathy, it's me, Jon. We're going to have to postpone our coffee this afternoon I'm afraid. Um, something's come up. I'll see you up at school later on and we'll … um … we'll work something out. I mean re-arrange it. Okay, sorry, again. I mean it: I really am sorry.'

∞

Jon arrived at school that afternoon with plenty of time to spare. He hoped Cathy would be there early too so they could talk and he could explain. Not that he knew exactly why he'd postponed their coffee but it had somehow seemed inappropriate when he was 'going out' with Tilly that evening. Telling Cathy that though would seem like an excuse. He wondered if he should make up a story about a neighbour that needed his help urgently. Or one of the dog clubbers maybe. He'd told her about the dog-walking gang. As far as she knew he was the only male – although that was no longer true since Bernard had joined the group – so it was quite plausible that Sybil maybe would need help and that he'd volunteered. And if she asked what it was then he could say something simple like a fuse that needed changing. That wouldn't take long but – he tried to visualise the situation – he could say that Sybil liked to chat and he knew she'd keep him there for ages. He nodded to himself. It sounded so convincing he was beginning to believe it himself.

He was going over the conversation in his head when the bell rang and noisy children began pouring out of school. Gracie had already appeared and Sophie was coming out through the door just as Cathy ran into the playground. She scanned the upturned faces before spotting her daughter who was looking around anxiously. Gathering Rosie to her she left without acknowledging Jon's presence. He scowled in the direction of what he had come to call 'the bitches' and, taking Gracie's and Sophie's hands walked them back to the car.

While they chattered away about what they'd done in school Jon thought about Cathy and the way she'd ignored him. He'd have to make it up to her he decided. Maybe take her some flowers when next he visited. Whenever that would be. He was vaguely aware of his daughter speaking to him. 'Yes, Sophie?'

'What's for dinner?'

'Pizza.'

'Cool.'

'And as a special treat you can have it on your laps while you watch television.'

'Yay!' Both girls cheered.

'Are you going to watch television with us too, daddy?' Gracie asked.

'No, Mummy and I are going out for dinner tonight.'

'Oh. Without us?'

'Yes but Mrs Taylor's going to come and look after you.'

'Oh goodie, I like Mrs Taylor.' Sophie beamed.

'She always gives us biscuits and milk before bedtime.'

'And reads us lots of stories.'

Jon glanced at his daughters in the mirror. They were arguing over what stories to ask Mrs Taylor to read. Sophie wanted one very long one while Gracie preferred lots of short ones. He smiled. At least they were happy. And he supposed he should be too. Going out to dinner with his wife was a rare treat these days. He tried to think back to the last time it had been just the two of them. They'd been to restaurants with clients and business partners for meals that went on the very generous expense account that Tilly had but he really couldn't remember them dining alone.

'When was the last time we did this?'

'Did what?'

'Ate out on our own together?'

Tilly shrugged. 'Can't remember. Your birthday?'

Jon shook his head. 'The girls had tonsillitis then and I was too knackered to go out.'

'My birthday then?'

'You said you'd rather we cooked for you – and then you had to work late.'

'Oh yes, but I did enjoy the cake you made!'

Jon sipped his wine. Tilly had automatically ordered the shiraz before stopping and asking Jon if he would prefer something else. When he'd said it was fine by him she remarked that it was a very good vintage.

'When did you acquire a taste for fine wine?' he asked.

'I think I've always had it,' she said.

'Not back when we drank Bulgarian £2 a bottle wine.'

Tilly laughed. 'Those were the days. Oh, do you remember Mick who lived in the flat downstairs and …'

'Always turned up whenever we had spaghetti bolognese for dinner. "I just happened to be passing," he'd say. Passing a second floor flat, yes, Mick, course you were.'

'But he'd always bring a bottle of Mateus Rose with him! That was probably where I acquired my taste.'

They both laughed, and Tilly raised her glass, 'Let's drink a toast.'

'To what?'

'To us and …' she paused, 'our family, which is soon to be bigger.' The words tumbled out rapidly and at first didn't register with Jon. When they sank in he frowned.

'What do you mean? Oh, the girls haven't been on at you again to get a cat, have they? I've told them Benji won't put up with a cat in his territory.'

'No, not a cat.'

217

'Another dog then? I suppose that would be better but I'm not sure if it's a good idea. I'm the one who looks after Benji now as it is, in spite of all the girls' promises that they'd look after a pet.'

'No, not a dog either.' Tilly took a deep breath. 'A baby.'

Jon stared at his wife, the frown deepening in puzzlement. 'A baby?'

'I'm pregnant, Jon. We're having another baby.'

When the words had finally sunk in Jon took a big swig of his wine. He started to speak then stopped. He swilled his words around in his mouth appraising them carefully before finally speaking. 'You're having a baby?'

'We're having a baby,' Tilly corrected him.

'But …' he stopped. Shook his head. 'I thought …'

The waiter stopped at their table. 'Are you ready to order yet?'

'No,' Jon waved him away. 'I don't understand. How has it happened?'

Tilly laughed. 'It's not that much of a mystery. We had sex and I conceived.'

'Yes, but I thought you were on the pill.'

Tilly was rubbing her neck, an old habit that showed how nervous she was. 'I was …'

'You were?'

'I am – at least I was until I realised I was pregnant - but don't you remember I was having severe period pains and the doctor changed my pill? He did warn me that in the change-over period we should use condoms too but I forgot to buy any and forgot to remind you and, well, things just happened.'

Jon was still in a state of shock. He couldn't believe that his super-efficient wife had let such a thing happen – and that, what's more, she seemed pleased.

Tilly reached across the table and took his hand. 'Are you upset, Jon?'

Jon wasn't sure how he felt. Surprised was putting it mildly. 'No, I'm not upset,' he said finally. 'Are you?' he added.

'No, I'm thrilled.' She was beaming now.

'But what about your job? Won't time off, even if it's just a couple of months, affect your chances of promotion?'

'Probably. It shouldn't of course, legally, but we lawyers know how to get around minor legalities. But I don't care. I really want this baby. I almost think …'

'What?'

'That I deliberately forgot to take extra precautions, that I hoped I would get pregnant.'

'But you didn't say anything. I had no idea.'

'No, I know and that was wrong of me. I should have discussed it with you. But I sort of excused myself by saying it was in the hand of fate. If it were meant to be and so on.'

Jon shook his head again. 'I need time to take this in. When's the baby due?'

'You've got just over seven months to get used to the idea.'

He nodded slowly. 'I've done it before so I suppose I can do it again. The girls are in school so it'll be fairly easy to work around their times. Yeah, we can do this.' He nodded more enthusiastically and, for the first time, smiled. 'So I'm going to be a dad again. I wonder what the girls will say?'

'The thing is, Jon, I'd really like to be at home with the baby myself. I feel I missed so much with the girls. I envy you your relationship with them.'

He smiled thinking about it and how precious it was. He could understand why Tilly would want to make up for missed time. 'But what about your job?'

'I was thinking I could go back to it part-time maybe when baby goes to school.'

'But you love it so much. Won't you hate being at home?'

'I might have been carried along by the cut and thrust of it but there are so many aspects I dislike, mainly, of course, working long hours and having to eat out with clients when I'd rather be having beans on toast with you and the girls. And yes, I'm sure there will be days when I am bogged down by the tediousness of it – you've said yourself some days are boring – but being there for all the firsts will make up for it I'm sure. But I'm making assumptions here. I'm assuming you'll be happy to give up your stay-at-home dad role. I'm also assuming that you'll be able to get another job. If you can't then …' she shrugged.

'We'll deal with it if it happens,' Jon finished her sentence for her. Suddenly he was seeing his wife for the first time in what seemed like years. Her eyes were shining and her cheeks flushed. Then he noticed there was a bright red stripe on her neck where she'd rubbed it so furiously. 'Have you been worrying about how I'd take this?'

She nodded. 'A bit. I've had a while to get used to the idea of being pregnant and, as I said, it was what I was secretly hoping for. But there were so many unknowns as far as you were concerned.'

He squeezed her hand. 'We used to talk about everything.'

'I know. And I know it's my fault we don't because I'm so busy and tired. And I hate that but I didn't want you to think I resented working or that I resented you staying at home. And I hate it that the girls seem to love you more than me and I never get time to do anything with them and you're such a good dad and you fit in and I won't know what I'm doing and I'll be useless and … oh dear.' She was close to crying.

'Hormones.' Jon nodded his head like a wise old sage.

'What?'

Hormones and hunger. We can't plan a nursery when we're hungry.' He signalled to the waiter. 'Let's order, shall we? We've got lots to talk about now.'

# Chapter 17

The next morning, after a night when they'd made love more passionately and tenderly than they had done for some time, Tilly helped Jon to prepare breakfast. By the time the girls got up the table was laid and everything out ready including, as well as their usual cereals, strawberries, blueberries, honey and thick Greek yogurt.

'Wow!' Sophie's eyes were wide. 'Strawberries and honey. I love strawberries and honey.'

'And blubrrries!' Gracie's favourite. 'Where did they come from?'

'We stopped at the supermarket on our way home last night. We thought as you'd been such good girls you deserved a treat.'

'Daddy, how did you know we'd been good girls?'

'Mrs Taylor told me so.'

'But you bought this before you got home.' With her chin down and her mouth pursed Sophie looked just as Jon imagined his wife would when she was quizzing a tricky witness. Tilly came into the kitchen and stood behind Jon, wrapping her arms around his waist.

'And why is Mummy still here?' Sophie frowned now.

'It's all right, poppet,' Tilly reassured her. 'We just wanted to tell you something.'

'What?'

'Well, let's sit down and start breakfast first, shall we?' Jon said. 'Otherwise we'll be late for school.'

When they were all settled with large bowlfuls of fruit, yogurt and honey, Tilly looked at Jon and mouthed, 'Go on, tell them.'

He put down his spoon. 'Girls, as Mummy said, we've something to tell you.'

'You're not getting a divorce, are you?' Gracie's little face suddenly wrinkled up anxiously.

'A divorce? Good heavens, no. Whatever made you think that?'

'Tania's mummy and daddy are getting a divorce. She's going to live with her mummy and only see her daddy at weekends.'

'No, no, in fact, it's just the opposite. Sort of,' Jon said. 'You tell them.' He winked encouragingly at Tilly.

'Well, we're going to have a new member of our family.'

'A kitten?' Sophie squealed. 'Oh yes!!! Can we call it Princess and buy it a big cushion to sleep on?'

'Um, no.' As Sophie's face fell Tilly added, 'I mean, we're not getting a kitten. We're having a baby.'

The two girls stared at their mum and then at their dad. At last Sophie said, 'A baby? A real baby?'

'Yes,' Tilly laughed. 'What other kind is there?'

'Wow! Wait till I tell the girls in school! They'll be so jealous!'

Gracie still looked unsure. 'Are you all right, Gracie?' Jon asked.

'Can we have a kitten as well?'

'No, I don't think so. Not yet. One day when baby's bigger maybe.'

'A baby's much better than a kitten, Gracie. We can help look after it, can't we, daddy? And feed it and change it …' she paused. 'Unless it's done a pooh. Daddy can change it then.'

'Come on, girls. Eat up. You've still got to get washed and dressed before school.'

When at last they'd finished questioning their parents and gone upstairs to get ready, Jon took his wife in his arms. 'That went okay, I think.'

'You don't think Gracie'll be too disappointed not to have a kitten?'

Jon laughed. 'She'll get over it.' He hugged Tilly. 'Have I told you lately that I love you?'

She smiled back at him. 'Not for a long time.'

∞

Maggi said she'd walk with Sybil while Bernard and Jon took the long route, taking Pixie with them. 'He looks like he needs a good romp,' Jon said. The two women watched the men as they marched briskly towards the hill, then they too, along with Bassett and Mitzi, set off along the lower route.

'Jon has a bounce in his step today, don't you think, Sybil? I hope he doesn't make Bernard walk too fast.'

'He does look brighter and more … himself than he has done for a while. I hope that's a good sign.' Sybil frowned slightly as she spoke.

'Why wouldn't it be?' Maggi asked. 'He's got a pretty good life.'

'Mm, yes, I'm sure you're right. Now, tell me, how did your date go?'

'Honestly,' Maggi laughed. 'I keep telling everyone it wasn't a date. Not exactly.'

Seeing Sybil's raised eyebrows she added, 'Well, a sort of date I suppose. And it was lovely. The film was very good. Do you like James Bond? I wouldn't mind seeing it again if you wanted to go.'

'I'm glad you enjoyed your date with Mr Bond but I am rather more interested in how you and Bernard got along, although judging by the way he took your arm back there when he thought you might trip, I'm guessing the answer is very well.'

The beaming smile on Maggi's face suggested that Sybil's guess was a good one.

'Oh, Sybil,' she sighed. 'It was lovely. Really lovely. So wonderful to be fussed over and treated well by a gentleman. It's been such a long time. Not that Jack didn't treat me well it was just … well, I suppose we were so used to each other a little of the magic had disappeared. Or rather a lot of the magic. We'd settled into a comfortable routine – as old married couples do - and there's nothing wrong with that. But it wasn't just the way he took care of me; it was our conversation and the way we laughed at all the same things. And our memories too. Not the same people but the same places and things. It was so nice just to sit and chat. We almost didn't make it to the cinema in time we were so busy talking.' She sighed again. 'Listen to me: I don't know if I sound like a silly teenager or a foolish old woman!'

'I'm so pleased for you, Maggi. You deserve someone like Bernard. Now tell me: did he kiss you goodnight?'

'Sybil! I'm surprised at you. I'd have expected that from Jemma but not you.'

'Why not me? I'm not so old that I've forgotten what happens on dates, you know?'

'No, of course not. Well, as I say we had a lovely evening. I managed to cook dinner without burning anything and Bernard said how nice it all was. He also complimented me on the comfort of my sofa – although that may have been more a comment on the fact that it sags quite badly – and he liked the way I'd decorated the kitchen and …'

'Maggi.'

'Yes, Sybil?'

'I am going to get cross in a minute.'

'Why is that, Sybil?' Maggi was trying very hard to keep a straight face.

'You know perfectly well why.' The older woman leaned in, 'Did he kiss you goodnight or not?'

Maggi linked her arm with Sybil's, 'Yes, he did,' she said and giggled. 'And what's more, I kissed him back.'

Sybil clapped her hands together. 'Marvellous. When are you having your next date?'

'Well, I have to work Saturday evening so Bernard suggested we could go for lunch on Saturday and then walk it off with the dogs.'

'How lovely. Have you decided where to have lunch?'

'We thought there's only one place we could go.'

'Jock's?'

Maggi nodded. 'As the dog club brought us together it seems an appropriate place for our first meal out.'

'And you can be sure Angela will take extra care with your paninis.'

They'd reached the lake and sat for a while on one of the benches overlooking the tranquil water. They watched as Bassett and Mitzi struggled to drag a fallen branch out of the reeds. The two dogs worked together well as team, one tugging this way and that before the other took over. Eventually they got the branch out and on to the side of the footpath. Mitzi lost interest now the challenge had been accomplished so Bassett settled down on his own to chew on the bark while the poodle headed in the direction of the ducks.

'Mitzi!' Maggi yelled. The dog looked around at her name. 'Come back here, Mitzi, there's a good girl. We can't have you chasing ducks.'

'She's very obedient, isn't she?'

'Angela has her well-trained. But to be fair, all our dogs are quite good.'

'Yes, that's true. Although Jock had his moments when he was younger. You never knew him in his naughty days.'

'Naughty days? I can't imagine dear little Jock having naughty days.'

'Don't you believe it! They all do really. Maybe we all do too.'

Maggi thought about this for a few minutes then she said, 'I'm not sure if I ever did. I went straight from being a schoolgirl to a wife almost. I didn't go through the typical rebellious phase of most teenagers. I seemed to miss out on that.'

'Perhaps it's time you caught up then.'

'Sybil! What are you suggesting?'

'I'm just saying that you don't want to waste any more time. Make the most of every minute and every opportunity you have to enjoy yourself. Grab what life offers you with both hands.'

'I think Bernard might be surprised if I grabbed him too hard.'

The two women laughed and then Sybil went serious again. 'I mean it, Maggi. Don't waste a second. How is your saving going for Australia?'

'Well, I have enough for the fare and a bit extra for spending money but I don't want to be a burden on Peter and Linda. I want to be able to pay my way while I'm there.'

'Pay your way?'

'Yes, contribute to the household bills. Food at least.'

'And do you think your son will take your money?'

'I don't know,' Maggi shrugged, 'but I want to be able to offer.'

'That is very admirable of you,' Sybil said. 'And very stupid.'

Maggi looked at her amazed. 'Stupid?'

'Book your ticket! Get on that plane and get out there. See your grandchildren before they forget who you are. And invite Bernard to go with you.'

If Maggi had been amazed before she was stunned by Sybil's last words. 'Invite Bernard? Oh, I don't think so; we barely know each other and ...'

'At least suggest it to him. See what he says.'

'I don't think so, Sybil.'

'Please, humour an old lady.'

Mitzi was showing signs of getting bored.

'Come on, we'd better carry on or she'll be back after those ducks,' Maggi smiled at Sybil. 'I'll think about what you said, I promise that much – but no more!'

∞

'Pregnant?'

'Yes.' Jon had told Cathy the news as soon as they'd sat down with their coffee.

'I didn't know you were trying.'

'We weren't. It was an accident although I'm not entirely sure that Tilly didn't exactly do anything to avoid it.' He grinned

'So is she going to keep it?'

'Yes, of course. She's delighted.'

'You say she's delighted. What about you? How do you feel about a new baby?'

'I was surprised at first but now I couldn't be happier.' And it was true, Jon realised as he said the words. He felt happier than he had for a long time.

'Oh.' Cathy stared into her coffee cup and then smiled. 'So, anyway, let's not talk about Tilly now. Let's talk about us.' She glanced upwards through her lashes in Jon's direction.

'Us?'

'There's no reason why Tilly's pregnancy should come between us. Not until she takes maternity leave anyway and even then ...'

She ran her tongue over her lips in what Jon assumed was meant to be a seductive fashion.

'Cathy, there is no us.' He was surprised he had to spell it out.

Her face changed and she frowned at him. 'What do you mean, no us? What about everything you said on the phone to me?'

It was Jon's turn to look down at the carpet. 'That was … a mistake. I shouldn't have said anything. I was feeling – I don't know, mixed-up and you were friendly and I was … stupid. I'm sorry.'

'Sorry? Is that the best you can do? You think you can seduce me and then drop me just like that?'

'I didn't seduce you!'

'Maybe we hadn't quite reached the physical stage but don't tell me you weren't imagining us together.' Cathy was shouting now. 'You said as much on the phone.'

'I told you: I was confused. And I'm sorry but I don't think this is all my fault.'

'Whose fault is it then? You're the one who's being fickle, changing your mind.'

'Things have changed,' Jon tried to lower his voice, to bring a sense of calm back into the conversation.

'Yes, your wife decides she wants a baby and goes about getting pregnant without even consulting you. What does that say? That she doesn't value your opinion – or you.'

Jon stood up. 'I'm going now, Cathy. I've said I'm sorry and, if you believe I've misled you deliberately then I am even sorrier but I didn't mean to.'

When she didn't move Jon put down his mug and left, closing the front door quietly behind him.

In the car he leaned back against the seat and took a deep breath. He hadn't expected the conversation to be easy but he hadn't expected such vehemence from Cathy either. He'd been a fool. He glanced at the clock. He had more than an hour before he had to pick up the girls. He decided he'd go to the library. They'd phoned him to say that the book he'd ordered was in and ready for him to collect. He hoped some semblance of normality would return to his day if he occupied himself with mundane matters.

∞

Having fought back waves of nausea that had swept over her almost continuously during her morning meetings Tilly decided she needed some fresh air at lunchtime. She glanced at her watch. Lunchtime? It was almost two o'clock. She leaned back in her chair and stretched her shoulders. She knew she'd been fortunate in her first two pregnancies to have experienced virtually no morning sickness. She'd had friends who'd had to take their beds for most of the early months. And what she was suffering now wasn't unbearable – as long as she didn't think about it. She hadn't actually been sick and keeping her mind occupied seemed to help. She didn't have another meeting until four so she'd take a stroll in the park, eat a banana and maybe even have a sandwich if they had one she fancied at the little café round the corner from her office.

She was standing up to leave when she had an idea. She picked up the phone and dialled home. The phone rang once, twice, three times until the answer-machine came on. 'You've reached the home of Jon, Tilly, Sophie and Gracie. We're having too much fun to come to the phone at the moment so please leave a message.' Tilly chuckled. Jon had taken great care recording the message and had got the girls to say their names and shout the 'too much fun' bit. She'd told him off initially. 'What if a client calls me at home? It won't sound very professional.'

'It's not professional to call you at home,' Jon had pointed out in return.

She was still chuckling when the beep to start recording came on. 'Hi Jon, it's me. I was going to suggest that you popped into town to meet me for a stroll in the park but you're obviously already out gallivanting so I'll see you later. I have a meeting at four but it shouldn't last long. I'll try and get home early. Love you.' She blew a kiss to sign off.

She chose a simple grilled chicken salad roll from the limited selection left in the shop and walked the few streets to the park. The sun was shining and the grass was littered with young couples. Tilly smiled at them and at the individuals, mostly students, who were scattered in amongst the lovers. That had been her once before she'd met Jon. Then it had been them. She smiled contentedly to herself and finding a spot under the shade of a large oak tree, settled down to eat her lunch and relax.

It was so peaceful sitting there in the cool deliberately not thinking about anything Tilly was tempted to phone her office and make an excuse to avoid returning, but, she reasoned with herself, there may be a need to take sick leave if the morning sickness got worse and she'd need time off for ante-natal clinic so better not to upset the bosses unnecessarily. Reluctantly she began to make her way back to the office. She was almost at her office door when a woman spoke to her. 'Hi Tilly, how are you?'

Tilly stared at the woman's face. It was one she recognised but had no idea of its context. Was she a client and if so on which side of the law, or was she a neighbour or school parent? She tried to play for time. 'Hi, I'm fine. How are you … all?'

'Good, thanks. Since the boys had chickenpox we've had a pretty ill-free time, which makes a change in our family.'

'Oh good, I'm glad to hear that,' Tilly took a chance. 'The boys are back in school now then?'

'Yes, thank goodness, they were driving me mad at home!' The woman paused. 'Everything okay with you?'

'Yes. Our girls, as you know,' Tilly crossed her fingers saying that, 'had chickenpox too and I think that drove Jon scatty but we're all well now.'

'Yes, it's lovely seeing Jon up at school. He's such a devoted dad.'

'He is, yes. The girls are very lucky – and so am I.'

'He gets on well with people generally too I've noticed.'

Tilly shrugged. 'I suppose he's quite sociable.'

'Well, I'm sure Cathy appreciates his … friendship.'

There was a reason Tilly was so good at her job: she could read subtext better than many of the barristers she dealt with. Her brain quickly absorbed and responded to the innuendo without a noticeable pause.

'Oh she does. She's told me many times how helpful he's been to her.'

'Oh.' Like a deflating balloon the woman seemed to shrink a little.

'Now I must be getting back to work. It's been lovely chatting to you. See you again soon.' Tilly kissed the air each side of the woman's face and had the satisfaction of seeing a stunned look, before she turned and swished her way through the door.

Inside she fell sideways against the wall. It felt as if she'd been punched in the stomach and she desperately needed air in her lungs. The nausea she'd been resisting rose now and tasted bitter in her mouth; she made it to the Ladies' just in time to heave her lunch into the bowl.

Now, it seemed, she had an excuse to finish early. She could say she had a bug: she didn't want her employers to know about her pregnancy at this early stage if she could help it. She sat on the floor of the cubicle, hugging her knees to her chest until she heard the main door being opened and another woman entering. She quickly sat herself down on the lavatory seat and waited until she was alone again before emerging and attempting to make herself look presentable. She washed her face, brushed her teeth with the toothbrush she always carried in her handbag for long days, and reapplied her make-up. By the time she'd done all that she'd made her decision.

Back in her office she called home again. This time Jon answered the phone, 'Hi honey, got your message. Sorry I missed you; I'd have loved to join you in the park.'

'Yes, well, I was just calling to say that something's come up and I'll have to work late tonight after all. I won't be home until after the girls are in bed. Give them a kiss goodnight for me will you?'

'Yes, of course. But they'll be disappointed. I told them maybe we could all take Benji to the park after tea while it's still light.'

'Well, you shouldn't have told them that. You'll have to take them on your own. I'll see you later.'

'Tilly? Are you ...'

But she'd put the phone down.

Jon frowned. Working late wasn't unusual nor was finding out it was necessary at the last minute. What was unusual was Tilly's tone of voice. She'd sounded ... he puzzled over it. Angry? Sad? A mixture of both. She'd sounded so cheerful on the phone at lunchtime; something must have happened to upset her. 'You and me both,' he muttered to himself. He was still shaken by his encounter with Cathy and it had taken him some effort to speak normally on the phone. There'd been a part of him that had wanted to blurt out the whole – or at least part of the - story. 'Tilly, I'm sorry, I've been a fool and came close to being an even bigger one but nothing happened and it's you I love, I realise that now.'

He took a deep breath: he couldn't do that; it wasn't fair on Tilly. 'Probably her hormones,' he said out loud to Benji. 'I remember what she was like when she was pregnant the last time. Up and down until I never knew if it were safe to come home or not.' He wagged his finger at the dog. 'You were lucky you didn't know her then. She'd have had your guts for garters as soon as look at you on her bad days.' Benji wagged his tail in return. Jon smiled then called the girls. 'Okay, girls, Mummy has to work late ...' there was a chorus of groans, 'so we'll have beans on toast now and take Benji to the park straight after. How about that?'

Going into the park Jon spotted Sybil at her bedroom window. Waving to her reminded him he'd not heard anything from the journalist he'd tried to contact in America; he'd check his emails when he got home and maybe try again. He wasn't going to give up straight away.

∞

'Claire, hi, it's Jemma.'

'Hi Jemma. How you doing?'

'Fine, well, you know, anyway the reason I'm calling is I realised I'd promised to invite you for a meal and I hadn't done and I didn't want you to think I'd forgotten because I hadn't I just wanted to be on my own, I don't mean on my own in that I don't want you here, but not my mother, I didn't want her here, but she's gone now not that it would have mattered really because it's only a thank you meal but she does tend to monopolise the conversation so I was wondering if, if you're not busy although I expect you are and it doesn't matter if you are, if you'd like to come and have something to eat with me. As a thank you.' Jemma finally ground to a halt and then added, 'And Pixie.'

'Pixie?'

'My dog. He'll be here too so I won't be on my own although a dog doesn't really count I suppose. For some people.'

'I'd love to.'

'What?'

'Come to your house for a meal,' she spoke slowly.

'Oh.'

'But can you manage? Would you like me to bring a takeaway?'

'No, I can manage. Anyway my mother's left me enough food in the freezer to feed a small army.'

'So you want to use some up,' Claire chuckled.

'No, no, I'll cook something. I, um, are you sure?'

'I'm positive. When would you like me to come?'

'Anytime. I'm always free. I mean now that I'm only just getting back to normal, that is.'

'Okay, well, you suggest a day?'

Jemma hadn't thought this far ahead. She'd expected Claire to make excuses. She nibbled her finger-nails as she pondered. To suggest that very evening looked a bit desperate and anyway she needed to tidy up the house a bit. Even by her none too scrupulous standards it looked a mess. How had she managed to create so much untidiness in the few short days since her mother had spring-cleaned so efficiently? At least she knew it was clean underneath the magazines and books.

'Jemma, are you still there?'

'Oh, yes, sorry, I was just working a date out.'

And it wasn't just the room that looked a bit uncared-for. She ran her fingers through her hair. As standing in the shower for too long was difficult she wasn't washing her hair as often as usual. She'd need to do that as well as all de-hair her legs, exfoliate her skin and lose half a stone. Sitting down for most of the day being looked after and very well-fed had done nothing for her figure. She sighed and reminded herself this wasn't a date, just a thank you meal.

'What about tomorrow evening?' Jemma asked tentatively.

'Sounds great. What time shall I come round?'

'Eight? Would that be all right?'

'Perfect, and I'll bring a bottle of wine. You can drink, can you?'

'Oh yes, like a fish.' Jemma screwed her face up in her hands as she realised how that must sound but Claire laughed. 'I meant, you're not taking any medication, are you?'

'Oh, no. I don't even need pain-killers most days.'

'Excellent. Then I'll see you tomorrow at eight. Bye, Jemma.'

'Bye.'

Jemma replaced the phone in its holder. She'd proclaimed to Claire how well she could manage but she hadn't needed to on her own so far. She wondered if she should get Gwennie in to help out with the preparations but then discarded that idea. 'You can do this,' she told herself. 'You've been sitting around long enough. Time to get back into action – before you turn into a pumpkin.'

# Chapter 18

By the time Claire knocked on her door the following evening the house was spotless, there was a lamb tagine slowly cooking and Jemma herself was looking and feeling more like herself.

'Mm, that smells good,' Claire sniffed the air appreciatively as she entered. 'Moroccan?'

'Yes, lamb. I forgot to ask if you were a vegetarian or allergic to anything so I hope that's okay?'

'Absolutely. Lamb is my favourite.' She handed her the wine. 'And I forgot to ask if you preferred red or white so I brought both.'

Jemma laughed. 'I like both as it happens, but maybe red would be best with Moroccan lamb?'

Pixie, who'd been in the back garden patrolling his territory, suddenly came charging in. He ran to Claire and jumped up, putting his dirty paws on her shoulders.

'Pixie, get down!' Jemma shouted and, hurrying to grab her boisterous pet, stood on his squeaky bone causing Pixie to jump suddenly, with the result that he tumbled backwards into Jemma, who in turn fell back, landing spread-eagled on the sofa with Pixie on top.

Claire burst out laughing.

'Pttf, get off me, Pixie! Get up, you great stupid animal. And it's not funny,' she added to Claire.

'Sorry but it is from this angle.' She leaned over to take Jemma's hand and help her up after Pixie had rolled off and had begun frantically licking his owner's face by way of apology.

Standing up, Jemma caught a glimpse in the mirror of her face, smeary where muddy doggy saliva had mixed with make-up and mascara, and she sighed. 'I was so determined to be a perfect hostess tonight.'

Claire pulled a handkerchief out of her pocket and gently daubed Jemma's face. 'It is clean,' she assured her. Jemma looked into

Claire's face, which she was desperately trying to keep straight, and began to laugh. 'No wonder my mother despairs of me.'

'I can't think why she should. You seem … perfect to me.'

'Oh no!'

Dead on cue Pixie, sensing a potential group hug, had thrust himself between them and was looking enthusiastically from one to the other. They both chuckled.

'Come on,' Jemma said, stepping back. 'You can open the wine while I put the water on the couscous and then we can eat in five minutes. I hope you're hungry; there seems to be quite a lot.'

'I'm hungry,' Claire nodded, 'and it looks as if Pixie is too.'

There was a long finger of drool dangling from the boxer's mouth.

'Forget it, you. You've already had your dinner – and you're in my bad books. On your bed, go on.'

The dog didn't move.

'Bed, Pixie. Go on! Now!'

Pixie again looked from one to the other but stayed sitting where he was.

'Pixie, I'm not telling you again: go to your bed now!'

The dog stood reluctantly, then turned and walked, head hanging down forlornly, to the living-room where he climbed onto the sofa, lay on top of Claire jacket, stretched out and issued an enormous 'how hard done by am I?' sigh followed by an equally enormous fart.

Jemma closed her eyes. Perhaps if she wished really hard the evening could leap back in time. Just by an hour or so. She opened one eye. Nothing had changed except Claire was studying her in a puzzled way. She opened the other eye. 'Would you like to leave now or are you intent on staying for the rest of the cabaret?'

Claire laughed out loud. 'You're not getting rid of me yet. I'm sticking around till the end of the show.'

She put her arm on Jemma's shoulder and steered her towards the kitchen. 'Come on, I'm hungry and I don't think that couscous is going to cook itself. Where do you keep your bottle opener?'

'But your jacket? He's lying on it.'

Claire shrugged. 'Let's look on it as him keeping it warm for me, that's all. Now come on, or I'm going to be eating this stew out of the pan.'

∞

'And we're going to the pictures on Saturday.'

Jemma was relating the events of the evening for the third time. She'd been subjected to an early morning cross examination from Gwennie, followed by interrogation from Sybil on their walk and now was having to tell Angela, Maggi, Bernard and Jon all about it over coffee in Jock's.

Jon chuckled, 'So Pixie didn't deter her then?'

'She took it all in his stride – even when Pixie insisted on lying across my lap when we adjourned to the sofa after dinner.'

'She sounds like a keeper,' Maggi nodded approvingly.

'She does sound rather lovely,' Angela agreed. She gave Maggi a meaningful look. 'Another romance for the dog club. We're becoming quite a dating agency!'

Maggi frowned at her but Bernard smiled and brought his arm up to rest his hand on Maggi's shoulder. 'My life has certainly changed since I began walking with you.'

'For the better I hope?' Angela said.

'Oh good heavens, yes. Much.' He beamed at Maggi who blushed furiously before saying, 'Anyway we've finally agreed on a date.'

The other dog clubbers all stared at her. Sybil paused, tea-cup halfway to mouth, Jemma put her lemon cake back on her plate and Angela, for once, was speechless.

Jon was the first to speak, 'Fantastic news! Congratulations!' He took Bernard's hand and began to shake it enthusiastically. Then the women all began to talk at once but Bernard, struggling to make himself heard, shouted, 'Hang on, hang on! I think you've got the wrong end of the stick!'

Maggi was staring one to the other. 'What stick? What are you all so excited about?'

'I think everyone misunderstood when you said we've agreed on a date, 'Bernard said gently.

There was a moment's silence and then Maggi burst out laughing. 'Oh my, I see! You thought I meant a wedding date!' She laughed again. 'No, no, a date for our Australia trip.'

'Ohhhh.' There was a general sigh of disappointment.

'For goodness sake, we've only known each other five minutes,' Maggi continued. 'We've both got happy marriages behind us and we don't want to rush into anything. We're not even thinking about anything like that!' She said it with great disdain and it was only Sybil who noticed the expression that flashed briefly across Bernard's face. He quickly recovered and said, 'Good heavens, no. We're free spirits off to travel the world.'

'That's right,' Maggi said grinning, 'although Peter was a little surprised when I told him I'd be bringing a friend with me. I don't think he's quite as free-spirited as we are. But, no, we're thinking about going on the 5th of next month. We've found flights that are reasonably priced and it seems unlikely we'll get any better so we're going to book today.'

'She wouldn't let me book last night,' Bernard grumbled. 'She said she wanted to sleep on it.'

'It's such a lot of money and, well, I've been dreaming of it for so long, it's frightening to finally have it within reach.'

'It'll be marvellous!' Angela exclaimed. 'I'm so delighted for you. I'm sure we all are.'

The others all nodded and then Jon said, 'What are you doing with the dogs while you're away?'

'Ah, yes,' Bernard said. 'We wanted to talk to you all about that.'

'I'll have Bassett,' Sybil said. 'He can stay with me but I don't think there'd be room in my little flat for Whisky too.'

'I'll have Whisky,' Jemma volunteered. 'He and Pixie get on well and I've got the room.'

'Are you both sure?' Maggi asked. 'We'll be gone for a month remember?'

'No problem,' Jemma said.

'And if it gets too much we can swap around, take it in turns to have them to stay,' Angela added.

'Yeah, course we can,' Jon agreed.

'As it is, they all get walked together. Look how you've all helped me and Jemma when we couldn't do it,' Angela said.

'I must confess I was worrying about putting Bassett in the kennels.'

'Do you know how much they charge? You'd have had to have saved for another year to manage that.'

'But you must let us pay you,' Bernard said. 'We can't …

The looks on their faces stopped him mid-sentence.

'We're friends and that's what friends do,' Sybil said, putting an end to that discussion. 'Now tell us what plans you've made so far. I assume you'll be travelling around Australia a bit as well as seeing the family.'

'Yes, Peter is going to take some leave and we're all going to hire a couple of camper vans and travel around. It's a huge country, you know; I hadn't realised. I thought we could see it all in a few days! But we're definitely going to go to see the Great Barrier Reef.'

∞

Jon found the email waiting for him in his Inbox.

"Hi Jon,

Good to hear from you. As an investigative journalist myself – albeit retired – I appreciate the effort you put in to tracing me. Yes, I did know a Sybil Wright many years ago. Now I have to ask why you're asking the question.

Yours,
Bill Walters."

"Hi Bill,

Great to hear from you too, especially to find out that you are the man I'm looking for. You ask why: well, it's a long story and it all begins with some dogs …"

The next morning Tilly was up and in the shower before Jon had come to. When he was getting the breakfast stuff out for the girls she came into the kitchen and poured herself a cup of the coffee she'd put on to percolate before she showered. She sipped it as she gathered her papers and briefcase together. Over her shoulder she said to Jon, 'So where were you when I phoned yesterday afternoon?'

'What?' Jon paused in his hunt for Gracie's favourite bowl. 'When?'

'When I called early yesterday afternoon.'

He burrowed his head deeper into the cupboard. 'Oh, um, I don't remember. Where on earth is her bowl? She won't eat anything unless she's got it.'

'You don't remember? It was less than twenty-four hours ago.'

'Oh then, yeah, um,' he emerged from the cupboard. 'Oh, yeah, I went to the library.'

'On your own? I thought you usually took the girls. In fact you went there last Saturday.'

'Yeah, I did but … I had to pick up a book I'd ordered.'

'What's it called?'

'The book? I er oh I can't remember the title, by whatisname who writes those thrillers – but what's all this cross examination? You're not in court now. If you've got time to spare you can help me find Gracie's bowl.'

Tilly pointed to the draining board. 'Is that the one you're looking for?'

'Yes! Why didn't you tell me before?'

Tilly shrugged, finished her coffee and pulled her coat on. 'Got to go. See you later.'

'Will you be working late tonight?'

'I don't know. Kiss the girls goodbye for me.'

And she was gone. Leaving Jon puzzled and slightly uneasy. His wife's manner seemed to have changed overnight – or rather over day. She'd been fine the previous morning. What had happened to change that? And why had she been so suspicious over his movements yesterday? It was almost as if she knew he'd been seeing Cathy.

Not that there was anything to know about that. Jon shook his head. Seeing Cathy. That made it sound far more exciting than it had been. They'd only ever chatted. Except for the one kiss. It wasn't even as if that was a big thing, at least not on his part. It was true he'd been tempted and flattered by her interest in him but … no, he put his hand to his head, who was he trying to kid? He'd have taken it further. He was just working up to it. It wasn't that he didn't love Tilly; it was simply the excitement that had attracted him, an excitement that had been missing from his relationship with his wife over the last few years.

'Daddy!'

Jon spun around to see his elder daughter sitting, book in hand, at the kitchen table. 'Oh morning, Sophie.'

'What were you doing, Daddy? I asked you a million times for some orange juice.'

'A million? As many as that? I'm sorry, Soph, here you are.' He handed her a glass of juice as Gracie tottered in, looking only half awake. 'Morning, Gracie. Do you want some orange juice?'

'Yes please, Daddy. In my Aurora cup.'

Jon showed her the cup in his hand. 'I'm already onto it. By the way, Mummy asked me to kiss you goodbye from her.'

'Oh, has she gone already? I wanted to show her my painting from school yesterday.' Sophie was disappointed.

'She'll see it tonight, sweetheart. She had to go in early.'

'Why does she always have to go in early?' Gracie grumbled.

'She doesn't always,' Jon said, 'and remember things are going to be changing so you'd better make the most of having your dad at home with you. Come on, get your cereal eaten; does anyone want any toast?'

∞

He was still thinking about Tilly's sudden change of mood when he was putting the dishes in the dishwasher before setting off with

Benji. There was no way she could have found out about his afternoon visits to Cathy. Yet something had obviously upset her. A sudden awful thought crossed his mind: Cathy had been very upset when he'd told her their liaison would have to stop; in her anger could she have phoned Tilly and told her? Maybe even made up some stories that would have made it sound worse than it was? But if that had been the case surely Tilly would have confronted him immediately? He thought about phoning Cathy but wondered what he'd say, then, glancing at the clock, saw it was time to set off to meet the rest of the dog club.

He took Benji's lead from the hook behind the door. 'Come on, Benji, let's go meet our pals.'

∞

Angela had decided that the café was running so smoothly now that she could afford to take a morning off and join the dog clubbers on their walk. She opted to take the uphill path with Maggi and Bernard to get the best exercise while Jemma, who was walking almost normally again, would follow the lower shorter route with Sybil and Jon.

They'd reached the lake when Jemma stopped. 'I think I'll sit here and wait for you while you do the round trip,' she said.

'Oh my dear, are we walking too fast for you?' Sybil enquired anxiously.

'No, it's not that. I just don't want to overdo it. Will you take Pixie with you though, please?'

'Yes, of course we will, won't we, Jon?'

When he didn't reply, Jemma looked at Sybil and frowned. She mouthed, 'Is he okay?'

Sybil nodded. 'Come on, Jon. Let's get these dogs exercised. You enjoy the lovely autumn sunshine, Jemma.'

Sybil and Jon walked on in silence for some way until at last Sybil said, 'Would you like to tell me what's the matter?'

Jon stared at her blankly. 'Matter? What do you mean?'

'You've hardly spoken at all on our walk and you're not yourself today. You don't have to tell me anything if you don't want to but I am a good listener.'

He sighed and shook his head. 'Am I that transparent?'

Sybil smiled. 'Transparency is a good thing.'

'Oh, Sybil, I've got myself into a right mess. And it's all my own fault. I can't blame anyone but myself. I've been stupid.'

'Well, Jon, perhaps you have but why don't you just tell me about it instead of berating yourself?'

They walked a little further in silence as Jon gathered his thoughts. At last he said, 'Tilly's pregnant.'

'Ah,' said Sybil. She waited for him to continue before offering congratulations in case they wouldn't be welcome.

'And that's marvellous,' Jon added quickly. 'We're delighted. It wasn't planned.' He frowned, 'At least I didn't plan it … but, anyway, Tilly was really happy and she wants to give up work to stay at home with the new baby and that's fine too. I'll have to start looking for jobs, maybe do a short course to update myself, and it seemed I was getting my wife back. But now she's acting funny.'

'I understand pregnant women often do behave unusually, even erratically.'

'I know about hormones and I've seen them in action often enough but this is … different. The thing is, well, like I said, I've been stupid.'

Sybil waited quietly.

Jon bent to pick up a stick to throw in the lake for the dogs. When he stood again he said, 'There's this woman, a mum at school. We're not having an affair or anything but I have been seeing her regularly, just for coffee.' He toyed with the stick in his hand. 'We kissed once. Just once and it was only a kiss. But I said some things and I probably would have taken it further soon – if Tilly hadn't announced her pregnancy.'

The dogs were sitting patiently at Jon's feet. He looked down at them not seeing them.

'I think they're waiting for you to throw the stick,' Sybil said gently.

'What? Oh yes.' He hurled it across the lake and the two dogs leapt in each determined to get there first.

'And Tilly has found out about this woman?'

'That's it: I don't know. I don't see how she could have done. Yesterday morning she was fine when she went to work; she was even going to come home early so we could come to the park together. But then later on she called to say she'd have to work late and we didn't speak again until this morning when she was definitely shirty with me.'

'Perhaps she had a bad day in the office?'

'No, I don't think so. She was quizzing me this morning about where I'd been when she phoned me yesterday afternoon. She wouldn't normally care and I couldn't think fast enough.'

'Why did you have to think fast?'

Jon looked embarrassed. 'I was with Cathy - but only to tell her I wouldn't be seeing her again.'

'I see,' Sybil said.

Pixie had returned triumphant, the stick in his mouth, and he was standing expectantly, hoping for a treat – or for the stick to be thrown again. Benji reached dry land a few seconds later and shook himself violently covering all three of them with muddy water.

'Aw, Benji!' Jon exclaimed. 'You've soaked Sybil, you stupid dog!'

'It's all right, Jon. No need to take it out on Benji.'

Jon's shoulders sagged. 'No, you're right, Sybil. I'm sorry Benj.' He bent and patted the downcast dog who instantly perked up.

'If only a pat would cheer Tilly up as easily,' Jon said. 'I don't know what to do. Should I tell her about Cathy? Come clean before she accuses me? Or keep quiet and hope I'm imagining it and it will go away?'

'Might Cathy have phoned Tilly out of spite?'

'I thought about that. I don't think she knows where Tilly works so it's unlikely. And anyway she wouldn't, would she?'

Sybil raised her eyes. 'No fury like a woman scorned, they say.'

Jon sighed again.

'I'm not being very helpful, am I?' Sybil said. 'But I'm not sure if I'm the right person to advise you. You know my history: the secret I kept from my husband for forty years. I don't think I ever lied to him but I didn't tell him the truth either. I justified it by telling myself it was kinder like that. Reg never knew and wasn't hurt; I bore my guilt – and pain - on my own. But if you're going to live with a secret you have to remember it constantly so you don't get caught out.' Sybil smiled sadly. 'Once I began to tell Reg that 'our' teashop had been taken over and was being refurbished. I was well into the story before I remembered it wasn't 'our' teashop at all, but mine and Bill's. I had to do some fast thinking then.'

Jon smiled. 'I bet.'

'And if she already knows then the question of whether to tell her or not becomes immaterial.'

'Unless I'm willing to not only be economical with the truth but to tell downright lies. And I couldn't do that.'

Sybil rested her hand on Jon's arm and squeezed it. 'I hope it all works out for you. Maybe you'll find there's a perfectly innocent and unrelated reason for Tilly's mood.'

'I hope so, Sybil. I really hope so.'

They had nearly reached the bench where Jemma was waiting for them.

Seeing her owner Pixie bounded up to Jemma who, sitting back with her eyes closed, was caught unawares when the large soaking wet dog pounced on her joyfully.

'Aaah, Pixie, you're drenched!'

'Sorry, Jem, my fault. I threw the stick in.'

'Don't worry about it,' Jemma grinned. 'He'd have gone in anyway if I know him. I'm used to being wet.'

As Jon walked on ahead Jemma raised her eyebrows enquiringly at Sybil and mouthed, 'Is he all right?'

Sybil nodded. It was best to keep her concerns to herself. And she really did hope it would be all right.

∞

Back in her flat, after she'd made herself a cup of tea, Sybil sat down in her chair. The weight of Jon's problem felt heavy on her. She didn't feel she was the right person to advise him. Keeping a secret from his wife was a huge potential problem in waiting. She knew how hard it could be.

When Bill had left, she'd been devastated. She still didn't know how she'd managed to keep it from Reg. It was as much as she could do to go about her daily chores when all she had really wanted to do was curl up in her bed and weep. But Reg hadn't even noticed. Or had he? Had Reg noticed something different about her in those days? He was a perceptive man, sensitive to her moods. How could he not have noticed?

This thought, which had never occurred to her before, made her sit up abruptly in her chair. 'Reg knew.' The sudden awful certainty hit her with a clarity she could never have anticipated. Oh maybe he didn't know the details, the who or the where, but he knew. And he waited. Waited for her to come back to him. She may not have left him physically but in those months with Bill her spirit, her heart, was far away. In a teashop in town, in a dingy bachelor flat, on a passenger ship bound for America, and, finally, in New York.

'Oh Reg,' she whispered his name. 'I'm sorry. I'm so sorry. I never knew. I was so bound up in my own misery that I never saw yours. Forgive me, my dear.'

She picked up his photograph that stood on the little table by her chair and holding it to her face kissed it through her tears.

# Chapter 19

'What do you think, Tilly?'

In the silence that followed all eyes turned in Tilly's direction. At last the senior partner spoke again. 'Tilly? Are you all right?'

'What? Oh, I'm sorry, did you say something?' She rustled the notes in front of her, hoping the words, which appeared as a meaningless blur, would spring into life and tell her what she should reply but the blur remained.

'I asked what you thought of the proposal?'

'Proposal?'

'To settle the Courtridge case. Are you feeling unwell, Tilly? You don't seem to be yourself this morning.'

'I'm sorry, yes, I think your proposal is excellent.'

'Excellent? They're suggesting our client settles for a quarter of what we proposed. I'd hardly call that excellent.'

'No, of course not. You're quite right. Actually, I don't feel all that well. I wonder if I might finish early today?'

'I think that would be beneficial for all of us, especially our client.' Her boss dismissed her with an impatient wave of his hand.

Tilly hurriedly gathered up her papers, dropped them again, grabbed as many as she could and left the room before she could do any more damage to her reputation. Pulling the door closed behind her she leaned back against it and took a deep breath. 'Right, woman, pull yourself together. You'll have no job to graciously resign from if you don't straighten this out.'

In the car she wondered where to go. Home? Jon would be there – at least he should be there – she felt her stomach clench in suspicion and considered ringing him. No, that wasn't the way. The park. The one he always took Benji to. She'd not walked there for a very long time. Perhaps she'd collect the dog and take him with her. No, not home. Straight to the park. Fresh air and some afternoon sunshine. That would do her good, help clear her head. Maybe she'd get a sandwich at Jock's. Jon was always going on about how good it was there. Yes, she'd do that.

In Jock's Tilly ordered a simple chicken panini and a cappuccino. She told Angela, who'd taken her order, that she'd be sitting outside when it was ready. Angela vaguely recognised her customer's face but as the woman showed no signs of wanting to chat, she didn't push it.

Waiting for her lunch Tilly leaned back in her seat and closed her eyes. It had been a tumultuous few days: her joy at her confirmed pregnancy, anxiety about Jon's reaction, delight, and now doubt and pain. The sun painted images on the insides of her eyelids and for a few moments she let her mind drift. She felt she could quite easily drop off and sleep for a month.

With her eyes closed Tilly didn't see the elderly woman going into the café and looking curiously at her. Inside Sybil, who was delivering one of her lemon drizzle cakes, said to Angela, 'Isn't that Jon's wife sitting outside?'

'I thought I recognised her face,' Angela exclaimed. 'But I only met her very briefly on the day we opened and I confess I might have been a little distracted then.'

Sybil smiled. 'I'm sure it is her. But I wonder what she's doing here this afternoon.'

'Well, I'm about to take her order out; do you want to have your cup of tea out there with her?'

'She might not want to be disturbed.'

'You could ask. Thanks, Tony.' She took the warm panini from her husband and added it to the tray with the cappuccino. 'This is hers. Come on.'

Sybil knew it was no use arguing with Angela and followed her out of the café.

'Your Panini and cappuccino. I hope you enjoy.' Angela carefully arranged the dishes in front of Tilly and then added, 'My friend and I here,' she indicated Sybil, 'think we know your husband. Jon?'

Tilly smiled and nodded, 'Yes, I'm Jon's wife.'

'I think we did meet before – you came to the opening of this café I believe …' Tilly nodded as Angela paused, 'But I didn't get a chance to talk to you properly. I was rather tied up, I'm afraid.'

'Quite understandable,' Tilly smiled again.

'And did you meet Sybil then?'

'Yes, I did. Hello Sybil. How are you?'

'I'm very well, thank you, my dear.'

'Sybil makes cakes for me, you know. She's a wonderful cake-maker. You must try some of her lemon drizzle; she's just brought a fresh one across and she's going to have a cup of tea. Perhaps she could join you?'

'Angela!' Sybil was appalled. 'Ignore her, my dear. I'm quite happy to sit elsewhere if you want to be by yourself.'

Tilly very much wanted to be alone but she knew how much Jon liked his unorthodox bunch of dog-walking friends and didn't want to appear rude. 'No, please, sit, join me.'

'If you're sure?'

'Yes, honestly. It's fine.'

Sybil, still frowning at Angela, sat opposite Tilly.

'I'll bring your tea out now, Sybil. Would you like a slice of cake to go with it? It's freshly made!'

Sybil shook her head. 'Honestly, Angela, you'll never make your fortune if you insist on feeding me the cake you've just paid me for.'

'What makes you think I won't charge you for it?'

Sybil merely raised her eyebrows to the sky. 'I wish you would.'

Angela laughed and returned to the café, returning quickly with a pot of tea and a large slice of cake. 'Is everything all right with your panini?'

'It's lovely, thank you.'

'Can I tempt you with some of Sybil's cake for afters?'

It looked so delicious and moist on Sybil's plate that Tilly nodded her head. 'Go on then.'

'I'll bring it out in a few minutes with another cappuccino.'

Pausing only to greet some regular lunchtime customers who were just arriving, Angela hurried back into the café leaving the two women laughing.

'She can be dreadfully bossy but her heart is very definitely golden,' Sybil felt obliged to defend her friend.

'Jon speaks highly of all of you,' Tilly said.

'And we think very highly of him too.' Sybil beamed and Tilly's heart lurched slightly.

Sybil noticed the flush that came to Tilly's face and to cover the other woman's discomfort took her time and made a show of pouring her tea. As she sipped it she carefully watched Tilly who was drawing a pattern in the swirl of foam left in her coffee cup. Her face, when not animated in conversation, looked drawn.

'I noticed you when I arrived,' Sybil said. 'You were lost in thought.' She smiled gently.

'Was I? Yes, I suppose I was.'

Their conversation was interrupted by Angela who brought another steaming cappuccino and an equally large slice of cake to their table. 'I'm sorry I can't stay and chat with you,' she apologised, 'but it's a busy period for us now.' The four tables outside were all occupied as were most of the interior tables.

'That's quite all right, Angela. We understand. You go and help your poor over-worked husband now.'

'Huh!' Angela would have said more but at that moment Tony's voice called out, 'Angela, we've got a queue building up here!' She made a face and rushed back inside.

Tilly forked a piece of cake into her mouth, savoured it then closed her eyes and sighed. 'Mmm, this really is delicious.'

Sybil smiled modestly. 'Just a simple recipe. Anyone could make it.'

'I bet I couldn't; I'm the world's worst cook.'

'It's just a question of practice.'

They fell silent again as Tilly enjoyed her cake. When she'd finished she licked her fingers and ran them over the plate to pick up the crumbs. 'So good.' She smiled at Sybil.

'He's a good man,' Sybil spoke softly.

'Who is?'

'Jon. A wonderful father, devoted to the girls. It's been so nice during school holidays when he's brought them to walk with us. They're so bright. You must be very proud of them.'

'I am.'

'You've done a good job bringing them up.'

'It's mostly Jon who's done the bringing-up when I've been at work.'

'But they are the product of both of you. And two fine young women they will be. And he is, of course, devoted to you too.'

'Is he?' The words were out before Tilly could stop herself. Slowly tears began to slide down her face. 'Is he really?

Sybil moved her chair around to shield Tilly from the gaze of customers on nearby tables, and put her hand on the young woman's shoulder. 'Oh yes, my dear. Absolutely. You must never ever doubt that. One only has to hear the way he talks about you to know that is true.'

'Really?' Tilly gazed into Sybil's eyes.

'Good heavens, yes.'

'It's just that,' she shrugged, 'I've been so engrossed in work and now I'm afraid he's …' She stopped, unable to continue. She took the pristine neatly folded handkerchief Sybil was holding out to her, and blew her nose. 'I see so much of it, every day, couples divorcing. It becomes just matter of fact; you don't pay attention to the hurt. But I'm scared he's got fed up of waiting for me.'

Sybil took both of Tilly's hands in hers. 'Let me assure you, my dear, that isn't the case.' She paused, uncertain whether to mention Tilly's pregnancy. She made up her mind. 'The two of us walked together only this morning and, I hope you won't be angry with him, but he told me your wonderful news.'

'Did he?'

'He is so delighted, so very happy and looking forward to your future together.'

'Did he say that?'

'Maybe not those exact words but that was very definitely the message. Now, shall I order you another cappuccino while you go and repair your make-up in the Ladies'?'

Tilly nodded. 'Please.'

When she'd gone into the cafe Angela, who was collecting dishes from the outside tables, walked over to Sybil. She'd noticed the tears. 'Everything okay?' she asked.

Sybil nodded. 'I think it's going to be.'

∞

Jon was waiting at the school gates when he felt a gentle tap on his shoulder. He looked around to see Tilly smiling at him. He turned and kissed her cheek.

'Hi love. This is a surprise.'

She took his face in her hands and kissed him on the lips. 'I didn't feel very well in work this morning so Mr Pearson told me to go home.'

'This morning? But you stayed in work till now?'

'No. I've been sitting outside Jock's for the last …' she glanced at her watch, 'couple of hours.'

'Oh. Why didn't you come home?'

'I needed to think.' Before Jon could ask her what about she continued, 'I met Angela and Sybil. Sybil sat with me and I had some of her lemon drizzle cake.'

'Oh.' Jon didn't know what to say. 'It's very good cake.'

'It is, fabulous. Sybil said she'd show me how to make it when I'm on maternity leave.'

Jon raised his eyebrows and was about to apologise when Tilly carried on. 'It's okay; I don't mind you telling her. She's such a sweetie I'd have told her myself anyway.'

He smiled. 'She is lovely.'

'And Angela wouldn't let me pay for anything.'

'No, she's like that.'

'But I had a panini, three cappuccinos and cake. I felt dreadful when she wouldn't take any money.'

'We're always telling her off but it's a waste of time. She says if it wasn't for the dog club she wouldn't have the café.'

'Jon, I'm not sure what's been going on and …' she held up her hand as he tried to speak, 'I don't want to know. We're a family and a family that's going to get bigger. That's what matters to me; is that what matters to you?'

'More than anything.'

'That's okay then.' This time she wrapped her arms around his neck as she kissed him.

'Oh purleese,' a small voice hissed at them. 'Do you have to do that here?'

They broke apart to see Sophie regarding them with great embarrassment. 'Sorry, Soph,' Jon said, smirking sheepishly, and taking two large steps away from Tilly.

'That's better. Why are you here anyway, Mummy?'

'I thought it would be nice to collect you from school for once.'

'Are we going to the park?'

'We could do, if you'd like that.'

'Yeah! Can we go to Jock's?'

'I'm afraid Angela always gives them ice cream,' Jon admitted.

'Maybe we can call in, but we'll go home and change and pick up Benji first, shall we?'

'Mummy!' A little whirlwind threw herself at Tilly's legs. 'I got a star for my sums today and my painting of Benji Mrs Richards put on the wall. And Lucy couldn't do her sums but I could do them all and I helped her.'

'Come on, Gracie, we're going to the park now.' Sophie was keen to leave.

'Are we going to Jock's?'

Tilly shook her head at her husband. 'Honestly, what do you get up to when I'm not around?'

For a moment Jon's heart seemed to stop but as he realised the question was innocent and she was smiling he grinned back at her. The children took her hands and chattered excitedly on the way to the car park. Jon, walking behind, watching them realised he'd had a close escape. He'd almost made a dreadful mistake with Cathy. He couldn't make any excuses not even to himself. Whatever had happened to disturb Tilly the previous day, she had made up her mind to put it behind them. Now he had to do the same. If he suffered a few heart-stopping moments like the one he'd just undergone it was small enough retribution for his behaviour. He wondered briefly if Sybil had had anything to do with Tilly's change of mood. He wouldn't be surprised.

∞

A few days later after their walk and the now obligatory cup of coffee in Jock's it was time for the friends to head off in their different directions: Angela back into the kitchen to prepare for the lunchtime rush; Jemma home to collect her camera for a dog portrait session; Maggi home to change ready for work; and Bernard to the library to collect the Australia guide he'd ordered. Sybil had waved them all off and was about to make her way back to the flat when Jon stopped her.

'Sybil, are you doing anything this afternoon? Early afternoon that is.'

'I don't have anything planned. I'll probably put my feet up and read – oh, did you want me to have Benji for you?'

'No, nothing like that but I was hoping you might come round to my house. There's something I'd like to show you.'

'What would that be?'

Jon hesitated. 'I'd rather not say just yet but it'll all become clear this afternoon. I'll come and fetch you obviously.'

'That won't be necessary; I can walk to your house.'

'No, you won't. I'll pick you up at about two, if that's all right?'

'Yes, I'll look forward to it.'

Promptly at two Jon collected Sybil who was waiting in the car park for him. He leapt out, opened the car door and helped her in. When he'd made sure her seat belt was properly fastened he set off. Sybil watched him carefully. 'You seem a little … nervous, Jon,' she said. 'Is everything all right?'

'Oh yes,' he beamed. 'At least I think it is. I hope you'll think so too.' He frowned. 'I really hope you'll think so too.'

When he'd told Tilly what he'd done and what he was planning she'd been concerned. 'She's an old lady, Jon. It might be too much of a shock for her.'

'She's a tough old bird,' he reassured his wife. 'You've not had a chance to get to know her properly. She's strong.'

'All the same, this coming out of the blue …'

'No, no, it'll be fine.'

'Would you like me to be here?'

'Why?'

'In case she comes over faint or something.'

'Tilly, last time you were pregnant you almost fainted each time you had to have a blood test. I'm not sure you'd be the best person to have on hand.'

Tilly laughed. 'That's true. Lord, I'd forgotten about the blood tests. They'll probably set the vampires on me at my ante-natal next week. Okay, then, what about one of the other dog-walkers? Angela or Maggi?'

'I told you Sybil said I was the only person she'd ever told. It might be awkward if they were here.'

Tilly sighed. 'Okay then, well, I just hope you're right about her. I'd hate to come home to find an old lady spread-eagled across my sofa in dead faint. Or worse!'

Jon recalled this conversation now as he led Sybil into the living-room. There was a buzz from the computer in the corner and the screen saver was alternating photos of Sophie and Gracie. Sybil noticed it straightaway and made for it.

'Don't touch that!'

She jumped back, startled. 'I was only going to look at the photos of your daughters.' She patted her chest. 'Dear me, you made me jump then.'

'I'm so sorry, Sybil; I didn't mean to shout. Look why don't you sit down and I'll make us a cup of tea. Please, sit here on the sofa.'

He helped her lower herself into the deep cushion and when she was settled, she laughed. 'I'll never get out of here again!'

'Don't worry, I'll help you. Now, tea? I've got the kettle on.'

'Not at the moment, thank you, dear. But why don't you tell me what this is all about?'

Jon paced the floor in front of her. 'Are you sure you wouldn't like a cup of tea? Or I could make coffee. But you never drink coffee, do you? Fruit juice? Apple or orange?'

'Jon, come and sit next to me and tell me what's got you so agitated.' She patted the cushion. He sighed and slipped reluctantly onto the sofa.

'Well you see …' He jumped up again. 'It's probably best if I show you. Come and sit here.' He pointed to the chair in front of the computer.

'Must I, dear? You'll have to give me a hand up out of this cushion then.'

Jon put one hand under her elbow and the other around her shoulders. 'One, two three, up.'

'These comfy chairs are all well and good but not made for the likes of me,' Sybil chuckled. 'Now, where do you want me to sit?'

He led her across to the desk chair and settled her down again. As he did so he knocked the mouse and the computer monitor flashed back into life. The image on the screen was of a bookcase except for a face in a small square at the bottom.

'Good heavens,' Sybil exclaimed peering at the face. 'Is that me?'

'Oh, yes, you see – look at this camera. Here, on top of the monitor.'

'That round thing is a camera?'

'Yes, and …'

Suddenly a man's face came into view in front of the bookcase and an American voice spoke 'Sorry, Jon. Wouldn't you know I'd have to go to the john at just the …' He stopped mid-sentence. 'Sybil?' The word came out as hardly more than a whisper. 'Is that you?'

Sybil frowned and peered at the man's face on the screen then she wriggled on to the edge of her seat to try and get a better look. She shook her head and turned to face Jon. 'Who is that? How does he know my name?'

'It's me, Sybil, Bill. Bill Walters.'

Sybil's eyes opened wide and she started backwards. 'Bill?' she gasped.

'Yeah, really it is me.'

'But … where are you? I don't understand.' She had gone very pale and Jon wondered if he should have listened to his wife and explained things to Sybil instead of presenting her abruptly with this face from her past.

'In New York. In America,' he added.

'I know where New York is. But I don't understand. How am I seeing you? How am I talking to you? Jon?' She looked around wanting an explanation from the man standing beside her. He was definitely flesh and blood otherwise she'd have been convinced it were a dream.

Jon squeezed her shoulder gently. 'It's one of the wonders of the internet, Sybil. It lets us hold conversations face to face even though there are miles between us.'

Sybil still looked pale. 'But … Bill?' She shook her head.

'Your fine young friend there set this up. He did a grand tracing job on me and asked me if I'd like to talk to you again,' Bill spoke gently, tenderly. 'And I told him there hasn't been a day in the last fifty years when I haven't talked to you in my head.'

'Oh, Bill.'

Her eyes filled with tears and she reached out to touch his face on the screen.

Jon found his own eyes were a bit watery too. 'Are you all right, Sybil?'

She nodded, still stroking the screen.

'I'll go and make that cup of tea now, shall I?'

Sybil nodded again and then spoke, 'Yes, please. Oh but wait, Jon, this must be awfully expensive.'

'No, it's all part of the internet service. You don't have to worry about anything. I'll go and put the kettle on and leave you and Bill to get to know each other again.'

When he'd gone Bill said, 'Jon told me your Reg passed away a few years ago. I'm sorry to hear that.'

'We had a good life together but …'

'No children?'

She shook her head and looked down. 'Oh Bill, I'm so ashamed of the way I treated you.'

'I wouldn't have missed it for the world. I loved you, Sybil.'

'And I you, Bill. But I loved Reg too.'

'I know and the better man won.'

'No, no, not better, just … first.'

They were both silent for a moment and then Sybil sat more upright and spoke again, 'But now, this is a wonderful surprise. Tell me what you've been doing with your life, Bill.'

'Where do I begin?' he laughed.

'At the beginning of course.'

'For a long time it felt as though my new beginning was really the end.' He paused as they both remembered the pain of separation. 'But my job soon became my career and ended up taking over my life. I made it, Sybil. I became the investigative journalist who won prizes. The one I always said I'd be.'

'I never had any doubt that you would, Bill.'

'You always did encourage me. It was partly your belief that helped me to move on. I might have seemed like a cocksure young fool but, inside, I wondered if I really had the ability. But you were so certain.'

'So you achieved your dream.'

'One of them anyway.'

They were both silent for a few moments as they remembered and then Sybil spoke again, in a determinedly cheerful voice, 'And did you marry a nice American heiress whose daddy owned a newspaper to help you on your way?'

'Now you come to mention it …' They both laughed.

'No, I never married, heiress or otherwise. I met a few girls along the way and had some fun but, well, my job took me all over the world including some war zones so it wasn't fair to ask anyone to wait at home for me. Anyway I never found anyone to match up to you, Sybil.'

'And what do you do now?' She spoke hurriedly to choke back the emotion that threatened both of them.

'I'm retired, of course, but I still write a weekly column for the local broadsheet and occasional guest posts in various magazines. I play a little golf when my knees start to creak and I fear I'm about to seize up if I don't, but mostly I read. And what about you, Sybil? How do you pass the time?'

'I manage to walk most days with the dog club; did Jon tell you about us?'

'Yes, he explained that's how he met you.'

'I live in sheltered accommodation, a small flat just next to the park, and, oh yes, most recently I've taken up a new career.'

'Is that right?'

'Oh, nothing as grand as investigative journalist!' Sybil smiled shyly, 'But I bake cakes at least three times a week for Angela, who runs Jock's café in the park. She's one of the dog clubbers; did Jon mention her?'

'No, he didn't, but tell me: are your cakes as good as the madeira in our tea-shop?'

Sybil laughed. 'Oh now that was good cake! I can't possibly say whether mine compares. You'll have to pop over and taste it!'

'I'd like to do that.'

She laughed again. 'You're not down the road now, Bill.'

'No, but there are hundreds of planes every week between New York and London.'

At that moment Jon brought in a cup of tea for Sybil. 'And it's easy getting from Heathrow to here.' He coughed. 'Oh, sorry, didn't mean to interrupt. I wasn't listening. Just caught the last bit of your conversation. Here's your tea, Sybil. I've got to go and collect the girls now but I won't be long.'

Sybil sipped her tea grateful for an opportunity to collect her thoughts. Bill spoke again, 'That's something I miss too.'

'What is?'

'A good cup of tea.'

Sybil laughed. 'Surely you can get that in America? I thought it was the land of plenty!'

'Oh it is – as long as you like coffee. Or cola. I buy tea bags but it never tastes quite the same as I remember it.'

'Maybe your memory is playing tricks.'

'I don't think so. You are just as beautiful as ever I remembered you.'

'Bill, now I know you're being foolish. I'm a wrinkly old woman.'

'You're beautiful to me, Sybil. You always have been and you always will be.'

They sat and gazed at each other for a few moments then Sybil shook herself. 'Listen to us! Like star struck teenagers.'

'What's wrong with that?'

'We're not teenagers!'

'So? We can be star struck geriatrics, can't we?'

Sybil laughed again. 'Oh Bill, you always could make me laugh.'

'Would you like me to fly over to see you?'

Sybil bit back her instant response. 'But that would be very expensive, Bill.'

'I'm a wealthy man, Sybil. Maybe not millionaire wealthy but enough to be able to do whatever I want. I want to come and see you but do you want me to?'

This time she didn't hesitate. 'Yes. I do. Very much.'

# Chapter 20

It was the Friday before Maggi and Bernard were to fly to Australia. They had arranged to meet over dinner to discuss their plans. It had been Bernard's suggestion and when Maggi had said that she'd cook a meal for them he'd declined, saying that he'd already booked a restaurant.

It was a little Italian bistro that they'd visited several times and Maggi, being Maggi, was on first name terms with the owner and his wife, Gina, who came over to greet them as they entered the restaurant.

'Good evening both,' she smiled warmly. 'Let me take your coats.'

'Buona sera, Gina,' Maggi had looked up the greeting out of the respect she felt for the couple who had worked so hard to make a success of their business.

Gina showed them to what they now considered their table in a corner at the back. She lit the candle and handed them each a menu. 'The special tonight is autumnal risotto.'

'Mm, that sounds good,' Maggi said, 'as long as it doesn't contain leaves or twigs.'

Gina looked shocked and Bernard quickly explained that Bassett had needed a trip to the vet earlier in the day after he'd got a stick stuck in his throat.

'Oh no! Is 'e all right?'

'Yes, he's fine now, stupid dog,' Maggi said. 'The vet said he might have a sore throat but it's the least he deserves after eating twigs. And causing me needless anxiety.'

Gina laughed. 'Oh well, soon you'll be in Australia and not 'aving to worry about 'eem.'

Maggi smiled but after they'd placed their order and Gina had left them to fetch the wine she said, 'I will worry about him though, probably even more now.'

Bernard stretched his hand across the table and took hers. 'He'll be well looked after by Sybil. She's well used to dogs and if she has any concerns she'll take him to the vet, you know that.'

'Yes, I know, I just wish he hadn't reminded me how stupid he is just before we go.'

Bernard frowned. 'You mean it's come as a surprise to you?'

Maggi stared at him for a moment and then burst out laughing. 'Yes, you're right: I'm being silly. He'll be fine, I know that. It's just that ...'

'You're going a long way away and for a long time, I know. But, honestly, Bassett will have a whale of a time on his holiday too. Didn't you say Sybil had already bought him a new dish and some toys?'

Maggi nodded. 'I know he'll be spoiled rotten. Jemma said she'd bought some of his favourite treats too – and some for Whisky of course.'

Gina returned with their starters, stuffed mushrooms for Maggi and bruschetta for Bernard.

'Mm, that looks good,' Maggi sniffed the air appreciatively. 'I'm going to enjoy this.'

'That's what you always say,' Bernard smiled at her. 'Whatever you have.'

'What can I say? I like my food.'

'And I'm very glad you do too. It makes me feel less ...'

'Less what?'

'I was going to say piggish but I realised that might not come out sounding right.'

Maggi grinned. 'It sounds fine to me.' She raised the glass of wine Bernard had poured for her. 'Here's to us two little piggies.'

'To us.'

After they'd eaten their autumnal risotto, which Maggi had declared to be the best food she'd ever tasted and Bernard had said, 'You always say that too!' they took their time choosing their desserts.

'I can't decide,' Maggi said, 'whether to have the panna cotta or the semi freddo.' She sighed deeply.

'Well, what if you have the panna cotta and I have the semi freddo and we can share?'

'But you always have tiramisu.'

'Time for me to have a change then.'

'Okay, sounds good to me.'

When they'd given Gina their order they both sat back in their seats and Maggi wriggled uncomfortably in her chair.

'It's no good: I'm going to have to undo my trouser button now,' she said. 'I can usually wait until after pudding but that risotto was very filling.'

'Nothing to do with the extra bread you requested to mop up the mushroom juices then?'

'Nothing at all.'

They both laughed and then Bernard once again took Maggi's hand across the table. 'Maggi, I ...' He was interrupted by the arrival of Marco, owner and chef of the restaurant.

'I 'ad to come and say good bye. You are going next week, yes?'

'Yes, but we'll be coming back, don't worry. You won't be losing two of your best customers just yet!'

Marco grinned. 'Eet is always a pleasure to serve you. Two people who appreciate fine food.'

'We certainly do that,' Maggi said.

Marco shook their hands enthusiastically. 'We will mees you but 'ave a good time.'

'Thank you, Marco. I'm sure we will.'

When Gina arrived with their desserts, they found each plate contained a portion of tiramisu as well as panna cotta and semi freddo. 'Oh good heavens,' Maggi declared, 'that looks so pretty but,' she peered closely at the plate, 'those are rather large portions.'

Bernard agreed. 'When we mentioned the tiramisu we didn't mean you to include it. And that's a full portion of panna cotta surely?'

Gina shrugged. 'You can't divide a panna cotta portion. Eet is individual. Ees too much for you?'

'Er, no, I shouldn't think so, would you, Bernard?'

'I'm sure we can squeeze it in. Thank you, Gina.'

Maggi took a deep breath and picked up her spoon. 'Right, I'm going in. We can do this. We don't want to appear ungrateful, do we?'

'Of course not.'

Some time later when they'd finally cleared their plates and Gina had removed them before bringing coffee, they again stretched out in their chairs.

'Phew,' Maggi blew out a long breath. 'I didn't think I'd manage that.' She licked her lips. 'But it was good, wasn't it? I can't decide which I prefer.'

'On the whole I think I'd come down in panna cotta's favour,' Bernard said thoughtfully, 'although on a hotter evening semi freddo might be more welcome and I can always eat tiramisu.'

Maggi ran her finger across the plate, wiping up the traces that remained. She licked her finger. 'Yes, I think you're right.'

Bernard grinned as he watched her. 'That's one of the things I love about you, Maggi. The way you enjoy life to the full.'

Maggi paused, her finger again on the edge of her plate. She looked hard at Bernard.

'What's the matter?' he asked.

'You said ... no, nothing. It's all right.'

'No, go on, tell me, do. I'll worry otherwise.'

'You said one of the things you love about me.' She said it hurriedly, to try to suggest it was unimportant. 'That's all. It just, um, surprised me.'

'Maggi.' It was Bernard's turn to take a deep breath now. 'Your appetite for life is one of the things I love about you, it's true.' He gulped, 'But there are many more things. I love the way you will help anybody, I love the way you make an effort for people, I love the way you work so hard yet always manage to make time for others, I've loved the last few months getting to know you, and, well, Maggi, I ... I love you.' He sat back in his chair. 'There, I've said it. I know you told the dog club it was much too early and that we'd hardly known each other for five minutes but I think I began falling in love with you the day you first spoke to me, asking me what had happened to Ned. You were so understanding. Now in what I know feels like the blink of an eyelid we are going to Australia together and I'm old-fashioned enough to prefer to do that with a ring on your finger. But if it's not what you want yet then I'm prepared to wait as long as it takes.'

∞

The following day Angela had invited all the dog clubbers plus Claire, Tilly and children, and Brenda and her husband, plus dogs of course, to a farewell tea party at Jock's after closing time.

Although Angela had offered to provide the food everyone insisted on contributing something. As the centrepiece of the table Sybil had made and iced a cake in the shape of Australia. When Maggi saw it she exclaimed, 'Oh my word, that's wonderful, Sybil.'

'Jemma helped me,' Sybil admitted.

'I only printed off a map of Australia for you to cut around. You did all the difficult stuff,' Jemma said.

'Thank you both,' Maggi hugged them. 'And I see the dogs have their own cake!'

'That's down to Jon,' Jemma said. He found a special doggy recipe.'

'Well, we couldn't leave them out, could we? And the girls helped me make it, didn't you, girls?'

'I weighed out everything,' Gracie said proudly. 'And helped mix.'

'And Benji licked the spoon,' Sophie said. 'And I think he liked it.'

'I'm sure they all will. It was very kind of you to make a cake especially for them.' It was the girls' turn to be hugged by Maggi.

'Oh dear,' she sniffed, 'I knew this was going to happen.'

Bernard handed her a large clean white handkerchief. 'I've come prepared.'

Wordlessly she took the handkerchief from him and he squeezed her arm gently.

'Come on then, everyone,' Angela spoke loudly over the chatter. 'Let's tuck in before Maggi's tears wash us away.'

They all laughed and filed across towards the tea spread, which looked enough to feed a moderate-sized army.

'Where to begin?' Maggi said, slowly and deliberately reaching out towards a plate of sausage rolls in the middle of the table.

'Oh,' Jemma gasped. Following her line of sight Angela was next to exclaim, 'Oh my goodness!'

Sybil gave a delighted little yelp while Jon looked from one to the other, bemused. 'What's up?' he asked. A smiling Tilly pointed to Maggi's hand. 'Ohhh,' he said, 'fantastic! Congratulations both!'

Food was temporarily forgotten as more congratulations, hugs and kisses were exchanged. 'When did this happen?' Angela asked.

'Last night. Bernard proposed to me in the restaurant and we got the ring this morning.' Maggi couldn't help beaming as she showed off her ring, a small ruby surrounded by pearls.

'It's so pretty,' Jemma said again. 'Is it antique?'

Bernard who was standing behind Maggi with his hand protectively around her shoulder said, 'I'm not sure about antique but it is old, yes. I was all for getting a huge diamond but Maggi insisted this was what she wanted.'

'Oh it's definitely more Maggi,' Angela said.

'Yes, it's beautiful,' Sybil agreed.

'But, Maggi,' Jon said, 'I thought you thought it was too soon.'

The women all looked at each other and shook their heads. 'Just when we think he's getting the hang of it he says something stupid again,' Jemma said. 'And then we remember he's just a man.'

'Hey, do you mind?' Bernard said. 'That's my sex you're so roundly putting down. We're not all like him, you know.'

'Excuse me? You're supposed to be on my side here,' Jon laughed.

Bernard patted him on the shoulder. 'Let's face it, Jon, you and I will never be on a par with women when it comes to understanding their wiles.'

'Wiles indeed? That's your fiancée you're speaking about.' Maggi put her arm through Bernard's and he bent his head and kissed her.

'And I wouldn't have her any other way,' he added.

There was a collective 'awww,' from the women present before Gracie said, 'Can I be bridesmaid?'

'Gracie!' Tilly tried but failed to sound stern.

'Well,' Maggi said, 'we won't be having a big church wedding but I don't think two little flower girls would be out of place anywhere, do you Bernard?'

He shook his head, 'Definitely not,' and Sophie said, 'Two?'

'Yes, of course. I'd need you both, if that's all right with you?'

Sophie's beaming smile gave the answer to that.

'Now,' Angela said, 'let's start on the food before the hot bits go cold.'

After they'd filled their plates and were sitting down, conversation continued again between mouthfuls.

'So, Sybil,' Jemma said, 'any more news on when Bill is coming over?'

She'd told them all the story – an expurgated version – of how she'd met Bill and how Jon had put them in touch again and it was to their shared delight that he had decided that he would definitely make the trip over from the States.

'Yes,' Sybil said.

'Oh when?'

'It had better not be when we're away!' Maggi cried.

'I'm afraid it's next Friday.'

'Oh no!'

'But it's all right because Bill's planning on staying at least a month, and probably longer so he'll still be here when you come back.'

'So soon?' Angela clapped her hands. 'How thrilling! Where is he staying? We could put him up, couldn't we, Tony?'

'That's kind, thank you, Angela, but there's a guest room in my apartment block and I've booked it for Bill.' Sybil still felt a surge of happiness each time she spoke his name aloud. She'd stored his name in her heart for so long, unable to speak it to others, that now, like a teenager in love, she said it whenever she could.

They questioned her some more but gradually conversation turned to other matters and a buzz of happy chatter filled the room.

'Maybe we could have a double wedding,' Maggi whispered mischievously in her ear.

Sybil blushed but her voice as she said, 'Really, Maggi!' betrayed her.

Maggi squeezed her hand and whispered, 'I'm so happy for you.'

'My dear, I still can't quite believe it,' Sybil confessed.

'You deserve it,' Maggi said, pressing her hand again.

Sybil wasn't quite sure that she did. But maybe, as Tilly had said when she'd told her the full story, she'd paid the price already, and now it was time to enjoy the moment. Sybil had spent so much time in their house on their computer – at Jon's insistence even though she'd said she and Bill could use the telephone to talk, an idea he'd pooh-poohed as far too expensive and not as enjoyable - she'd felt obliged to confess to Tilly. And in her she'd found an easy confidant – and new friend.

'Who'd have thought,' she said now to Maggi, 'that at my age I'd be making new friends and finding old ones? And it's all because of the dog club.'

'That's true,' Maggi agreed. 'I somehow doubt I'd ever have saved enough …' She noticed Sybil's eyebrows rise, 'okay, plucked up the courage' she grinned, 'to go to Australia without everyone's support and encouragement.' She glanced lovingly across at Bernard who was showing Gracie and Sophie how to make paper planes. 'Or met Bernard.'

Jemma had wandered across to join them and heard the last part of the conversation. 'Are we talking about the dog club?' she asked. 'My life has changed significantly. My dog portraits are becoming so popular I'm doing at least two a week. It's becoming my main source of income and I'd never have thought of taking photos of dogs if I hadn't started with Jock.'

'And I do love my photo of him. You really captured his spirit so well. Even though he was old and frail at that time, in his portrait, I can see the young pup all over again.'

Jemma beamed with pleasure. 'Good, I'm glad.'

'More to eat anyone? Come along, eat up, there's plenty,' Angela held out a plate of daintily-trimmed prawn sandwiches. 'Get off, Pixie, they're not for you!'

The boxer hung his head sorrowfully and Angela relented. 'Oh go on then, here's one.' It disappeared without touching the sides. 'No more now or your mummy will be telling me off.'

Jemma grinned. 'He could eat the plateful without even noticing. But, Angela, we were just talking about the dog club and how it's changed our lives.'

'Oh my word, yes. Who'd have thought it? Here we are running a café – and presently,' she looked around the room, 'entertaining our best friends before two of them set off on an adventure on the other side of the world and another has an adventure without leaving home.' She could feel tears coming to her eyes. 'So, anyway,' she blinked rapidly, 'come on, eat up. Or the dogs will be having a field day with the left-overs.'

Jon excused himself from the conversation he'd been having with Bernard and Tony to move to his wife's side. Tilly was standing slightly apart and looking around at all the faces.

'You okay?' he asked her. 'Not feeling sick, are you?'

'No, not at all. I'm just … people-watching.' She smiled at her husband. 'You're all so different.'

Jon leaned back against the wall next to her and considered the people in the room. 'Yes, I suppose we are. All we have in common is that we're dog-owners.'

'And yet,' Tilly paused, 'in a comparatively short period of time, you've all played a part in each other's lives in one way or another.'

Jon's brow furrowed. 'I don't think of it as playing a part as much as becoming friends.'

'Yes, that's what I suppose I mean.' She tucked her arm through her husband's. 'And I'm looking forward to getting to know everyone as a friend too – when I take over from you.' She glanced sideways at Jon. 'A new chapter in our lives.'

Jon kissed her on the tip of her nose. 'And I'm really looking forward to reading it.'

**THE END**

42478136R00160

Printed in Poland
by Amazon Fulfillment
Poland Sp. z o.o., Wrocław